"STOP TEASING AND KISS ME," she demanded. The voice sounded nothing like hers—so throaty and hot—but it inspired the reaction she wanted.

"Careful what you wish for, Red." He lifted her onto the island counter, yanked her forward, and stepped between her thighs. "You just might get it."

Her body went up in flames as he took her mouth in a kiss meant to devastate her feminine senses.

Oh. My. God.

His tongue… Lizzie didn't know they could move like that.

She fought to keep up, her nails digging into his scalp as he ravaged her inside and out. No way did she regret this request. She'd demanded, and he delivered.

His palms slid up her sides, scattering goose bumps in their wake and hardening her nipples. When he reached her neck, she was putty in his hands, allowing him to do whatever he wanted.

He tilted her head to an angle that allowed deeper entry into her mouth while aligning his lower body with hers.

A jolt of electricity shot up her spine from both shock and something carnal. No man had ever touched her *there*, but she could feel him through the thin barrier of her panties.

Because she was in a dress.

With her legs wrapped around a man.

In his kitchen.

How deliciously wanton.

IMMORTAL CURSE SERIES

BLOOD HEART

AN
IMMORTAL CURSE
NOVEL

LEXI C. FOSS

Editing by: Outthink Edits, LLC & Jacy Mackin

Cover Design: Phatpuppy Art Studios

Typography: Covers by Julie

Published by: Ninja Newt Publishing, LLC

Print Edition

ISBN: 978-0-9993709-7-1

To Laura—For still being my best friend despite my inclination to kill people. No, I mean characters. Right.

Oh, and for understanding the following words/topics: Bush. Tree. Wall. Yep. Infamous NYC Eiffel Tower. 47. Pig Latin. "Relaxing" vacations.

Please say hi to Stas & Lizzie for me next time you're on 79th. <3 Pizza is forever; cheeseballs are too.

BLOOD HEART

BOOK THREE

A NOTE FROM THE AUTHOR

Blood Heart is the third book in the Immortal Curse series and picks up right after the events in *Forbidden Bonds*. It's strongly encouraged, but not required, to read these books in order. For those new to the Immortal world, I'm including a glossary of key terms and definitions.

Cheers,
Lexi C. Foss

IMMORTAL CURSE SERIES

GLOSSARY

PRETERNATURAL BEINGS

Fledgling (noun): The child of a male Ichorian and a human female, who has not yet been reborn as a Hydraian; they do not typically possess supernatural or psychic gifts until their immortal rebirth.

Hydraian (noun): An immortal offspring of a male Ichorian and a human female, who possesses two supernatural or psychic gifts and does not require human blood to survive.

Ichorian (noun): An immortal being of unknown descent who possesses one supernatural or psychic gift and requires human blood to survive.

Immortal (noun): A general noun designating a being who does not age and is immune to natural human death.

Seraphim (noun): A being who belongs to the highest order of angelic hierarchy. No known Seraphim are in existence today.

KEY TERMS

Arcadia: Notorious Ichorian club in New York City that also serves as the primary meeting location for the Ichorian government.

Blood Laws: A series of ordinances created by the Ichorian governance board in response to the Treaty of 1747.

Catastrophic Relief Foundation (CRF): A global humanitarian aid organization headquartered in New York City with a secret paramilitary unit designed to destroy rogue supernaturals.

Conclave: The Ichorian governing board.

Elders: The original Hydraians who also serve as the Hydraian governing board.

Nizari: Ancient Ichorian assassins who hunt and kill fledglings.

Nizari Poison: A green substance notorious for killing fledglings and preventing their rebirth.

Sentinel: A soldier in the CRF unit designed to slaughter rogue immortal beings.

Treaty of 1747: An armistice agreement between Hydraians and Ichorians to cease fire and live in their designated areas. Those who opt to cross these boundaries do so at their own risk.

TOP SECRET
(SECURITY CLASSIFICATION)

HANDLE VIA

CRYPTO-VARIUM

CHANNELS

ACCESS RESTRICTED
CATASTROPHIC RELIEF FOUNDATION LEVEL 9

ASSET FILE: 4-7
GENOTYPE: NONHUMAN
PROJECT NAME: REBIRTH

WARNING NOTICE
TOP SECRET EYES ONLY
GLOBAL SECURITY INFORMATION
UNAUTHORIZED DISCLOSURE SUBJECT TO CRIMINAL
SANCTIONS

TOP SECRET
(SECURITY CLASSIFICATION)

CHAPTER ONE

Pepperoni Pizza Party

Subject displays signs of unnatural
beauty, a requisite of the program.
Project benefactor is pleased.

—Entry Log 110.09.4-7

Bang.

Bang, bang.

Lizzie Watkins glared at the ceiling. Reviewing spelling tests for first graders was a daunting enough task without the gladiator theatrics going on above her.

She blew a raspberry. Clearly, the new owner on the third floor had finished moving into his condo. Lizzie hadn't even known her upstairs neighbors had moved out until she saw the relocation company carrying boxes through the lobby for the new resident.

Crash.

She set the papers aside with a huff and climbed to her feet. Normally, she welcomed new tenants with cookies, but this one had touched her last nerve.

Thud.

"For crying out loud!" She slid on a pair of pumps by the door, grabbed her keys, and stomped off toward the stairwell.

One flight of stairs later, she stood outside the new tenant's home and waited for the horrid song to change over before introducing her fist to his door. Repeatedly.

"Just a second!" The male voice sounded deep and masculine.

She tapped her foot while waiting, arms folded, eyebrow quirked, mouth ready.

"Sorry," the voice continued as the door opened. "Had to finish my set."

Abs.

That was the first thought that registered.

Because the man had greeted her shirtless.

A pair of navy gym shorts sat low on his lean hips, leaving his muscular physique on full display. The trail of moisture licking a path over his chiseled chest suggested he'd been working out. At least that explained the clanking and banging.

"Um…" Lizzie met a pair of soft brown eyes and faltered.

Milk chocolate, her cook's brain supplied.

I don't care what color they are, she snapped back.

Or that his gaze appeared to be roaming shamelessly over her body right now.

No.

Focus.

We're here to yell.

2

Right.

She cleared her throat and leveled the attractive man with a look she used on her misbehaving students. "I live in the condo beneath yours, and your—uh—workout, is, well, it's distracting me from my work."

Yes, Liz. That's a wonderful lecture.

"Is it?" He didn't sound apologetic, and his gaze had yet to return to hers. He seemed fascinated by her breasts. Damn man.

"Yes, it is." She inserted a little more force into her tone, which only seemed to amuse him.

"Hmm, I'll try to keep it down," he murmured. "And I would apologize, but there wouldn't be much truth in it."

She gaped at him. "Excuse me?"

"Well, I can hardly feel bad about attracting you to my door, especially dressed like that." He waved a hand over her body, causing Lizzie to consider her attire.

Black pumps, tiny blue sleep shorts, and a rose-colored tank top with no bra underneath. With her roommate out for the night, Lizzie had slipped on her pajamas before starting on her paperwork. And she hadn't bothered to change before scurrying upstairs.

"Oh." Her cheeks burned from mortification. Even her hair was a tousled mess. If her mother caught her out in public like this, she'd throw a fit. "Right. Uh, thanks for keeping it down. Nice to meet you."

She turned to walk away, quickly, and cringed as his chuckle followed her down the hall. He probably thought she was nuts. Great. Well, she didn't like him much, either, with all that racket.

"I'll try to keep it down," she scoffed, doing a poor impersonation of his deep voice.

She slammed her front door with more force than necessary, kicked off her shoes and wandered to the master bathroom.

"Awesome." As she suspected, her makeup was fine, but the long auburn strands she always wore styled in

3

public were a hot mess on top of her head. And her pink camisole top left nothing to the imagination thanks to her oversized boobs. No wonder he'd been so enthralled.

"At least we're even," she muttered. He'd given her an eyeful of his perfectly sculpted chest as well. "Can't complain about that."

Feeling naked, she pulled on her favorite New York University sweatshirt and tromped into the large kitchen to search for something to eat. Her parents had gifted her this condo on the Upper East Side after college graduation. She suspected it was a way to keep her at a distance. As if she would move back in with them.

Although, with her roommate working all day and spending almost every night with her new boyfriend, Lizzie felt lonelier than ever. She wanted to be happy for Stas, but she didn't trust the Catastrophic Relief Foundation (CRF). The world-renowned humanitarian organization always struck her as wrong, and after Tom died on one of their missions—

Knock. Knock.

She blinked. "What now?"

Closing the refrigerator, she wandered over to the front door and groaned upon peering through the peephole. A now-clothed muscular giant stood in the hallway. She pressed her forehead against the wood and grumbled under her breath before calmly twisting the handle.

"Yes?" Not her most eloquent greeting, but the circumstances weren't exactly favorable.

A pair of adorable dimples flashed at her as the man braced his forearms on the door frame over her head. "Do you like pepperoni?"

"Excuse me?" Apparently, that was her go-to phrase in this guy's presence.

"Pep-per-oni," he repeated slowly and arched a brow. "Well?"

"Who doesn't like pepperoni?" she asked, flabbergasted. *And why the hell are you asking me about it?*

4

"My thoughts exactly," he replied as he breezed past her into the condo like he owned the place. He kicked off his sneakers onto the mat beside the door before glancing around her living area. A couch, two big chairs, a coffee table, and an entertainment system. Nothing too extraordinary, but she liked it.

He seemed to focus on her curtains as he murmured, "It's a little pink for my tastes, but otherwise nice."

"Glad you approve," she replied from the still-open door, startled. "Is there something I can help you with?"

Before I call the cops, she added to herself. Lizzie had half a mind to scream, but her manners kept her in check. He was a neighbor, after all, in an exclusive condo building with security downstairs. Still a stranger, but not quite, given their residential situation.

"Do you frequently barge into other people's homes like this?" she demanded.

"Yes." His dimples flashed as his eyes crinkled. "Do you have any beer or wine?" he asked as he started in the general direction of the kitchen. His navy shorts and white shirt looked very out of place as he crossed through her formal dining room.

Lizzie kicked the door closed as she chased after him. "What are you doing?"

"You're not very observant, are you?" He grinned over his shoulder before opening her fridge. "Wine coolers." He shut it with a shudder. "No, thank you."

Her brain started working again as he went through her cabinets.

"Okay, mister, I don't recall inviting you inside, nor do I even know you. So, if you could kindly leave…"

His responding chuckle silenced her. From anyone else, she might have enjoyed that sound, but she didn't like it from *him*. She should have felt afraid, not irritated. But he kept using those dimples and chuckling.

Ridiculous charmer.

"I think we know each other well enough, Red."

She bristled at the unoriginal nickname. All her life people had commented on her red hair and lack of freckles. "You can go now."

"Don't be like that," he murmured as he found her wine stash. "Finally. I was beginning to think I lived above a puritan." He pulled out a bottle of her favorite cabernet and set it on the counter. "Perfect."

"Are you going to make me call security?" Because she would. The doorman downstairs was a good friend thanks to her obsession with baking. Lizzie brought him cookies at least once a week.

"Sure." He selected two wine glasses from her cabinet. "I like Dennis."

Great. Maybe I'll invite him up here to drag your butt home.

Her gaze dropped to said butt. Pure muscle, as were his long legs. He had to be close to six and a half feet tall. Poor Dennis didn't really stand a chance. Which should have terrified her, but didn't.

It's his smile.

A ridiculous reason to trust a muscular giant in the kitchen.

Fair point.

Okay, plan B.

"How do you feel about the cops?"

"Depends on the district," he replied flippantly as he uncorked the bottle. "Are you a half-glass or full-glass kind of girl?" His chocolate gaze danced over her bare legs and sweatshirt. "Definitely a full glass."

Her phone buzzed before she could bite off a response to that.

Where are you, Elizabeth? Her mother's condescending tone underlined the text message. Tonight was the CRF's annual gala. Her family went every year due to her father holding one of the highest positions within the organization, but Lizzie couldn't stomach attending tonight. She used to look forward to the event because it meant seeing Tom.

Her heart ached with the sensation of loss.

No.

She refused to think about him or the organization he devoted his life to. Literally. Or the fact that Stas was currently attending the event in misguided support.

Fruity notes touched her nose as the stranger wafted the glass beneath her chin. His eyes grinned down at her, clearly oblivious to the turmoil stirring inside of her.

"Thanks," she managed to say and took a healthy sip. Then she remembered that this was *her* wine in *her* glass in *her* condo. She shook her head and slammed the stem down on the marble countertop. "Okay, buddy, just who do you think you are?"

"Jayson Masters," he replied without missing a beat. "And you?"

She blinked, taken aback. This... this... *man* acted like no other person she'd ever met. He was rude, arrogant, and pushy, gave her one hell of a headache... and was smiling at her with the most charming expression she'd ever seen.

She shook her head again. "You need to go."

"Why?" he asked. "Do you have plans for the evening?"

"Well, no, but—"

"Are you expecting someone?"

"No, but that's—"

"Have you eaten?"

She frowned. "No, you interrupted me while I was trying to find something to cook."

"Then my timing is perfect. Dinner should be here in about"—he checked the clock over the stove—"twenty minutes, give or take. Hopefully, you like San Dinos. I've heard good things, but it's my first time."

"You've never had San Dinos's pizza before?" It was one of the best places in Manhattan. Everyone loved their New York style of thin crust, cheese, and light sauce.

"I've only been in the city six weeks, Red, and I've spent most of that time working." He sipped his wine and murmured, "This isn't bad."

"It's fantastic," she corrected. "And stop calling me Red. It's unoriginal."

"Give me something else to call you and I'll consider it," he countered, reminding her that they didn't know each other.

"I'm sorry, but why are you here, again?"

"Dinner," he drawled. "It's this activity where two people enjoy decent drinks and food and sometimes socialize. Perhaps you've heard of it?"

"Of course I have, but why are *we* having dinner?" She gestured between them as if *we* needed a definition.

"Consider it my way of apologizing for being too loud." He winked and turned toward the dining area again, bottle and glass in hand. "Can you grab some plates and napkins? We'll need them."

She gaped after him. How had her quiet night alone turned into a meal with a stranger who lacked boundaries?

Her phone vibrated again on the counter.

You're late, Elizabeth. You know how I feel about tardiness.

Lizzie snorted. That was the understatement of the decade. She picked up the device and typed out a message.

Something has come up. I can't make it.

She turned off the power and tossed the phone into the breadbox. Her mother would call incessantly for the next hour at least, and then the messages would start. Lizzie would delete them all tomorrow.

The television flickered to life in the other room.

"Seriously, no boundaries," she grumbled as she started toward the living area. Suddenly, she thought better of it and grabbed the plates and napkins he requested—as well as her wine—and found him sprawled out on her leather couch.

"Favorite movie genre?" he asked.

She set all the items on the coffee table in front of him, folded her arms, and considered tapping her foot again. "You seem to enjoy choosing things for me, so why don't you pick?"

He flipped to her movie history and cringed. "Chick flicks. Given all the pink decor, I should have known."

"Romantic comedies," she corrected, irritated. Stas liked to remark on all the rosy room accents as well, but Lizzie thought it brightened the overly modern condo. No one would ever convince her otherwise. "And that genre sounds perfect," she added for good measure.

His disheartened expression almost pulled a smile from her. *Almost*.

"Hmm." He looked her over, considering. "Okay. We'll watch a 'romantic comedy,' but only if you tell me your name."

"Oh, now you want to get to formalities? After taking over my condo?"

"I did ask earlier, and I introduced myself." He pointed to his chest. "Jayson, remember? And you are…?" The twinkle in his gaze matched the playfulness in his voice, causing her exterior to crumble slightly.

He's actually pretty cute.

Hot, her hormones corrected. *Off-the-charts hot.*

And possibly crazy, her brain pointed out.

Can't have it all.

With a shake of her head, she finally gave in to him. "Lizzie."

"There. That wasn't so hard, was it?" He started surfing through the options as he added, "Most women prefer giving their name before showing up at my place half-dressed, but I think I prefer your method."

She sputtered. "You're one to talk, answering the door shirtless." *Yes, great comeback, Liz.*

God, was it her, or had the temperature in her condo gone up ten degrees? Rather than turn on the air conditioning—something that should not be needed in late September—she walked across the room to switch on the overhead ceiling fan in an attempt to hide her discomfort.

"True, but at least I was inside my own condo." Jayson

selected a film before continuing. "You were wandering the halls with your assets on display for the neighborhood to see. Not that I'm complaining. You're obviously gorgeous."

Her tongue forgot how to function.

How did she even begin to reply to that?

And "gorgeous"?

Please.

Sure, she had an okay figure and her skin rarely blemished, but she was far from being anything extraordinary. Something her parents reminded her of daily. She looked nothing like them, which they considered her fault.

Familiar music started on the television as the film rolled to life. Of all the movies in her library, he'd somehow picked her favorite.

Jayson patted the cushion beside him, distracting her from analyzing that coincidence too deeply. "Come relax with me, Lizzie."

She wanted to ask whether or not he'd showered after working out, but the jibe felt childish.

Besides, he didn't smell all that bad. If anything, he smelled quite nice. Not that she'd noticed the underlying hint of cedar he'd introduced to her apartment or the fact that, despite having just worked out, his thick brown hair looked perfectly tousled.

Nope. She didn't acknowledge any of those things.

With a sigh, she settled onto the cushion she'd vacated earlier and curled her legs beneath her.

"For the record, I'm only agreeing to this very bizarre dinner because you ordered from my favorite pizza place. Turning down San Dinos would be a sin, and I consider myself a good New Yorker."

His laugh lines crinkled, suggesting he smiled often. "Whatever you say, Lizzie."

She picked up the papers from earlier and sifted through them. Might as well get some work done in the process. Or try to, anyway.

~*~

I'm in.

Jayson typed the two words into his phone and hit Send while pretending to focus on the television. He'd waited until after the pizza arrived to inform the team of his progress. It seemed only fair to spend some time with the woman he had been admiring these last six weeks before having to bail.

Not that Lizzie Watkins had spoken much while pretending to work and eat. She had traded her half-eaten slice of pizza for some paperwork, but she didn't seem to be making much progress.

She pinched her lips to the side while she focused on the same sheet of paper she had pulled out ten minutes ago. Jayson suppressed a smile.

The woman had surprised him with her fiery response earlier tonight. Lizzie came off as politely sweet during all his observations, especially when volunteering with the youth center in the Bronx. She was a female of means with a heart of gold, and Jayson found his respect for her growing every day.

But he didn't enjoy her movie preferences.

He'd selected the boring romance because his notes indicated this to be her favorite. That's also why he chose San Dinos. The pizza wasn't bad, but not the best he'd tried either. Granted, his experience vastly outweighed the woman beside him, in more ways than one.

Mateo's reply flashed on the screen. *Brilliant. Engage in sixty seconds.*

Jayson eyed the clock and started counting. On the minute mark, he flicked the trigger on his watch. Now the fun would begin.

He finished his wine and set it on the table before relaxing into the couch.

When he volunteered for this assignment, he hadn't expected to enjoy it. Babysitting a spoiled rich girl sounded about as fun as spending a month in an Ichorian den. But Lizzie Watkins continued to surprise him.

Six weeks of observing her taught him a lot about her habits, gentle mannerisms, and innate innocence. The request to officially infiltrate her life came two days ago after several failures to understand Lizzie's genetics.

She wasn't human; that much they knew based on the CRF's obsession. But she also didn't appear to be an Ichorian or a fledgling and definitely not a Hydraian or a Seraphim.

Whatever she was, the CRF considered her an important asset.

Hence today's little test.

How fast would they react to the blocking mechanism radiating from Jayson's wrist?

Lizzie Watkins's condo was under constant electronic surveillance, but he didn't know how strictly the CRF monitored her or who had been assigned to her personal detail. Jayson suspected the amount had increased now that her roommate was dating a renowned Ichorian. They were very careful not to discuss anything pertinent in the condo as a result.

This experiment, however, would provide them some interesting answers.

"Are you going to eat that?" Jayson asked, nodding to her plate.

Lizzie blinked alluring brown eyes up at him. "Yes. I'm just trying to finish grading this homework."

"What grade do you teach?" He knew the answer already but liked her voice.

"First grade," she murmured.

"Yeah? Do you like it?" Kids weren't his thing, but his observations of Lizzie suggested she enjoyed mini-humans.

"Well…" She nibbled her lip again. Such a sexy little quirk, not that she seemed to realize it. "I like it so far, but it's only my third week. I graduated with a master's degree in education from NYU a few months ago." All things he read about her, but they sounded far more interesting now.

"Congratulations," he murmured, meaning it. He saw how hard she worked despite having everything handed to her on a silver platter. Lizzie Watkins was blessed with a good heart, one he knew would be devastated when she learned the truth someday. Fortunately, he wouldn't be the one responsible for that part. He was here for information-gathering purposes only.

"What do you do for a living?" she asked. "Other than create a lot of noise and break in to your neighbors' apartments, I mean?"

He smirked at her little jibes.

Jayson had decided the best way to establish contact with the asset was to force her to come to him, so he had thrown some weights around to grab her attention. He never in his wildest dreams imagined she would show up at his doorstep in that revealing tank top and shorts, but he harbored no complaints. The woman possessed the body of a lingerie model and the face of a goddess.

Too bad she was strictly off-limits or he would consider acquainting himself with her more intimately.

"I work in acquisitions," he replied vaguely. His usual cover when on assignment. "It's not very exciting." *Unless hot redheads are involved.*

"I wouldn't call teaching exciting, but I do find it rewarding," Lizzie murmured as she swapped her paperwork for her plate. "Thank you for dinner, by the way." Even after barging into her apartment like a Neanderthal, she still thanked him. That alone said so much about her.

"My pleasure." And he meant it.

The phone lit up again. *Jackpot. Three Sentinels en route.*

Jayson slid the metal into his pocket and stood to stretch his arms over his head.

"I should probably get going." They were only an hour

into the movie, but he needed to work. "We should do this again, Red. I like spending time with you."

She laughed. "Yeah? You don't even know me."

Oh, if only you knew, sweetheart. "Maybe I'd like to."

Her humor subsided as a splash of pink brightened her cheeks. "Oh, uh... I..."

Most women jumped at the chance to follow him up on an offer like that. It intrigued him that she didn't. Jayson knew what he had to offer both in the looks department and in bed, and she'd had more than an eyeful of his assets.

And likewise.

He cleared his throat. "We're neighbors, and neighbors hang out. You know, as friends."

"You're really not from the city, are you?" She smiled and shook her head. "Where did you move from?"

He bent to lace up his tennis shoes before replying, "I'm from all over." Considering his three-thousand-plus years on Earth, that wasn't necessarily a lie. "But work brought me to the city."

"Oh, okay."

He stood upright, shoes in place. "So, dinner again? As neighborly friends?"

"Sure." She shrugged. "Just, you know, maybe ask to come inside next time."

His phone vibrated again. A final warning.

"What would be the fun in that?" he teased as he walked over to the door. "Make sure you lock up, Red. You never know what other crazy neighbor might barge in here and demand a pizza date." He said it in jest but meant every word. Especially about the locking-up part. She needed to be careful, not that she understood that yet. One day, she would.

"Funny." Her brown gaze held a touch of happiness that warmed his heart. Watching her grieve these last few weeks had been an uncomfortable experience. She hid it well in public, even within herself, but she wore the sorrow in her eyes.

If only she knew the truth.

"Anyway, I'm sure I'll be seeing you, Red." He gave her a salute rather than a handshake and showed himself out.

"Not if you keep calling me Red," she retorted.

He waggled his brows. "It'll grow on you."

"Doubtful."

"We'll see, won't we?" Because he couldn't stop calling her that. She probably assumed the nickname referred to her hair, but it didn't. Those rosy cheeks of hers had turned a delicious red after realizing her lack of attire in the hallway, and the image would remain etched into his memory for a long time.

Jayson loved women of all kinds, but a gorgeous redhead was his kryptonite. And Lizzie Watkins definitely hit the mark.

He winked at her before starting toward the stairwell. "Lock up, Lizzie," he reminded, knowing full well she'd watched him move down the corridor. "Good night."

She muttered something before closing her door, and he paused to listen for the latch. When he heard it, he continued his mission, heading down the stairs instead of up. He wanted to be seen leaving the building. It would coincide with the release of the electronic interference in her condo.

Jayson engaged his gift for concealing his physical appearance as he hit the lobby and strolled past the Sentinel waiting for him.

Pretending to get the mail. Could you be more conspicuous?

The CRF needed to improve their training.

Two more Sentinels stood twenty feet down the sidewalk outside, pretending to chat like old friends. Their open stances and vigilant behavior proved that to be a lie. They could have at least feigned having a smoke or something.

Jayson continued shifting his facial traits as he moved past them. He kept his stride casual while searching 79th

15

Street for anything else out of the ordinary. The last thing he needed was to invite a hunting Ichorian to the party.

As per the Treaty of 1747, Hydraians who entered New York City did so at their own risk. Considering the place was overrun with Ichorians and home to the CRF headquarters, most of Jayson's kind weren't keen on paying a visit. But he could alter the perception of his physical appearance. For that reason, Luc had assigned this mission to him. The Sentinels could see and pursue him, but once he lost them, they would remember his traits differently.

Hence his ability to blend in, in a city overrun by his enemies.

He turned the corner onto Columbus Avenue and sensed the two juveniles from outside following. As much as he would enjoy killing them, he couldn't. He needed the CRF to think the interference was a fluke and maybe send in a technician to review all the connections. Nothing more.

Jayson paused beside the American Museum of Natural History. He pretended not to see his stalkers as he stretched out each of his quads. *Just going for a run, boys.*

He glanced at his watch.

One hour until his rendezvous with Mateo and Tristan.

That gave Jayson twenty minutes to play.

Let's see just how good of shape you Sentinels are really in.

He rolled his neck and shoulders, jumped up and down a few times, and took off at a light jog toward Central Park.

Game. On.

CHAPTER TWO

Bloody Good Times

Subject's intelligence levels are above average, but sympathy for humanity is abnormally high.

—Entry Log 114.1.4-7

Friends.

Lizzie leaned against the door, considering the term as the movie continued.

She had several *friends*, most of whom she rarely saw anymore because of her current hermit status, but all of them were female. Stas, Cam, Kristin, and now… Jayson?

She shook her head.

What a weird evening. Most of her neighbors were friendly, but not like Jayson Masters. A hello or a wave about covered the camaraderie of the building.

"We're neighbors, and neighbors hang out."

Lizzie giggled. "Definitely not from here."

She settled back into the couch and finished her slice of pizza. Her stomach hadn't allowed her to eat much with Jayson sitting so close. His presence seemed to consume the entire room, something she noticed as the evening progressed.

The man had entered as a decent-looking irritant and left as a hot-as-hell "friend." That's what he called this, anyway.

"He must be really lonely," she half joked. Lizzie made friends easily, but didn't usually befriend gorgeous men. Except for Tom, but he didn't count.

She grimaced at the unwanted reminder, and a sense of deep longing soured her good mood. His untimely demise haunted her every thought. It didn't help that the details of his death were classified by his employer, the damn CRF.

When she asked his father for information, he'd just given her a sad smile and said Tom died a hero overseas. No comment as to where or how, just a one-sentence story that meant nothing. Stas's similar response firmly placed Lizzie on the outside. She didn't even qualify as need-to-know.

The wine disappeared from her glass as she inhaled every last drop. Then she poured herself a fresh one. She took another healthy sip and cringed as someone knocked on her door.

"Seriously?" Just as the tears started, too.

The knocking turned to pounding.

Okay. She enjoyed dinner with Jayson, but he couldn't just keep coming down here and demanding entrance into her personal space.

Her blood heated as the man jiggled her knob.

Too far.

She stomped over to the door and threw it open. "Now, you listen—Oh!" She cleared her throat. "Uh, hi, Charlie."

"Miss Watkins," the Sentinel replied, all business. "Sorry for the intrusion, but your father requested I stop by to check on you."

Charlie worked for the CRF's paramilitary unit. They specialized in saving people in complex situations all over the world and, apparently, sidelined as errand boys for her parents. She knew him reasonably well as a result.

"You mean my mother told him to send someone." She shook her head and started toward the bread box to find her phone. Oh, her mother wasn't so much worried as pissed. The Sentinel at her door served as a warning that Lizzie had stepped out of line by refusing to attend the gala.

Well, screw her.

She powered up the mobile and snorted at the myriad of messages filling the screen.

Ridiculous.

Sending a babysitter to check up on her like she was ten years old and not twenty-four.

Delete, delete, delete.

She didn't even bother reading a single one. They would all say variants of the same thing.

We're so disappointed in you. Why can't you be a better daughter? Is this because you can't fit into the dress I sent you? I told you to start dieting.

Blah, blah, blah.

She turned to find Charlie leaning against the entry to her kitchen, blocking her path to the dining area. His familiarity and ease with entering her condo created a stir of unease inside—different from Jayson, who merely irritated her. The Sentinel boasted a presumptuous air that left a sour taste in her mouth.

"Everything okay, ma'am?" he asked in that professional tone.

All the Sentinels addressed her in this manner.

Well, except Tom. He always teased her the way an older brother would, but that had to do with them being raised together.

As for the others, she suspected her dad had something to do with it. Or maybe Tom's father, John—who was their boss and the CRF's CEO—had told the Sentinels to address her formally. The man treated her like a daughter, a habit formed out of being best friends with her father.

"I'm fine," she replied. "Thank you for stopping by." Years of practice in being polite kept her tone even and calm, despite her innate need to scream. It wasn't his fault her parents sent him here to check up on her.

She escorted him back to the foyer where he had closed and locked the door, but he paused upon seeing the pizza boxes and wine on her table.

"Do you have company, ma'am?"

"I really hate when you all call me that," she grumbled. "It makes me feel old."

He didn't smile or react but continued to stare at her while waiting for an answer. The professional act felt cold and sterile. She could be naked and he'd probably still address her the same way.

"I had a friend over, but he left," she finally said. "Do you want to take some of the pizza with you?" Jayson had ordered two boxes, one of which he finished himself and the other still had seven of the eight pieces left.

"No, but thank you, ma'am. What was the friend's name?"

She blinked. "What does it matter?"

"Just trying to provide a full report back to Mister Watkins."

Uh-huh. Her father couldn't care less. This had her mother's touch all over it.

"Well, you can tell my father that if he wants my friend's name, he can call me himself." She opened the door while speaking and cast a saccharine smile at Charlie.

"Since you don't want any food, I imagine you'll be going now."

The Sentinel cast an uneasy glance around the condo. "Is your friend still here?"

"Do you see him here?" she countered, irritated.

"Right." He tipped his blond head at her and exited. "My apologies for the interruption, ma'am."

"You're forgiven, *sir*," she retorted as she closed and locked the door.

Now her mother would get an earful on Lizzie's lack of manners. Her parents could add it to their pile of her shortcomings.

And they could add this text message as well.

You can call off the CRF lackeys, Mother, she typed. *I'm fine.*

The reply came five minutes later, indicating Charlie had already delivered his report.

What male friend did you have over?

Of course her mother wanted that information. *No one you know.*

Clearly, no one I want to know if he felt you need to indulge in pizza. That is not a solution to being unable to wear your dress, Elizabeth. I'll schedule an appointment with Doctor Schwartz next week.

The nutritionist.

Great.

Have a good night, Mother.

Lizzie threw her phone onto the table, grabbed a pillow, and screamed. She hadn't bothered to try on the size four dress because she knew the damn thing wouldn't fit her boobs.

Lizzie wore a solid six. It had been that way since high school, much to her willowy mother's chagrin. Over a decade of ballet and strict eating hadn't stopped her curves from flaring, and the last five years of eating how she wanted hadn't added to her body, either.

"Cheers." She toasted her mother with a slice of pizza from the table and enjoyed it with more wine.

21

So much for her productive evening.

~*~

Fifteen minutes.

That's how long the Sentinels lasted at Jayson's pace through the park. He ran in circles for another half hour before exiting near *The Pierre*—a favorite meeting place over the last century.

Jayson nodded to the doorman at the Fifth Avenue entrance before skipping up the checkered stairs to the first-floor lobby. He wandered through the plush seating area and found Tristan waiting in the elevator bay with a female hotel employee.

Always flirting, Jayson thought, grinning.

"Ah, here's my friend now," the Ichorian murmured with a wink to the blonde beside him. "Thank you, lovely, for keeping me company. Perhaps we'll meet again?"

The woman simpered, as they always did in Tristan's presence. His Irish lilt, seductive charm, and rich demeanor embodied the female dream, and his reasonably good looks, athletic form, and dimpled smile helped, too. What his conquests failed to notice was the incredibly lethal nature lurking behind those forest-green eyes.

Or maybe they did realize it and enjoyed the potential challenge of taming the predator.

Her reply was lost to the arriving elevator. Jayson gave the lady a nod while Tristan brushed a kiss against her wrist—an intentional move to test her pulse.

"Hungry?" Jayson joked as the doors closed.

"Starved," Tristan replied. "But I'll handle my appetite later."

"Well, she certainly seems willing."

"Most of them are," the Ichorian replied as the doors opened to the 17th floor. "How was your run?"

Jayson shrugged. "Uneventful."

"Pity." Ichorians loved blood, but Tristan thrived on

violence. Still, Jayson trusted the Ichorian despite his proclivities and immortal race, because of ancient family ties.

But that didn't mean he always liked the sadistic leech.

Mateo opened the door before they could knock, and let them inside. Luc and Balthazar stood near the windows, observing the skyline, while Jacque relaxed on the bed and flipped through channels on the television.

Jayson grinned at his best friends, happy to see them after six weeks of living in solitude above Lizzie Watkins's condo. All their planning sessions and conversations were over the phone due to the danger of them visiting in person, something they clearly ignored tonight.

"You need to get laid," was Balthazar's greeting. Typical. The notorious god of deviance probably pitied Jayson's temporary vow of chastity. But he couldn't afford any distractions, women included.

"I'm missing Brazil right about now," Jayson admitted.

Balthazar nodded solemnly. "I'm already planning your return party."

"Excellent." Jayson focused on Luc and folded his arms. "*You* shouldn't be here."

As the leader and king of the Hydraian race, venturing into New York City was a serious risk. Ichorians would love a reason to kill Luc—not that he would ever give them one—but his presence here put several lives at risk. Specifically, Mateo's and Tristan's.

Ichorians had strict laws about fraternizing with Hydraians. Just being in this room sentenced Mateo and Tristan to death, not that they seemed bothered.

Centuries of skirting the rules and meeting in private bolstered their confidence, but chatter in the immortal community suggested Ichorians were falling under harsher scrutiny by their governing power, the Conclave.

But what concerned Jayson more were the rumors about immortals actively looking for ways to break the tenuous balance of power between Ichorians and

Hydraians. Killing Luc, the leader of his kind, would be an excellent way to ignite chaos and start a war. Something everyone in this room preferred to avoid.

"Next time, send Jacque to collect me and we'll meet somewhere safer," Jayson continued. "For all our sakes."

"A hundred bucks," Jacque boasted from the bed, his silver gaze on Mateo.

"I didn't accept your bet," the blond Ichorian replied flatly. "I owe you nothing."

"Jacque guessed you would demand that," Luc explained. "And I'm perfectly safe at the moment." The stubborn brute crossed his strong arms and narrowed his emerald orbs at Jayson. "I'm here to reiterate that although you've established contact with the subject, you can't fuck her."

"Seriously?" Jayson was almost offended. He glanced at the more reasonable of the two. "It's like he doesn't trust me, B."

Balthazar shrugged. "I've told him it's a ridiculous edict, but you know how inflexible he gets."

"True. Maybe he's the one who needs to get laid?" Jayson suggested.

"An accurate assessment," his friend agreed. "By a certain dark-haired fledgling, maybe?"

Jayson's eyebrows inched upward. *Eliza?* he asked silently, knowing his mind-reading friend would hear him.

Balthazar nodded in confirmation.

Interesting. All of the exchanges Jayson had witnessed between Luc and Eliza were heated debates where she questioned his authority.

It surprised them all, considering her experience with a hoard of sadistic Ichorians and her less-than-pleasant attendance at a recent Conclave, but the woman possessed an ironclad will to survive. Her personality started to resurface after a few weeks of feeling safe in Hydria. Some of it was a result of Balthazar using his gift for emotions to assist her in the healing process, but most of it stemmed from her innate strength.

I'm sorry to be missing the fireworks, Jayson admitted.

"It's quite a show," Balthazar replied, grinning. "I'll send you updates."

Please do.

"Are you two done acting like children?" Luc asked, his emerald gaze flickering with irritation. "And I already told you that's never happening. Eliza's a child." He turned to the blond Ichorian in the corner. "What are our next steps?"

And back to business already.

Mateo glanced up from his phone. "I want to check our surveillance in her condo since we put it there over six weeks ago—I know the CRF hasn't detected it, but it never hurts to refresh the equipment. And I'd suggest you all use it as an opportunity to look for anything related to the serum."

Ah, the reason for all of this. Whisking Lizzie off to Hydria and telling her the truth would make all this easier, but the Hydraian Elders, Jayson included, had voted to withhold the information from her while they assessed the situation.

Tom, the son of the CRF's CEO, was a recently acquired ally with a wealth of helpful information. Part of his debrief included information regarding Lizzie. She required some sort of medication to stay alive, but no one knew what or how the organization administered it. Hence Jayson's purpose in New York City.

He had observed her for six weeks to no avail, and their contact on the inside hadn't gathered anything useful. Luc opted to escalate the plan because time was running short. They needed answers—and fast—before they could decide how to proceed with Miss Watkins.

"When?" Luc pressed, his focus still on the blond.

"Issac suggested Tuesday," Mateo replied. "Something about Stas working late with Stark and Jonathan."

"Excellent." Luc turned his intelligent gaze on Jayson. "We'll need you to distract Elizabeth while Stas handles

CRF interference."

"Oh, I'll distract her plenty." *And enjoy every minute.* "But you can't search her condo, Luc. Send someone else." Luc might be his leader and king, but on this, Jayson would not falter. "It's too dangerous."

In a rare moment of seriousness, Balthazar said, "I agree. We'll send Grace and Ash with Jacque." His brown gaze met and held Luc's as a one-sided debate ensued between them. "We'll send Alik with them, too." Silence. A nod. "She'll say yes, and you know it."

Those final words helped Jayson follow the debate. "Grace is ready," he said. "Saying otherwise is an insult to her training." Which he took personally, since he'd been the one to provide it.

Sparkling green eyes met his and narrowed. "I refuse to risk one so young."

"Nine hundred is hardly young, Luc." Jayson shook his head. "You can't do everything, and I'm confident she'll handle it. Besides, her ability to read the history of objects will come in handy."

Balthazar ran his fingers through his dark hair and shook his head at whatever Luc was thinking. "I'll work on him, Jay. For now, we need to get moving."

Luc refocused the discussion. "Anything else to report on?"

Always so serious.

"He does need to relax more," Balthazar agreed. The mind reader never gave anyone any privacy, something that used to irritate the hell out of Jayson, but after three thousand years of knowing the bastard, he was used to it. Besides, his ability to hear thoughts made him the best wingman imaginable. "I love you, too, Jay."

Jayson grinned before recalling Luc's question. "I'm good for now."

Luc nodded his blond head as if he expected as much. "I wish we could stay longer, Jay, but..."

"You shouldn't have come to begin with," Jayson

finished for him. "Get going before the bloodsuckers track you down."

"I take offense to that," Tristan murmured, speaking for the first time since entering the room.

"Says the one thinking about his meal downstairs," Balthazar remarked, amused. "She sounds delectable."

"Oh, she will be." Tristan grinned. "Does that mean I'm dismissed to enjoy my evening?"

Mateo rolled his eyes. "Sure. I'll report to Issac on your behalf."

"Brilliant. I'll escort Jayson downstairs before I seduce my snack."

"How gentlemanly of you," Jayson joked before nodding at Balthazar and Luc. "Go home."

They returned the nod while Jacque hopped off the bed. "Teleporter at your service." He gave a mock bow before extending his hands. "Nice to see you, Jay."

"Likewise," he replied as the three of them disappeared into thin air.

Bye, old friends.

A touch of envy caressed his chest.

He didn't so much miss home as his people.

And his own bed. And his pool. And the food.

He sighed. The sooner he solved this case, the better.

Jayson faced the Ichorians. Tristan stood ready, his expression bored, while his counterpart remained focused on his phone.

"We're all set for Tuesday," Mateo said as he typed something onto the screen. "Issac says to have Lizzie out by six in the evening."

"It's a date," Jayson replied. "Shall we?"

"Indeed." Tristan fixed his already immaculate suit jacket and tie and led the way.

With nods to each other, they parted from the elevator, and Jayson left the Ichorian to his evening of seduction.

Jayson walked most of the way home, his eyes vigilant as he moved through the park. He was almost disappointed to find no Sentinels waiting for him on 79th Street.

Another early night for me.

He nodded to the night doorman, wondering only briefly how the Sentinel had gotten past him to enter. Probably a show of identification, or perhaps the man was on a guest list of sorts. He'd check that later.

Three flights of stairs later, he was at his door and paused.

A shift in the air provided him a millisecond of warning before someone fired a bullet.

From inside his condo.

In the direction of his head.

Jayson engaged his affinity for metal as he fell to a crouch.

"Fuck," he muttered as he caught the succession of bullets too late. They pelted his door with soft thuds, denting the wood. "Damn it."

At least it wasn't CRF issued. Those fuckers would have exploded into flames. Incendiary bullets were the organization's deadliest invention yet, and Jayson hated them.

But that meant a non-Sentinel was in his condo.

And the bastard had deadly aim.

Jayson located the source of the mayhem and bent the gun with his mind as he entered his condo and dove into the dining room. Two knives graced his palms as he found them beneath the table, and he threw them at the source.

But the asshole caught them in midair with one hand and paused to examine the craftsmanship. "Beautiful," the Ichorian murmured. "I'll be keeping these since you just destroyed my favorite pistol."

"Perhaps you shouldn't have fired it at me," Jayson growled.

The uninvited visitor stood to his full height. "I had to ensure you were still a worthy opponent, and you proved as qualified as ever, Jedrick."

God, that name. Jayson hadn't heard it in over a millennium. "I go by Jayson now, or Jay."

The black-haired immortal shut the front door before leaning against it and folding his lean arms. "Really? Why?"

"You don't ever change your name, *Ezekiel*?"

He laughed. "Actually, it's Kiel right now."

"Kiel," Jayson repeated. "Like *kill*?"

"A brilliant play on words, no? Can't say the same about Jayson. A bit boring, if you ask me."

"I wasn't asking." Jayson pushed off the floor and wiped his hands on his shorts. "And I preferred Zeke," he admitted, referring to an old nickname. Though Kiel suited the Nizari assassin well. "What are you doing here?"

"Ah, now isn't *that* the question of the night?" Ezekiel shrugged out of his leather jacket and hung it on the door. All-black clothes lurked beneath, befitting the immortal's profession of choice. He was one of the most renowned fledgling assassins in history and Jayson's notorious rival, yet the two of them had a strange camaraderie, as well; an unspoken agreement that should one of them die it would be by the other's hand.

"You know, I amuse myself in the oddest of ways," the immortal continued. "Like stalking Sentinels for sport. I followed three here earlier tonight. Imagine my surprise upon sensing you, a Hydraian Elder, leaving the building shortly after." The Ichorian cocked his head to the side. "Blood laws dictate I kill you now, but I say, what would be the fun in that? I'd much prefer to know what has you so intrigued by the alluring redhead downstairs that you're willing to risk your existence so openly."

Ice drilled through Jayson's veins. Not because Ezekiel knew about Lizzie, but that her condo had attracted his attention. A fledgling lived there.

Stas.

The moment an Ichorian learned about Stas's existence—and, more importantly, her abilities—she would become the target of the immortal world.

29

Something she knew and refused to acknowledge, ergo her insistence on staying with the CRF and trying to learn more about Lizzie.

Jayson would admire her courage if her choices weren't so suicidal.

"Now…" Ezekiel relaxed into one of Jayson's oversized chairs and crossed his long legs in an elegant way that belied his words. "I'm already aware of Elizabeth's relation to George Watkins and that her intriguing roommate is a Sentinel—who is also romantically involved with Issac—but why are the Hydraians so interested?"

If you know about the inhabitants, then I doubt you were following the Sentinels for sport, old friend, Jayson thought. *How very informative of you.* Meaning the assassin had given him the intelligence for a reason. Ezekiel never did anything without thinking five steps ahead.

Does he already know about Stas?

Jayson crossed his arms and cocked a hip against the dining table, feigning a boredom he didn't feel. "I'm sure you have a theory, Zeke." *Tell me more.*

"Oh, I have several." Ezekiel smiled, and it was positively lethal. "Elizabeth Watkins looks nothing like her parents. I'm sure you've noticed? Oh, I can see you have. She's gorgeous, isn't she?"

"Get to the point." *Before I kick your ass.*

"Don't worry, old friend, she's not my type," Ezekiel purred. "But I can see she's definitely yours."

Jayson didn't take the bait, but a fire brewed inside— one created by a protective instinct he hadn't felt in a long, long time. He feigned a yawn to hide his sudden drive to throw a blade at the Ichorian's head. "Sorry, I'm bored. What do you want, Zeke?"

The assassin smiled. "Nothing yet. I'm too curious."

That sounded ominous, especially coming from Ezekiel. He was the notorious right-hand man of Osiris, the head of the Conclave and the leader of the Ichorian race. Except Ezekiel had been off the radar for the last century or so.

"I thought you were dead," Jayson remarked. "Where the hell have you been?"

"Oh, here and there," he replied flippantly with a wave of his hand. "Off seeing the world and all that jazz."

"Right." Jayson believed that about as much as he believed Ezekiel had a heart. "So you dropped by to say hi? Reminisce about old times?" *By trying to shoot me.*

"Sure." Ezekiel stood and smoothed his button-down shirt. "I also wanted confirmation."

"Of?"

"Your feelings for the girl below," he replied as he retrieved his jacket. "I'm looking forward to our new game, Jedrick. It's been too long." He slipped on his coat and pulled his long, dark hair from the collar to lay it over his back. Ezekiel clearly hadn't received the fashion guides for this century, or perhaps he enjoyed the old "vampy" style. His pale skin and black, gold-flecked eyes only added to the nefarious appearance.

"What if I don't want to play?" Jayson asked, wary.

"Oh, but we've already started." He held up the blades. "Thanks for these. I'll be putting them to good use." He opened the door and grinned over his shoulder. "See you soon, old friend."

I certainly hope not. "Try to work on your aim in the interim," Jayson suggested.

Amusement flickered in Ezekiel's eyes. "And you work on keeping that poor girl safe. It would be such a shame if she fell into the wrong hands, Jedrick."

He disappeared into the corridor before Jayson could reply. Mostly because his throat had clogged with an emotion he didn't feel often.

Fear.

It paralyzed him inside while pissing him off at the same time. Jayson lived through more horror than most immortals his age, and yet this minute detail gave him pause? Unacceptable.

31

She was just a girl.

A beautiful, smart, tenderhearted one who may or may not be human.

Most likely not human, anyway.

"God damn it," he muttered.

Lizzie, through her connection to Jayson, had just earned herself a lethal admirer. One with a propensity for killing brutally.

Not exactly true. Ezekiel already knew about her through her connection to George Watkins and the CRF itself. But he hadn't been *interested* until Jayson arrived.

And that put Stas in danger too.

Fuck.

Jayson closed the door and dialed a number from memory.

A cool British accent came over the line two rings later. "One moment."

Loud music and conversation flowed over the line while Jayson waited, and the dimming suggested Issac was walking away from the source of the commotion. "Is Elizabeth all right?" he asked.

"She's fine, but an old friend just dropped by uninvited."

"Who?"

"Ezekiel."

Silence met that proclamation.

"He suspects I'm here for Lizzie, and he's intrigued," Jayson added. "And he mentioned Stas. He knows she's a Sentinel and commented on your relationship with her."

"I see," Issac replied, voice devoid of emotion. "Does he suspect her heritage?"

"His history of tracking and slaughtering fledglings suggests that, if he doesn't yet, it's only a matter of time before he does. Especially now that he's fascinated." Which meant Stas needed to get the hell out of New York City. Now.

"Issac?" Stas's voice flowed in the background, as did

the click-clacking of heels. Jayson pictured her walking toward the suit-clad Ichorian. Their relationship concerned him, mostly because it would only end in heartache. Not that it was his place to comment.

"What's going on?" she asked, voice concerned. "Is Lizzie okay?"

"Jayson has just had a visit from a renowned Nizari assassin."

"What?" Her voice held a touch of fear. As it should. "I thought you said they didn't exist anymore."

"Their purpose is moot due to a lack of known fledglings," Issac clarified. "But some of them are very much alive, and the one who visited Jayson is the deadliest of them all. And he knows about you."

More silence. Jayson guessed they were either embracing or staring each other down.

Issac proved it to be the latter as he said, "It's time, Aya. We need to get you out of the city."

"Absolutely not." Stas's tone was resolute and brooked no argument. Not that it stopped Issac.

"It's not safe for you here."

"You've been saying that for months, and while I agree with you, there is no way in hell I'm leaving Lizzie behind. Or you."

"Stubborn woman," Jayson muttered. Because he understood and admired that level of loyalty. It was why he agreed to venture to New York City despite it being a likely death sentence. He had a responsibility to his kind to investigate and help Lizzie, especially if it meant bringing her in as an ally. The Hydraians needed all the help they could get.

"Aya…" Issac sighed. "Jayson, keep an eye on Elizabeth."

The line went dead.

"Well, that went as expected." He shook his head and dialed Luc.

It was going to be a long night.

CHAPTER THREE

A Blood Promise

"Aya," Issac repeated, this time with a little more force in his tone.

Astasiya stopped near the stairwell, her spine rigid. "I'm not debating this."

He caught her hip and pressed his chest against her exposed back. Her sapphire gown hugged her curves in all the right places, giving him quite the uncomfortable evening. But now was not the time for such indulgences.

"I may not be well versed in relationships, but I believe communication to be a fundamental point. Yes?" His lips brushed her ear with every word.

She melted against him on a groan. "I hate when you do that."

He grinned. "On the contrary, love, I think you quite enjoy it." He nipped her pulse and slid his palm to her lower abdomen to stop her from moving away from him again. "We're discussing this, Aya. You promised me you would relocate to Hydria at the first sign of danger."

Not that she seemed all that enthused with upholding her end of the bargain. He had tried to convince her to leave the CRF once they saved his sister from Jonathan's clutches, but Astasiya used her roommate as an excuse to stay. Her arguments were sound, therefore, he didn't press his opinion, but every moment she spent in this city, he worried. Endlessly. Never had he cared so much for a woman other than his next of kin, and it hurt on a level he didn't know existed.

Astasiya turned in his arms and placed her hands on his shoulders as he grasped her waist, holding her flush against him.

"Okay, a Nizari assassin told Jayson he knows about me, but he hasn't done anything yet. Is it because he doesn't suspect me, or is it something else?"

"Ezekiel's intentions are cryptic at best, but he's notorious for playing with his food." The Ichorian was renowned for his cruelty and lethal intelligence. His ability to track by blood type increased his notoriety. He was part of the short list of beings Issac considered to be a true threat.

"But he hasn't come after me yet," she repeated.

He arched a brow. "And so you would prefer to wait for such a moment?"

"No, but I'm prepared to deal with one."

"Your training with Gabriel may be far superior than I

anticipated, but that does not qualify you to handle an assassin of Ezekiel's caliber."

Astasiya's eyes widened. "I'm pretty sure that entire sentence was an insult."

"No, it was a rational statement. You are still new to this world and do not know Ezekiel like I do, nor are you prepared to fight him. He will win, you will die, and I do not accept that outcome." His grip unintentionally tightened, but he couldn't seem to loosen it. She was here and real, and he refused to let go. Life without her... "I can't lose you, Aya."

Her serious mask crumpled as she wrapped her arms around him and buried her face in his chest. "You won't."

A lie. They both knew he would lose her eventually. She couldn't remain a fledgling forever, but he would rather her live an immortal life without him than lose her forever.

"It's time," he said again. "You know it's time."

She shook her head against him. "She's my best friend, Issac. I won't leave her behind."

He threaded his fingers through Astasiya's beautiful blonde hair as he returned her embrace. His lips found her forehead as he suppressed the urge to sigh. He could never deny her, even when he needed to.

"She's well-guarded by Jayson," he murmured. "And I'll be here too."

"How would you explain my disappearance to John?" She pulled back enough to meet his gaze. "And Osiris?"

Two excellent questions. "I'm not concerned about Osiris." Not in the way she mentioned, anyway. The ancient Ichorian showed an uncanny interest in Astasiya during the Conclave but had yet to reach out to inquire as to her immortal status. If he thought of her at all, it could be months or years down the line. Time passed in a unique way for immortals of his age.

"And John?" she pressed.

"Would likely inquire about your disappearance and

perhaps cause a nuisance, but I'll handle it."

Her eyes expressed admonishment. "You're allowed to be cavalier about your life, but I'm not at liberty to risk mine." She cocked her head to the side. "This is a relationship, Issac, where we both care for each other. If you stay, I stay."

"Oh? And if I opt to move to Hydria, will you come with me?"

"Do you want to move to Hydria?"

"That belies the point. Would you move?"

She stared him down, as if contemplating his sincerity, and he let her see the truth in his gaze. He truly wanted to know. Would she follow him?

"Issac…" She closed her eyes and sighed, long and slow. "I know you're worried, and I am too, but she's my family. Would you leave Amelia?"

His chest ached with memory as he forced himself to answer honestly, "No." Issac had left his sister once, though not intentionally. He had thought she was dead, only to find out Jonathan had played him for a fool. "If I had known she was alive at the CRF, I never would have left her there."

"That's how I feel about Lizzie," Astasiya replied, opening those enchanting eyes once more. "I know your bond is by blood, but she's my person. I love her, Issac. And I won't leave if I can help her."

"But can you help her?" he countered.

"Could you have helped Amelia?" she tossed back, eliciting a growl from him.

"Aya—"

"No, listen to me. Those runes at the headquarters would strip your gift for illusion, yet you would have tried everything to breach them to save her, even if it cost your life. That's how I feel about Lizzie, but unlike you, I'm in a position where I can help her. I just need more time."

"To do what? You're not any closer now than you were six weeks ago." He pulled away to run his fingers through his hair. "This is madness, Aya. An assassin was in your building tonight. Does that hold no bearing on your thought process?"

She bristled. "Don't talk to me like I'm a child."

"Then stop acting like one," he retorted. "This is your life we are discussing, not some Sentinel mission or game."

"This is Lizzie's life too." Liquid fire lit her green eyes, stirring arousal deep inside him. Not a fantastic time to react, but she resembled a goddess in these moments, and his soul yearned to take her in every way. *Mine.*

"I understand the risk," she continued. "But it is my decision. And yes, perhaps I'm not equipped to handle an assassin in combat *yet*, but he's never faced a fledgling like me. All I need is my voice."

Power underlined her tone, exciting him more. She'd grown beautifully in the last few months, not just in physical strength but in mental ability, as well.

"I know you all think I'm being selfish and immature," she added. "Your centuries of experience trump mine, and I respect that, but I cannot ignore my instincts, Issac. Asking me to flee is not in my nature. To stay is ridiculous and dangerous, and I understand all that, but I can't be put in time-out while everyone else risks their lives for my best friend. That's not who I am."

The air thickened as her words lingered between them. So strong and courageous, the embodiment of a warrior. He admired her for it, even as he yearned for her safety and for her to see reason.

She failed to realize this wasn't solely her decision since it impacted him just as much. If Ezekiel discovered her secret, it would be Issac's life on the line as well. He didn't fear the Conclave, but he did worry about how far he would go to protect her.

But she was right. Asking her to sit on the sidelines would break a fundamental part of her. And Issac could never be the one to extinguish the light that burned so fiercely inside her.

"Can we compromise?" he asked softly.

"It depends on your terms." She sounded so regal but seemed unaware of it. This was the cause of Luc's intrigue—he saw the potential for her to lead. And her ability to compel only enhanced that interest.

Issac pushed the thought aside and forced himself to live in the present, to enjoy what time he had left with this incredible woman. For the time being, she belonged to him, as he did to her. And he refused to let the future intrude.

Time for a little game of persuasion.

"My terms," he murmured as he advanced on her. She stepped backward, causing the predator in him to grin. He cornered her in the nook beside the stairwell door, placing them out of sight for anyone who chose to enter this vacant corridor of the hotel.

"I will agree to you staying in New York," he said as he aligned his body with hers, trapping her against the wall. "If you promise to spend every night with me. Whether it be at your place or mine, I want to know that outside the CRF, you are safe."

She swallowed. "Using seduction to distract me isn't fair, Issac."

"You use your gifts; I will use mine." He ran his hands up her sides. "I love this dress. Tell me what you're wearing beneath it."

"That's not relevant... to... our negotiation," she whispered as she arched into him. He loved how her body responded to his every touch as if trained specifically for his brand of pleasure.

Issac caught her lip between his teeth and nibbled. "On the contrary, I find it very relevant." He started pulling the fabric up her legs. "I want to know what I'll be removing later when you come home with me."

She shuddered against him as he exposed her thighs. "Issac..."

"Aya," he replied, his mouth at her neck. He traced her

pulse with his tongue. "Tell me you agree, love."

Her nails dug into his shoulders. "You're not playing fair."

"Never with you," he whispered. She meant too much to him. He would break every rule to keep her safe, and he would concede to her wishes if it meant keeping her happy. But he needed this in return. "Please, Aya."

She softened in his arms, her head falling back against the wall. "I need at least one girls' night with Lizzie."

He grinned against her neck. "Granted, so long as I can sneak in after she goes to bed."

"How very teenage boy of you," she teased. "But I concede that point."

He tasted her sensitive skin. "Then we have a deal?"

"Are we making a blood vow?" The taunt in her voice teased his baser instincts.

"Mmm." He sunk his canines into her neck and luxuriated in the sweet essence beneath the skin. Her blood hit the back of his throat, and a growl he couldn't contain slipped out as she clung to him. After two shallow pulls, he released her from his bite and whispered, "Careful what you wish for, Aya."

"Issac…" She shook against him as the endorphins from his lethal kiss worked their way through her system. "Fuck." Another convulsion of hers vibrated his body. "Fine. Yes. I agree to your terms, not that it's a hardship."

His lips curled. "Oh, I think you'll find it to be quite a bit of work, love." He nuzzled her throat and reaffirmed his grip on her dress by inching the fabric upward to expose more of her thighs. "Fancy a preview?"

"Does it involve you biting me again?" she asked, her voice whisper-soft and drowsy with gratification.

He licked the still-open wound. "Yes."

"Then yes, please." She arched her neck. "Take me, Issac."

"Always." He soothed the mark on her tender skin with his tongue before dropping to his knees.

She knotted her fingers in his hair, forcing him to meet her gaze. "Wh-what are you doing?"

He grinned as he revealed her midnight-blue panties. "You did not express where you wished to be bitten, Aya."

"Oh, God…"

"Hold on to that thought, love. You'll be needing it again soon."

Chapter Four

"Not a Date" Is a Date, Except When It's Not

Subject appears reliant on familial approval. Habitat and accommodations should be revisited in future iterations.

—Entry Log 118.05.4-7

Lizzie pressed sweaty palms against her navy-blue shift dress and checked her appearance once more in the mirror.

"You're being ridiculous," she whispered. "It's not even a date."

Yet she had tousled her hair into perfect auburn waves. Her eyes popped with the eyeliner, and a sheen of cherry lip gloss graced her lips.

Her sorority sisters, especially Cam and Kristin, would approve. Stas, however, would laugh at her.

And that's why Lizzie considered her the closer friend.

She grinned at the thought as she sent a text off to Stas. *I'm grabbing dinner with that new neighbor I told you about.*

Jayson had slid a note under her door Sunday night asking if she wanted to grab dinner tonight. He'd left his number at the bottom, and like an idiot, she'd programmed it into her phone and sent him a confirmation via text message.

A really stupid decision.

Lizzie didn't go out on Tuesdays, or any weeknights, because of work. But her lesson plans were already done for the month due to all her evenings alone.

Try to behave, Stas teased. Lizzie had given her the full description of their overbearing man upstairs. *I'll be home around ten tonight. Stark is forcing me to work late again.*

You should kick his ass.

Oh, believe me, I'm trying.

See you in the morning for breakfast? Lizzie asked.

They used to eat with each other every day, but things had changed over the last few months with Stas working so much. Tom's funeral hadn't helped, either. It was probably in Lizzie's head, but her friendship with Stas felt stilted. Cold, even.

Her phone dinged with the reply, *Coffee? :)*

Lizzie grinned. Caffeine was the way to Stas's heart. *Obviously*, she replied.

Count me in.

See you then.

It's a girls' date, Stas promised.

Lizzie smiled. *Sounds great.*

She loved that her best friend had finally found happiness, but missed their girl time together. They used to enjoy pizza once a week and binge-watch chick flicks, but now Stas spent most weekends with Issac. Lizzie couldn't fault her for it; her best friend deserved happiness and more.

And yeah, a tiny part of her also hoped Issac might be able to convince Stas to leave the CRF and pursue other opportunities.

Which, of course, made Lizzie a horrible person.

Her hatred of the organization stemmed from an irrational sensation of fear that increased every time she neared the corporate headquarters. She visited her father a handful of times in his top-floor office, mostly when he needed her to sign something. The last time had been some paperwork for her trust fund.

For whatever reason, he preferred to do everything at the CRF instead of at home. Probably because he rarely left his desk unless it involved doing something for work. As the Chief of International Affairs, he traveled often. As a kid, she rarely saw him, which probably contributed to her dislike of the organization. Killing Tom and stealing her best friend didn't improve matters.

There went Lizzie's happy mood. Just in time for the knock on her door.

Six o'clock on the dot.

Lizzie liked a punctual man.

Not that this was a date.

Friends, she reminded herself.

That didn't stop her heart from fluttering upon opening the door. Because, wow, Jayson cleaned up nicely.

Designer jeans, a deep-red sweater, artfully styled dark hair, and grinning chocolate eyes, all wrapped up in a muscular package most women only dreamed about.

Not a date.

Just neighbors.

A man like him wouldn't be interested in you anyway.

That last voice sounded a little too much like her mother.

And I've been staring at his chest for two solid seconds.

"Hi," she managed.

Those adorable dimples peeked at her. "Hi," he returned. "Ready?"

"Yep." She grabbed her purse from the table in the foyer and slipped on her heels. They added three inches to her five-foot, six-inch height, leaving her forehead around his lips.

Stop thinking about his mouth.

Right.

She followed him down the hall to the stairs and said nothing as he led her outside.

Lizzie didn't have a lot of experience with men outside her small social circle. She dated occasionally, but it never blossomed into anything. A few kisses here, some touches there, all of which led to nothing memorable. Only one man ever tempted her to go beyond light petting.

Tom Fitzgerald.

Her crush began at the ripe age of thirteen and continued through the years, though it waned a little in college. She watched him with other women and started to realize he would never see her as anything other than a sister. All hope she harbored of him wanting her died the day of his funeral.

Jayson tugged on the loose strand of hair hanging by her face. "Long day, Red?"

God, they were already a block away from their building and hadn't said more than four words to each other. Instead, she'd trod down a melancholy path that had no place in their evening plans.

Lizzie cleared her throat and forced a smile. "It's been a long few weeks." No sense in lying about it. "But I'm managing."

"Want to talk about it?"

"Not really."

He shrugged. "All right, let's talk about dinner instead. I know you love San Dinos, but I've heard rumors of a better pizza place."

Her eyebrows sprang upward. "That's blasphemy!"

Jayson laughed. "I say we test it and decide for ourselves."

She narrowed her eyes. "What's the name of this supposed restaurant?"

"It's a real restaurant," he replied. "And I think it's called Magilinos or something."

She'd never heard of it. "Where is it?"

"Uh, it's in Brooklyn." He gave her a sheepish smile. "I hope you like the train."

~*~

Lizzie Watkins was trying to kill him.

First, she wore a dress that ended midthigh, revealing those sexy-as-hell legs to the world.

Second, she added fuck-me heels and handled them like a runway model.

And now she sat across from him, moaning.

Oh, he knew the pizza here totally kicked San Dinos's ass, but he hadn't expected his *friend* to react with sexy little noises after each bite.

Luc's unnecessary reminder about keeping the relationship professional with Lizzie didn't help. Jayson knew his job and respected it, but a growing part of him started to see this assignment as a challenge. One he wanted to see naked in his bed.

Not. Going. To. Happen.

"Okay," Lizzie said after polishing off her third slice. "I was skeptical, but you win. That was amazing."

Mmm, he certainly enjoyed those words rolling off her plump lips. Too bad the context was all wrong. The woman maintained the innocence of an angel, and that only increased the allure. Her every move seemed to radiate erotic appeal without even trying. Anywhere else, and any other time, he would seduce her out of the dress, leave on the heels, and give her a night to remember.

Alas, he had work to do, as the buzzing against his

thigh constantly reminded him.

We need at least another hour, the last message had read.

Sixty minutes of small talk ought to do it. He could handle that.

"So, you've never heard of this place?" he asked, feigning surprise. Lizzie's high-society upbringing sheltered her from the simple pleasures in life, such as finding off-the-beaten-path pizza pubs.

"I have now," she replied cheekily. "Not that I'll get out here much with that forty-five-minute train ride."

He chuckled, remembering her expression when he mentioned their destination earlier. Shock had mingled with horror at the idea of leaving her cocoon in Manhattan, but she'd been a good sport about it.

"It was worth it." He referred to both her initial reaction and the subtle jibe at their long journey. "Okay, so far I've learned you're a teacher who enjoys decent pizza and rarely leaves Manhattan. Oh, and you dislike loud music—can't forget that bit." He folded his arms on the small table, leaning toward her. "Tell me more. How long have you been in the city?"

"First," she said, holding up a finger. "I have no problem with loud music, just neighbors who like to throw weights onto the floor above my head. Music and I happen to get along just fine, thank you very much."

"Yeah? I bet you listen to pop crap."

She snorted. "And you clearly enjoy men screaming at unfashionable levels while banging on drums."

"There is nothing wrong with metal, Red."

"Says the man who has to throw his weights around just to be heard above the commotion."

He could apparently add witty to her long list of positive traits. The smile on his face actually hurt. It'd been there most of the evening because of her. "I guess I need to cross 'attend a concert' off the idea list for future neighborly activities."

She giggled. "Most New Yorkers consider waving to be

the extent of activities that should occur between neighbors. Where did you say you were from, again?"

"Now hold on, I believe I asked you that first." He needed this conversation to be about her, not him. Because although he could lie, he didn't want to, and there were only so many ways to twist the truth. "How long have you lived in the city?"

"All my life," she replied. "Born and raised in Manhattan, attended Columbia for undergrad and NYU for grad school. And you know where I live now."

"So, your family lives in the city too?" He phrased it as a guess but already knew the truth. "Any siblings?"

He kept it light to appear politely interested, but inside, he was dying to know more about her relationship with George and Lillian Watkins. Stas had provided some of the sordid details, but maybe Lizzie could give him some minute detail that would help crack this case. Doubtful, but worth a shot.

Some of the amusement left Lizzie's expression, but her tone remained pleasant. "I'm an only child, but yes, my parents live in Manhattan."

"Do you see them a lot?" A natural follow-up question.

She pinched her lips to the side, considering. He caught the moment she decided to say what she wanted rather than the polite response.

"I do," she admitted. "Usually often, but not very much lately. We're not really getting along right now, but I have to see them this Sunday. It's tradition."

"Tradition?" he repeated, curious.

"Yeah, it's this monthly brunch, except it actually happens every four weeks, so it's technically thirteen times a year, not that it matters." A delectable pink caressed her cheeks, endearing her to him even more. "Sorry. It's silly. It's just a late breakfast with my parents and my dad's best friend."

"And you can't skip it?"

"Uh, I mean, I could, maybe. I've never actually tried.

The Sunday brunch fell over Christmas one year, and we all still went." She laughed without humor. "Pretty sure my mom would kill me if I ever skipped."

"And you always go to the same restaurant? Even the time you went on Christmas?" He tried to maintain an innocent curiosity in his tone, but her revelation floored him.

This has to be related to the CRF somehow.

Lizzie nodded. "Yep. I don't know how my parents managed it, but the restaurant opened just for us. It couldn't have been cheap, not that money would ever stop them." Her crimson cheeks darkened deliciously, solidifying her nickname. "You probably think I'm some spoiled rich kid now, don't you? Living in a condo I obviously couldn't afford on my own and telling tales about my parents buying out restaurants."

Her gaze fell to where her hands were clasped in her lap. A telling gesture that confirmed his suspicions regarding her fragile confidence.

"I'm not in the habit of judging people based on their familial relations, Lizzie." Otherwise, they wouldn't be having this dinner. "I mean, my father is a dick." Understatement of the millennium. "And my mother passed a long time ago." Because his Ichorian sperm donor killed her for sport. "But I'm my own person, and I don't associate who I am today with either of them." *And haven't done so for about three thousand years, to be precise.*

"I'm so sorry," she said, meeting his gaze. "About your mom, I mean."

Her apology surprised him. He hadn't thought of his mother in ages, but of course Lizzie wouldn't realize that. His facial appearance, which he didn't bother altering in her presence, likened him to a thirty-year-old man, maybe even younger. She would assume his mother passed in the last decade or so.

"I've long reconciled with her passing," he answered carefully. "But thank you." Time to switch it back or she might ask how his mother died, and wouldn't that be a fun conversation? "So, why every four weeks?"

"The brunch?"

"Yeah."

"Uh, it's always been that way. My father's best friend is also his boss, John Fitzgerald. Do you know anything about the CRF?"

He forced a confused expression. "The humanitarian organization?"

"That'd be the one." A note of sarcasm underlined her words, amusing him. It seemed she wasn't a fan. Something they definitely had in common. "Anyway, John is the CEO. My dad works for him."

"And they always go to brunch together, huh?" Stas had mentioned something about this, but no one thought much of it. A mistake on their part.

"Every four weeks," she replied. "You're welcome to join me Sunday if you like uncomfortable conversation and salad." That blush worked its way up her neck again. "Oh, that sounded like an invitation to meet my parents, and that's so not what I meant. I know we're just friends, that this isn't anything, obviously, and… and yeah, I'm going to shut up now."

She hid behind a glass of water and drank it with a little too much vigor while he chuckled.

The woman was adorable.

And charming.

And very off-limits.

Damn it, Luc.

"Actually, I think I'd enjoy going with you." Just to see the look on Jonathan Fitzgerald's face. "But I'm leaving for a work trip on Sunday."

The first blatant lie of the evening. Oh, he would be working, but in New York City. And very likely at her brunch. Because his curiosity was piqued.

Every four weeks.

That couldn't be a coincidence.

The records Tom—Jonathan's son—found stated she needed some sort of serum to stay alive. What Jayson hadn't deduced yet was *how* the CRF gave it to her, because in the last six, almost seven, weeks of watching her, he had yet to see them intervene in her life other than Friday night after he blacked out their surveillance.

But maybe it was simpler than that and didn't require her visiting headquarters.

Just a brunch.

"Oh, are you off to somewhere fun?" Lizzie asked, referring to his trip.

"No, definitely not." Anything dealing with the CRF could not be classified as enjoyable. "But I won't be gone for long. A few days maybe." More like hours.

Relief touched her expression, and it warmed him that she didn't bother to hide it. Or maybe she couldn't. "A few days of peace and quiet? I can handle that."

Oh, the little minx! "Darling Red, I do believe you're asking for trouble now."

"Me?" She batted innocent eyes at him. "Never."

"You know what? I think our next date will be at a concert after all. One of my choosing."

"That's a *date* I'll turn down," she tossed back.

"Yeah?"

She nodded, her expression underlined in certainty.

A sense of challenge swept over him.

Okay. He couldn't bed her, but a little flirtation never killed anyone.

Her triumphant grin faltered as he stood and walked to her side of the table. By the time she realized his intentions, he was already behind her, hands on her chair, and leaning down to whisper in her ear. "You can resist me that easily, can you?"

Her chest rose and fell in quick succession as her pulse beat an unhealthy rhythm beneath his chin. Mmm, not so unaffected after all, it seemed. Not that he was any better. Being this close to her felt too right for his liking. Not to mention she smelled far too sweet for his taste. He suddenly had a desire to indulge in a new fantasy—and the forbidden undertone was not helping.

She swallowed and tried to catch his gaze by looking sideways. "I might be persuaded," she admitted. "If you promise to bring me earplugs." As unnerved as he clearly made her, she still managed to maintain an air of wit.

It was fascinating, and he loved it.

And he wanted to push it one step further.

He nuzzled her neck and luxuriated in her sharp intake of air. It lifted her ample breasts for his viewing pleasure, something his lower half enjoyed far more than it should.

His fingers itched to knot in her hair and introduce his mouth to hers—just for a second—but the buzzing against his thigh reminded him of his purpose.

Attractive or not, she was still an assignment.

And he had better control than this, not that his hardening member downstairs seemed to accept that.

Damn.

"Consider it a future neighborly date," he whispered, unable to resist. And straightened to check his phone.

Never mind. There's nothing useful in the condo. We'll be done in about thirty minutes. Sorry to disappoint you. Grace's defeated tone bled through the text. He would have to call her later to let her know it was fine. Jayson never expected her to find anything, only hoped. But he'd gotten what he needed through the art of old-fashioned conversation, and then some.

~*~

Lizzie fought to breathe.

What just happened?

Jayson had leaned so close she could almost taste his woodsy aftershave. Now he stood just behind her as he typed something into his phone. She glanced up to see him grinning—not at her but at his screen.

52

Another woman, maybe?

He could easily be a player. She knew little about him other than he enjoyed barging into his neighbor's condo and demanding pizza dates. But his easy candor and smooth lines suggested a comfort level with women that required a lot of practice. Pair that with his gorgeous exterior, and yeah, he likely slept around a lot.

Not that it mattered.

They were friends on a *neighborly date*, as he had called it.

And so what if his lips grazed her ear while he spoke? That could hardly be considered romantic. Even if it did set off a flurry of butterflies in her lower belly.

"We should probably start heading back," he said, his focus still on the phone in his hand. "It's getting late, and we both have work in the morning."

Right. He went from flirting with her to wanting to leave. Either she'd misread the signals or she had done something wrong. Maybe a mixture of both?

Irritated with herself for overanalyzing a very straightforward situation, she shoved her chair back into Jayson's legs.

"Oh!" She rotated to look up at him and cringed at his pained expression. "I'm *so* sorry!"

He cleared his throat and took a step back to allow her to stand. "No problem." Except it certainly *sounded* like a problem. She had pushed back with more force than necessary, but it shouldn't have hurt that much.

Unless the chair had connected with more than his legs...

What a typical way to end an otherwise decent evening. With Lizzie being a klutz.

Heat overwhelmed her cheeks and neck, even her breasts, as she wished teleportation existed so she could pop herself home and hide under her bed.

"I'm sorry," she said again, helpless.

His warm gaze met hers. "I think I'll live, Red."

She couldn't even argue the use of that dreadful

nickname. Although it did come off as more of an endearment when he said it. Or maybe that was just her imagination.

He picked up her purse and slipped it over her arm. "You just caught me by surprise, which was my fault for focusing on my phone." His fingers danced down her wrist, and then he linked his hand with hers. "Shall we?"

So casual.

Like holding her hand was the most natural and platonic thing in the world.

He led her outside and toward the nearest station.

The temperature had dropped, cascading goose bumps down her exposed arms and legs. Her dress's short sleeves were enough to keep her comfortable in the restaurant and during the early hours of the evening, but they had stayed out later than she anticipated.

"Sweater or arm?"

Lizzie blinked up at the strange man. "Excuse me?"
There's that awesome phrase again.

"Shall I choose?"

Uh... "Sure?"

"Excellent." Jayson's hand left hers as he draped his arm over her shoulders and pulled her close.

Oh, well, this is nice.

His body felt strong and warm against hers. And who knew cedar smelled so good?

"Better?" he asked as his hand ran up and down her arm.

Her mouth forgot how to form words, so she nodded instead.

Friends were allowed to keep each other warm, right?

Yes.

Okay.

This wasn't date territory at all. Just a friendly gesture to keep Lizzie from freezing her ass off. Stas would do the same and had done so on several occasions, because Lizzie had a penchant for dresses, even in winter.

Tom would have done it, too, her heart helpfully reminded.

She shoved that thought in a closet and kicked it closed. No sense letting the past ruin a mostly enjoyable evening with a new friend.

Jayson's touch left all too soon as they settled into a pair of seats on the train. They made small talk for a bit until he asked Lizzie why she chose teaching as a profession. Her standard reply about liking kids seemed to stick in her throat, not because of nerves, but because, for some inexplicable reason, she wanted to give him more.

The truth.

"Children are so impressionable at that age," she murmured. "I think having a positive influence means everything, and I want to provide that since one wasn't provided to me."

He stretched his arm along the back of their seats and shifted slightly to face her. It caused their knees to touch, but he didn't seem to mind. "Did you have bad teachers while growing up?"

His tone held a note of incredulity. Obviously, he assumed her wealthy parents had provided her with a reasonable education, and they did. But that's not what she meant.

"I attended private school, and my teachers were all exemplary, but when money is involved, they tend to look the other way." And they did. All the time. "Like when a student misses classes to attend beauty pageants or is spending more hours taking ballet lessons than studying, you would think a teacher might intervene, right?"

"They didn't?"

"Nope." The word popped in her mouth, but he didn't smile.

"I assume the ballet and beauty pageants refer to you?"

She nodded. "It was a constant in my life until college."

And even then, her mother had tried to force her into the adult pageants. However, after Lizzie turned eighteen, she exercised her legal right to refuse. But she never quit dancing. Not completely, anyway. She attended classes for fun now whenever she had time, which wasn't much lately.

His brown gaze roamed over her, and he smiled. "I bet you won often."

She didn't return his amusement. "Occasionally." And when she didn't, her mother never let her hear the end of it. She studied her hands and sighed. "I went into teaching to help children like me, to help those who might be suffering from emotional or physical abuse." Because that's what it was, even if her mother would never admit it.

He lifted her chin with his thumb and stared deep into her eyes. "I think that's very admirable, Elizabeth. And I'm sorry."

She blinked. "For what?"

"For making a joke of something that clearly pains you so deeply, and that you had to go through that. Childhood is the time for fun and games, though I know from experience that's not always the case." He traced her jaw with his fingertip before extending his arm behind her again and relaxing. "My parents, or rather, my father, had certain expectations for me as well. Needless to say, I didn't abide by his wishes."

"But you're obviously doing well for yourself," Lizzie replied. If he could afford a condo in her building, then he wasn't horribly off. Unless his father bought it for him, too, something she highly doubted.

"Oh, I'm definitely doing okay without him, perhaps even in spite of him." Jayson chuckled to himself and shook his head. "Hmm, I believe this is our stop?"

Lizzie smiled. "Still acclimating yourself?"

"It's a huge city."

"Uh-huh, and you still haven't told me where you're from originally."

He stood and held out his hand for hers, tugging her upward. "I think I'll keep it a secret for now, Red." He waggled his brows. "Gotta give you a reason to hang out with me again."

"Oh? You mean I'll have a choice?" she teased as they ascended the stairs. Next time they went out, she would remember her cardigan.

"You had a choice tonight," he reminded.

"I only agreed so you wouldn't barge into my condo again."

His arm fell over her shoulders as he yanked her into his side. Her palm went to his abdomen to keep from falling. His chuckle vibrated the arm she wrapped around his waist to steady herself. "I see the thanks I get for buying you pizza. Twice."

She tried really hard to focus on his words and not the rock-hard muscles bunching beneath her fingertips. Seeing them was one thing, but feeling them? Quite another.

He kept walking, and she hobbled along with him as she searched for her brain.

"Thank you?" She thought that's what he wanted her to say. Maybe. She really didn't know. Being this close to such a fine specimen of male short-circuited her thoughts. It was a miracle she didn't fall on her ass with these heels.

At least she wasn't cold anymore.

"That almost sounded believable, Red."

"Sorry?"

He laughed again and led the way to their building while she focused on remembering how to walk.

What the heck is wrong with me?

Stas always called Lizzie boy crazy because of her obsession with boyfriends and marriage, but a lot of it was said in jest. Lizzie wanted her best friend to be happy, while never really considering her own happiness because she always wanted Tom. Or she thought she did.

But Jayson left her questioning everything; the way she felt around him was decidedly different. Not love drunk, but happy and protected. And warm.

She barely acknowledged the night doorman and navigated the stairs in silence with Jayson right behind her. When she stopped at her floor, he waved her on, and she laughed.

"Oh, this is the part where you demand entry for dessert."

He grinned. "No, this is the part where I ensure you're safe before I go upstairs."

"Well, that's good, because I haven't baked in days."

"You bake?"

She turned to relax against her door and stared up at him. "I'll neither confirm nor deny my hobbies until you tell me where you're from."

"I see what you're doing." He leaned his forearm over her head, caging her between the door and his solid form. "If you bake me cookies, I'll tell you more about all the places I've lived."

"Why cookies?"

"Because Dennis tells me they're amazing."

Damn it. The doorman was giving away her secrets but she had to laugh. "He loves chocolate."

"I do too," Jayson murmured, holding her gaze. "But then again, I like a lot of things."

She swallowed, unsure how to respond to that. The innuendo in his tone left her breathless. Most men who stood this close to her only left her uncomfortable— including the ones who had kissed her—but something about Jayson was different. She experienced happiness with him, an emotion few people had ever evoked from her.

"I had fun tonight, Red."

"Me too." She swore her pulse was louder than her voice right now. It sounded like a drum in her ears.

Thud, thud, thud.

And she'd thought his music was obnoxious. Ha! She couldn't even think over this pounding.

"I'll text you after I get back from my trip next week, and we'll plan that concert. Or maybe a movie."

She nodded on autopilot, unsure what she was saying yes to exactly, but agreeing nonetheless.

His chuckle tickled her lips, sending tingles through every limb.

"Friends can kiss good night, right?" he asked as he brushed his mouth over hers.

Another nod, because no way could she argue with that logic.

His opposite hand lifted to cradle her cheek as he pressed his lips to hers in a firm but chaste kiss. He stepped back all too soon, leaving her dying for more, and his smoldering gaze suggested the feeling was mutual.

"Good night, Lizzie," he murmured. "Don't forget to lock up."

Right.

Door.

Somehow she managed to open it and mumble, "Good night."

That kiss left her quivering long after Jayson left.

She sat on the couch, staring at nothing and feeling everything.

It was as if he'd imprinted himself on her soul, which sounded ridiculous even to Lizzie. But his presence melted into her blood, leaving her a trembling mess of uncomfortable need.

Over a single kiss!

Not even Tom's hugs had made her stomach twist like this, nor had any of her previous experiences.

Friends can kiss good night, right?

Not like that, they don't.

I'm in so much trouble.

CHAPTER FIVE

A Game of Cups

Day eight without human food and
subject's vitals fall within adequate
levels. Next phase will include blood
ingestion.

—Entry Log 105.02.4-7

Lizzie's skin crawled as she stepped into the elevator of the last building she wanted to be in right now. She much preferred her silent condo on a Sunday morning, but her mother would kill her if she skipped brunch.

Stas's hand found hers and gave it a gentle squeeze. "It's going to be okay, Liz."

"The last brunch wasn't," Lizzie muttered. Tom

skipped several family brunches while he was deployed, but this one he had missed for an entirely different reason. One his father and her parents refused to talk about during their last brunch because it contradicted her mother's etiquette rules.

"Well, this one will be different," Stas promised. "Because I won't put up with the Evil Bitch's shit."

Lizzie's lips twitched. Her best friend had given her mother that nickname after their first meeting. "How did you convince Issac to come to this?" They had been an item for a few months, but he never attended previously.

"Doctor Fitzgerald asked him to attend."

"He did?"

"Yep. So you have at least two of us on your side, Liz. Because Issac won't tolerate Lillian's bullshit, either."

The elevator announced their arrival before Lizzie could reply. Issac Wakefield stood just outside the door, waiting for them in the lobby in one of his hand-tailored suits. Black on black today, which paired nicely with his dark chestnut hair and striking blue eyes. He didn't smile as they exited, but his gaze glimmered with satisfaction as it slid over Stas's navy dress and matching heels.

"Aya," he murmured as he tugged on one of her blonde strands of hair. "I missed you this morning." Stas brushed a kiss against his cheek and whispered something in his ear that caused his lips to curl upward.

They weren't outwardly touchy-feely, but a genuine love radiated between them. Not the fuzzy, quick-and-easy kind, but the soul-destroying, heart-wrenching kind. It almost hurt to watch. A connection like that didn't exist between normal people, and it certainly didn't apply to the older couple watching the exchange from the reception desk.

Lizzie's happiness died upon spotting her mother's overly done profile. The woman needed to loosen a few brown curls and maybe stop using eyeliner altogether. It seemed to have permanently damaged her face. Or maybe that was from the frown lines.

She appeared positively petite next to Lizzie's well-fed father. He wasn't necessarily overweight, just a little chubby in the belly, especially when compared to the lithe, blond male beside him.

Her chest ached to behold him. He resembled his son in every way, and it didn't help that he didn't look a day over forty despite having to be in his midfifties by now.

"Hello, Elizabeth," Issac greeted. His English accent gave her name a sexy appeal she didn't hear often. "How are you, love?"

She forced a smile. "I'm okay. You?"

"Eager to get this over with," he admitted quietly. "Shall we?"

His honesty was refreshing and just what she needed. She nodded.

Stas looped her arm through Lizzie's and took on the role of bodyguard as they approached the waiting party. Formal greetings followed despite everyone already knowing each other very well before they claimed their usual table near the windows.

Let the countdown to two o'clock begin.

~*~

Jayson's heart ached for Lizzie. Discomfort and sadness radiated from her as her mother whispered in her ear again.

Verbal poison.

Stas sat to her right, irritating Jayson even more. The woman should be in Hydria, not at a brunch in the middle of Manhattan. Apparently, she'd worked out some sort of arrangement with Issac that Luc had begrudgingly approved.

But she seemed to be the only one keeping Lizzie from crying and also appeared to be as pissed off as Jayson. Her eyes were narrowed, and Issac's hand had disappeared beneath the table ten minutes ago in an attempt to either calm her down or, more likely, to prevent Stas from leaping over Lizzie and kicking Lillian's ass.

The two other men at the table seemed oblivious, or perhaps didn't care.

Jackasses.

Jayson wanted to introduce Lillian to the oversized windows by tossing her through the glass. Alas, he had work to do in the kitchen.

Issac's admirable ability to manipulate vision worked well in situations such as this. He could tap into everyone's visual receptors and alter reality, and he easily manipulated hundreds of people at a time. The Ichorian once likened it to a row of televisions, saying he merely selected the channel he wanted everyone to watch.

Centuries of experience had only perfected his craft.

Right now, it allowed Jayson to move freely through the dining room without anyone noticing him, including Lizzie.

The only one immune to the manipulation was Stas. She was marked with a rune of sorts that blocked Ichorian gifts. Whoever put it there and why remained a mystery, but it served as the reason the two lovebirds initially met.

Jayson slipped into the kitchen and followed the blonde waitress who had just taken the drink orders from Lizzie's table. He had arrived thirty minutes early with Issac to investigate the restaurant but found nothing useful. They decided on plan B, which included Jayson supervising every second of the meal and looking for anything out of the ordinary.

So far, nothing.

But their brunch had just begun.

The short waitress punched all the meals into the system, including Lizzie's green salad with no dressing and dry chicken breast.

That sounds horrible.

What happened to his pizza-loving redhead who

63

enjoyed greasy pepperonis as much as he did?

Stas ordered two pasta dishes with extra garlic bread.

Nice.

Issac had chosen well.

Not that they had a future, but that wasn't for Jayson to worry about.

He trailed after the petite waitress to the refreshment station, where she poured five drinks. She pulled a phone from her pocket and typed one word.

Ready.

The response was immediate. *Here.*

She left the drinks unattended and wandered to the back entrance with an empty glass in hand. The solitary service elevator held her focus. Jayson hoped Issac was seeing all this; otherwise, his cover would be blown as soon as the door opened.

He leaned his hip against the wall and left his hands loose in case he needed to fight. His affinity for metal would help, as would the knives tucked into his suit jacket.

The gentle *bing* sounded a second before the metal slates slid open to reveal a blond male with broad shoulders and a bored expression.

Sentinel Stark, Jayson recognized. He was Stas's primary trainer at the CRF.

The man's light green eyes flickered Jayson's way, but his lack of an outward reaction confirmed Issac's interventions.

Stark stepped forward with a glass of water in his hand.

"Hi, Stark," the waitress greeted.

"Bridget," he returned as they swapped items. "Your assistance is appreciated, as always."

She smiled. "It's not a very hard job."

He didn't return the smile as he moved backward into the still-open elevator. "See you in four weeks."

Jayson wanted to kick himself for missing this obvious connection. Stas had mentioned the brunches, but no one thought a damn thing of it.

He was still shaking his head when the blonde turned around, shrieked, and dropped the glass. It shattered into a bazillion pieces between them.

Apparently, Issac had decided now would be a good time to drop the visual charade.

Jackass, Jayson thought. His lack of a warning caused their best lead to explode all over the fucking floor. And now he had to deal with a hysterical woman. Because no way could he pretend to just be wandering around the employee-only area.

His instincts fired.

He grabbed her, placed his hand over her mouth, and pulled her into a corner mere seconds before two other employees rushed into the back area.

"What the hell?" A stocky male in a chef's hat eyed the broken glass and surroundings with annoyance. "Seriously, what the fuck?"

The brunette beside him scratched her long nose and glanced in Jayson's direction. Her lack of a reaction set his body at ease.

Thanks, Issac, he thought. Not that the Ichorian could hear him.

"Get a broom," the chef said. "Clean it up."

He didn't wait for a response as he left the back area.

"Asshole," the brunette muttered as she grabbed a mop and broom and proceeded to take her sweet-ass time picking up the sharp pieces.

All the while, the waitress in his arms tried futilely to escape, but Jayson wasn't a rookie at restraining a woman. He kept one arm locked around her middle, trapping her arms to her sides, and used his other hand to cover her mouth. Her legs flailed uselessly as he held her off the floor. She managed a few decent back heel kicks, but pain was an old friend.

By the time the pseudo janitor finished cleaning, the blonde was exhausted.

He waited a full minute before pushing out of the

corner and carrying his ward with him to the door, where he closed and locked it quietly.

"Now." He rotated the blonde to face him and read the absolute terror etched into her expression. "I'm not going to hurt you, but I do need you to do me a favor."

Her eyebrows shot upward as tears streamed down her cheeks.

"Okay, let's get one thing straight," he continued. "Screaming will just result in my holding you captive again, and as you've, hopefully, already deduced, your coworkers won't see us. So I recommend you stay quiet and hear me out. Then you can scream later to your little heart's content. All right?"

He had her pinned up against the door with one forearm across her abdomen and the opposite keeping her silent with his palm. But she didn't appear to be fighting anymore. He took that as a good sign.

The horror radiating from her blue eyes, however, would remain for a while.

Humans didn't take well to learning about the supernatural. Her mind would supply her with a multitude of excuses for what just happened, none of which would be the obvious. Her reaction, though, answered at least one burning question.

She had no idea that Ichorians and Hydraians existed.

Which meant she knew nothing about the true nature of the CRF.

He slowly removed his palm from her mouth and waited for her to react. When she didn't scream, he dropped his hand and loosened his hold on her.

"Thank you," he said quietly, meaning it. She was obviously terrified, but intelligent as well. He could respect that. "Now, about my favor. I need you to call the man from the elevator and tell him you need another glass of whatever it is he brings you."

Her eyebrows inched upwards. "You... What?"

"Do you have any idea what's in that glass he gives

you?"

She shook her head slowly.

"But you give it to the redhead, right? Every four weeks?"

Some of the color returned to her cheeks as she nodded.

"I assume they pay you," he continued.

Another nod.

"Great. I need you to text him and tell him you accidentally dropped the glass. And I want you to do it on speakerphone so I can listen."

"I... I..."

"Look, I don't exactly have a lot of time. And all I need is that simple phone call. Then I'll disappear." Afterward, she could tell whomever she wanted about him. With him distorting his features, she wouldn't be able to describe him, and the security feeds were already altered thanks to Mateo's intervention. All avenues were covered.

She swallowed but otherwise didn't move.

He took back his assessment regarding her astuteness. The shock had clearly fried some brain cells.

"Unlock your phone and hand it to me." He held out his palm, waiting.

Her hand shook as she complied.

Jayson scrolled through her text messages from Stark and reviewed some of their previous exchanges to understand their usual cadence. Short and to the point. He could do that.

I accidentally dropped the glass. What should I do?

"I suspect he's going to call." And likely not be very pleasant. "I need you to talk to him. Mention me, and you won't like the consequences. Understood?"

She gave him a short nod as the color drained from her cheeks again.

Jayson knew he could evoke fear when he wanted to, but this was just ridiculous. Aside from holding her still, he'd done nothing menacing. It was the Sentinel she should worry about.

The phone rang within seconds, flashing with the name: Gabriel Stark.

Well, here we go.

Either she helped or she didn't.

Jayson selected the Talk button and raised an eyebrow at her.

"H-hello?" Her nerves were expected and appropriate. Stark would assume she was startled by dropping the glass and worried about his reaction.

"You dropped the glass," he repeated emotionlessly.

"I... I tr-tripped."

"Indeed."

"I-I'm sorry."

"That I believe," Stark replied. "Obviously, you won't be paid this month."

Tears welled in her eyes. "C-can't you just b-bring me another one?"

"No." His flat reply reverberated through the room and was followed by a click as Stark ended the call.

Bridget cast big doe eyes up at Jayson. Clearly, she expected the worst from him and he couldn't necessarily blame her.

"Excellent. See, that wasn't so hard, right?" He pushed away from her and waved a hand at the door. "You're welcome to go."

"Th-that's it?"

"I told you I just wanted a favor."

She frowned. "You meant it?"

"I try to keep my word when I can," he replied as he punched the service elevator button. "Oh, but a piece of advice. Find a new job and change your number."

"What? Why?"

"Because Stark? He's bad news. When he grows tired of you, you'll be replaced. And I don't mean fired." He stepped into the elevator as it opened. "Have a good afternoon." He gave her a salute before pressing the button to take him down to the ground floor.

His phone slipped into his hand as the doors closed, and he had it at his ear a second later.

Jacque answered on the first ring. "'Sup?"

Jayson loved military technology, and that adoration extended to telecommunications.

Hence his perfect signal inside the metal box.

"I need a teleport," he said.

"From the coordinates you sent me?"

"Yep." Jayson anticipated something might go wrong, and it never hurt to have a backup plan.

"Peace." The phone went dead.

Jayson shot a text off to Issac while he waited for the elevator to continue descending. *Heading to Hydria for a debrief.*

Regroup at 16:30, was the reply as the doors opened.

Jacque stood in the building's lobby, leaning against a column with his hands in his jeans. His rock band shirt and floppy black hair brought a smile to Jayson's face.

Home.

~*~

Lizzie looked at the clock for the thousandth time.

Brunch should have ended thirty minutes ago, but thanks to their waitress's disappearing act, they had just finished eating.

Lizzie handed her half-eaten salad off to their replacement waiter and folded her hands in her lap. Her mother had commented three times so far on Lizzie's choice to wear black.

Such an unflattering color on you.

Why would you wear black with your red hair, considering that it's so close to Halloween?

Really, Elizabeth, it's like you're in mourning.

Lizzie wanted nothing more than to shove a fork down her mother's throat.

But she remained proper, quiet, and hyperfocused on the flower arrangement in the middle of the table.

Stas squeezed her thigh, grabbing her attention. "How do you feel about Friday night, Lizzie?"

Uh... "As in this Friday?"

Stas nodded. "Is that enough time to prepare for a dinner party?"

Lizzie's eyebrows inched up. She'd clearly missed an important conversation. "Depends on what you want to eat." *And who I'm feeding?*

"I've always enjoyed your cooking," Doctor Fitzgerald replied.

"Likewise," Issac murmured. "Is there anything Gabriel won't eat?"

Who the hell is Gabriel?

Doctor Fitzgerald shrugged. "I'm certain whatever Lizzie decides will satisfy him."

"Sentinel Stark," Stas whispered while Issac and Doctor Fitzgerald discussed a time. "They want to come over for dinner Friday."

"Why?" Lizzie whispered back.

Stas shrugged. "I don't know. Doctor Fitzgerald received a call and inquired about dinner afterward, saying Stark wants to meet you."

"Why?" Lizzie repeated.

"Probably because I've told him so much about you, or maybe he wants to come over and beat me some more," Stas muttered.

"It's quite rude to whisper at the table when dining with company," Lizzie's mother stated loudly.

"Really? Because you seem quite fond of whispering things in Lizzie's ear," Stas snapped back.

Oh no.

Her mother locked gazes with Stas, but before she could say a word, Issac spoke up.

"Does seven work for you, Elizabeth? Or will you require more time for a party of five?"

So my parents won't be attending. Good. Not that she really wanted company anyway, but she could tolerate an evening with Stas and her coworkers.

"Seven is fine," she replied.

Lizzie loved to cook, but lately, she hadn't wanted to be anywhere near her kitchen. Even to bake cookies. Which was the primary reason she had yet to deliver chocolate sweets to Jayson.

That and the fact that he hadn't bothered to text her once since their non-date five days ago. And now he was traveling, so who knew when or if she'd see him again.

Just friends, she repeated for the millionth time.

He owed her nothing, and she barely even liked him anyway.

So what if she had dreamt of him every night this week. She was just lonely.

That kiss hadn't meant much, either. Her lips may have tingled for an hour afterward, but that was because she hadn't kissed anyone in over a year. Of course she reacted to it.

"Lizzie," Stas murmured. "Is everything okay?"

"I'm fine." The phrase rolled easily off her tongue, just as it did every time someone asked how she was feeling.

Because it was the expected reply.

The man I've been in love with for most of my life just died, but I'm fine.

My mother enjoys battering my self-confidence, but I'm fine.

You just invited the man who resembles the dead love of my life over to dinner Friday night, but I'm fine.

My best friend has decided to work for the very company that ruined my childhood and killed Tom, but I'm fine.

Our new neighbor kissed me and never called me afterward, but I'm fine.

Fine.

A lie.

Lizzie most definitely wasn't fine.

And she hadn't been for a very long time.

"I'm fine," she repeated for good measure. Because if she said it enough, she'd believe it. Someday.

CHAPTER SIX

When a Ghost Invites Himself to Coffee

The benefactor's associate who
supervised today's experiment suggested
the subject's social training be
expanded. We're taking it under
advisement.

—Entry Log 109.04.4-7

He missed her.

He shouldn't.

It was ridiculous.

But he did.

Jayson flipped his phone around a few times in his hand, debating. What could it hurt to pay her a short visit? Say hello?

They were neighbors.

Friends, even.

I kissed her.

Though he could hardly call it a kiss. B would send him to sexual therapy for considering it anything other than a platonic gesture.

Jayson didn't chastely kiss women. He devoured them.

So this hardly counted. No rules broken; forbidden ribbon intact.

One week since he'd last spoken to Lizzie. He protected her every day, but she didn't know, nor did she have a clue he'd been at the restaurant two days ago.

Her forlorn expression that morning still killed him. He usually ran in the opposite direction at the first sign of emotion from males and females, but her heartache called to him on a level he didn't know existed.

"Shit," he muttered, standing.

He needed a good run.

Or a fuck.

Maybe both.

The celibacy was screwing with his head. He never went long without sex. Jayson enjoyed all varieties, types, positions, and kink. Had even shared women with men and vice versa.

Three thousand years was a long time to be alive not to vary it up every now and then.

A knock at his door had him springing up off the couch, hopeful that a certain redhead had come up to say hello. Instead, he found Ezekiel leaning against his doorjamb, looking bored. He didn't ask to come inside. He just stood there, legs crossed casually at the ankles, black eyes gleaming.

"You want to get a drink?" he asked, surprising the shit out of Jayson.

"Is that an innuendo for something?"

Ezekiel flashed a row of perfect teeth at him in his version of a smile. "No, not tonight."

"Let me change." Jayson left the door open while he retreated to the bedroom to don a pair of jeans, a sweater, and several knives. When he returned, he found Ezekiel in the same spot by the door. "If you try to kill me, you'll fail."

The Ichorian shrugged as if to say, *Perhaps*.

Jayson locked up his condo and followed the leather-jacket-wearing assassin down the hall and stairs. The fact that he presented his back to Jayson was a sign of trust, a way of returning the favor for agreeing to the impromptu drink rather than slamming the door in the man's face.

"How is your wooing of the sexy redhead going?" Ezekiel asked casually as they walked.

"I'm not wooing her."

"Oh, I agree it's not going as expected," the Ichorian replied, nodding. "A pity after that pizza date in Brooklyn went so well. Perhaps you should try calling the woman more? I hear they like that."

Jayson resisted the sudden urge to drive a blade down the other man's throat and focused on keeping his voice calm. "I had no idea you were so bored, Zeke." *Or that you followed us to Brooklyn.*

How could he keep Lizzie safe if he didn't even sense a lethal assassin trailing their every move?

"More like *curious*." Ezekiel flashed another one of those terrifying grins. "Still, what gives? Why woo her one night and ignore her the next? That sounds like a woman's game."

"I'm not trying to woo her," Jayson said again.

"Right you are, Jay. Because you're doing a shit job of it." Ezekiel shook his head as he stopped in front of a coffee place only a few blocks from the condo. "Shall I show you how it's done?"

Over my dead body.

Jayson swallowed his desire to throttle Zeke and redirected the conversation. "When you said you wanted a drink, I thought you meant at a bar."

"This is a bar of sorts. They just happen to serve coffee."

Suspicion tightened his chest. He may have lost touch with the Ichorian over the centuries, but he knew the assassin's proclivities did not include relaxing in casual locations.

"What are we really doing here, Zeke?"

"Playing," he replied as he opened the door. "After you."

This isn't going to end well.

And that thought was confirmed when he spied Stas and Lizzie sitting on a couch across from the entrance. Big brown eyes met his, widened, then narrowed.

"Ah yes, she's sour with you indeed." Ezekiel nudged Jayson's arm. "Let's see if I can't help fix it?" The Ichorian started toward the duo with a confident swagger.

Fuck.

He knew Ezekiel had a game in mind, but he didn't expect this one. It took all manner of control to keep a straight face as he trailed behind the sadistic assassin. Lizzie's glower didn't help, and neither did the concerned expression on Stas's face as she glanced up from her coffee mug.

"Jayson?" Lizzie asked, her expression confused and tinged with hurt. "I thought you were traveling on business."

"We were," Ezekiel replied before Jayson could utter a word. "We just returned this evening and were searching for a place to have a drink when Jayson saw you inside." He gestured to the giant glass windows overlooking Broadway.

Well, at least he didn't call me Jedrick.

Lizzie peered at Ezekiel, her eyebrows inching up slightly. "You're coworkers?"

"More like business rivals," the assassin replied smoothly and extended a hand. "I'm Kiel, by the way."

She pinched her lips to the side, but manners won as

she accepted his gesture and shook his hand. "Lizzie."

"I know," Ezekiel replied. "Jayson won't stop talking about you."

Wow.

If Jayson didn't want to kill him before, he did now.

"When he saw you from outside, he suggested we ask to join you, but now he's being shy." He tsked. "It's very unlike him. I daresay your beauty has tied him up in knots. Scared him speechless, hmm?"

Oh, for fuck's sake. He'd painted Jayson as a pansy. A knife between those black eyes would make for a fantastic facial ornament. Maybe he'd add another to the man's groin. Ezekiel always did fancy metal decor, hence the random lip piercing.

"What Kiel is trying to say is that we're here for a cup of coffee and will be leaving you alone in a minute." Jayson gestured to the counter, but of course, Zeke didn't move.

"Oh, but you've told me so much about her. I want to learn more. You wouldn't mind if we joined you for a bit, would you?" Ezekiel's placating tone made Jayson's skin crawl.

Damn it.

Say no, Red.

"Uh…" Lizzie looked to Stas for approval, but the blonde was focused on Ezekiel's profile. "I mean… I think that's okay?" She seemed to be waiting for Stas to speak up, but her lips were firmly closed, her attention on the leather-clad Ichorian.

Could she sense the lethal air surrounding Ezekiel?

All the Hydraian Elders wanted Stas out of the city. It was dangerous, but she ignored their wishes. Would this finally force her to see reason? Not exactly his preferred method, but fear could be one hell of a motivator.

"Excellent," Ezekiel murmured. He relaxed onto the couch cushion catty-cornered to Lizzie. "Get us a round, yeah?"

Jayson folded his arms, unamused. "It's not a pub, Kiel."

"Right. I'll take a cappuccino."

His eyebrows inched upward. "And I'm paying?"

"Obviously." Ezekiel turned to Lizzie and Stas. "Would you ladies like anything?" He eyed Stas's mug. "Perhaps another latte, darling?"

Her knuckles went white around the ceramic as she met his gaze. And all the color drained from her face.

No response.

Lizzie frowned at her friend before gazing up at Jayson. "I'm okay, thank you."

"I say, are you all right?" Ezekiel asked, his tone holding a touch of amusement as he studied Stas. "You look like you've seen a ghost."

She cleared her throat. "No. Sorry." She stood suddenly. "I'm just going to grab a water."

"Jayson can do that for you," Ezekiel offered.

"I'm good," Stas said, waving him off. "I'll be right back."

Lizzie frowned after Stas as she walked stiffly over to the counter.

"You should go with her, Jay," Ezekiel encouraged. "Order our drinks."

Jayson narrowed his gaze. *If you touch her, I will kill you.*

Isn't this fun? Ezekiel seemed to reply. "Go ahead. I promise not to bite or misbehave while you're away." He flashed a conspiratorial glance at Lizzie. "He's terribly overprotective."

Funny, Jayson thought, irritated. "I'll be right over there." He spoke the words for Lizzie alone. One scream and he would be here.

"Okay," she replied, her brow furrowed. She likely thought he was insane. Not for the first time, Jayson wished Lizzie knew the truth.

He kept her in his periphery as he moved through the coffee shop and flinched when Ezekiel made her laugh.

No way would this end well.

Nails bit into his bicep through his sweater, distracting him from his mission, and he met a pair of terrified green eyes. His arm slipped around Stas's shoulders on instinct as he maneuvered her out of sight of Lizzie and Ezekiel.

"What's wrong?" he whispered.

She clutched her phone to her chest as if it were her only armor.

"Talk to me, sweetheart," he said, voice low. No one had noticed the strange embrace yet, but it was only a matter of time.

"He... That man..." She shuddered and pressed her forehead to his chest. If Lizzie saw this, their cover would be blown. Jayson wasn't supposed to know Stas.

Ezekiel oozed a lethal air that she'd obviously picked up on, and he was particularly deadly to her as a Nizari assassin. "You recognize him."

She nodded vigorously.

"Because Issac gave you his description, or is it a sense?" he asked, curious. Fledglings were so rare these days that their innate abilities remained a bit of a mystery, and Stas was far from typical.

"No." The single word sounded so broken he had to pull her away to study her face.

Tears, horror, and such deep sorrow.

"Okay, I really need you to talk to me, Stas." This woman had faced other immortals with similar dispositions without reacting like this. She had survived a Conclave, for crying out loud. A Nizari assassin should scare her, but this went beyond fear.

She hiccuped. "Jay..." She squeezed her eyes closed and took a deep breath. "That..." Another breath. "That's the Ichorian who killed my parents."

~*~

"So, you work in acquisitions?" Lizzie asked, curious.

Kiel's long black hair, lip piercing, and leather jacket appeared more rocker than businessman.

He smirked. "I do, yes. For a rival company of sorts."

"But you're friends?"

"Yes, I suppose we are, in a manner of speaking." He crossed one leg over the other and relaxed against the arm of the couch. "You could say we have a long history."

"Did you go to school together?" she asked.

"We trained together, yes."

That was an odd way to phrase it, but most of his mannerisms and phrases were different. So was his accent. "Where are you from?"

He chuckled. "That's a complicated question. Define *from*."

"Uh, like where you were born?"

"Babylon," he replied, not missing a beat.

She blinked at the too-familiar name. "Like the ancient city?"

"The very one. And you?"

"Okay, but hold on, are you saying you're from the actual city of Babylon, as in the area from, what was it, the Mesopotamia period?" Lizzie didn't major in history, but that sounded right. "Or do you mean a city called Babylon?"

He leaned closer to her, his black eyes smoldering with gold embers. "What do you think?"

"That you clearly mean a city named after Babylon." His pale skin suggested northern roots, and no one would refer to that area in the Middle East as Babylon. They would call it Iraq, or whatever city it was now called in that country.

"Sure." He smiled. "And where were you born?"

"New York City."

"Are you sure about that?" he asked.

She stared at him. "Yes."

He nodded. "I see. Fascinating. And you've lived here your very short life?"

Another odd phrase, but she went with it. "Yes, in Manhattan."

"Do you ever tire of it?" he asked, those hypnotic eyes captivating hers. She wouldn't call him handsome as she would Jayson, but sexy, in a very dark way.

"Sometimes," she admitted, recalling his question. "But I don't know where else I would live."

"Greece, I imagine." Another quick reply that left her baffled.

Of all places to mention… "Why Greece?"

His Cheshire-cat grin reminded her of the devil. Alluring, yet evil. But whatever he planned to say was silenced by Jayson setting a tray of cups down rather loudly on the end table between their couches.

"Cappuccino," he said flatly.

"Brilliant. Thanks, mate." Kiel plucked it off the tray and took a sip. His nose wrinkled, but he didn't comment.

Lizzie glanced at the counter for Stas but didn't see her.

"Your friend is making a phone call," Jayson explained as he took Stas's vacated seat beside Lizzie. "She introduced herself then asked me to let you know. Something about work."

Of course. The CRF owned her best friend's soul now. "I see. Kiel was just telling me I should move to Greece."

"Was he?" Jayson murmured. "Well, it is a beautiful country with fantastic weather and the islands are nice, but I'm not sure why Kiel would recommend it. I don't believe he's been there often."

His friend peeked at them over his coffee cup. "Oh, I've been there more than you realize."

"I bet." Jayson reached over Lizzie for his own coffee mug, brushing her breasts in the process.

A surge of heat crept up her neck, stemming from her hardening nipples.

Crap. Her thin, lacy bra and violet dress wouldn't hide the reaction well. *Maybe he will think I'm cold.*

Or not notice at all.

He didn't show any outward reaction as he balanced the mug against his thigh with one hand. "How was your week, Red?"

"Uh, fine." *Boring. Long. Sad. Lonely.* When did it get so hot in here? She cleared her throat and searched for a safe topic. "How was your business trip?"

"There was a minor break in the plan, but I think we're close to finishing up our project."

Kiel leaned forward with interest. "And what project is that, Jay?"

"None of your business, Kiel."

"Oh, if only that were true," he replied with a twist of his lips. He finished his cappuccino and set it on the table. "That was mediocre at best."

"Grabbing a drink was your idea."

"Yes, yes, it was." The lean man stood and stretched long arms over his head before sighing. "I think I may go scout for a proper drink elsewhere. I assume you would prefer to stay here?"

"The company is significantly better," Jayson replied. "So, yes."

"You wound me, old friend." Kiel didn't appear wounded at all, just amused. "Please tell your friend I'm sorry we didn't get to properly meet. Perhaps next time. I'll try not to appear so ghostly."

Lizzie's brow furrowed. "I'm not clear on what that was about, but I'm sure she'll be happy to meet you at some point." Not that she had any idea when that would be or if she would ever see this eccentric man again.

"Oh, I doubt that, but time will tell," he replied cryptically. "Jay, as always, a pleasure. Stay sharp, yeah?"

Jayson rested his arm across the back of the couch, behind Lizzie's head, and gave his friend a meaningful look that she couldn't interpret.

"Likewise, Z," Jayson said.

"Cheers, Jay," Kiel murmured. "Lovely to meet you, Lizzie. I'll see you again soon."

"Uh, nice to meet you too." *And when?*

He winked and sauntered toward the exit without a backward glance.

"Jay," Lizzie repeated after the man disappeared through the door. "Is that your nickname?"

"Yeah, most people call me Jay." With one hand, he swirled the coffee in his mug against his thigh while his other arm remained stretched out behind her head. "Of all my friends for you to meet, that's not the one I would have chosen to introduce you to first, or even last."

"Why not?"

Jayson focused on his cup as if it held all the answers. "Let's just say, he's bad news."

She nodded in understanding. That much she had gathered from his demeanor, though there was a charm to him as well. "He's certainly different."

"That's an understatement." He sipped his coffee with a grimace and set it on the table. "I hate to agree with Kiel, but that's crap."

Lizzie grinned. "Is the coffee in Greece better?"

"It is."

"Which you know because you've lived there?" She kept the question light and innocent, not letting on to how much she truly wanted the answer.

But he saw right through it.

"Oh, Red." His arm fell to her shoulders as he leaned into her personal space. "I believe you owe me cookies first."

"I didn't know when you would be back." A sad excuse since she never intended to bake them anyway, but he didn't know that.

"Uh-huh. You could have called to ask."

"And you could have texted me at any point to say hello, but you didn't."

His chuckle was low and sexy, and far too intimate. "So what you're saying is, if I want cookies, I need to message you?"

She swallowed, her mouth dry. Somehow this man had turned baking into a seductive topic. Visions of him drizzled in chocolate swept through her mind. *Yes, please.*

But the clearing of a throat interrupted the moment.

Issac stood in front of them with his arm around Stas. They both wore matching expressions of disapproval.

"Uh, hi, Issac."

"Elizabeth," he returned. "Introduce me to your friend."

She bristled at the demand in his tone. "Introduce yourself."

"Fine." He stared straight at Jayson. "Issac Wakefield."

"Jayson Masters," her *friend* replied with an easy smile. He didn't remove his arm from her shoulders but did shift slightly to give her more space. "You seem uptight. Maybe you need to sit down."

"Funny," Issac replied. "I was about to escort Aya back to her flat. You should join us."

Jayson chuckled. "Yes, sir."

"What if we're not ready to leave?" Lizzie snapped, irritated. She didn't know what the hell had gotten into Issac or why her best friend wasn't calling him on his bullshit, but Lizzie wouldn't stand for it. Billionaire or not, he couldn't tell her what to do.

"It's okay, Red," Jayson murmured. "We can go."

"Please, Liz," Stas said. "Can we hang out at the condo? I need something stronger than a coffee."

Lizzie noted the puffy circles beneath her best friend's eyes and the slight redness to her cheeks. Almost as if she'd been crying. "Did something happen?"

"Nothing I can't handle, but I would feel better at home." Stas gave her a pleading look, one she rarely used.

Girl code took over.

If Stas needed to go home, for whatever reason, Lizzie would agree. And she wouldn't ask questions. She learned a long time ago that they rolled right off Stas. Her best friend was the type to open up, but only when ready.

"Sure," Lizzie said. "Yeah, we can go."

Jayson stood first and held out his hand for Lizzie to help her up. She didn't really need it, but she accepted anyway. When he didn't let go and linked their fingers together, her heart skipped a beat. Issac's glower at the obvious display of affection only worsened the effect.

They were friends.

But not.

Or more?

Would he kiss her again?

Probably not with Issac giving him that glower.

Just stop.

Jayson squeezed her hand as they walked in silence, and she looked up to find him grinning. "You still owe me cookies."

She returned the smile. "Only if you tell me about Greece."

"Deal."

Stas halted on the sidewalk in front of them but didn't turn around. "What about Greece?" she asked, her voice thick with emotion.

Lizzie frowned. "Uh, Jayson used to live there. Even though he won't admit it."

"Kiel, an old associate of mine, implied it, but I've neither confirmed nor denied it."

"He used to live there," Lizzie confirmed. "He's just playing hard to get because he wants me to bake for him."

Jayson dropped her hand and wrapped his arm around her shoulders, pulling her close. "You're trouble, Red."

"You both are," Issac interjected. "In trouble, I mean."

"You really need to relax, Wakefield." Jayson gave him a pointed look. "Keep walking. We're right behind you."

"Leave it alone." Stas nudged Issac onward. "It'll work itself out."

"Oh, something will be worked out," Issac replied, causing Jayson to chuckle.

"I don't know why he's acting like that," Lizzie

whispered up at him. "He's usually a lot more pleasant."

"He's protective," Jayson whispered back. "But don't worry, Red. He doesn't scare me." His easy smile left in the next moment as he tripped and let out a curse.

Issac caught Jayson by the arm as he started to fall. "Easy there, mate," he said, his voice holding an edge to it. "Pavement can be tricky."

"You know what else is tricky?" Jayson breathed. "Metal."

Issac flinched. "Noted."

"Escort us home," Stas demanded. "Now."

Issac's resulting smile reached his eyes. "Certainly, Aya."

Jayson didn't seem to be nearly as amused, but he laid his arm across Lizzie's shoulders and started walking again. It felt colder and less intimate, and he didn't look at her again.

His behavior baffled her. He seemed to be attracted to her, or so her minimal experience with men suggested, but he also treated her as only a friend. Like Tom did.

But Tom never kissed her on the lips, only on the cheeks.

Except Jayson hadn't truly kissed her, either, not in the passionate way a man who desired a woman would, anyway.

It was chaste and friendly.

Why is this so complicated?

The doorman of the building greeted them all by name. Lizzie smiled but said nothing as Jayson led her to the stairwell and up to their door.

"I think Issac and Stas can take it from here," he said softly.

"You don't need to go." The needy note in her voice left a sour taste in her stomach. Was she that starved for attention that she had to beg? Ouch.

"It's okay, Red. We'll catch up later over cookies." He brushed a kiss against her temple. "Chocolate, please." He pulled back with a wink. "Talk to you soon, Liz."

"Chocolate," she repeated. Right. She swallowed the lump in her throat. "Okay. Night."

His leaving shouldn't have bothered her as much as it did, but she had finally enjoyed herself a little, only to have it ripped away like everything else in her life. A few stolen moments of flirtatious words and laughs.

Was that all she could expect? Or would there ever be more?

As he walked off toward the stairs, she worried she would never know.

A melancholy thought, but if she had learned anything over the last few months, it was that life was short.

The next time she saw Jayson, she would tell him how she felt because she refused to make the same mistake with him as she had with Tom. He died not knowing she loved him, and though she may not love Jayson yet, she didn't want to risk not telling him that she liked him. Perhaps even more than a friend.

She stepped through the open door and locked it behind her.

"I'll be in my room if you need me," she said to the couple standing inside the foyer.

"Liz…"

"It's okay, Stas. Enjoy your time with Issac." She gave them both a small smile before leaving them to their own devices. At least her best friend was happy. She deserved it more than anyone Lizzie knew, even herself.

CHAPTER SEVEN

Secrets and Lies

Stas collapsed against Issac, her heart breaking for so many reasons.

"Not here," he whispered against her ear, reminding her of the surveillance in the condo. He led her into the hallway without a word, guiding her to who knew where. She barely registered him locking the door.

She hated everything.

The CRF.

This world.

Fate.

The monster who killed her parents.

Issac's arms held her upright as her legs buckled beneath her. Just as he'd done outside the coffeehouse. He'd arrived within minutes of her call, indicating his nearby presence. It should have infuriated her that he felt the need to babysit her, but she'd never been more thankful for his unwavering protection than she was tonight.

And he was right. Staying in the city was a suicide mission. But she couldn't leave Lizzie. Especially not with an assassin lurking around the corner.

She shuddered. It'd taken all her strength to walk back into that coffeehouse for Lizzie. But by the time they returned, the man who stalked Stas's memories was gone. She'd tried to put on a smile for Lizzie's sake, but it felt false. Wrong.

He's real.

And he was not only the villain of her past but also the one who wanted to destroy her future.

"Aya," Issac murmured, bringing her to the present. They were standing in the stairwell, locked in an embrace she never wanted to leave. Ever. "Lucian has requested a meeting."

"About…?" She couldn't finish, couldn't say *his* name.

Understanding flashed in his midnight gaze. "Ezekiel."

She swallowed and forced a nod.

"In Hydria," he added. "Jacque is coming to retrieve us."

She nodded again, unable to speak. The terror she felt tonight… She shivered and hugged Issac tighter.

He'd been right.

She was no match for the assassin. He would rip her to shreds, and enjoy it.

That smile… Oh God, that smile…

Issac pressed his lips to her temple and rubbed her back. She knew what he wanted to say. *It's time.*

She agreed but couldn't leave Lizzie behind. "What about Liz?" They couldn't run off to Hydria and leave her unprotected.

"Jayson has requested one of his Guardians watch over her while we are meeting with Luc. Jacque is dropping her off right now."

"Oh."

From what Stas understood, the strongest Hydraians were part of the Elders' personal security teams. Jayson had requested his remain in Greece due to the threat of Ichorians in the city and him being the only one capable of concealing his identity. That he and the others felt it necessary to send someone in his absence spoke volumes about how they perceived Lizzie. They wanted to protect her too.

That small insight helped calm some of her nerves.

They really do care.

"'Sup," a deep voice greeted from behind them. Stas had gotten to know the teleporter well over the last few months and usually grinned upon seeing him. But not tonight.

"Hello, Jacque," Issac murmured as one of his hands left her back. "Thank you for the lift."

"Anytime."

The world shifted around them, churning Stas's stomach as her scenery changed. Issac released her from his hold, allowing her to gain her own footing. Then she turned to face several familiar immortals, all of whom were seated at a long wooden table. No drinks or food. No games. Only stern expressions, a whiteboard, several computers at the back wall, and a basket of phones.

It seemed to be the Hydraians' equivalent of a war room.

"Stas. Wakefield," Luc greeted from the head of the table. "Have a seat."

"Lucian," Issac replied as he pulled out a chair for Stas. "Have you called Aidan?" He settled into the seat beside her and laid an arm over her shoulders. So casual, yet so meaningful. A sign of partnership and care, and one she desperately needed right now.

"Yes, I conferred with him earlier," Luc said. "He feels Ezekiel is playing a game of strategy and is very much aware of Stas's bloodline."

"That is my opinion as well," Issac murmured, his thumb drawing a pattern against her upper arm. "Did he have a recommendation?"

~*~

"He thinks we should play along," Jayson informed them, irritated. Aidan had clearly lost his damn mind. Engaging Ezekiel in a game was the last thing any sane person would ever do. "I happen to disagree."

"What were Aidan's reasons?" Issac asked, his expression blank.

"Put simply, we need more information." Luc scratched his jaw. "Our best course of action is to continue gathering intelligence while Elizabeth remains ignorant, and as it seems Ezekiel has no intention to harm her—"

"Yet," Jayson added, unable to help himself. He understood the assassin better than anyone at this table, not that they were listening to him.

Luc blinked those all-knowing eyes at him, an indication that he was in full omniscient mode. "Ezekiel's penchant for violence is renowned, yet he chose to carry on a conversation with Elizabeth instead of killing her for sport. I would love to know why, wouldn't you?"

Stas cleared her throat. "Honestly, no, I don't really want to know why." Her voice seemed softer than normal, almost hoarse, but her spine straightened with every word. "But I would like my best friend relocated and protected."

LEXI C. FOSS

"We cannot protect her properly without the serum,"
Luc pointed out. "And without it, we risk killing her."

Stas's shoulders fell, causing Issac to pull her closer.
His sapphire eyes went to Luc, communicating something
only the two men seemed to understand. They shared a
father, in a manner of speaking, anyway, which created a
brotherly bond between them a few centuries back. It
didn't quite rival the one Jayson, Luc, Alik, and Balthazar
had formed over their thousands of years together, but the
connection between Luc and Issac was one of loyalty, love,
and family. And it showed now.

"We can't help Lizzie until we know what the CRF—
my father—did to her," Tom said, his voice quiet.
Normally, new Hydraians weren't allowed in these sorts of
conversations, but his knowledge on the subject qualified
him to be here.

Issac gave the man a measuring look and nodded. "I
agree with Thomas. Taking Elizabeth now could put her at
risk. We need more information regarding her origin
before we proceed."

Jayson cursed inwardly.

Logic.

He knew that.

But their flawless reasoning did little to dispel his inner
turmoil over the events of tonight. Although he agreed
that they needed more details before liberating Lizzie from
her situation, a growing part of him longed to tell her the
truth.

The hurt in her gaze when he left her standing in the
hallway nagged at him all the way upstairs. Had Jacque not
been waiting in his condo, Jayson very likely would have
ended up back at Lizzie's door, begging for a good-night
kiss.

What the fuck is wrong with me?

Jayson didn't pine after women. He dated sporadically,
but most of his dalliances were for a night or two only.

Yet this redhead had him all tied up in knots.

It was her innate goodness. After six weeks of observing her tender treatment of others less fortunate—like the homeless man she gave her lunch to that one day on the subway—Jayson couldn't help but feel a little for her.

And the nurturing relationships she'd formed with her students; even from afar, he could see their affection for her. Children were excellent judges of characters, and they adored her.

Because she's genuine.

He ran his fingers through his hair and looked at the ceiling as the memories rolled through his thoughts. All those beaming expressions directed at a woman who never expected them.

Fuck.

Lizzie deserved so much better than this.

He actually felt guilty for doing his job, which made little sense. It wasn't his responsibility to tell her the truth. That task belonged to Luc, Stas, and Tom. Jayson's purpose was to observe, report back, and protect as necessary.

Damn it.

Lizzie had to feel alone right now, and they were all to blame. Grace was in Jayson's condo right now, protecting Lizzie from above, but his Red had no way of knowing or understanding that.

But Luc and Issac were right.

They would need a safe place to take Lizzie after she learned the truth, which required a better understanding of her genetic makeup. "We need the serum," he muttered.

"Indeed," Issac agreed. "Which, I believe, is the purpose of our dinner Friday night."

Jayson nodded. Jonathan had requested the gathering at Lizzie's condo shortly after the fiasco at brunch; inviting Stark to tag along only confirmed the plans.

"But that requires Stas to go back to the city," Jayson added. "Where Ezekiel is likely to be very aware of her."

Silence as all eyes turned to the woman in question.

She cleared her throat as she straightened her shoulders again. "It's a necessary risk to help Lizzie. I'll be better prepared the next time I see him." Her tone lacked the usual confidence, indicating that—for the first time—she actually understood the danger she'd put herself in.

She's learning. Finally.

"Forgive my insensitivity," Luc murmured, his gaze on Stas. "But are you certain Ezekiel murdered your parents? I ask because his methods have always been quiet and reserved, not one of passion and mayhem. Yet, from my comprehension, your parents were burned alive. That strikes me as quite different from his usual methods."

She remained quiet, her shoulders and back still. After several beats, she nodded. "I'll never forget the way the flames glowed in his black eyes. It was him. I'm certain of it."

Luc's forehead crinkled in a way Jayson recognized after millennia of knowing one another. *Doubt.* The facts weren't adding up in that omniscient mind of his, leaving him puzzled, but he didn't question her further.

"I'm sorry, Stas. I can imagine this is painful for you, but it is the logical course. We will help Lizzie in due time. You have my word."

Stas would have no way of knowing just how powerful a statement that was coming from the leader of the Hydraian race, but Issac and Jayson understood. Luc had just made a blood vow of sorts, and he took those very seriously.

She said nothing, but Issac answered for her with a subtle nod of gratitude.

"It's settled," Luc murmured. "Dinner Friday night."

Jayson stretched his arms over his head. "Looks like we get to play another game of hide-and-seek, Wakefield."

Issac smirked. "My favorite."

"Try not to drop the charade too quickly this time," Jayson suggested, referring to the part where Issac let the waitress see him on Sunday without any warning.

"Perhaps you should try working on your reaction time," Issac replied.

Jayson shook his head and shifted his focus to Jacque. "I'm ready."

"Stay alive," Luc said as the teleporter appeared at Jayson's side, his hand at the ready.

Jayson nodded once in agreement. "Likewise."

CHAPTER EIGHT

Playing Hide-and-Seek

Project benefactor requested additional
supplements be added to the subject's
regimen. Observation required.

—Entry Log 103.11.4-7

Jayson threw a baseball up in the air, caught it on its way down, and repeated the action.

"Anything new?" he asked as Jacque paced beside the couch. It'd been a few days since they saw each other last.

The teleporter shrugged. "Amelia and Tom broke ground on their home over the weekend."

"Yeah?" Jayson grinned. "That's good. I'd like my

house back when I return." It would require a thorough cleaning since the two lovebirds had used it as their own for the last few weeks, but at least they had put it to good use during his time away from the island.

The ball landed in his palm, and he lowered it to his stomach. He'd chosen to lie on the couch while he waited for Issac's call, but his legs were restless. Jonathan and Stark would be over any minute to enjoy Lizzie's company under a false promise of friendship. Similar, he supposed, to him asking her to go to dinner as a way to lure her from her condo. But while they wanted to drug her with some unknown substance, Jayson actually enjoyed her company.

Would she ever understand the difference?

Or would she hate him once she knew the truth?

He didn't want to be bothered by such trivial questions, but the notion of displeasing her unsettled him.

She's just a woman.

An attractive one he wanted to see naked, but that was par for the course with most females he met.

Except this one had gotten under his skin.

It's the guilt, he decided. Jayson prided himself on always telling the truth, and although he hadn't quite lied to her outright, he had withheld pertinent information.

To protect her.

"Okay, what gives?" Jacque demanded.

Jayson stopped throwing the ball. The teleporter stood beside his head, arms folded, silver eyes glinting. His uncharacteristically serious expression kept Jayson from cracking a joke at the man.

"What do you mean?"

"You're seriously distracted, Jay. I'm over here telling you about what Eliza did to Luc, while you're over there in la-la land thinking about fuck knows what." He started pacing again while studying his oversized watch.

"Uh…" Jayson didn't even realize the teleporter was talking. "Sorry." He sat up, planting his feet on the floor, and gave Jacque his undivided attention. "What's up?"

"No, that's my line. What's up with you?" He paused again and cocked his head to the side. "Is it the girl? Has she gotten to you?"

Jayson snorted. "No, nothing has gotten to me. It's an assignment like any other, except with a little added risk." He stretched his arms over his head and relaxed into the cushion behind him. "But I am feeling a little antsy being stuck here all day and night."

He rarely left the building as a safety precaution. If he did, it was to follow Lizzie to work and observe their surroundings. Not the most exciting pastime considering her steadfast routine.

Jacque nodded in understanding. "Why don't you go out tonight? After the task, I mean. Just go let loose for a while and have some fun. Stas can watch the chick downstairs. It's her roommate, after all. Right?"

Jayson rubbed a hand over his face. The thought had crossed his mind more than once to enjoy either a night in Hydria or one on the town. He needed to do something other than sit here in solitude. Working out only expelled so much stress from the body.

"I'll consider it," he muttered. His body craved the freedom—a night of bliss and pleasure, losing himself in a woman, without thinking…

It'd been too long since he felt that sweet relief. A few weeks he could manage, but two months without it was a record of sorts for him. At least in this century.

It would have to be a redhead.

Brown eyes.

Legs for days.

Enough curves to fill his hands.

He would of course think of her.

Wrong.

His fists clenched as a sense of responsibility overrode the desire thickening his blood.

You can't leave Lizzie.

And you can't have her, either.

His job was to learn more about her, but even more than that, he needed to protect her. One night, hell, one minute, could change everything.

Jayson's phone buzzed, giving him the distraction he needed to cease his internal debate. He would decide how to spend his evening after crashing the party downstairs.

"We're up," he said, standing.

The four of them worked out a plan earlier. Jacque would teleport Jayson to Stas's bedroom. Then Jayson would wander around the condo like he did at the restaurant with only Stas and Issac being able to see him. Once he gathered the information they needed, he'd meet Jacque in the bedroom again and return to his condo.

Easy.

He grabbed the teleporter's shoulder and braced himself for the tunneling sensation. It barely registered due to the small distance, unlike his longer trips to Hydria. Those were hell on his stomach. It beat flying any day of the week, though.

Jacque collapsed onto Stas's bed, jean clad legs crossing at the ankles as he pulled out his phone and tucked one arm behind his head. Apparently, that's how he planned to spend the next hour or so.

Jayson smirked and slipped out the partially open bedroom door. Voices trickled down the hall. From the sound of it, Jonathan and Issac were engaged in a conversation regarding the financial market.

Fascinating.

Jayson left those decisions to Luc. He was a mastermind with investment strategy. His funds alone could sustain all of Hydria for centuries, pending any unforeseen disasters.

Such as an Ichorian invasion or an attack from the CRF.

He paused on the threshold of the kitchen. One more step and the party in the dining room would be able to see him.

Wakefield better have brought his A game tonight.

Here goes nothing.

He stepped as quietly as possible onto the marble tile. Lizzie stood near the oven, waiting for the timer to sound, while everyone else was seated at the table.

No one looked at him.

Jonathan kept rambling on about business markets while Issac, Stas, and Stark listened. Jayson eyed the Sentinel dressed in jeans and a button-down.

He knew very little about the man other than Jonathan considered him a leader on the unit and Tom referred to him as a cold son of a bitch. That description seemed apt. Stark appeared neither amused nor interested in his superior's dialogue, but his stiff posture suggested he was alert and very aware of their surroundings.

Jayson lifted his arm up and down, waiting for a reaction.

None.

With a shrug he moved farther into the kitchen and admired Lizzie's bare legs. The dark red dress hugging her gorgeous form left him wishing he was here for other reasons.

She stilled, her nose twitching, as he silently moved behind her. He meant to take another step, but her reaction intrigued him.

"I'm losing it," she whispered to herself, eliciting a grin from Jayson.

She sensed him, or perhaps caught a whiff of his aftershave.

The recognition pleased him immensely, as did her tight dress. It clung to her curves in all the right places. His hands itched to explore every inch of her, but the oven's buzzer had him moving quickly to the counter beside the sink.

Stas started to stand, but Stark waved her off with a gruff "Allow me." He pushed away from the table with an air of authority and strode with purpose into the kitchen.

"How can I help?" he asked, his tone and expression emotionless.

"Umm…" Lizzie tugged that plump lip between her teeth, driving Jayson wild. He longed to complete this mission just so he could have the right to know her mouth. Even if for only a moment.

Dude, what the fuck is wrong with you?

He shook his head. Maybe he could ask Jacque or one of the Hydraian Guards to babysit Lizzie while he sought some necessary relief. Because this pining business needed to end.

Drooling over a woman like a dog over a bone.

Pull it together.

"Can you grab the salad and rolls?" She sounded so sweet and shy, her demeanor almost demure. The dominant in Jayson enjoyed this side of her, while the man in him craved the feisty woman underneath.

Where's my confident Red?

"Sure." Stark picked up the bowl and the basket beside it and took the items to the dining room. Lizzie trailed after him with what appeared to be homemade lasagna.

Jayson glared up at the ceiling.

He didn't believe in a deity, but he had to ask: *Did you create this woman just for me?*

Because, seriously, the woman boasted a body built for sin and enough intelligence to entertain him for days, and she loved food. If he believed in soul mates, he'd consider her his, but his thousands of years of experience kept him logical.

Love existed for very few, and even in those rare cases, it never lasted forever. Most people grew tired of each other after several years, decades if they were lucky. And Jayson's kind lived forever.

Immortals didn't do long-term romance, but he wasn't opposed to repeating sexual encounters. And with someone like Lizzie? Yeah, he could enjoy a few rounds with her.

She set the dish on the table and turned in to Stark's chest.

Jayson moved forward, ready to intervene, but logic froze him on his second step.

What the hell are you going to do? Yank him off of her?

He ran his fingers through his hair.

This mission was fucking with him in a bad way.

At this rate, he'd need Balthazar to take him out for the night. Maybe hit Rio again or jump up to Dublin. He needed a trio of redheads, at a minimum, to help cure this itch.

Shit.

This feeling would only grow worse as the mission continued, and he desperately needed his focus. A woman should not have him reacting against instincts. Ever.

He settled on his perch again and pulled out his phone to text Grace. *I need a night off when this thing with Wakefield is done. Arrange it and tell B.*

After ensuring his sound and vibrate features were off, he returned the device to his pocket and watched as Stark helped Lizzie into her seat. The touching really wasn't necessary. Surely she could manage sitting on her own.

"I haven't gotten the glass—"

"You've already done enough," the Sentinel interrupted. "I'll grab them with the drinks."

Drinks, huh? Jayson thought. *How convenient.*

"This looks amazing," Jonathan murmured, distracting her from replying as Stark pushed in her chair.

"Oh, uh, thank you," Lizzie replied, her attention falling to the notorious Ichorian. She would see the CEO of the CRF. All Jayson saw was a murderous traitor who had murdered Eli, one of Jayson's oldest and closest friends.

I'll kill you someday, Jonathan.

Stark's broad shoulders blocked Jayson's view, reminding him of his purpose. He relaxed his hands and arms, just in case he needed to fight.

The kitchen was large enough for an island but didn't have one. The oversized counters and open bar overlooking the dining area gave it an airy feel, yet Stark's presence consumed the space as he opened the fridge.

Danger poured off him, and not just because of the six metal blades Jayson sensed on him. It was in the way he moved, like he knew he was the most lethal predator in the room.

He retrieved a bottle of white wine from the fridge.

"Where do you keep the glasses?" he asked, his focus on Lizzie.

She pointed to the cabinet on the opposite side of the sink from Jayson. He considered moving but worried that even the slightest rustle of clothing would alert Stark to his presence.

The man seemed too attuned to his surroundings, as if he could feel things he shouldn't. Tom's report mentioned the possibility that Stark may have undergone CRF enhancements. From the way he acted, Jayson had to agree.

A row of wine glasses appeared, followed by Stark uncorking the wine and serving equal portions. Normally, that bit would be done at the table, not beside the sink, but the purpose became obvious when he pulled a vial of clear liquid from his pocket.

And there it is.

Stark poured a quarter of the contents into one of the glasses, closed the small container, and set it on the counter. He swirled the wine twice before picking up a second drink and turning towards the table.

Jayson caught Issac's gaze before slipping off the counter to open the same cabinet Stark had used. Hopefully, Lizzie wouldn't count her crystal stemware later.

He didn't waste time glancing over his shoulder. If someone noticed his antics, he would hear their reaction, but more importantly, he trusted Issac to have his back.

The little jar contained a few ounces at best of the serum. He couldn't take it all without being obvious, so he settled on roughly the same amount Stark had poured into the wine glass and hoped it would be enough. He carefully placed the vial right where he found it and returned to his spot, glass in hand, with a few seconds to spare.

Stark picked up two more drinks, delivered them to the table, and returned for the final one. He slipped the vial into his pocket without looking at the contents.

It occurred to Jayson as the Sentinel walked away that the casual way he had left the item sitting on the counter seemed a bit too convenient. Almost as if he had done it on purpose.

But why would he do that?

Stark had no way of knowing Jayson stood there waiting for such an opportunity. Unless he sensed him.

The Sentinel took his seat without a backward glance, his expression as passive as it was when he poured the wine.

No.

Stark couldn't sense him. If he did, there would be a fight, yet the Sentinel seemed almost bored.

With a shake of his head, Jayson made his way back to Stas's room, where Jacque waited on the bed. He didn't glance up from his phone as he lifted his elbow in the air. Jayson grabbed it and chuckled as his living room appeared around them. The teleporter managed to land perfectly on the couch, with his legs crossed and phone still in hand, while Jayson stood beside him.

"I remember when you couldn't walk five feet without accidentally shooting off somewhere. You'd return several hours later with this mien of terror on your face."

Jacque shrugged. "I've mastered the craft."

"Clearly." He set the glass carefully on the coffee table before checking his messages from Grace.

You know I love you, but babysitting is not my job. x

He grinned at the joke. All the Elders kept a personal

security team of Hydraians with unique abilities. Jayson had five on his protective detail, and one of them was Grace. Jacque primarily served Luc, but his insane skills tied him to everyone.

"Be right ba—" Jacque disappeared before finishing the sentence.

See you soon, G, Jayson typed, knowing Jacque was on his way to retrieve her.

He considered changing out of his jeans and tee in the interim but didn't know what Balthazar would have in mind. Probably a European nightclub given the midnight hour overseas, or maybe they could find something in the States to keep him occupied.

Either way, it would be a fun night of debauchery, as usual.

The smile he anticipated at the thought never came. Instead, a strange sort of ache radiated from his gut.

"This is insane," he muttered.

Because that bizarre pain reminded him of guilt, something he had no business feeling. He owed Lizzie nothing and vice versa.

Except he wanted to owe her something.

A lot of things, really.

It's the forbidden thing, he decided. Jayson loved a challenge, and being told he couldn't have someone only encouraged him to want her more. Paired with Lizzie's innate innocence and alluring features, no wonder he had plummeted down the rabbit hole.

He palmed his neck and glared at the floor. "Fuck."

"Yes, I believe that's exactly what you need," Balthazar murmured from beside him. He'd appeared at the perfect time, as always. "Where to first, Jay?"

~*~

Three glasses of wine did little to dull the headache forming behind Lizzie's eyes.

She tried so hard to smile and enjoy the conversation, but it was difficult when every topic revolved around the CRF and political affairs.

I don't care, she wanted to say more than once.

But this latest topic regarding Stas's training had Lizzie's stomach in knots.

"She's ready for the next stage," Stark was saying. "Shadowing."

"Yeah? You're tired of kicking my ass every day?"

The blond smirked, or at least Lizzie thought he did. From what she had observed, his facial expressions rarely changed. "That'll continue until you beat me. So you should expect that to continue forever."

Stas nudged Issac. "See, I told you he occasionally makes jokes."

"I believe this is the part where I should be disturbed, yes? Discussing another man harming my girlfriend?" Issac asked with a grin that didn't quite reach his striking eyes.

"She defends herself well enough," Stark replied. "Lately, at least. When we first began, I thought she preferred lying on the ground to standing."

"And I've also told you he's a jackass too, right?" Stas added.

Doctor Fitzgerald shook his head with a laugh, while Lizzie concentrated on her wine. This evening would have to end eventually.

She used to love a reason to host a dinner, especially when it involved inviting Tom and his father over, but her interest waned over the last year or so. It started when Stas accepted her internship with the CRF and intensified when she decided to join the organization full-time after graduation. Now she was a Sentinel, just like Tom, and would probably end up in a grave too.

Lizzie's grip on the crystal stem tightened with the thought.

How could no one see the issue here?

They were all blinded by the CRF's innate goodness

and ignoring the very real possibility that Stas could end up hurt, or worse.

All of them were chuckling about her painful training and the next step in her shadowing Stark abroad. Like this was some damn comedic play instead of a tragic one.

She shook her head, trying to clear it, but the anger only grew.

Did they feel no remorse at all?

Tom's father sat two seats down, *smiling*. It'd been eight weeks since the funeral, and he seemed completely unfazed, while Lizzie sat here with a broken heart, worrying that everyone she ever loved would die horribly.

And no one cared.

The conversation carried on around her in a vacuum of sound that tunneled through her ears.

All about the CRF.

Nothing regarding Tom's death.

No sadness.

No guilt.

No memories.

Just a general discussion on Stas's future with the organization that consumed Lizzie's father, leaving her to fend for herself with Lillian Watkins.

Endless ballet classes, beauty pageants, and lectures on how to properly behave in society. There was also the encouragement not to eat and the general disapproval over having a future in any profession other than being the perfect housewife.

As a child, Lizzie hated her father for never protecting her and loathed the job that took him away from her.

She understood, as an adult, that it was never really the CRF's fault, but that irrational hatred never left, giving her an uneasy feeling anytime she went near the headquarters.

And then Tom's demise brought it all back, coupled with Stas's employment and her decision to join the very same unit that killed him.

They didn't understand how painful it was to sit here

and listen to them all chat about an organization she detested—to be the only one sitting in misery while they laughed and smiled and *enjoyed.*

I hate them.

Such an irrational thought.

She knew that, but it reverberated through her mind over and over until a scream built in her throat. A swallow of wine shoved it back down to where it belonged inside her heart. Her mother taught her how to hide emotion well, one of the only useful gifts from her childhood.

Needing something to do, Lizzie set about cleaning up the dishes without a word. She could feel Stas's worried gaze on her as she moved, but she refused to acknowledge it.

Being angry with her best friend felt wrong, yet right. They used to be so close, confiding in each other over everything and spending quality time together, but lately, Lizzie felt like she was living with a stranger.

Stas rarely came home, and when she did, she brought Issac or stayed for a few minutes before leaving again. Their weekly girls' nights were now monthly and stilted, and always ended early. Lizzie just didn't see a point anymore.

She felt so alone.

A tear threatened, but she swiped it away.

I'm being a child.

Emotional.

Irrational.

She needed a distraction.

And maybe to grow up a little.

Tom always saw her as a child because she behaved like one, and sulking in the kitchen certainly proved him right.

She set the last of the plates in the sink.

This was the part where she hand-washed them meticulously and set them out to dry, but her hands refused the task.

Why do I do this to myself?

Not even nine o'clock on a Friday night and she stood alone in her kitchen, staring at a pile of plates.

A giggle blossomed in her chest at the absurdity of it. *Twenty-four-years-old going on fifty.*

To hell with it.

She would clean the dishes later. Maybe even tomorrow.

The minor change in her routine lifted an invisible weight from her shoulders. All the stress and disappointment of dinner left her on an exhale.

A sense of freedom and bliss overwhelmed her as she realized she could do whatever she wanted.

There were no papers to grade, no work in the morning, and no commitments except for the guests at the table. But none of them were talking to her anyway, so why stay?

Maybe she could call Cam or Kristin. It'd been a while since she saw her sorority sisters. Why not meet them at a bar and let her hair down a little?

Or she could go out alone and meet a stranger. That sounded scandalous. She liked it.

With a smile, she went to her room, freshened up, slid on a pair of stilettos that paired well with her red dress, and grabbed her purse.

The sound of her name stopped Lizzie in the hallway beside the dining room.

"Yes?" she asked, turning.

"What are you doing?"

"I'm going out," Lizzie replied with no destination in mind. Her mother would be furious when she heard about this, but she couldn't bring herself to worry. She more than earned this reprieve from social niceties. "Enjoy your evening."

"Wait, Liz—"

But Lizzie had no intention of waiting for anything or anyone.

She opened the door and let it slam behind her with

finality. Her feet were moving in the direction of the stairwell before she realized what her heart had in mind.

Jayson Masters.

Why should he be the only one allowed to stop by unannounced? Lizzie could be spontaneous, too, and if he happened to be out, she'd figure out plan B.

Her lips curled with the challenge.

Yes, this was what she needed to be doing—enjoying life.

She'd start by telling a certain overbearing neighbor how she felt. Not with words, but with her mouth.

CHAPTER NINE

Running Domestic Errands

Subject appears ready for human
interaction trials. Meeting with
moderator tomorrow to discuss
parameters and requirements.

                    —Entry Log 117.12.4-7

"You ready?" Balthazar asked from the bedroom doorway. He'd left with Jacque to deliver the mysterious liquid to Luc's team for research. His delayed return suggested their omniscient friend had several questions. Typical.

"Just about." Jayson fixed the collar of his gray dress shirt, leaving the top button undone, and added a light jacket to the mix. His dark jeans lent a casual feel that suited their destination. Balthazar was dressed similarly, minus the jacket.

"Fewer clothes to take off later," he murmured, responding to Jayson's mental observation.

"That's half the fun, B."

"And see, this is why I've missed you. The others just haven't achieved our level yet." He clapped Jayson on the back. "Let's go have some fun."

"Don't let Luc hear you talk like that." The trio had a history of competition, and Luc more than held his own. "He owned that syrup challenge last year."

Balthazar grinned as they walked toward the living area. "That was an excellent week."

"How he managed to get those two women in that position..." Jayson whistled at the memory. "That was a sight to behold."

"He earned that win," Balthazar agreed. "Hands down."

"Or up, as it were."

Balthazar chuckled. "Indeed."

"I still want to hear about what went down in Brazil," Grace said from the couch. She had her bare feet up on the coffee table and a bowl of popcorn in her lap.

"Jay, several times."

Jayson's eyebrows hit his hairline. "And you didn't?" The whole damn competition started after Balthazar and Luc disagreed—again—about waffles and pancakes. The debauchery that ensued as a result satisfied Jayson for several weeks.

"I assumed that was self-explanatory." B winked at the now-blushing Hydraian on the couch. "Grace knows how I handle women in the bedroom, don't you, sweetheart?"

There were some things Jayson didn't want to know. This was one of those things.

"I think we should go before I lose my interest." *Just need to find Jacque.* The teleporter was probably in the kitchen, stealing his food.

"Mmm, I highly doubt that's about to happen anytime soon," Balthazar replied with a secret smile.

Jayson didn't like that look. He knew what usually followed. "What—"

A knock at his door cut him off.

"You should probably answer that." Balthazar relaxed onto the couch beside Grace. "Might be important."

Lizzie. If it were anyone else, Balthazar would have opened the door himself.

A peek into the hallway confirmed it.

He twisted the handle and grinned at his favorite redhead.

She dove right into the conversation without waiting for him to begin.

"I've decided that you're not the only one who can stop by unannounced." The confidence in her voice and lack of a greeting deepened his smile.

"Well, hello to you too, Red."

"Hi," she added as an afterthought. "I don't actually know what I want to do, but I want to do something."

His eyebrows inched upward. "Yeah? Like what?"

"Dancing." She slipped past him as she spoke. "And maybe more drinking…"

Her voice trailed off as she spied the couple on the couch.

"Oh…" That delectable red graced her cheeks and neck as she spun to face him. "I'm so sorry. Oh God. That was so rude of me. I didn't realize you had company, but of course you do. I'll… uh…" She tried to slide past him again, but Jayson blocked her exit.

"Dancing and drinking," he murmured, repeating her requests. "Does that mean you're ready to attend that concert with me?"

She snorted, her gaze meeting his again. "I said I want to dance, not bang my head against a wall."

He covered his heart. "You wound me, Lizzie."

"Somehow I doubt that," she replied with a saucy little

grin. "And you never texted me to plan the concert, so I think that means you owe me another movie night instead."

He leaned into her personal space. "I definitely prefer drinking and dancing over that option," he admitted softly. "But if you insist, then it's a date."

"Hmm, I give it a five-point-two," Balthazar murmured as he strolled up next to Lizzie. The words would go over her head, but Jayson understood the implication behind them.

Give me a break, B. She's an innocent. If he laid it on any thicker, she'd run downstairs.

Balthazar's expression said, *Let me show you how this is done.*

"You must be the beautiful neighbor Jay won't stop thinking about." He held out a hand. "I'm Balthazar, Jay's oldest and dearest friend. Lizzie, right?"

"Uh, yeah." She accepted his hand.

"Lovely to meet you." He brought her wrist to his lips.

"Likewise?" Lizzie's breathless voice sizzled over Jayson's skin.

He never cared how women reacted to Balthazar. The man could send lovers to their knees with a look, something that made him the ideal wingman and provided them both with endless entertainment and pleasure. But hearing Lizzie react to his friend in that same way undid something inside of him.

Balthazar released Lizzie's hand far too slowly for Jayson's liking as he asked, "I assume you're staying for the party?"

"Party?" she repeated.

What are you doing?

Shh. I've got this, Jay, his eyes seemed to say.

Oh, I bet you do.

"Jay didn't tell you?" Balthazar tsked. "That's just like him. He doesn't know how to properly host." That last part was whispered conspiratorially at Lizzie, eliciting a giggle from her.

Now you're just being a dick.

Balthazar's gaze glimmered deviously. "Like even now, he still hasn't offered you a drink." He shook his head in mock reproach. "What can I get you, sweetheart? A glass of wine, perhaps?"

Jayson closed the door because, clearly, Lizzie would be staying for the party he had no intention of throwing. It shut a little louder than intended, not that anyone seemed to notice.

"Um." Lizzie licked her lips. "I do like wine."

"Excellent," Balthazar murmured. "You make yourself at home while Jay and I procure the drinks. A beer for you, Grace?"

"Obviously," she replied from the couch. Her legs were still kicked up on the table, but the popcorn had been set to the side.

"Come on, Jay." Balthazar nodded at the kitchen. "Time to play host."

"Sure," Jayson replied. "Lizzie, this is Grace. I promise she's mostly harmless." He winked at his favorite Guardian while he said it and pushed away from the door. "Be back in a minute." *I need to go kick my best friend's ass.*

Balthazar chuckled. "You'll need more than a minute."

"We'll see, won't we?" he muttered while following his friend through the dining room.

They rounded the corner to find Jacque sitting on one of the counters with a pizza box in his lap.

Jayson eyed the now-empty container. "Do they not feed you in Hydria?"

"Your fridge is full of leftovers. I'm just helping you clean it up," the slender teleporter replied around a mouthful of food.

"Charming," Jayson muttered.

"I could say the same about you, Jay. What was that back there?" Balthazar demanded. "Half-assed flirting? I've taught you better than that."

"Come on, like you've taught me anything." Jayson opened his fridge to look for a bottle of wine he knew didn't exist. "We both know I can hold my own just fine, B."

"Did I hear something about a party?" Jacque interrupted. "'Cause you're going to need more liquor."

"And people," Jayson added. "What the fuck were you thinking inviting her to stay for a party?"

"You let me worry about that." Balthazar grinned knowingly. "First things first, we need a bottle of wine. Jacque?"

"On it." He disappeared in a flash.

Jayson palmed the back of his neck and blew out a breath. "So much for a night off." Something he blamed Balthazar for more than Lizzie.

"When have I ever let you down?" his friend asked. "I've got this."

"A new challenge?" Jayson guessed with a laugh. "Do tell."

"Oh, no. This one is personal and all my own, but you'll be thanking me in the morning." The promise in his voice was one earned by centuries of perfected experience.

He shrugged. "All right." When Balthazar set his mind to something, it happened, and on this, Jayson had no complaints.

Assuming it doesn't hurt Lizzie.

He frowned at the thought. Why would it? They didn't owe each other anything. He liked her, sure, but she was forbidden fruit—an asset—that he couldn't touch.

She doesn't know that.

"That's quite a conundrum," Balthazar mused. "She has you tied up in knots, my friend. But don't worry. We'll get it straightened out." He clapped Jayson on the shoulder just as Jacque reappeared with a bottle of wine in each hand.

"Didn't know what you'd prefer, so I grabbed two from Wakefield's cellar." The teleporter set them on the counter and turned to Balthazar. "I assume we're off to pick up some people and more drinks?"

"We are indeed. Let's start with Maria." He extended a hand as Jayson's mouth fell open.

"You can't be—" But it was too late. Balthazar and Jacque had already disappeared.

Fuck.

Maria specialized in altering short-term memory, which could only mean one thing: Balthazar planned to pick up random humans from bars and teleport them here. To Jayson's condo. In the middle of New York City.

He inwardly groaned at the idiocy of this plan. They might as well post a sign out front welcoming the Ichorians to their party.

"Do you need any help?" Lizzie asked as she rounded the corner. She glanced at the two unopened bottles before eyeing Jayson's position against the counter. He'd leaned against it while lamenting about his situation. "Where did your friend go?"

"He's working out some party details," he replied vaguely.

"Oh, okay. Um, do you want me to help you get ready?" The hopeful note in her voice endeared her to him even more.

"I can open the wine." He went to search for a corkscrew. Mateo and Issac had furnished the condo for him. There had to be one somewhere.

The fridge opened beside him, causing him to look questioningly at Lizzie.

"I'll help," she explained with a sweet smile. The woman seriously had no idea how her beauty affected others. "With the food prep, I mean."

"Food prep?"

"Yeah. You know, like cheese and crackers, fruit…" She trailed off as she eyed his mostly empty shelves. "Or… not." She closed the door and lifted one eyebrow. "How do you expect to throw a party without any food?"

"Uh…" Most of his parties ended in the bedroom, not the dining room.

Both brows rose now. "You don't plan to serve anything other than beer and some wine?"

"Well." He palmed the back of his neck again. "I wasn't exactly…" The fiery glimmer in her eyes sent his thought process south. Would her pupils dilate like that in his bed?

"Jayson Masters," she chastised. "You cannot throw a party without food!" She shook her head. "What time are you expecting people?"

He considered Balthazar's intentions and shrugged. "Thirty minutes or so?"

Lizzie huffed a breath. "Hardly enough time, but we can manage." She set the white wine in the fridge, near his personal beer stash, and left the red on the counter. Jayson knew Balthazar would bring more alcohol, but the amount in there would be enough to at least kick-start the party.

"Let's go." She grabbed his hand and gave him a good tug, forcing him to follow. His dick wanted to go in the opposite direction, toward his room, but it seemed she had other ideas in mind.

"Where are we going?" he asked.

"There's a twenty-four-seven market open on Seventy-seventh and Broadway. Let's go grab a few things." She was already at the door. He spied her purse on the end table, but she made no move to grab it. Good thing he had his wallet—not that he would ever let her pay anyway.

"Have fun." Grace waved, her amusement palpable. "I'll just babysit your place until you get back."

"Cute," he returned.

She flashed him a wide grin. "I try, Jay. I do."

Lizzie yanked him into the hallway before he could reply and guided him down the hall. "Now, how many people are having you over?"

Knowing Balthazar… "At least twenty." And most of them would be women.

"I can work with that."

He watched her ass as she descended the stairs before him. Yeah, he could think of worse pastimes than letting her boss him around. Except in the bedroom. He enjoyed control too much for that.

She listed several "party snack" ideas on their way to the store, and he agreed to each one just for the hell of it. Her definition of entertaining differed significantly from his, but he didn't mind.

All of her formalities reminded him a bit of Amelia, or at least the former version, anyway. The one who returned to Hydria two months ago seemed less enthusiastic about social gatherings. Not that he could blame her. Torture changed a person.

Jayson grabbed a basket at the door and followed Lizzie's commands throughout the market. Then he handed his card over to the cashier, with a bemused smile at the total his redhead had managed to rack up in less than ten minutes of wandering.

"You certainly know how to shop, Red," he murmured.

"Oh, this is nothing," she replied. "You should see me with my sorority sisters."

"Yeah? Tell me more about these sisters." He picked up the reusable bags Lizzie insisted on buying in addition to the food. She claimed they were important for the environment, which he couldn't exactly argue against.

"You want to hear about the lingerie parties and pillow fights, don't you?"

"Absolutely."

"Sorry, but that doesn't happen."

Not true, Red. He'd attended several over his lifetime. "Sounds like a bucket list item that requires checking."

She snorted. "No, thank you."

"Not even with me?" he teased.

Her cheeks flushed. "Uh, I…"

"I'm joking, Red." *Not really.* Her virginal ears weren't ready for his suggestions yet. "Now, tell me, why did I need flour again?"

Her lips curled. "Cookies."

"For me?"

"For your guests."

"Oh, Red, that's not going to work. I never share what's mine." And that applied to more than just cookies. Sure, he'd enjoyed a woman, or several, over the years with both Luc and Balthazar, but never the ones he wanted for himself. Like Lizzie. Not that they were talking about that right now.

"Who said they're *your* cookies?" she taunted, her eyes shining with mirth. This playful side of Lizzie appealed to him on a base level. He would even say he found their banter fun.

"First of all, you promised to bake me cookies," he reminded. "That's the only way I'll tell you more about where I've lived. And secondly, I paid for the ingredients. So they're my cookies, Red."

"You paid for the groceries because this is your party. And technically, you owe me for saving your butt and helping you provide snacks for your guests." A taunt glimmered in her gaze. "Furthermore, maybe I'm no longer interested in learning more about you."

"Oh, we both know you're interested," he countered. "Don't lie to yourself."

"That's not cocky at all."

"Darling Red, you haven't even skimmed the surface of my cockiness, but feel free to explore me more in depth at your leisure."

"How very *neighborly* of you."

"Hey, I try to be hospitable." He showed her the four bags in his hands. "Proof."

She laughed and shook her head. "Do you want me to carry one of those?"

"Now she asks, as we round the corner to our block." He shook his head in mock disappointment. "And she calls me a bad host."

Her mouth opened and closed. "Crap. I should have offered... I'm—"

"I'm joking, Lizzie. Like I would let you carry these for me. I might not be the best host, but I do know how to behave like a gentleman." *Even when all I want to do is drop these bags, shove you against the wall, and fuck the hell out of your mouth.*

She skipped ahead to open the door to the building and flashed Jayson a triumphant grin. "Now I'm being socially acceptable."

"Pretty sure you're always acceptable," he replied with a nod to the doorman, who stood behind Lizzie with a welcoming expression. "Hi, Dennis."

"Evenin', Jayson. Lizzie." He tipped his hat and secured the front area after they walked through it.

Jayson considered giving him a heads-up about the party, but Lizzie was already on her way to the stairwell. Her ballerina legs sure were quick when she wanted to move them.

He trailed after her with a chuckle and took the stairs two at a time to keep up. When they reached his hallway, he sent a prayer above for the silence. Either Balthazar wasn't back yet or he'd recruited fewer people than expected for their little soirée.

"It's probably open," he said as they approached.

Lizzie twisted the handle and froze as sensual music spilled into the corridor. "You said maybe twenty people..."

He peeked over her shoulder. "I said at least twenty." It appeared to be closer to thirty or forty. He recognized several Guardians in the crowd. They were loyal to a fault. As long as they didn't leave the condo, it would be okay. The rest of the attendees were harmless mortals, if a little loud. Not an Ichorian in sight, with the exception of Tristan.

That explains the sound control in the hallway. Clever man.

Lizzie elbowed him. "We need more food, Jayson."

"It'll be fine, Red," he assured. "Jacque can hop out to get us more if needed."

"Jacque?" she repeated.

"'Sup." The teleporter appeared in front of her. Literally. Not that she saw it, because her eyes had been on Jayson.

"Oh." Lizzie took a step backward, pressing her back to Jayson's chest. "Hi."

"Hi," Jacque returned. "You rang?"

Jayson lifted his grocery-laden arms, bracketing Lizzie between them. "Can you please *walk* these over to the kitchen, Jacque?"

His friend grinned cheekily. "Sure, Jay. I'll walk them over." He grabbed the bags and skipped away a little too quickly. His energy levels were through the roof.

"That's Jacque," Jayson murmured as he wrapped his arms around Lizzie's waist. She hadn't stepped away from him, so he interpreted that as an invitation. "He's a good friend who happens to enjoy running errands."

"Oh," she said again, her body warm against his. "Okay."

"We should go inside," he whispered against her ear. A trail of goose bumps stamped a path down the column of her neck, encouraging him to take it a step further. He pressed firmly into her backside as he forced her forward into the foyer and kicked the door closed behind him. The scene before them matched what he anticipated.

Dancing.

Drinking.

Debauchery.

Typical Balthazar. He went by Bacchus once, a few thousand years ago. His legend still haunted mythology books, though Dionysus was the more popular version of the name thanks to the Greeks. He had perfected his party-throwing skills throughout his very long life, and the scene in Jayson's flat proved it.

The music was pitched at just the right volume to allow

casual conversation while also encouraging everyone to move to the sensual beat, and the lighting was bright enough to see while also lending an erotic feel to the air. Almost like a nightclub and a lounge combined, but in a residential flat.

Incredible, really.

The notorious god approached with a woman on each side, his expression welcoming in more ways than one. "I hear you left us for some domestic shopping?"

"Lizzie insisted we grab some snacks for the party," Jayson explained as he eyed the two gorgeous brunettes under his friend's arms. *Argentinian?*

Balthazar winked in confirmation before saying, "That was a lovely thought, Lizzie."

"Thank you," she replied, sounding quite pleased with herself. "You were very right about Jayson being a poor host."

Oh, the little minx.

"Careful, Red," Jayson murmured into her ear as he tightened his hold. "Or I'll show you how I usually host a party."

Her cheeks warmed against his nose.

Mmm.

What other parts of her body could he make blush? Her breasts, definitely. And her thighs would redden beautifully beneath his attentions, as would other more intimate parts of her. His cock woke up at the thoughts overriding his brain, and he didn't bother to hide it. What was the point anymore? She had to know he wanted her, even if he couldn't have her.

His hormonal drive tonight proved how badly he needed to get laid, but it seemed only one woman would satisfy the fire Lizzie evoked inside him. Good thing he had that woman in his arms.

"Without food?" she guessed, her voice breathier than when she teased him seconds before. That she was able to focus enough to answer his taunt said he needed to up his game.

He nibbled her ear before whispering, "Depends on the menu." Her responding shiver pleased him immensely.

"Operating at a level six now," Balthazar said, interrupting the moment. "I approve."

You and I both know that I operate at an eleven on your scale of one to ten, but I'm toning it down out of necessity, Jayson replied mentally as he smiled against Lizzie's neck. Her floral scent teased his baser needs and invited him to explore more.

Balthazar merely grinned. "Well, now that you're both back, we can get this party started properly." His sinful gaze fell to the woman at his right. "This is Delfina"—he looked to the left—"and Sofía." Those lips curled into the picture of seduction as he gestured to Jayson. "Ladies, this is the friend I told you about."

Two sets of amorous, light-colored eyes fell on Jayson, which should have triggered all manner of sordid thoughts yet didn't. He smiled but didn't quite feel it. Not the way he did ten minutes ago while bantering with Lizzie, anyway.

"Ladies," he greeted as he openly appraised the women. Their sky-high heels and short dresses suggested Balthazar had picked them up at a nightclub, likely in Buenos Aires. The majority of the humans here appeared to be from various parts of South America. All gorgeous with curves for days and reminiscent of his last trip to the southern continent.

Nice work.

Of course, his friend's eyes replied, cocky as ever.

Jayson murmured a few complimentary words in Spanish that the women returned in kind. He loved a sexy accent, but his focus shifted as the redhead in his arms tried to step away.

"I'll, uh, leave you all to chat while I get the snacks ready," she said when his arms locked around her waist. He'd been going for polite, not interest, which she'd clearly misinterpreted.

This isn't going to work, B. Not with her here.

Or perhaps even then. Only one woman seemed to be tickling his fancy lately, and that was the one trying to escape his unyielding hold.

"Lizzie promised me some cookies." He skimmed his nose over her neck to calm her down. "And I owe her a glass of wine."

"Really, it's okay. I can manage on my own." She tried again to leave, but his arms remained locked around her.

"I hate to break this to you, Red"—he threaded his fingers in her hair and angled her head backward to hover his lips over hers—"but I'm not ready to let you go yet."

Her pupils flared in the way he wanted. Tonight had been about sating his lust with a random female or two, but Lizzie's presence changed everything. The notion of being with another woman no longer appealed to him, which meant he was in for a painful evening. But at least he could satisfy some of his cravings by spending time with his favorite redhead. His fixation would pass once the mission ended and he took some well-deserved time off.

He brushed his mouth over hers and smiled when her breath fluttered over his lips. At least he wasn't the only one fighting the desire between them.

"Wine?" he asked softly.

"O-okay."

"Good." He spoke the word against her mouth and followed it with a gentle kiss because he couldn't help himself. "Let's go, Red."

Jayson righted her and started to say something to Balthazar and his guests, but the trio had melted into the party scene again. His friend stood in a circle of women, including the duo from before, dancing and managing to make each of them feel equally adored.

He lifted his gaze in a way that said, *Enjoy your evening, Jay.*

A show of solidarity, respect, and understanding. Lizzie was forbidden fruit, but if Jayson took her to bed, there would be no judgment from Balthazar. His ability to sense and control emotion, as well as read thoughts, granted him a deeper insight than most.

Jayson acknowledged the acceptance with a nod. Not that he would do anything about it. His steadfast control would serve him well.

But there were other ways to sate his needs.

Maybe he would explore some of those.

CHAPTER TEN

A First Time for Everything

Sensation and pleasure are incomprehensible to the subject. Benefactor is displeased and requests hormonal updates. Lab technicians are working on a cocktail to fix the oversight.

—Entry Log 116.03.4-7

Lizzie needed more wine. The three glasses from earlier had worn off after her walk to the store with Jayson, and this new one wasn't enough to dull the insanity spiraling inside her.

Every touch set her blood on fire.

Every seductive glance elicited goose bumps.

And, oh God, the kisses.

She clenched her thighs.

What is he trying to do to me?

Never in her life had a man worked her into a frenzy like this. Not even Tom. She didn't know how to handle it, and the wine seemed to do nothing to cool her off.

"What do you want me to do with these?" Jayson asked, showing her the bag of grapes she'd picked up at the store. Even those simple words seemed underlined in suggestion. She had to be misunderstanding him.

But all the touching... is irrelevant.

A man who craved the kind of relationship Lizzie wanted did not openly flirt with other women in front of his romantic interest. And he'd certainly flirted with those models in the other room. Not that she could blame him—they were gorgeous.

Just friends, she reminded herself and focused on his task.

"We need to wash them and put them in a bowl." She pulled one from the cabinet and handed it to him. "I'll focus on the cheese and crackers." Lizzie had thought wine snacks would be appropriate given his drinks of choice, but his friends didn't seem very interested in food, as they were too busy bumping and grinding.

To each her own, she supposed. Lizzie would set some food out on the table for those interested and leave Jayson to host his party. She doubted he wanted her to stay. These were his friends. She understood that.

Maybe she would call Kristin or Cam. She still owed them a girls' evening out, and it wasn't too late. They were probably out drinking somewhere. Lizzie preferred to join them over returning to her lonely condo. Issac and Stas were probably still there, and after the way she'd left, Lizzie didn't want to see them.

She finished arranging the cheese and found Jayson watching her. "What?"

He stepped into her space and gently pressed his thumb to the area between her eyes and started to massage it in slow circles. "I'm trying to figure out who or what put this frown here. I thought we were having fun."

"We are... No... I mean, it's not." *For crying out loud!* His hands really impacted her ability to form proper sentences. She cleared her throat and tried again. "My mind was wandering."

"Do you need help bringing it back?" His warm fingers plucked the knife from her hand and set it aside as he crowded her against the counter. "Because I'm happy to help with that."

Her heart skipped a beat as she forgot how to breathe. "Okay," she somehow managed.

His lips lightly caressed hers in another one of his infamously chaste kisses. Oh, she enjoyed them, but each one only deepened this feeling of need churning inside her, and she couldn't handle much more. It felt like an inferno—curling, flaring, and dying for an outlet only he could provide.

She slid her hands up his arms, luxuriating in the Italian silk of his blazer. Lizzie adored the sleek and sexy look, and Jayson wore it so well. She traced the collar of his shirt before dragging her nails up his neck and into his luscious hair.

All their previous kisses were controlled by him, but she desired more.

She locked her fingers in his thick strands and leaned into him.

"Stop teasing and kiss me," she demanded. The voice sounded nothing like hers—so throaty and hot—but it inspired the reaction she wanted.

"Careful what you wish for, Red." He lifted her onto the island counter, yanked her forward, and stepped between her thighs. "You just might get it."

Her body went up in flames as he took her mouth in a kiss meant to devastate her feminine senses.

Oh. My. God.

His tongue... Lizzie didn't know they could move like

that.

She fought to keep up, her nails digging into his scalp as he ravaged her inside and out. No way did she regret this request. She'd demanded, and he delivered.

His palms slid up her sides, scattering goose bumps in their wake and hardening her nipples. When he reached her neck, she was putty in his hands, allowing him to do whatever he wanted.

He tilted her head to an angle that allowed deeper entry into her mouth while aligning his lower body with hers.

A jolt of electricity shot up her spine from both shock and something carnal. No man had ever touched her *there*, but she could feel him through the thin barrier of her panties.

Because she was in a dress.

With her legs wrapped around a man.

In his kitchen.

How deliciously wanton.

Never in her wildest dreams did she expect this, yet it felt so right and natural. And positively terrifying at the same time.

The mixture of emotions traveled from her mouth to his as she tried to return his kiss with equal skill. But she knew her experience paled in comparison to his, as was evidenced by the easy way he dominated her mouth and controlled her body with a few practiced moves.

She couldn't bring herself to care, not when it produced this level of euphoria. His fingers knotted in her hair, tugging just enough to keep her grounded while he continued his sensual lesson.

Her legs tightened around his hips as she fought for something she didn't quite understand.

Friction.

Heat.

More.

He broke the kiss with a curse, his breath hot against her lips.

"Come now, don't stop on my account." The unfamiliar voice sent ice cubes dancing down Lizzie's spine.

Jayson's embrace had erased all thought and reason, including the fact that they were very much not alone in his condo. Something she hadn't even considered while he consumed her on the countertop.

And, apparently, they had acquired an audience of at least one.

Jayson combed his fingers through Lizzie's hair before lowering his hands to her sides. She expected him to step away, but he didn't. Part of her wished he would so she could stand up and straighten her dress, while the other part of her felt protected by his possessive stance.

The conundrum left her speechless, if a little mortified at having been caught in the act, but at the same time, hot and bothered. Lizzie never broke etiquette rules—they were ingrained in her after years of training—but Jayson had plowed right through those barriers with his addictive kisses. And she didn't regret it for a second.

"Pity," the voice murmured as he opened the fridge behind her.

"Tristan," Jayson growled. "Is there something I can help you find? The door, maybe?"

"I wanted to top up my wine but found myself distracted by the show." The fridge closed with a snick. "You know how I feel about voyeurism."

Jayson's grip tightened. "Take your kink elsewhere."

"Since when do you mind an audience?" Tristan asked with a slight lilt. *Irish, maybe?*

Glass clinked against granite as the man went about pouring himself wine on the same island Lizzie sat upon. She could feel the coolness of the bottle near her ass, sending a chill down her spine. Or perhaps it was the stranger's proximity that unsettled her.

"I seem to recall you being quite fond of a little exhibitionism," he continued. "Don't tell me you're

131

undergoing a change, as well. I don't think I can handle losing two of my mates to pets. Although, I admit, this one is quite lovely."

A finger trailed down her arm, causing Jayson to yank her closer.

Her hands grasped his shoulders for balance as she finally peered over her shoulder at the tall man behind her.

Vibrant green eyes held her captive.

"Yes, quite lovely." His smile could only be described as wicked. He looked over her at the man between her legs as he added, "But I can see you're not up for sharing, so I'll find a snack elsewhere."

"That would be wise," Jayson replied. "And try not to spill anything."

"Now you're just insulting me, Jay. I know better than to imbibe in your personal space." He returned the wine bottle to the fridge and turned to pick up his glass. "Can I make one suggestion?"

"You're going to anyway."

"I am," Tristan agreed. "Perhaps move this interlude to a more private location if you don't want to invite others. It could confuse those of us who know you well."

Lizzie swallowed and returned her focus to Jayson.

His friend kept referring to sharing and watching, and she inferred he meant in a sexual context. But to what extent?

Her limited experience extended to a male here or there, and never anything below the waist. She couldn't possibly live up to whatever Tristan had just implied.

"Thanks for that," Jayson said, his focus on the other man. "Now go back to being useful in the living area. It's getting loud."

"Oh, I have a feeling it'll be far louder later, old friend." The taunt in Tristan's voice had Jayson's eyes narrowing. "But don't worry. I'll control it for you, because that's the kind of friend I am."

Lizzie had no idea what they were talking about but

guessed it was some sort of inside joke between them, though the expression on Jayson's face suggested that might be the wrong term.

"As if you're not getting something out of this," Jayson returned.

"Indeed," Tristan murmured. "Why else would I agree to put my talents to use for such a frivolous affair?"

"Because you're such a good friend?" Jayson suggested.

"I do appreciate your humor, Jay. Enjoy your evening. I know I'll be enjoying mine." He trailed a finger down her arm again, or tried to, anyway. Jayson caught his wrist before Tristan reached her elbow.

"Stop playing," Jayson said, voice low.

Tristan grinned as he twisted his hand free. "Maybe next time." His green eyes glimmered wickedly as they met hers. "Nice to meet you, love. I do so adore a silent woman."

Her lips parted, but by the time she could even formulate a reply, he had left the kitchen with his wine and the bowl of grapes Jayson had prepared.

Warm hands caressed her cheeks, pulling her attention back to the man between her thighs. "I'm sorry, Liz. He's a bit of an ass."

"You have really weird friends," she blurted out. First that coworker, Kiel. Then Balthazar—who wasn't so much weird as impossibly good-looking and far too charming for his own good—and now Tristan. "How do you know them all? And didn't you just move here? Who are all those people? And you speak Spanish?"

She couldn't seem to stop the word vomit—a consequence of being startled, embarrassed, and slightly overwhelmed.

"I need my wine," she decided.

He stopped her from twisting, reached around her to pick up the glass, and handed it to her.

"Balthazar is visiting from where I lived before, and Tristan is an old mutual friend who lives in the city. As for all the others, I recognize a handful, while the rest are Balthazar's acquaintances since he wanted to throw this party, and I speak a lot of languages." He tucked a piece of her hair behind her ear as he smiled. "Did that cover everything?"

She finished what was left of her wine while trying to formulate a response.

"The, uh, sharing thing?" She didn't have the aplomb to clarify that any further, and her face heated just from mentioning it. Or maybe that was the alcohol. "I need more."

She gave him her glass, and he eyed her speculatively. "How much have you had to drink tonight, Red?"

Not the answer she expected. "Are you accusing me of being drunk?"

"No." He set the glass off to the side. "I'm checking because I want you to stay sober."

"Why?" Wasn't drinking the whole point of throwing a party?

He cupped her cheek and forced her to meet his gaze. "Because I need your consent."

She frowned. "For what?"

"For the things I want to do to you." He traced her bottom lip with his thumb. "But we'll determine your limits first."

Her mouth went dry at both his words and the smoldering tenor of his voice. It erased all the awkwardness from Tristan's interruption and rekindled that foreign sensation heating her veins.

"I like you," she said on impulse. "That's why I came up here tonight. To tell you I like you."

Very mature, Liz, she thought with a mental cringe. How old was she? Twelve?

Fortunately, he seemed more amused than annoyed.

"Yeah? I think you've made that clear." He kissed her softly before adding, "The feeling is mutual."

He pulled her off the counter and fixed her dress.

"Follow me, Red."

~*~

Fuck it.

Jayson was going to hell anyway. He might as well enjoy himself on the way there.

He didn't meet Balthazar's gaze as he pulled Lizzie toward his bedroom, but he felt the mind reader's eyes on him. Satisfaction radiated from the man because this had clearly been his plan all along.

When have I ever let you down? He seemed to ask.

Never.

And tonight was no exception.

Fine. Jayson would indulge himself a little. He deserved it after two months of focusing on this mission. If Lizzie didn't want him, he wouldn't touch her, but those little mewls of desperation in the kitchen confirmed all his suspicions.

She hadn't even realized her own reactions or that her body had been on the verge of cresting into orgasm after a few innocent touches.

He bit back a groan at her inexperience. It floored him.

This desire between them was an all-consuming insanity. And something needed to be done about it.

But there would be rules—for him, not her.

Lizzie required a slow introduction into his bed, and he refused to overwhelm her. She deserved better than that.

And he couldn't fuck her the way he wanted to until she knew the truth.

Shit, he shouldn't even be willing to go this far without telling her everything, but his sense of honor had taken a backseat after that interlude in the kitchen.

This would be about making her feel good and nothing more.

She'd forgive him for that, right?

He escorted her into his bedroom and locked the door

behind them.

"So, um…" She gazed up at him through her thick lashes as color brightened her cheeks. "You mentioned limits?"

"Yes, I did." He backed her up into the wall, placing his palms against the hard surface on either side of her head. "No sex tonight."

Her jaw hit the floor. "Wh-what?"

"Right. That reaction is exactly why we're not having sex tonight." He traced every inch of her deep-red dress with his eyes before meeting her gaze again. "But I'm open to other options if you are." *Like taking off this dress and exploring the flesh beneath with my tongue.*

That pretty pink tongue darted out to lick her lips, and he wondered idly what it would feel like against his cock.

Not that they would be doing that tonight.

This was about her.

He ran his nose over the blush of her cheeks to her ear. "Let's start with easier questions," he suggested. "How do you feel about me removing your dress?"

She shivered, eliciting a smile from him. "Mmm, you approve, as do I. What else, Red? What else am I allowed to remove?"

He dropped one hand to her waist, sliding it upward to thumb the underside of her breast. "Your bra?" he whispered. Another tremble, followed by a soft little moan, encouraged him to travel downward to where the fabric ended on her leg. He explored the hem before gently prodding the inside of her thigh.

Her breathing escalated, causing him to pause.

"A limit," he murmured. "Mmm, I can work with this."

"I…" She shuddered even as her body tensed. "I-I don't know."

Because she'd never been touched there. He understood.

"That's why we have limits, Red," he said in a soothing tone. He would never force her or any woman into an uncomfortable situation. That went against his personal code.

"I'm not... sure." Another shudder, this one less erotic and more emotional.

He worshiped her neck with his mouth, easing her back into him as he removed his hand from her leg and brought it up to tangle with her hair. "I would be content to kiss you all night, Elizabeth. With or without clothes. It will always be your choice." His lips sealed over her pulse, sucking lightly and coaxing one of those needy noises from her.

That's it, sweetheart. Come back to me.

Her nails dug into his arms, pulling him closer. He pressed his hips to hers, testing another boundary. She reacted by arching into him. His dick ached at the contact, but he shoved his needs aside to focus on her. He could enjoy a long shower afterward.

"Mmm, I think we can begin." He pulled back to capture her gaze. "Tell me if I go too far, Red. One word and I'll stop. Understand?"

Her dazed expression and little nod didn't work for him.

He tightened his hold in her hair and gave it a subtle tug. "Elizabeth, I need to know you'll speak up, or this won't work." He could read all her body cues well enough, but vocal participation was a requirement.

She swallowed, sobering enough through the haze of arousal to focus. "Okay."

"Not good enough." He nipped her jaw. "What will you say if you need me to slow down? If something is too intense?"

She blinked up at him. "To, uh, stop?"

His heart warmed at the genuineness of her response. He would have so much fun training her in the art of seduction and sex. Perhaps even too much fun. "We can start with that if you want, but you may want to word it differently at some point."

Her lips curled downward. "Why?"

He pressed his lips to her ear again. "Because, Red, at some point, your pleasure will be so intense you'll beg me to stop even though it's the last thing you actually want."

~*~

"But we'll explore that later, when you're ready." The words burned against Lizzie's sensitive skin.

Oh. My. God.

He could do that to her?

How?

His hot mouth went to her neck again, sending shivers down her spine. As if it wasn't enough to be caged between him and the wall, he had to add his talented lips to the mix.

I'm in so much trouble.

The best kind, though.

Or so she hoped.

Because, oh God, he was doing those things with his hands again, gently tracing her sides and stopping just beneath her breasts. She wanted to force him higher but didn't know how.

"Turn around," he murmured. "Put your hands on the wall for me."

She didn't know what to think or how to feel but abided the command because she wanted more. Butterflies took flight in her abdomen as he gathered all her hair and pulled it over her shoulder. He traced the line of her zipper from the base to the top, setting her blood on fire.

"Breathe, Red." He pressed a kiss to her nape that scattered goose bumps down her spine. Or maybe that was the result of him exposing her skin inch by inch. She didn't know. Didn't care. Couldn't focus.

He's going to see me naked.

It's just like being in a swimsuit competition.

Totally not the same thing.

God, what underwear had she worn?

Maroon.

Right.

To coordinate with her dress.

Panties, not a thong, and a matching silk bra. Just like a bikini, only with more cleavage. She could handle this.

Her dress fell to the ground.

Oh, God.

Heat flared across her back as he pressed his palms to her bare skin. "You're killing me, Lizzie." He slowly rotated her to face him, and the arousal darkening his gaze knocked her off balance.

She'd never had a man look at her like *that*.

Ravenous.

Hot.

And so incredibly sexy.

It triggered something buried deep inside of her—a confidence she didn't know she owned.

He wants me. She could see it in the way his chocolate eyes roamed over every inch of her skin in unabashed admiration.

Lizzie had no idea what to do with that knowledge, but she wanted to kiss him so badly it hurt. She didn't wait or ask but used her heels to her advantage and pressed her lips to his.

He responded immediately, taking control of the kiss with his tongue and flattening her against the wall. She moaned into his mouth as he parted her legs with one of his.

So good.

She needed more.

That fire was brewing again, so addictive and consuming.

His fingers knotted in her hair once more, tugging her back to the angle he wanted as his opposite hand went to her hips to force her pelvis forward. She jolted as the sweet spot connected with his muscled thigh.

Oh. She liked that.

Jayson awoke something inside of her that she knew very little about. Pleasure and desire were concepts she understood but rarely felt. Even alone at night when she tried, nothing happened. She felt attraction—love, even— but never anything like this.

She kissed him harder, and he returned the embrace in kind, all the while keeping his leg lodged between hers and applying pressure where she desired it most.

What is happening to me?

She felt wanton, dirty, and so very alive.

Her nails dug into his scalp as the sensation mounted, and he grinned against her lips. "What do you need, Red?"

She couldn't articulate a response, because she didn't know.

He cupped her breasts, and she arched on instinct.

Okay, yes, that she wanted. Very much.

"Skin," she managed as fire danced over her senses.

Her bra disappeared, and she moaned as he gave her what she desired. But it still wasn't enough.

"Shh, I've got you," he murmured against her mouth. He lifted her into his arms and carried her over to the mattress, where he laid her down far too gently. His palms slid down her legs to her ankles. He slipped off each of her heels and let them drop to the floor.

Every part of her yearned for more, causing her to squirm uncomfortably on the bed. Jayson watched with a hungry expression while slowly removing his jacket and laying it over the chair in the corner.

She froze when his hand went to the top button of his dress shirt.

Her brain conjured an image of what existed beneath, dampening the space between her thighs.

Oh, yes, please.

He slowly unfastened each button while observing her reactions with that same voracious look.

"What are you doing to me?" she asked with a groan.

"Prolonging the moment," he replied, tilting his head to the side with a knowing smile. "Trust me. You'll thank me for it later."

"Right now, I want to kill you."

"No, sweetheart. You want to fuck me. I can see how you might confuse the two, but they're unrelated." He finished removing his button-down and the fitted shirt beneath, and began loosening his belt.

Her lips fell open at the implication, causing him to pause, but she didn't have it in her to tell him to stop. How could she turn down a naked Jayson?

Whatever he saw in her expression must have appeased him, because he continued and rid himself of his jeans.

Black boxer briefs.

Even mostly naked, the man still had excellent fashion sense. Not in the way of most men who favored suits, but one who enjoyed European fashion. Lizzie more than approved, especially as he strolled toward her with all those muscles flexing and clenching.

Her breathing escalated as he crawled over her.

"You have the most gorgeous breasts," he murmured against a stiffening peak.

His gaze held hers as he slowly took her nipple into the hot cavern of his mouth. She bowed off the bed in response, causing him to chuckle.

"Mmm, you approve." He switched to the other and sucked it harder, eliciting a tortured sound from her throat.

The sensations were too much, yet still not enough. She didn't understand what she needed, just that she *wanted*. Oh God, did she *want*.

He kissed a path down her stomach while she writhed beneath him, and it wasn't until he settled between her thighs that she realized his intention.

Stop was on the tip of her tongue when he did something with his mouth that she never could have predicted.

There, her mind supplied as she dug her nails into the

bedding beneath her.

That was what she craved.

Her body shuddered under the onslaught as he tortured her most intimate flesh through the red silk of her panties and applied pressure with his tongue.

Magic.

The man held a mystical touch.

That's what caused all this. Even when she touched herself *there*, it never felt anything like this, nor did she ever enjoy it.

But she *really* enjoyed that twirling thing he was doing right now.

"Jayson," she whispered, uncertain.

He reached out to take her hand, and she squeezed the hell out of it. This feeling hurt so good, and the flames consumed her every thought.

His rhythm, heat, and presence were all she knew.

And the inferno spinning inside her in that secret area she'd never been able to access until now.

It rippled through her and combusted without warning, shooting her soul into the stars as light flashed behind her eyes. Ecstasy reverberated through every inch of her being and poured from her mouth in an endless scream.

She should have been ashamed, but she didn't have the energy. Not after whatever he'd just done to her.

How many times had she tried to achieve the same feeling and failed? She usually gave up before starting, knowing it wouldn't work, but Jayson had played her body like a master. And she'd responded in kind.

Her breath came in pants as he moved over her again. His lips tasted sweet, and she realized with a gasp that it was her essence on his tongue—a sinful treat that thickened her blood and clouded her judgment.

He'd fully and completely corrupted her, and she didn't mind in the slightest. All she wanted was… "More."

"All night, Lizzie." He deepened their kiss and slid a thigh between her legs. "Whatever you need."

She shook her head. "Naked." She wanted to feel his tongue everywhere, not through a silk barrier.

He tsked. "Now, Red, we set limits at the beginning and agreed to keep our underwear on tonight." He nuzzled her neck. "Feel free to renegotiate that next time."

Her blood heated at the thought of the future, and she found herself nodding vigorously. His responding chuckle vibrated her chest in the most amazing way. And then he was kissing her, silencing all her thoughts and using pressure to drive her insane with lust all over again.

All night, he'd said.

Oh, yes.

CHAPTER ELEVEN

Breakfast

Jayson's plan backfired.

He thought a night in bed pleasuring Lizzie would help cure this temptation, but it only fortified his craving. Her passion had sprung to life in a way he hadn't expected, driving him all the wilder. Even now, as she snuggled into his side, he could feel the heat radiating from her. The

144

woman had transformed into a sensual goddess under his touch, and he fucking loved it.

He needed more.

So much more.

He palmed his forehead and blew out a breath. This wouldn't end well. He knew that. The second she learned the truth, everything would end, yet he couldn't bring himself to take this any further without her knowing the reality of their situation. It wasn't fair to her.

The conundrum left him with a throbbing headache and a raging hard-on.

He needed a long shower, preferably with the redhead using his shoulder as a pillow.

His steadfast control had never been more important than it was last night when she begged to touch him and reciprocate. It took more energy than it should have to refuse her, mostly because he quieted her requests by exhausting her sexually.

She passed out on top of him around five this morning, hence the early afternoon hour. He'd slept more than he expected and woke with the overwhelming urge to flatten her beneath him and claim her.

Fucking bizarre.

Jayson enjoyed naked women in his bed and usually entertained them with another round of pleasure in the morning, but this desire was unnatural. It went far deeper than a carnal yearning and scared the shit out of him.

He wasn't a "love them and leave them" type but more of a "love them and maybe love them again later" type.

But with Lizzie, he thought he could be a "love her and only her" type. Especially after the way she came apart in his arms. She had responded to his touch like no one else in his long memory.

It has to be a trick.

Something to do with her genetics?

He'd have to ask the others if they felt this strange draw to her. It was messing with his head. Both of them.

Her thigh shifted over his, lifting upward to settle where he wanted her touch most—as if her body knew his needs without asking.

The woman was clearly created to test his control and destroy him.

He bit off a groan as she pressed her ample breasts into his side.

Heaven. That's what she felt like beside him. And every sinful part of him begged to pull her under him and unleash his darkest cravings. But she was nowhere near ready for him, and not just because of all the secrets.

Her leg slipped lower, then higher, and before he could react, Lizzie straddled his hips and stared down at him through hooded eyes.

"Good morning," she murmured in a voice thickened by sleep and lust. It sounded amazing coming from her. And that look? Pure, unadulterated sex.

He settled his palm on her waist. "Good afternoon," he corrected with a smile. "Sleep well?"

"Mm-hmm." She rocked her hips over his erection with the murmur, sending pleasure straight to his aching balls. He tightened his hold to cease her movements, but she rebelled by flattening her chest against his and pressing little kisses to his jaw. "It's a new day, and I'm ready to renegotiate."

Fuck.

"Lizzie…"

She silenced him with a kiss and, with her tongue, unleashed everything he'd taught her last night. It blew his mind how quickly this woman caught on to his preferences. However, she'd neglected to remember one major element to this relationship between them.

He rolled her beneath him and pinned her arms to the mattress on either side of her head. "You're forgetting something important, Red."

Big brown eyes stared up at him as a beautiful flush painted her cheeks. "What's that?" she asked in a breathy voice.

"You're not in charge, sweetheart." He nipped her lip in silent reprimand before pressing his mouth to her ear. "And I say we're not renegotiating yet." He drew his tongue down the column of her neck to her collarbone and farther, until he reached the rosy peak of her breast.

They could test one more limit before breakfast.

Rather than suck the tender nipple into his mouth, he grazed it with his teeth and smiled when she bowed off the bed. A harder pinch elicited a strangled noise of need that sent a jolt of desire straight to his dick.

It seemed Lizzie Watkins wasn't averse to a little bit of pain mingled with her pleasure. He would enjoy evoking more of that at a later time.

He laved her abused breast before placing an open-mouthed kiss to the other and left her alone on the bed.

She blinked up at him in confusion. "Where are you going?"

"Brunch," he replied. "We need to eat." And his gifted nose told him someone was hard at work in the kitchen.

"But…" Her tongue darted out to lick her lips as she ogled at his barely contained cock. He fought the urge to grin. She looked ready to devour him. If only he could allow it.

"That's not on the menu, Red." He selected a pair of boxers from his dresser drawer and a white shirt. "Here."

She ignored the clothes. "I'm not hungry."

"Your eyes say otherwise." He pulled a matching tee over his head before finding a pair of sweatpants. "Get dressed."

The little rebel narrowed her gaze. "Can't we eat after?"

He planted his hands on either side of her head and stared her down. "You're forgetting who is in control again."

She frowned. "I never agreed to that."

"Not true, sweetheart." He brushed his lips against hers. "You agreed the moment you stepped into my bedroom. And"—he pressed his mouth to her ear—"you like my commands." He smiled against her warming neck. "Now get up so we can eat."

If she were lying on her stomach, he would have followed it up with a light swat to her ass. Instead, he gently bit her pulse before standing upright and cocking a brow.

She glowered at him, but her beautiful flush and stiff nipples told him all he needed to know about her aroused state. Lizzie wanted him to finish what he started, but he'd opted to force her to go without—his way of reminding her who called the shots.

And maybe because he wanted her to live through a slight variation of his agony.

Was it fair? Hell no.

Was it necessary? Yes. Because he needed a break before he did something stupid, like fuck her into oblivion.

He would need to talk to Luc today not just about the vial of liquid from last night but about his evolving relationship with Lizzie. This couldn't continue, not with her being kept in the dark. She deserved better.

Jayson immediately regretted his wardrobe choice for Lizzie as she pulled on his clothes. He dressed so many women in this fashion and never cared, yet somehow she captivated him.

His white shirt fell past her hips, ending just above the boxer shorts. The fabric hung loosely on her, but her curves peeked at him in the subtlest of ways. He would definitely be fantasizing about this later. After she left.

"Happy?" she asked.

He threaded his fingers in her hair and allowed a sliver of his arousal to rise to the surface as he kissed the hell out of her. His tongue silenced hers while he unleashed his desire and marked her the way he wanted. Her nails dug into his arms, spurring him on, until he left her panting before him. "I am now," he whispered, responding to her inquiry into his happiness. "Let's eat."

"You're killing me," she breathed.

"Likewise, Red." He swept his tongue over hers once more before sliding his hand into hers and leading her to the door. She followed without argument, her fingers curling around his as he guided her down the hallway and into the kitchen, where Balthazar stood in a pair of boxer briefs and nothing else. He flipped a pancake onto a plate as they entered, and turned to set it on the island.

"A seven-point-six, Jay. Nicely done." Mirth danced in his wicked gaze as he took in Lizzie's disheveled state. "You look famished, sweetheart. Why don't you take the first plate while I finish up the rest?"

Jayson counted the plates on the island while Lizzie stood frozen beside him. Balthazar's physique did that to most women. Men, too, for that matter.

"Are Grace and Jacque still here?" Jayson asked, curious.

"They're in the living area catching up on their American television shows," B replied as he flipped another pancake.

Eight plates, minus the ones for Lizzie, Jay, and the two in the living area, meant that Balthazar had four for himself. *You only took three of them to bed?*

A shrug from the immortal at the stove.

Not the correct assessment. Maybe he wasn't planning to eat. *Four?*

"You need more plates, Jay," Balthazar said as he grabbed one from the counter. "I believe twelve is the standard, but in this case, I need ten."

Five? Jayson grinned. *Nice.* "Yeah, I'll keep that in mind."

"Do." He handed the pancake-layered plate to Jayson. "Luc invited us over for drinks later."

Is he done reviewing the serum? Jayson asked.

Balthazar lifted his chin in the affirmative before saying, "He wants us over as soon as we're free. Does that work for you?"

"Yep." He picked up Lizzie's untouched plate and bumped his hip against hers. "Let's eat, Red."

"Uh, yep." Lizzie picked her jaw up off the floor and managed to follow him to the dining room.

"I clearly didn't do my job right if you find Balthazar more interesting than me," he said as he sat beside her rather than across from her.

"He's practically naked," she whispered.

He selected a set of silverware from the middle of the table—Balthazar seriously thought of everything when it came to the kitchen, and the bedroom for that matter—and handed it to Lizzie.

"Balthazar enjoys all aspects of sexuality, including exhibitionism," he replied. "I'm honestly shocked he bothered to put on boxers at all." He suspected the only reason he wore them was for Lizzie's sake. Everyone else in this condo had seen him naked countless times.

She gaped at him. "So this is normal?"

"For Balthazar? Definitely."

"And for you?" she asked.

He shrugged. "It's not a daily occurrence, but Balthazar has a thing for pancakes."

"No, I meant to throw parties and…" She trailed off as Balthazar left the kitchen with two plates and went in the direction of the bedroom. An array of giggles followed, causing Lizzie to frown. "How do you know all these people, again?"

He told her this last night, but perhaps not with enough detail.

"I don't know most of them," Jayson admitted as he grabbed a knife and fork for himself. "Balthazar is an old friend from Hydria, which is the Greek island I lived on prior to moving here for work." He gave her a pointed look. "You still owe me cookies."

"What about the others?" she pressed rather than agreeing. He'd circle back to the cookies later.

"Jacque and Grace are from Hydria, as well, and are

visiting for the weekend with B. Tristan was the only one you met last night from the city."

"And all the women?"

"Balthazar's friends." He found the syrup B had left out for them and grinned at the familiar label. Jacque had clearly procured this from Luc's private stash. Their supreme leader had a thing for pure maple products.

"Do you want any?" he asked, hoping to return her mood to the sexy banter from before.

"Uh, sure."

He drizzled the syrup over her pancakes while she watched before doing the same to his own. "Looks like B decided on chocolate chip today," he mused.

"So, he throws parties like this often?"

Jayson chuckled. "Yeah. I guess you could say it's his specialty."

She didn't return his amusement. "And he usually makes breakfast for everyone the next morning?"

"Sustenance is important after an evening of vigorous exercise," Balthazar replied as he returned to the kitchen to pick up the rest of the plates. "It's the hospitable thing to do," he added as he left for the bedroom again.

Lizzie gaped after him before refocusing on Jayson. "So it's routine for you all to sleep with women and feed them the next morning." Not a question.

"I wouldn't call it routine—"

"But it happens often?"

Jayson palmed the back of his neck. Most of the women he took to his bed understood his no-strings-attached terms, but Lizzie was different for several reasons.

"I don't know about often." As it depended on her definition.

"How many times in New York?"

"This would be the first."

"And in Greece?"

"Depends on the week." He wouldn't lie to her, but he

wouldn't elaborate, either.

Her eyes widened as the first ounce of emotion graced her features, and it wasn't one he ever wanted to see on her. *Pain.* "Always with different women or the same ones?"

He sighed. "Lizzie, what are you really trying to ask here? How often I take women to my bed? The last time I was with a woman? What do you want to know?" Because he would tell her, within reason.

Balthazar chose that moment to return again. "The ladies want syrup," he murmured with a wink and sauntered off as Lizzie's eyebrows jumped to her hairline.

"How many women are in there?"

"A few," he replied vaguely. At least they'd switched to Balthazar's sex life as a discussion. That should take some of the heat off Jayson.

"And that's normal?" she asked.

"Yes."

"For you as well?"

"I don't tend to entertain five women in my bed at once, if that's what you're asking." He regretted speaking immediately.

"Five women?" she repeated. "You've had... a... a... 'sixsome' before?"

Fuck. This was not going well at all. "Look—"

She shoved away from the table and out of his reach before he could react. Not that he'd been about to touch her—experience told him that would only make it worse.

"How many, Jayson?"

He knew what she meant—a number of bed partners. "You don't want that answer," he told her honestly.

She wouldn't be able to comprehend it, not without understanding his age and everything else first. And besides, he didn't have a figure to give. He stopped counting a millennia ago.

"Oh God." She blinked rapidly. "Tristan mentioned sharing. He meant..." She covered her mouth while

Jayson cursed inwardly.

Fucking Ichorian.

"It's not..." Okay, there was no safe way to answer that. *Not what you think* would be a blatant lie because it was exactly what she thought. "It's not something we will do," he settled on instead. Because he had no interest in sharing Lizzie with anyone.

She shook her head. "I... I..."

The moisture pooling in her eyes broke his heart. "Lizzie—"

"No, I'm not... I don't..." Her lips trembled, and he hated himself a little in that moment. He would never apologize for his past—he didn't regret a second of it—but seeing what it did to her now hurt far more than it should.

"I need to go," she said abruptly and spun toward the foyer.

He hopped to his feet to follow her, but a hand on his shoulder stopped him.

"Give her space," Balthazar whispered, appearing behind him in that uncanny way of his. He'd no doubt heard all the thoughts going through their heads.

"We both know that's the worst thing to do in these situations," Jayson replied as he started after her again.

The grip turned unyielding. "Although I agree, her case is anything but normal. Let her cool off."

"I can't let her leave like that, B."

"And I can't let you go after her."

"What the fuck is that supposed to mean?" He rounded on his oldest friend as the front door slammed. "Since when are you okay with letting a woman suffer on her own?" Balthazar was always the first to provide compassion and understanding, mostly because of his ability to read thoughts and control emotion.

"As I just stated, nothing about this situation applies to the norm," Balthazar replied in that irritatingly calm voice of his. "And you're not in the frame of mind to handle it."

"Excuse me?"

"You want to tell her the truth," Balthazar continued. "And don't deny it, Jay. You've been thinking about it all night, and your emotions right now can't be trusted. You'll break."

Jayson's gut reaction was to punch his best friend in the face, but reason held him in check.

"Fuck..." He rubbed his hand over his face before grabbing the wooden chair beside him and squeezing until it cracked. "Fuck."

"That's exactly what I told you to do last night," Balthazar muttered as he finally let him go. "And with any other woman, you would have done it. But not her. Tell me why that is?"

Jayson shook his head. "It's wrong, and you know it."

"The attraction is mutual, clearly. So how is it wrong, Jay?" Balthazar waited for a response, but Jayson couldn't articulate one fast enough. "Because you're worried she'll never forgive you for it—something you would never concern yourself with for any other woman."

"I'm not an ass."

"And I'm not calling you one," Balthazar countered. "I'm saying you usually wouldn't consider a future with a woman, but you're thinking about one with Lizzie. That's why you won't give in to your desire and also why you can't go after her right now. You're too tempted to tell her everything, and although I can condone sating the needs of you both, I can't allow that. Not without the others agreeing first."

Jayson knew he was right, but fuck if he didn't want to ignore logic and chase after Lizzie.

The hurt in her eyes... He'd put that there. Not because he meant to, but because he hadn't been quick enough to explain.

"I hate this," he admitted. "All of it."

"We'll sort it, Jay," Balthazar murmured. "But first I need thirty minutes to finish up in the bedroom.

Afterward, we'll head out to meet Luc."

"Thirty minutes?" Jayson repeated with a half-hearted laugh. He couldn't exactly be amused with Lizzie hurting downstairs, but he tried anyway. "You tired, B?"

"The ladies started without me," Balthazar replied with a shrug. "I gave them an objective, and they're living up to the task."

"Right." Jayson shook his head, irritated. "Not even that appeals to me right now." And it fucking should because he knew syrup was somehow involved. "I'll be here when you're done."

~*~

Lizzie threw her purse onto her mattress and collapsed beside it. She'd been an idiot to leave it unattended on Jayson's foyer table all night and an even bigger idiot for going to bed with him.

Or maybe it was the losing her shit over nothing that qualified her for Idiot of the Year?

A sob tore from her chest as she curled into a ball.

How had her night of bliss and passion ended so horribly? She'd let her insecurities out to play at the worst possible time, but seeing how unfazed he was by his friend's bedroom antics hit a nerve. Their night together—which she more than enjoyed—proved him far more skilled than her, but hearing how experienced he was scared the crap out of her.

Exhibitionism.

Sharing.

Erotic parties ending in ménages of unknown quantities, with breakfast the following morning.

I don't tend *to entertain five women in my bed at once.* Meaning he'd done it before.

Her chest rattled, forcing her to breathe.

How could she ever satisfy a man like that? No wonder he hadn't wanted to renegotiate this morning.

All that talk about the future had given her hope that he wanted more, that he was easing her into their passion out of respect for her inexperience. But his proclivities existed on a level she could never reach, and he surely realized that last night.

Was she just a diversion? The virgin neighbor he wanted to corrupt and deflower?

God, she hoped not. His touch had awakened something foreign in her. And he hadn't hidden how much he wanted her.

Unless he looked at all women that way.

"Damn it," she whispered as more tears fell.

Even if he did want her, she couldn't live up to his expectations. And after the way she'd just acted over breakfast, he surely knew that.

She'd more than overreacted.

But five women at once? That couldn't be normal. What did one even call that? A ménage à six?

And if he didn't *tend* to entertain that many women, how many did he bed on a regular basis?

You don't want that answer.

He was right. She didn't.

Jayson had been the first man to ever really touch her, and she had wanted so much more. She'd ruined that chance by reacting like a prude in his dining room.

Maybe it was for the best. Lizzie never planned to wait until marriage but had never met anyone who tempted her enough for sex. Other than Tom. Except now she wondered if that was true.

The feelings and sensations Jayson had aroused in her over the last few weeks were nothing compared to her past. Tom's hugs gave her girly butterflies, while Jayson's kisses set her on fire.

Her phone dinged, sending a jolt of hope through her heart, followed by a shiver of dread. She'd left her dress and shoes in his room. He probably wanted to drop them off, or worse, needed her to come get them.

156

Another ping had her groaning and digging through her purse for her phone.

The text on the screen was not what she expected.

OMG! You'll never guess what Cam did!

Oh, and you better be free tonight, Liz. It's been ages since I saw your face, and I need a girls' night.

A second later another message appeared.

Seriously, you need to call me ASAP. I'm dying over here!

Lizzie pressed her face into the bedding and muttered unintelligibly to herself.

She'd been relieved and saddened to find the condo empty. Breaking down in front of Stas would have been mortifying, but also therapeutic. Kristin did not offer the same outlet. She was a fun friend, not a close friend.

Another chime had her peeking at the phone.

Did Kristin tell you about the tickets?

Cam added a bunch of excited emojis afterward, including wicked devil faces and lips. A photo of a fallen angel outfit arrived next, followed by another text.

You still have that outfit from the Alpha B&W party our senior year, right?

Lizzie sat up on her bed, her interest piqued.

Yes, she typed back.

Little dots appeared from Cam seconds before her response popped up on the screen.

Good! Wear it tonight. It's fucking hot, chick.

Lizzie flipped to the conversation with Kristin. She considered texting but decided calling would be easier. After several deep breaths, she cleared her throat and hit dial.

An excited squeal came over the line, forcing her to pull the phone away from her ear.

"Are you sitting down?"

Lizzie cleared her throat again before saying, "Yes."

"Cam scored us tickets to some exclusive Halloween party tonight, and you're totally coming with us. No arguments, Liz. I haven't seen you in like two months, and

I know how you feel about dressing up."

Lizzie grimaced. The idea of playing dress-up for anything right now did not appeal to her in the slightest, but she couldn't exactly say that. Not without Kristin requiring a reason and demanding Lizzie go out anyway.

"The fastest way to get over a guy is to get under another one" was one of Kristin's favorite sayings.

"What time?" Lizzie asked.

"Cam says to be at her place by nine, and she wants you to wear that sexilicious costume from that black-and-white party. You know, the one where she hooked up with Dean?" She rattled off some additional details and a comment about her own outfit before ending with, "Any questions?"

"Where's the party being held?" Lizzie didn't really care but thought it might be good information to jot down in case Stas came home later.

"The Arcadia," Kristin replied. "It's supposedly a hot club, though I've never been there, and they throw an annual Halloween party with exclusive clientele. Cam says we should expect celebrities."

Those words would have excited her a few months ago. Now she just wanted to hide. "Sounds good," she managed. "I need to start getting ready."

Kristin would interpret that to mean Lizzie wanted to ready herself physically, but really, she required the time to regroup mentally. Because she couldn't put on a happy face and enjoy an evening out with the girls while moping over Jayson.

"Awesome. Toodles, Liz."

The line went dead.

Lizzie stared at her reflection in the mirror over her dresser.

Maybe this will be good for me, she thought.

She never did anything like this anymore, not since Tom's death, and she so desperately needed to let go of the pain.

Some alcohol and dancing would chase away the shadows beneath her puffy eyes.

A little harmless flirtation could help her forget Jayson temporarily, too.

Hanging out with her old friends would help her feel less lonely. Stas wouldn't like it because she didn't care for Lizzie's sorority sisters.

"But she's not here," Lizzie murmured to herself. "She's never here."

So why not go out and enjoy a little fun? Nothing held her here except herself. Jayson clearly didn't care that she'd run off, or he would have stopped by or called by now. Going out with friends seemed like the natural cure. She already had the outfit and shoes; she just needed the hair and makeup to go with it.

"I can do this," she told herself.

Experiencing a new club wouldn't be a hardship, and if she didn't like it, she'd come home. Easy.

"Now I just need to find that costume."

CHAPTER TWELVE

Angels and Demons at the Costume Ball

College enrollment complete.
Benefactor is eager to see how subject
acclimates to the social environment
and extracurricular activities.

—Entry Log 118.06.4-7

"Estrogen?" Jayson asked, incredulous. Could that be why he found Lizzie irresistible? He adored women, but something about her drew him in like no one else ever had, which was saying a lot for a man his age. "Are they trying to turn her into a succubus or something?"

Luc leaned against the wall beside him with his hands in his pockets. "She's quite alluring, but I don't think that's the purpose."

"She's a gorgeous woman," Balthazar added. "But I don't find her irresistible." The pointed glance and word choice said he'd been playing in Jayson's thoughts. It was the mind reader's way of confirming that Jayson's feelings were his own and not the result of scientific intervention.

But that didn't mean the serum wasn't at least partly responsible.

"What were the chemical properties?" Anything addictive, perhaps? Because that's how Jayson would describe his desire for Lizzie—an infatuation. He craved her presence and wished he was in New York with her, not here in Hydria. He'd left her with a guard again, but if she left the condo, the Hydraian wouldn't be able to follow. And that left Jayson antsy and anxious to return.

Luc scratched his jaw, gaze thoughtful. "The solution is primarily composed of estrogen and a few filler ingredients."

"So it's like a birth control pill?" Stas guessed. She stood across from them with Issac at her side.

Neither of them had greeted Jayson favorably, likely because they didn't approve of Lizzie spending the night at his place last night. *Well, too fucking bad.* His only regret was the way she had left this afternoon, something he would rectify as soon as they finished this conversation.

"Not quite," Luc replied. "Nothing in the chemical makeup prevents conception. It's more of a hormonal regimen, but for what, I'm not certain." He shifted his focus to Tom. "I don't see how this serum is keeping her alive."

"I never said it was." Tom folded his tanned arms. The newly turned Hydraian was clearly spending a lot of time near the pool with Amelia. "All I overheard was the mention of a monthly dose, and we all jumped to conclusions that Lizzie required it to live. Your research states otherwise, unless hormones are now required for breathing?"

"It's moot," Luc said. "We can replicate the serum, but I need a blood sample before we go any further."

"From Lizzie?" Stas's tone and expression dared anyone to answer that, but of course, Luc enjoyed a good challenge.

"Yes." Flat, straight to the point, and underlined in authority.

"No," she said immediately. "No. What we do next is tell her the truth. You have her serum. Replicate it, and let's bring her to safety."

"That's not your decision to make," Luc murmured, expression and stance professionally polite. Only those who knew him well would see the tick in his jaw, suggesting his urge to assert dominance.

"Maybe not," Stas agreed. "But I'm not going into her room like some vampire and stealing her blood without permission." She flashed an apologetic look at Issac, who merely shrugged in response. She blew out a breath and refocused on Luc, her expression still contrite but for a different reason.

Luc and Stas had disagreed with one another since day one, mostly because she feared her future and he found her behavior to be selfish. Jayson suspected it would only grow worse once Stas changed into a Hydraian—her innate gift for controlling people undermined Luc's natural sovereignty in Hydra.

"I'm done lying to her, Luc," she said, her tone lacking the confrontation from moments ago. "We agreed that we needed more information about her, and now we have it. Meanwhile, Lizzie's alone in New York with more than one lunatic, and that's unacceptable. It's time to tell her everything and move her somewhere safe before"—she paused to clear her throat, her eyes darkening—"before *Ezekiel* decides on his next move."

Jayson nodded, agreeing with every word but also keeping his mouth shut. His place in this discussion was jeopardized by his selfish reasons for wanting Lizzie to know the truth. Something Balthazar wouldn't hesitate to point out if it came down to an even vote.

"Stas is right," Tom said, but with a touch more reverence. "We've been searching for two months, and all we've found are some hormone-laced drinks. It's not a lot to go on, but we can gather more details from her once she's in Hydria—where she'll be safe."

Luc remained quiet, considering, and met Issac's gaze. "And you?"

"I do not believe Elizabeth to be a threat to anyone other than herself," he replied. "Informing her of our world and her potential place in it will not go over well, and I worry about her reaction—not for us, but rather, for her."

"He's right," Balthazar murmured. "You'll need me to numb her emotions, or she may do something rash."

"Alik?" Luc asked, his focus shifting to the silent man in the corner of the room.

"I recommended we bring her here two months ago, while you all agreed to send Jayson to play babysitter." Alik unfolded his arms to place his hands in the pockets of his leather jacket. "That should answer your question."

Luc acknowledged the response with a nod before fixing his gaze on Jayson. "And you?"

"Balthazar would tell you that my feelings on this subject prohibit me from offering an unbiased response," he replied honestly. "But I agree with the others that it's time to tell her the truth."

"So you all believe on varying levels that she's ready." Luc's carefully pitched tone suggested he didn't agree but would trust their opinions.

"She's not." Issac wrapped his arm around Stas as she reacted to his frank reply. "But I believe we are at an impasse. We require her cooperation to learn more, and the only way for that to happen is to tell her the truth. And I do not believe waiting for Ezekiel's next play is our smart move."

Jayson agreed with a nod, as did everyone else.

"Well." Luc clasped his hands and shrugged. "I guess that leads us to the next topic of discussion. Who is going to tell her and how?"

~*~

The reason for Cam's request to wear their black and white outfits became clear almost immediately.

Angels and demons.

Not an original Halloween party theme, but a classic nonetheless.

Most of the guests wore sinister outfits with leather and chains, giving the club a gothic feel. The music blaring overhead added to the dark atmosphere, as did the low lighting.

Definitely not Lizzie's usual hangout, but perfect for a spooky evening filled with drinking and dancing.

"Ladies," the bartender murmured as he dropped off their cocktails.

Cam simpered at the handsome man while Kristin handed over her card to start a tab. They alternated nights throughout college, something that had continued after graduation. Lizzie had covered their last girls' night out, and tonight was Kristin's turn.

"You're glowing," Cam said around her straw.

Lizzie grinned. "It's the black light." Her pure-white outfit of a miniskirt, knee-high boots, and a tank top were all glowing a purple color. "If only I had wings." She'd resemble a violet angel.

"Your bra is completely visible," Kristin teased. "We should have worn white too, Cam." They were both wearing black—Cam in a skirt that barely covered her butt and a see-through shirt, revealing her lacy bra, and Kristin in leather pants and a halter top.

Two demons and their pet angel, Lizzie.

"We're too sinful to wear white," Cam replied.

"Besides, Liz is the only virgin here."

"Hey! That's not…" Her cheeks flamed as memories of last night rolled through her thoughts. She cleared her voice before finishing with, "True."

"Has something changed in the last two months?" Kristin asked, eyebrows waggling.

"Maybe she's been shacked up with a guy and that's why she's been MIA," Cam said.

"Yes!" That excited Kristin. "I think you might be right. Is she, Liz? Is there a man keeping you busy?"

Lizzie shook her head. "You're both being ridiculous." But thoughts of Jayson crept into her mind, sending another rush of heat down her neck, followed by a chill when she remembered how they left things.

No calls.

No texts.

Nothing.

Not that she should expect it. She'd acted like a crazy person earlier. So what if the man was a little more experienced than her?

Try a lot *more.*

Okay, true, but couldn't that be a good thing?

"Oh my God, Cam's right. You've been hooking up with someone." Kristin set her drink down on the bar and gave Lizzie her full attention. "Spill. Tell us everything."

"Uh, well, I have this new neighbor. It's nothing, really, just, I don't know. He's hot, and we've kissed a few times." She swallowed several pulls from her straw in an attempt to cool off her cheeks, but the alcohol only seemed to warm her more. "It's really not a big deal."

"Jayson would be so disappointed to hear that," a male voice said directly behind her.

She turned in to a muscular chest encased in a leather jacket and lifted her gaze to a pair of ebony eyes tinged with gold flecks.

"Kiel," she breathed. "Hi. I didn't mean, that is, I…" Lizzie cleared her throat as he studied her with an amused

165

expression. He clearly thought she was an idiot, and rightly so.

"Ignore me," she muttered.

"On the contrary, Little Red, I find you impossible to ignore." He curled a long finger through one of her loose pieces of hair and gave it a little tug. "Introduce me to your friends."

"Right, of course." As if she could appear any more incompetent, she'd forgotten her manners. He remained behind her as she rotated to face her gaping friends. "Cam, Kristin, this is Kiel. He, uh, works with the neighbor I just mentioned."

"Hello, ladies," he murmured over her shoulder. "Can I introduce you to some of my friends?"

Cam's eyes brightened even more at the prospect. "Yes, I think you should," she replied in that flirtatious way of hers. Kiel's rocker image didn't fit Kristin's usual type, but Cam rarely discriminated. If the man boasted confidence and good looks, she gave him a chance. And Kiel certainly met both requirements.

"Brilliant." His hand appeared over Lizzie's shoulder as he signaled some friends from one of the booths lining the club's walls. The seating seemed to stretch all around, minus the area where the stairs led to a VIP lounge on the second level, and a dance floor took up most of the middle. The bar near the entrance was where they decided to start after surveying the interior. Kristin liked to begin with a few rounds to help loosen up before chatting with random men, but Cam had no problem initiating conversation while sober, as she did now.

"What do you do for a living, Kiel?" she asked while the two other men approached. Unlike Kiel, they were wearing all-black suits. Lizzie recognized the expensive brand with an inward smile. Kristin would be all over these guys the second she saw them.

"I'm an assassin," Kiel replied in that easy way of his.

Cam and Kristin laughed at his Halloween-inspired

joke, while Lizzie shook her head. An assassin didn't really fit the theme, and his leather jacket was the same as the other night. Not all that original, but maybe he didn't enjoy dressing up.

"I'm a devil," Cam replied and used her fingers to form horns over her blonde head.

"Are you?" Kiel sounded impressed. "In the sheets or out, I wonder."

"Why not both?" Cam replied, her expression coquettish.

Kiel's chest was close enough to Lizzie's back that she felt his responding chuckle. "I think you're going to have an enlightening evening, darling," he said as his friends arrived.

"Zach, Lars, meet Cam and Kristin." He curled an arm around Lizzie's waist as he added, "And this is Lizzie, but she's off the market."

Lizzie twisted to stare up at him while the others made their introductions. "I am?" she asked, incredulous.

"You are," he replied. "Your relationship with Jay is far more important than you realize, young one."

She blinked. "Has he talked to you?" Her tone betrayed a hopeful note she would have preferred to hide, but she couldn't help it.

"Not quite." His gaze danced over her in a curious way. "There is so much you don't know—it's radiating in your innate innocence."

She frowned at his bizarre words. They should have left her feeling uncomfortable, but instead sparked her interest. Nothing about Kiel struck her as normal or safe, yet he didn't strike her as dangerous. He was friends with Jayson—or acquaintances, anyway. Perhaps that's why she trusted him. Knowing her sorority sisters were at her back helped too.

"Would you like to know more, Lizzie?" he asked, tilting his head to the side. "About Jay? About our world?"

"You mean your business?" That didn't sound all that

interesting, but she wouldn't mind learning more about what Jayson did every day.

Kiel's lips curled. "What has Jay told you we do?"

"Acquisitions."

"Is that all?" He tsked. "My dear Lizzie, we have so much to discuss."

He nodded at his friends, and she glanced back to see Cam and Kristin being escorted onto the dance floor. So much for girl code. They must have assumed she was safe with Kiel since they already knew each other. Still, they could have asked.

"Do you want to join them?" Kiel asked, his lips at her ear. "Or would you like to know more about our world?"

Our world...

What bizarre phrasing, except it seemed par for the course with Kiel. He was a walking complex—handsome, charming, generally jovial, but with a lethal air, a don't-fuck-with-me vibe, and an accent she couldn't place.

She met his gaze again. "What do you mean by 'world'?"

"Come with me and find out." He let go of her waist and held out a hand. "I promise not to bite."

"All right," she agreed, pressing her palm to his. "But only if we're staying in the club."

His eyes sparkled with a mixture of mirth and secrets. "As the lady requests."

She expected him to maneuver them over to the booth his friends had vacated, but instead, he headed toward the heavily guarded staircase. A nod at the men dressed in black wearing earpieces had them standing aside for the couple to ascend, causing her nerves to sing with unease.

"Where are we going?" she asked, but he didn't hear her over the music. She considered trying again when the electronic beats quieted upstairs, but her new surroundings piqued a stronger curiosity.

Another bar, as well as a variety of more decadent booths with velvet interiors and glass tables, graced the upper balcony. Kiel meandered over to a vacant booth overlooking the dance floor below and gestured for her to slide in first. She did so while he flagged a waitress wearing a string bikini top and chains for a skirt.

Several of the other women up here boasted similar outfits and were all watching Lizzie with curious expressions.

I'm clearly overdressed for this level.

Or perhaps they wanted to know what qualified her to join the VIP lounge.

Lizzie forced a smile, but no one returned it.

"You know what I want," Kiel said. He hadn't taken a seat yet. Rather, he remained standing with his hands in his pockets as the curvy waitress approached. "My friend here would like something fruity, but spike it nicely. She'll need it."

The brunette trailed polished nails up his jacket and grinned. "Anything for you, love."

He caught her fingers and brought her wrist to his mouth. "Anything?"

"Tease." Her tone held a touch of admonishment. "We both know I'm not to your taste."

"Mmm, sadly true." He let her go after nipping the base of her thumb. "But I may need you for a demonstration later."

"Oh?" Her eager gaze went to Lizzie before returning to Kiel. "You let me know when, and I'm your girl."

"Thank you, sweetheart." He kissed her on the cheek before settling on the other side of the booth and fixing his gaze on Lizzie. "We'll begin once Cynthia delivers our drinks. In the interim, what do you think of the Arcadia?"

"Um, it's not my usual scene."

He chuckled. "No, I should think not. You strike me as a country-bar kind of girl, or perhaps a disco?"

"A disco?" she repeated with an ineloquent snort. "I like dancing, but I need something current."

"Disco isn't current?" He frowned as if puzzled by

that. "Forgive me, but the decades run together. Hell, sometimes the centuries do as well, though this technology era is quite fascinating."

She gaped at him. "How old are you?" Because he didn't look a day over thirty, but he spoke about time in such a weird manner. Just like everything else.

How is this guy friends with Jay, again? They seemed like very different people.

Kiel smiled. "Oh, we'll get to that very soon, darling. But would you mind terribly if I made a call? It will only be a moment."

"Uh, sure." Lizzie searched for her friends downstairs while he fiddled with his phone.

She could see the throng of gyrating bodies from her perch beside the glass railing, but making out individual faces in the flashing lights was impossible. The booths along the walls were easier to identify, as were the people inside them, but she doubted Cam or Kristin ventured there. At least not yet. Cam worked fast, but not *that* fast.

"Evening, Jedrick," Kiel drawled in a tone that drew Lizzie's attention. It held a sinister feel to it that he hadn't used in her presence before.

"Not a good time? Then I'll make this brief. I have something that belongs to you." He listened, his ebony gaze gleaming with a sinful emotion that unsettled Lizzie's stomach.

The playful charmer from before had been replaced by someone far more wicked.

This was a bad idea.

Too late now, Liz.

"No, not quite." He grinned. "Would you care to say hello to Jay, Little Red?"

~*~

Jayson's blood ran cold as he gripped the phone impossibly tighter. "Lizzie…"

"Jay-Jayson?" Her innocent voice came through the receiver underlined with confusion. "I don't—"

"Listen to me very carefully, Lizzie. You need—"

Ezekiel's tsk came over the line, silencing Jayson's attempt at a warning. "Now that's not a good sport, Jay. I offer you a chance to say hello, or perhaps goodbye in this case, and you try to ruin my fun? Where's the sportsmanship in that, hmm?"

The lamp shattered beside him as he knocked everything off the end table in Balthazar's great room. "If you fucking touch her—"

"You'll what, kill me?" Ezekiel chuckled, his amusement palpable even over the thousands of miles that separated them. "I daresay I underestimated your feelings for the woman. This is going to be quite fun."

Jayson gritted his teeth and forced the words out that he needed to say. "What do you want?"

"To see just how bad you want her back," Ezekiel murmured. "Would you like to know where we are?"

"You know I do," Jayson managed through his aching jaw. *So I can shove a blade between your eyes.*

"The Arcadia," he replied simply. "One of Lizzie's friends managed to procure an invitation to tonight's party, perhaps not by coincidence. But imagine my delight when your gorgeous Red waltzed in wearing a buffet of white. Oh, thank you, Cynthia. That looks lovely. I'll buzz you if we require anything else, such as the demonstration. Thanks, love."

"What are you doing?"

Jayson fell to his knees at the terrified note in Lizzie's voice, his will crumbling to his feet. He never should have left her alone. Not with Ezekiel on the loose. What the fuck had he been thinking visiting Hydria while she remained unprotected in New York?

He'd failed her in the worst possible way.

The Arcadia?

Fuck.

171

What the hell happened to her guard detail?

Ezekiel's cool reply didn't calm his nerves in the slightest. "Trust me, darling, this is for your own protection, as I suspect there will be a great deal of screaming in our near future."

"If you—"

"Hold that thought, Jay." The music died in the background, replaced by a scuffling that suggested a fight—one that ended with a muffled shriek and Ezekiel sighing. "Calm down."

"I won't calm down!" Lizzie snapped. "You just sealed us in a glass bubble!"

"For reasons you'll understand once I hang up the phone. Now sit silently, or I'll be forced to silence you."

A gasp came from Lizzie, filled with shock and fear.

Oh, fuck no.

Jayson would slaughter Ezekiel for this.

His fists clenched as he envisioned ripping the Ichorian limb by limb and burning each piece while forcing the asshole to watch.

Unspoken truce or not, he would end him.

Slowly.

Permanently.

He tried to voice his threats, but words failed him. Agony, fury, and a twinge of helplessness overwhelmed reason, paralyzing him in a shell of fear and loathing.

"I've given you our location. I suggest you act quickly, Jay." The line went dead, and Jayson sent his phone crashing into the wall. It shattered into a million fucking pieces just as Balthazar and Luc ran into the house.

The Arcadia was the one place in the world Jayson couldn't go, and Ezekiel knew it.

"Fuck!" Jayson pounded his fury into the floor, not caring at all for the skin cracking across his knuckles. It would heal in a minute. The same could not be said for Lizzie.

"What the hell is going on?" Luc demanded.

"Jay's losing it," Alik replied from his perch on the couch. "Reminds me of that time in Rome…" His voice trailed off at the glower Jayson flashed him. "Right, you remember."

Alik shrugged and went back to whatever the fuck he was doing on his phone. Jayson had the sudden urge to rip it from his hands and throw it, along with Alik, against the wall in response, but a hand on his shoulder steadied him.

"Talk to me," Balthazar demanded as he knelt beside him.

Jayson still couldn't form a coherent sentence, so he replayed the conversation through his head while clenching and unclenching his fists against the wood.

Violence unlike anything he'd ever experienced lanced his thoughts, slicing his need into two parts. One vied for sanity, while the other craved a suicide mission to New York.

"Ezekiel has Lizzie at the Arcadia," Balthazar translated for those who couldn't hear. "Get Wakefield, and we need to find out what happened to Jennifer."

Jennifer. Lizzie's supposed guard.

Why the fuck didn't she tell me Lizzie went out?

"Already on my way," Luc said as he left the house.

"He won't kill her," Alik said in that irritatingly calm way of his. "There's no entertainment value, and she's worth more alive. He's fucking with you, and winning." He hopped off the couch. "I'll be in the pool if anyone needs me."

Balthazar's hand tightened when Jay considered reacting by tossing a blade at one of his oldest friends. It wouldn't be the first time they fought, or the last, but Alik usually won. His ability to inflict pain mentally far surpassed their own, not to mention his telepathy. Powerful bastard.

"He's trying to redirect your rage," Balthazar murmured after the door slammed.

"It's working."

173

"Good. Now get up off the floor and act like the warrior I know you are." Balthazar pushed away from him and turned off the television before walking over to the kitchen. Jayson took two deep breaths, forced himself upright, and accepted the water bottle Balthazar handed him on his way to the dining area.

"Alik is right," B said. "Zeke is goading you for fun. He won't kill Lizzie."

"You can't know that for certain. He's a fucking assassin, for crying out loud."

"Who has had multiple opportunities to take her out and hasn't bothered. No, there's something else going on here." Balthazar took another swig of water and focused on the door just before it flew open. Issac and Luc walked in, followed by Stas and Tom.

"Jennifer fell asleep," Luc said flatly.

"She fell asleep?" Jayson repeated, his tone lethally soft.

"Yes, she thought Lizzie was staying in for the night." Luc's expression indicated he was not pleased by that excuse. "I'll deal with Jennifer after we fix this issue."

"Do so. Or I will." And a demotion would be the least of her concerns.

Falling asleep on the job.

Fuck.

If Lizzie dies because of this…

His hands curled into fists at the thought. He'd never forgive Jennifer, or himself.

"What's the plan?" he demanded.

"Mateo and Tristan are already en route," Issac informed. "What do they need to know?"

"Zeke has her in some sort of glass bubble," Jayson growled. "It drowned out all the noise."

Issac nodded. "VIP lounge. All the booths have sound control for purposes I'm sure don't require elaboration. Anything else?"

"He plans to make her scream." Jayson's hands fisted again, this time destroying the plastic bottle in his hand.

Balthazar handed him another one without missing a beat. "That's not going to happen, Stas. Wakefield goes alone." He must have been responding to her thoughts, because her eyes narrowed.

"She's my best friend." The fire in her gaze was admirable, but shadowed by heartache. No way could she go in there and think clearly. Jayson understood because he felt the same. Emotion superseded reason. "And he killed my parents," she reminded them, sounding broken.

"Which is why you won't react rationally when you see him," Balthazar replied softly. "You won't be helpful; you'll be a hindrance."

"The only way Issac will be able to focus enough to get Elizabeth out of there alive is if he knows you're here safe and sound," Luc added, his logic infallible. "Otherwise, you risk never seeing your best friend again."

"Lucian's right," Issac murmured. "You remember the Arcadia, Aya. We barely survived your first trip, and if forced to choose, it will always be you." He cupped her cheek and pulled her close. "I need to do this alone, love. You know that as well as I do, just as you know this is something I'm doing only for you."

"You're also too valuable. I'm all for you making your own decisions, but this would put your life at an unnecessary risk. If you walk in there spouting commands, Ezekiel will slaughter you on sight, and I will not allow that to happen." Luc's voice was uncharacteristically soft, but underlined in authority. He always chose his battles wisely, and this was one he would fight if she demanded it. Jayson would fight with him, as would Balthazar and Alik, if needed.

Stas pressed her forehead to Issac's chest as Balthazar nodded, his way of subtly letting everyone know she'd agreed to Luc's implied edict. Even with her emotions running high, she could perceive and admire logic. The woman would become a fine Hydraian one day, whenever she chose to accept her fate.

"What will you do?" Tom asked with a quiet intensity. "I've read Ezekiel's file. He won't just hand her over to you."

Issac ran his fingers through Stas's hair and kissed her gently on the forehead before taking a step back, his game face firmly in place. "I'm not concerned, Thomas."

Not so much arrogance as well-earned confidence. Issac knew how to handle this type of situation, but it killed a part of Jayson to sit back and wait. He ran a hand over his face and fought the urge to break more shit in Balthazar's house.

This furious reaction was so unlike him. Not even news of Amelia's captivity had impacted him like this, and he'd definitely been angry then. Yet he'd been able to remain levelheaded and calm while thinking through a solution.

Meanwhile, Lizzie had him wanting to go to the Arcadia himself to retrieve her—something he knew defied reason and comprehension. Just seconds ago he'd been commending Stas's ability to remain intelligent in this situation, and now he craved his own version of vengeance all over again.

Something is seriously wrong with me, B.

The nudge against his arm said they would work it out.

If only Jayson believed him. The notion of Issac saving Lizzie on his behalf grated. Walking into the Arcadia would be a suicide mission for any Elder, even one who could distort his appearance. Jayson understood that on a level, but relying on someone else to do it for him—

"Is the smart plan," Balthazar whispered, answering Jayson's thoughts. "You try to go with him, and Alik will knock you out."

"I'd like to see him try," Jayson muttered.

"He's waiting outside," Balthazar informed, voice pitched low for Jayson's ears alone. "That man knows all of us better than he'll ever admit."

"Doesn't make him any less of an asshole."

"Truth," B agreed and took a swig of his water to hide

176

his grin. Leave it to the mind reader to provide amusement under otherwise damning circumstances.

"You rang," Jacque announced as he appeared in the middle of the living area, wearing a pair of pajama bottoms and nothing else.

"Elizabeth decided to visit the Arcadia while we were discussing how to break the news to her tomorrow," Luc explained.

Issac smoothed a hand down his tie as he added, "Yes. It seems I require a lift back to the city."

CHAPTER THIRTEEN

Let's Play a Game of Truth

> Subject appears to be acclimating to
> collegiate life as expected.
> Cataloging all social interactions for
> future review.
>
> —Entry Log 118.10.4-7

"I'm not going to hurt you," Kiel said as Lizzie paced the small area between their table and the solid glass wall.

It had all happened so fast that she'd barely had a chance to react. Not that she'd gotten far. Kiel's arm had felt like granite around her waist as he yanked her backward into the space she explored now—a rectangular path, measuring/approximately three feet by two feet, beside the booth.

The club goers were all completely unfazed. A few watched her as one might an animal in a zoo, while the others went about their business as if this happened every day.

Because makeshift pods were apparently normal here.

Lizzie rubbed her arms in a poor attempt to warm them and continued exploring her little nook. The glass appeared solid and thick and impenetrable for all intents and purposes. Whatever switch Kiel had used to deploy it remained hidden to her, but if she found it, she could escape.

And then what? Run?

She almost laughed. Kiel had already proven his reflexes far surpassed hers. Lizzie was stuck here until he either let her go or got to the point.

"What do you want?" she demanded, or tried to, anyway. It came out far softer and a little shakier than intended.

"Desire plays no part in why we find ourselves in this situation, darling. I'm merely here to give you information and nothing more."

"Yeah?" She finally looked at him. "Information about what?"

"Let's start with Tom Fitzgerald. He's a friend of yours, yes?"

Goose bumps filed a path down her spine. She didn't want to talk about this with anyone, certainly not with a stranger who had trapped her in a glass box. "Did you know him?"

"Not personally, no." Kiel paused to sip his deep-red drink and gave her a sinister smile. "What would you say if I told you Tom is very much alive and well?"

She frowned. "I'd call you cruel and heartless."

"Both adequate adjectives, I assure you, but in this instance, neither are applicable. Because although you and the rest of the human race were led to believe he died heroically on some mission, I'm here to give you the truth. Would you like that?"

"I'd like you to let me out of this cage," she countered.

He clucked his tongue. "That wasn't what I asked. What if I could provide proof, right now, that Tom is alive? Would you listen to me then?"

She gaped at him. This had to be some sort of twisted joke, but she couldn't see the purpose. He already stated he didn't know Tom, yet he implied he knew about her friendship with him—something she never mentioned to Jayson, and certainly not to Kiel. She barely knew them both, but this man seemed to be insinuating he knew a whole hell of a lot about her.

"Who are you?"

"Ah, now we're getting somewhere." He sounded pleased by that. "But try rephrasing that question using *what* as opposed to *who,* and we'll move along at a far more acceptable speed."

She blinked, more confused than when this all began. Cam and Kristin were off dancing and having the time of their lives, while Lizzie was stuck in a glass container with a madman.

One who was friends with her neighbor.

Whom he called a few minutes ago with their location.

None of this made a lick of sense!

If only she had her purse. Cam had suggested they leave their things at her place since Kristin was on bar tab duty. All Lizzie had brought with her was an ID to enter the club. Not very helpful.

But she hadn't expected to be imprisoned in a soundproof booth with a maniac.

No music sounded through the walls, not even the base. Which meant her screams couldn't be heard, either, something Kiel had implied earlier while speaking to Jayson.

She needed to play this smart and hope like hell her

neighbor would come for her or her friends would notice her absence.

Doubtful on both accounts, but she could consider them her backup plan.

Still need a general plan.

Thank you, Captain Obvious.

Maybe if she went along with this asinine game, Kiel would let her go.

Doubtful.

That's unhelpful.

Kiel grinned and sipped his drink, tilting his head slightly as she considered her next move. He was clearly waiting for something. *A question*, she thought.

Who are you? she'd asked.

He'd replied with something about rephrasing.

"What are you?" She couldn't help the uncertainty in her tone, because obviously, he was a man. But Kiel seemed fond of twisting words and sentences into his own strange language.

"Sit down, Lizzie."

"Why?"

"I'm answering your question." He gestured to the seat she vacated when the walls came down. It would put her directly across from him with her back to the balcony, neither offensive nor defensive. If he wanted to harm her, he could just as easily do so with her standing.

Might as well rest her legs in case he gave her a chance to run. Although, that seemed unlikely in their little prison.

She slid into the booth and folded her arms on the table. The waitress had brought a pink, fruity concoction that would usually appeal to Lizzie but didn't tonight.

"My real name is Ezekiel," he murmured. "I've only recently taken on the name Kiel, as I like to switch things up every now and then. Living forever gets boring, you see. It's the small things that keep us entertained."

She nodded. "Sure." *You're insane.*

"Your Jayson went by the name of Jedrick when we

first met—that would have been around 1700 BC in Babylon, by the way. We were born in very different circumstances, myself to an impoverished woman raped by a soldier, and Jedrick to a military god. His father, Artemis, wasn't really a god but an Ichorian with a knack for controlling metal and a thirst for blood. But we'll come back to that.

"My mother died of disease when I was nine years old, thus forcing me to learn quickly and efficiently how to take care of myself. To say I had a particular flair for survival would be an understatement. You see, identifying easy prey and assassinating them quietly are strengths, Lizzie, ones I mastered in my youth."

He paused to sip his drink while Lizzie fought the urge to laugh hysterically.

First, he claimed to be from Babylon—the original city.

Second, to be, what, over three thousand years old?

And now he was making up words like "Ichorians," claiming Jayson to be the son of a god, and stating he, Kiel or Ezekiel—whatever he preferred to be called—was an assassin.

The man was a lunatic wrapped in a sane man's skin.

Unbelievable.

"Osiris approached me as a youth," he continued. "You haven't met him properly yet but will someday. Regardless, he appeared to me as a god and stated I was endowed with a unique skill set that suited his needs. He introduced me to his son, Sethios, and encouraged our friendship. Being of similar ages, we bonded quickly, and I essentially found myself in a new home, surrounded by unique principles that did not apply to humanity but to a greater universe."

He smiled, and it chilled her inside and out. "Would you like to know a secret, Lizzie?"

She cleared her throat, but the cobwebs sticking to her vocal cords rendered speech impossible. Probably a good thing, as she couldn't trust herself to speak.

Lizzie nodded, because she suspected a denial would disappoint him, and she had no intention of pissing off a crazy person without having an escape route.

"I have known of your existence for quite some time, even before you met Astasiya. But that's not my secret, actually." He waved a hand and smiled, amused with himself. "What I mean to say is, I arranged for you both to live together your freshman year. It was a result of laziness on my part, but I do believe it worked out for the best, wouldn't you agree?"

The thrumming in Lizzie's ears couldn't be healthy. She never gave him or Jayson Stas's full name.

"Who are you?" she whispered again.

He relaxed into his booth with a sigh. "You're not listening to me at all, are you?"

"I-I am," she stammered. *But you're crafting some sort of fictional tale that holds no relevance in reality.*

Except he knew Stas's full name. "Astasiya" was too specific to be a guess.

"I suspect we're running out of time, so let's try a new angle," Kiel said while spinning his half-finished drink on the table. "Tell me your thoughts on the CRF. Do you ever wonder what their paramilitary unit really does? How a Sentinel like Tom could be killed on a humanitarian operation?"

"He…" She finally gave in and tasted her drink—a strawberry daiquiri. The logical part of her cringed, but she needed something for her throat—it felt stuffed full of cotton balls.

"You work on that, and I'll answer for you, love. The CRF is not what the public thinks it is, which I know won't surprise you. Every time you go near headquarters, your instincts tell you something is wrong. Am I right?"

If he didn't have her attention before, he had it now. Because that feeling he just described was one she'd never told anyone about. Not even Stas.

"How do you know that?" she managed, her voice

raspy.

"Because I've seen you in that building countless times over the years and observed the changes in your biology. You're terrified of the CRF, and justifiably so. It's called muscle memory, darling. The things they've done to you are unspeakable, and although you possess no memory of it, your body does."

She swallowed. "Wh-what do you mean?" She rarely visited the headquarters, even as a child. But he was right about her innate reaction. The building horrified her for inexplicable reasons.

"I wish we could go into more detail, but our intimate meeting is nearly over, and we haven't even gone over the basics yet." He captured her gaze and held it. "You asked who I am, and I've told you. Now, as to what I am, I'm an Ichorian, just like Jay's father. Osiris turned me as an eighteenth mortal birthday present, granting me immortality, and before you comment, yes, I do appear to be closer to thirty-five. Mortals these days age far differently from the era I grew up in."

She hadn't been about to say anything at all, but she nodded anyway. Because sure. Why not? He did resemble a man in his thirties, but maybe immortality had something to do with his aging? Or lack thereof...?

Am I really believing any of this?

"I should add that there's one minor caveat to being an Ichorian—we require mortal blood to survive." He passed over his drink. "Have a peek inside and see for yourself."

Lizzie hesitated, especially after his flippant remarks, but did as he suggested, with a frown. "It looks like a Bloody Mary." A strange beverage for a coffee mug, but everything about this place struck her as unordinary.

"No, darling, it's blood from one of my favorite donors in the back. If you don't believe me, take a sip."

She sniffed instead and scrunched her nose as a wave of nausea overwhelmed her.

It certainly didn't smell like vodka and tomato juice.

But he couldn't be serious.

Blood? Gross.

"Like a vampire?" It came out as a squeak.

He chuckled. "A myth, I assure you, but a similar concept. Try not to use that term too loudly outside our glass walls, though, darling. My kind do not take lightly to being compared to vile creatures of the night—our ancestry is much lighter."

Lizzie gripped the edge of her seat. "You're... This is... Impossible. It's not..." She shook her head as she frantically tried to clear it. "I can't..."

Vampires aren't real. The supernatural isn't real.

"I can bring Cynthia in for a demonstration, if you'd like." He sounded so reasonable and normal, like he spoke about immortality and vampires on a daily basis. "Or you could peek over your shoulder into the booth below us near the dance floor, but if you could keep the screaming to a minimum, my ears would thank you for it."

Another sip from that damn bloody mug of his while he waited for her to choose.

If she asked for a demonstration, he would have to lower the glass. In which case, she could escape.

"Your eyes telegraph your thoughts beautifully, Lizzie. If you opt for the live feed, I will restrain you first, and trust me when I say that is more for your protection than anything else. Because a woman of your standard wandering through this club won't last more than five minutes without ending up in one of the booths, whether by choice or not."

She gulped. The way he said that was both unnerving and terrifying. "Why are you telling me all this?"

"Ah, that is an excellent question." He set his mug down with a genuine smile. "My motives are my own, but irritating Jayson is considered quite the bonus."

"He knows about all of this?"

"Of course. As I said, we grew up together. Jay's father, Artemis, is an Ichorian and a close friend of Osiris's, which was how Jay and I eventually met. Our shared proclivities for war and destruction created a competitive bond of sorts that came to a head about five centuries back. You see, my kind realized our progeny, Hydraians, carried lethal bloodlines that could destroy the Ichorian race, and, well, not to go into detail, but a lot of immortals died as a result."

Lizzie couldn't form words. It all sounded so real, yet improbable.

Hydraians?

Did Kiel enjoy making up words?

Except Jayson mentioned a word that sounded similar to that this morning. Hydria, was it? The place Jacque and Grace were visiting from?

Her eyes widened. Could *Hydraian* stem from *Hydria?*

She shook her head. This was all too much. To even believe this hysteria would qualify her for a mental institution.

Yet... Kiel's statements about the CRF and her feelings were spot on, though his casual comment about watching her freaked her out. And he knew things about Stas...

Lizzie gave in to the pull to survey the club, as he recommended, and turned to observe the booths below. Nothing too crazy, just a couple making out.

She squinted as the lights flashed overhead, illuminating their positions.

Is that...?

She covered her mouth with her hand.

A brown head.

There was a man, under the table, between the woman's bare legs with his mouth on her inner thigh. Lizzie expected him to move higher, but he didn't.

The female's body seemed frozen in time as the male beside her shifted his mouth to her neck to lick the trail of blood leaking from her wound.

Lizzie stood, her hands going to the glass, to scream for help when she realized the booth beside them held a similar picture. As did the one beyond it.

"Oh God…" *Cam and Kristin…* She needed to find them, to warn them.

"Your friends will be fine," Kiel murmured. "Zach and Lars may use them for a snack, but I've instructed them to see the girls home safely afterward."

"Why?" *Why would he do that?*

"Consider it my show of good faith," he replied. "Besides, most mortals leave this place with memories of a euphoric evening and nothing more. It's our way of maintaining a healthy food supply, though there are those who would prefer blood farms."

Lizzie turned to see him shrug.

"I see both sides of the argument, but we are digressing again. Shall we talk about Tom now? The friend you buried, who is indeed very much alive?"

Her legs threatened to buckle beneath her, forcing her to return to her seat across from him. Ten minutes ago, she'd called him cruel for even suggesting it. Now, she felt a beacon of hope followed by severe sadness.

Would Tom truly let her mourn his loss while living a life without her?

They were friends.

She loved him.

Why would he do that to her?

"To clarify, Hydraians are the result of an Ichorian father fornicating with a human female. Your friend Tom is the result of his Ichorian father, Jonathan Fitzgerald, coupling with a human woman named Anna."

Kiel draped his arm over the booth, his long fingers drumming a tune she couldn't hear, not with all the blood pumping through her ears.

Tom isn't human? John is an Ichorian?

This… No.

It's ridiculous and not real.

An elaborate story. A ruse.

"Tom staged a scene with several Hydraians and a few

Ichorians out in the middle of the woods at his mother's old cabin. His father believes one of the Sentinels shot Tom with an incendiary bullet—thus killing him—but it was all an illusion orchestrated by Issac Wakefield."

"Issac?" she repeated. *He's part of this too?*

"He's an Ichorian—I'll prove that in about a minute—and he helped save your friend's life. I imagine it was a gift for Astasiya, as he is quite fond of the talented woman, but there you have it. Tom is alive, residing in Hydria, and yes, Stas knows as well. Now that brings us full circle, yes? And why they've kept all this from you? I have theories on that, but unfortunately, we are out of time."

"We are?"

"Indeed." He cocked his head toward the bar. "Your rescue is here roughly ten minutes earlier than I anticipated. I'm impressed."

Lizzie followed his gaze to where Issac and two other suit-clad men were walking purposely up the stairs to the VIP section. Issac flashed the bartender a grin that spoke of familiarity and also nodded at several others, who all returned the gesture in kind.

Proof, Kiel had said, that Issac was an Ichorian.

He knew all the members of the club.

She could chalk it up to his billionaire status and say he knew all these people through high society, except Lizzie didn't recognize any of them, and she was very familiar with the elite crowd in New York City.

The Arcadia boasted an opulent air and old wealth, the kind she was raised to recognize. Yet she only knew the man approaching their enclosure.

"Lizzie, if you value your life at all, you'll remain calm throughout this interaction. I may have no intention of harming you, but I cannot speak for the others here. If you cause a scene, they will silence you, and not in a polite manner."

Ice slithered through her veins, freezing her in place as the glass slid upward to its home in the ceiling.

Even if she wanted to scream, she couldn't.

Her airways burned from a lack of oxygen.

Part of her thought this might be a very bad dream, but Ezekiel had remained so calm and collected throughout. The bearer of information, which was expressed in a concise, truthful way, meant to do what? Terrify her? Placate her? Teach her? She didn't know.

As their enclosure disappeared, she shivered not because of the air but because of the loss of protection.

Kiel had told her all of this in a soundproof chamber—he meant to keep her safe in the event that she reacted.

But why?

He clearly didn't care about her.

What was his goal?

To irritate Jayson.

Because Jayson didn't want her to know the truth. No one did, including Issac and Stas.

And Tom.

Her heart ached at the betrayal.

Everyone knew about this except her.

"Evening, Issac," Kiel greeted. "Care to join us for a drink?"

Issac slid into the booth next to Lizzie, his thigh brushing her frozen one. He steepled his fingers on the table, his focus on Kiel.

"I mean no disrespect, Ezekiel, but if you do not release Elizabeth to me right now, I will be forced to react in her best interest."

The quiet lethality lurking beneath his words sent a chill down her spine.

He sounded like a predator.

A villain.

A vampire.

She bit her lip to keep from reacting, but the terror rattling around in her chest begged to be let out.

Because her roommate and best friend was dating a monster, one who seemed completely at ease in this club, where they served blood in mugs and feasted on arteries downstairs.

How could Stas keep this from her?

"Hmm, I believe her best interest requires you not to react at all," Kiel replied as he finished his drink. He set it aside with a smile. "Well, if you don't fancy a drink, then how about a walk?" He glanced at the two men standing guard beside the booth before meeting Issac's gaze again. "Just the three of us ought to do." He smiled at Lizzie. "I imagine you are craving some fresh air right about now, sweetheart. Am I right?"

Her lips formed a response that her voice failed to deliver. If he meant to guide her outside, she wouldn't argue. Anything to leave this horrible place.

"I believe that's her version of acquiescence," Kiel said. "Shall we?"

Issac stood with a nod at his two friends and held out his hand for Lizzie.

Two days ago, she would have accepted.

Maybe even an hour ago.

But now?

No.

Maybe Kiel was a lunatic with a wild imagination.

Maybe she would wake up in five minutes.

Maybe unicorns were real.

She had no idea, but she did know one thing: she didn't trust Issac Wakefield. Or Tom Fitzgerald. Or Jayson Masters. Or Stas Davenport.

I truly am alone.

"What have you done?" Issac demanded, his words directed at Kiel.

"We may have enjoyed story time while you were on your way, but let's continue the discussion outside. I would hate to draw attention from anyone of import."

Issac closed his hand into a fist and dropped it to his side. "Indeed," he growled as he stepped away to give Lizzie a wide berth to exit the booth.

She did so carefully, her legs unsteady beneath her. All those years of dancing failed her tonight. She hobbled about like an old woman with frail limbs caused by years of misuse.

Kiel stood directly beside her, his warmth a comfort in the otherwise freezing club.

What did that say about her sanity?

She trusted the one man she shouldn't, but he'd told her the truth.

He also mentioned being an assassin.

Jesus... She would never move on from this moment.

If it was all true, she'd... How would she...?

Lizzie shuddered.

Where did she go from here?

Kiel had only just begun to talk about the CRF, but even his brief words confirmed her worst fears. Evil lurked there. He implied she had reason to fear them, but didn't elaborate.

No time now.

He led the way down the stairs as she moved on zombie-like feet behind him with Issac at her back.

The bodies gyrating on the dance floor passed in a blur, as did the bar.

She didn't bother looking for Cam and Kristin.

What could she do? Scream about vampires? They would laugh, and she would probably die.

Kiel said they would be safe. She wanted to believe him; he hadn't lied to her yet. Even in the coffeehouse, he'd told the truth.

Babylon.

He meant the real city. The one that existed thousands of years ago.

How was this even believable?

Jayson is the same age, maybe even older...

Her brain couldn't wrap around that logic. It ceased to comprehend. She'd made out with... with... a walking mummy.

LEXI C. FOSS

Or a god, she thought. Not that it made her feel any better.

The tear ducts behind her eyes attempted to function and failed. Shock rendered her useless.

"Ah, it is a lovely evening for a stroll," Kiel proclaimed as they exited the club. He gazed upward with a grin. "Glorious. Let's meander this way, yes?"

Issac stepped up beside Lizzie, but he refrained from touching her. She followed on autopilot—like a marionette being controlled by an invisible string linked to Kiel.

It took two blocks before Issac finally spoke. "What game are we playing, Ezekiel?"

"Why must everything be for amusement? Perhaps I'm helping you."

"I highly doubt that."

He chuckled. "You might be right, but I'm not the one playing a game here. That would be you, and it's a dangerous one, I might add."

Issac yawned and tucked his hands into his pockets. "Your riddles bore me."

"Do they?" Kiel finally stopped and rotated to lean against the side of a building. "How about a suggestion instead?" He folded one ankle over the other, his gold-flecked eyes serious. "Move Astasiya out of the city before the Conclave discovers her secrets. And I'm not referring to her Sentinel training."

The air chilled between the two men while Lizzie struggled to breathe. This was all too much. The underlying threats, comments on immortality, the realization that everyone she knew had lied to her...

Do I really mean that little to them?

"Why haven't you acted?" Issac asked, his voice quiet but edged with lethality. It trailed goose bumps down Lizzie's arms.

Dangerous.

Predator.

"My reasons are my own," Ezekiel replied as he pushed

192

off the side of the building. He fixed his gaze on Lizzie, eliciting a shiver from deep within.

Run.

But where would I go?

She couldn't trust anyone.

"I'll see you again soon, sweetheart, though I fear our next meeting will be under less favorable circumstances." He managed to sound both contrite and unapologetic at the same time. And she had no idea how to reply to that.

"Have fun fixing this one, Jedrick," he added as he caught something a second before it would have hit his nose. "Another memento. How thoughtful." He slid the metal item into his jacket and disappeared into a shadow.

Literally.

Lizzie gaped at the display of inhuman behavior as her knees buckled beneath her. Issac's arm around her waist kept her from falling, but she spun away on instinct, placing her back to the wall as she tried to locate Kiel.

"Where…? How…?" One moment he was walking, and the next he wrapped a cloak of darkness around himself and vanished into the night.

In the middle of New York City.

On the street.

How was that even possible?

"Lizzie." Stas's voice drew her attention to the left where she approached with Jayson and that Jacque guy from last night.

"Ezekiel has been talking," Issac stated flatly. "How much he revealed, I'm uncertain, but it was clearly enough."

Lizzie stumbled back as Stas reached out to touch her.

"Oh, Liz…"

Lizzie met her best friend's gaze—the woman she'd known for seven years.

Trusted.

Loved.

"Tell me," Lizzie whispered, needing to know. "Tell me

that it's not true." She'd just seen a man vanish, for crying out loud. But it had to be an illusion.

All those things Kiel said had to be a lie. Right?

Vampires didn't exist.

"Tell me it's a lie," she repeated, a little more desperate this time. "Tell me he's insane. Please."

Stas glanced at Issac, her lips opening and closing, and Lizzie's heart beat unsteadily in her chest.

Oh God.

Her best friend wouldn't keep something like this, would she?

No.

She couldn't.

But everything Ezekiel said...

"Is Tom alive?" Lizzie's voice held a weird raspy quality to it and sounded foreign to her ears. "Is it true? Is it all true?"

Stas visibly swallowed.

And then nodded.

"He's..." Stas paused and cleared her throat. "Yes. Tom's alive."

"And Issac's a vampire?" It came out on a squeak. "And Jayson..."

God, she couldn't continue.

Insanity.

Complete and utter insanity.

Stas stepped forward. "Liz..."

No!

Lizzie's hand reacted of its own accord, slicing across Stas's cheek with a crack.

It felt so good to hit something, or rather, someone.

She wanted to do it again, only harder.

Everyone had lied to her.

Everyone.

"I deserved that," Stas muttered. "But, Liz—"

Lizzie cut her off with a scream. It'd been building in her chest for hours, days, maybe even months, and exploded in a rush of sound she couldn't contain.

Agony.

Fear.

Fury.

Hurt.

Pain.

They all culminated in that single moment, and she didn't bother to hide it as she collapsed on the sidewalk without any care other than to release it all.

And release she did.

Over and over and over again.

Until she felt a strange sensation surround her.

A whooshing.

It knocked her out of her spell and into a new, dizzying one of dancing light and surreal sound.

Then she landed in a new reality.

On a beach at night with waves rolling in the distance.

"It's okay, Red," Jayson murmured. "You're going to be okay."

What craziness was this? A dream? A shift in dimensions? Her lips parted on a question when a drowsy spell hit her out of nowhere.

"She needs rest," Issac said in response to something. A question, perhaps? Something Jayson... Maybe...

Oh, but sleep sounded nice.

A nightmare. That's all. She'd wake tomorrow.

Everything would be fine.

Yes.

"I've got you," Jayson whispered as warmth wrapped around her.

Floating.

Starless night.

Heaven.

CHAPTER FOURTEEN

Was It a Dream?

Subject's collegiate curriculum is not providing a sufficient challenge. It's suggested that future iterations undergo a less rigorous academic regimen during the development phase.

—Entry Log 119.04.4-7

"It's going to be okay," Jayson whispered as he tucked Lizzie into his bed. No one had argued about the placement, not even Stas. He tucked a red strand of hair behind Lizzie's ear and pressed his lips to her forehead. They lingered a second longer than needed, but he couldn't help it.

196

She's safe.

"I'm never leaving you unprotected again," he vowed. She couldn't hear him, but it didn't matter. The promise was more for himself than for her because he suspected when she woke she would want nothing more to do with him.

And that realization hurt a hell of a lot more than he ever would have anticipated.

He brushed his knuckles over her cheek and stepped away reluctantly to join the others in his living room. Amelia and Tom were seated on the love seat, their expressions grim. Stas stood in the corner, her face buried in Issac's chest, and Luc sat in Jayson's favorite recliner, sipping a cup of tea.

Balthazar wandered in with two beers and handed one to Jayson. "Figured you could use this."

Alcohol didn't impact immortals at all, but he accepted the drink anyway. He could use the refreshment.

"She's never going to forgive me," Stas said, her voice pitched low for Issac but reverberating in the eerily quiet room. Even the strongest women required a moment of weakness, and this was it for Stas.

The anger and hurt resonating from Lizzie had been palpable. And that scream... Jayson would have nightmares about that sound. So much agony and pain wrapped up in a piercing shriek meant to wound. He winced at the memory and rubbed his chest on impulse. It did little to ease the foreign ache growing deep inside.

Stas's statement about forgiveness applied to him as well. It was never Jayson's decision to keep Lizzie in the dark, but he had engaged in a relationship with her under false pretenses, which made him a bit of an ass.

"Right. We need to know exactly what Ezekiel told her. Obviously, he mentioned Tom and Issac, but what else?" Luc set his mug aside. "I say we wake her up."

"She'll scream," Jacque warned as he appeared behind the recliner. He must have been listening from the kitchen.

"And it's loud," the teleporter added with a shudder.

Luc lifted a shoulder in response. "B has a fix for that."

"We can't," Stas said, her voice lacking its usual confidence. She pulled away from Issac, her green eyes tired as she addressed Luc. "We've taken everything else away from her; we can't take this too. She's earned her pain, and we all deserve to feel it with her."

Jayson rubbed a hand over his face and sighed. Stas was right. Dulling Lizzie's emotions would be taking away yet another choice, and they had already fucked this up enough.

"Regardless, we're solving nothing by keeping her in a coma." Luc glanced questioningly at Issac. "Unless you're speaking to her in her dreams?"

"Given the way she reacted to me at the Arcadia, I believe she would consider that a nightmare rather than a dream," the Ichorian replied.

Silence settled over the living area.

The soft introduction they all agreed on earlier no longer applied. Ezekiel had thrown Lizzie into the deep end without a flotation device and expected her to know how to swim.

Fucking prick. Ezekiel may not have harmed her physically, but he sure as shit hurt her mentally.

"I agree with Luc." The somber note in Tom's words described the atmosphere in the room. "We've hurt her enough. It's time to live with the consequences of our decisions."

"You were protecting her," Amelia murmured, her hand on Tom's chest.

"Perhaps, but she won't see it that way." Tom kissed her on the cheek before standing. "Let's wake her up. I'm ready."

"I'm not," Stas whispered. "You didn't see the way she looked at me."

"My guess is that look will be nothing compared to how she will treat Thomas," Issac said.

"Thanks, buddy," Tom replied with false sincerity.

Issac merely shrugged, unbothered.

"I have an idea," Balthazar said. "One that might make her more agreeable when she wakes up and won't involve any of us taking her choices away. It may also give us some insight into what Ezekiel told her."

Everyone stared at him, waiting for him to elaborate.

"But it will only work if Jayson is up for the challenge," Balthazar added with a gaze Jayson knew all too well.

Anytime Balthazar mentioned a challenge, it always ended favorably, but that wouldn't be the case with Lizzie. This task would be difficult, perhaps even hurt Jayson in the end, and his friend was asking him now with his eyes if he had the heart for it.

Jayson set his beer on the coffee table and raised a brow. "What did you have in mind, B?"

~*~

Lizzie floated in a cloud of cedar, man, and heat. Her legs stretched against the silky sheets as she nuzzled deeper into the muscular pillow beneath her head.

Jayson, she thought with a smile, then frowned as trickles of memories surfaced behind her lids.

The Arcadia, and Kiel telling her stories about immortality and blood. She flew upright and blinked into the darkness.

"Red?" Jayson murmured, his voice thickened with sleep.

Confusion riddled her thoughts.

How had she ended up in his bed again?

Unless…

Was it all a dream?

Lizzie ran her hands over her clothes—boxer shorts and an oversized T-shirt. Her feet were bare. No white clothes or boots.

A warm palm caressed her lower back as Jayson sat up

beside her. "You okay?" he asked, his voice low and sexy.

"I..." She licked her lips. "I don't know." It had all felt so real, except that last part with the whooshing and the blackness. The end of a nightmare, maybe?

She turned and placed a hand on his bare chest. Okay, *that* was definitely real. Her fingers danced over the muscular planes to his abs before dropping to her side.

"I had the strangest dream," she admitted. *I think.*

Had it all been a figment of her imagination? Lizzie could come up with a lot of crazy things, but this seemed extreme.

"What was it about?" he asked with a yawn. The hand against her back moved in soothing circles, melting the remains of her tension. She leaned into him, seeking more of that comfort. Her dream had really rattled her nerves.

"You'll think I'm crazy," she said, shaking her head. He slid his palm up to her shoulder and unleashed magic with his fingers. "That feels good."

"Here." He shifted her to relax between his legs and put both hands to work on her upper back. "Now tell me about your strange dream, and I'll decide if you're really crazy."

She groaned at both his words and his skilled touch. Lizzie had no idea she was so tense. The dream must have really worked her up. Maybe talking about it would help.

But not all of it.

She didn't mention the disastrous breakfast conversation or the pancakes and skipped ahead to the part about the Halloween party at the Arcadia.

"It was pretty normal until Kiel showed up," Lizzie murmured. "His friends invited Cam and Kristin to dance. Meanwhile, Kiel asked if I wanted to know more about your world." Such a weird term, one she herself would never use, yet Kiel had used it repeatedly in her dream.

Unless it wasn't a dream at all.

Jayson tugged on a strand of her hair. "Don't leave me hanging here, Red. What did he say about our world?"

Right. A nightmare. Nothing else.

She cleared her throat. "Uh, well, he told me a story about growing up with you in Babylon, as in the original city"—something she obviously pulled from her conversation with Kiel at the coffeehouse—"and he said your dad was a war god. Actually, he called him an 'Ichorian.' I must have made up that term in my head after his original reference and the blood talk because, you know, *ichor* and *Ichorian* sound similar, right?"

Except, was that the order of the conversation? She couldn't remember; it'd all been so insane and—

"You're familiar with ichor?" he asked, his surprise palpable.

"Uh, yeah. I learned about it in school at some point." Why would that shock him?

"Ichor," he repeated, sounding incredulous. "That's something they teach in the New York City private schools?"

"Yeah, in high school, I think." Most of her knowledge came from an ambiguous background, due to all the traveling for beauty pageants and learning on the fly. Lizzie could never recall the specifics of when she learned a subject; she just knew the information, which was all that mattered in the grand scheme of things.

"Anyway, he also said something about knowing me before Stas." Lizzie attributed that bit to the coffeehouse as well since he'd met Stas briefly. "Afterward, Kiel drank blood in front of me, which was gross." She shuddered at the too-real memory.

"And he called you an immortal 'Hydraian.'" She forced a laugh. "I'm guessing I created that term from your comments about Grace and Jacque being from Hydria…" She trailed off as she thought back to *when* he had said that.

During their disastrous breakfast.

Which never happened…

"I'm not normally this creative," she added, puzzled.

Jayson never mentioned Hydria, but geography was another one of those subjects she just understood. The small island in the Aegean Sea belonged to Greece. But how had she picked that location specifically?

She finally focused on her surroundings, beyond the silky sheets and the sexy man behind her.

Something didn't feel right. Not the temperature or atmosphere. This was definitely Jayson's space, but...

It's too quiet.

"There's no city noise," she realized. "And you have curtains." They went from the ceiling to the floor. Did she miss those before? She'd been a bit preoccupied, but they seemed out of place somehow. As if they were hiding a very large window, something she knew their condo building didn't include.

"Lizzie," Jayson murmured, his hands sliding to her arms. "I need to tell you something."

She focused on the silk curtains and the rustle of cloth at the bottom. *Fresh air?* Impossible.

His fingers went to her chin, tilting her head back to meet his gaze. They resembled mysterious orbs in the dark room. "I'm sorry."

Her gut twisted with those two morose words. "Why?" she managed, her mouth dry.

"Because it wasn't a dream," he replied. "And from what you've said so far, Ezekiel told you the truth."

She blinked. His words were clear but didn't fully register. "So you're..." She couldn't finish. Because no. He must have misunderstood.

"I'm a Hydraian, and we're in my room. In Hydria."

She pushed away from him, and he let her, his hands dropping away. She went to her knees and faced him on the bed.

"In Greece." She couldn't help the incredulity in her voice. "You knocked me out and flew me to Greece?" Because airport officials wouldn't frown upon an unconscious woman being flown across international borders at all. Not one bit.

"Jacque teleported you here. He's a Hydraian, too, as are Balthazar and Grace."

"Turn on the lights," she demanded, requiring proof.

The silk sheets swooshed as he moved, and a lamp popped on beside them. Rich, cream walls and mahogany furniture tumbled into view with a vivid blue curtain, blowing in the night breeze.

"It's a balcony," he murmured. "Overlooking the Aegean Sea."

Lizzie slid off the mattress and padded over to the door, needing to see it for herself.

The doors were open beyond the curtain, revealing a star-filled sky hanging over a rolling ocean. She grabbed the ledge for stability as her knees threatened to buckle again, and Jayson moved in behind her.

"You're... this..." She swallowed. The fingers of her free hand lifted to prod her neck as an image of the booths at the Arcadia soured her thoughts. "Y-you drink blood?"

"No," he murmured. "Hydraians don't require the mortal essence to remain alive. It's one of the many things Ichorians hate about us." He moved to rest his elbows on the balcony, his shoulders falling as he gazed out over the night. "The only time I've ever lied to you was about my job, Lizzie. Otherwise, I've always been truthful, just not very forthcoming. Keeping everything from you wasn't my decision, which sounds like an excuse, but it's merely the truth."

"I-I don't understand. Why? How?" All of Ezekiel's claims settled over her at once, forcing her to squeeze the door hinge hard to stay upright. She didn't know whether to cry, scream, run, or jump. Every emotion rattled inside her at once.

"We're not a threat to you," he said as if sensing her rising fear. "Quite the opposite, actually. I was sent to New York City to protect you."

"Protect me?" she squeaked. "From what?"

"The CRF." He twisted to face her and leaned against the balcony. His bare chest glowed in the starry night, giving him a regal flair she would have admired in a better situation.

"I've spent the last two months trying to determine what it is they've done to you, as has Stas, and our discoveries are minimal at best. We planned to tell you this week, to include you in the research, but Ezekiel had his own plans in mind."

"Research?" she repeated.

"Into whatever the CRF did to you as a child," Jayson replied, his voice low. "Did Ezekiel explain the true nature of a Sentinel?"

Lizzie shook her head, both at his comment about her childhood and at the mention of the prominent paramilitary unit.

"The humanitarian missions are a cover for something far more sinister and deadly. Sentinels are trained to hunt and kill rogue immortals, both Hydraians and Ichorians. It's Jonathan Fitzgerald's pet project."

"Kiel said he's an Ichorian," Lizzie whispered. "Issac, too."

"Both statements are true, but while Jonathan is a monster, Issac is an ally. He's been working with Stas to gain more information about you—or at least, he's tried."

Lizzie finally let go of the door to rub her arms. Despite the warmer air, she felt cold and so very alone.

"Everyone knew," she murmured, more to herself than to Jayson.

They all kept this from her. Jayson, Issac, Stas, Tom...

"Is he here?" she asked. Kiel told her he was alive. Everything else he said had proven to be true; would this as well? "Is Tom here?"

"Yes," Jayson replied quietly. "In the living room."

She nodded, her feet already moving.

Lizzie didn't bother checking her hair or her attire. She didn't care. Nothing mattered. These people had lied to her, kept secrets from her, and allowed her to grieve on her own. Were they ever really her friends?

She sensed the change in Stas months ago. Was that when she learned the truth? All this time, Lizzie had been nothing but supportive, a *good* friend, the best, and Stas had lied to her at every turn.

But none of that compared to the biggest deceit of them all.

Tom.

His funeral had broken her. She had cried alone in her room for days, because Stas had been too busy working. Lizzie thought her best friend just didn't care about Tom the same way she did, but no, that wasn't it at all. Stas didn't grieve because she knew Tom was still alive. And no one told her.

She followed the light in the hallway to an open space filled with people she recognized. At the moment, however, they all resembled strangers. Especially, the one in the middle watching her with a concerned expression.

Lies existed in those dark brown eyes.

She thought he loved her at least a little bit, but this proved all her emotions wrong.

Anyone who cared about a person would never put her through the pain of such a loss and say nothing.

But this man did.

The one she admired growing up, whom she thought she loved more than anyone else in existence.

Betrayed.

"Lizzie," he whispered as she approached him. "I'm—"

Her fist met his jaw with enough force to send him back a step, and a part of her was pleased with that hit, while the other part wanted to collapse under her grief. Because touching him made him real and alive.

All of it was true. She knew that, but to have proof changed the story entirely. "How could you?" she accused, her vision blurring with tears. "*How could you?*"

"It was the only way to keep you safe," Tom

whispered.

"We needed John to believe he was dead," Stas said as she tried to approach, but one look from Lizzie froze her in midstep.

"You've known all along and didn't tell me." Her voice lacked the anger brewing within, something she chalked up to exhaustion. "I want to go home. To my condo. To be alone. Now."

"I would not advise that," Issac murmured. He sat beside a brunette with matching blue eyes.

His sister, Lizzie realized. A woman Issac had told her was dead over breakfast a few months ago. "All of it has always been a lie," she said, shaking her head.

"Amelia was only recently found alive," a voice said from her left. Balthazar cocked his head to the side, studying her. "When Issac told you she was dead, he believed it."

"He believed... But you... Did you just read my mind?" She shook her head. "Never mind. Of course you can hear my thoughts. You probably all can." She couldn't help the hysterical note of sarcasm, or the laugh that followed. "Take me back to New York."

Issac folded his arms. "As I said—"

"I don't care what you said," Lizzie snapped, her patience gone. "I've had enough for tonight. Let me go. Unless I'm a hostage?"

"Of course not," a blond man said from a recliner. "You're a guest for as long as you wish to be one."

"She can't go back," Stas whispered. "Not until she understands."

"You were the one who requested we stop taking away her choices, were you not?" the blond asked, arching a brow. "Her request is to return home, and I suggest we acquiesce." He stood, his height and strength reminding Lizzie a little bit of Jayson. "You are welcome back anytime, Elizabeth. We're but a call away." With that, he left the house.

"I'll get Jacque," Jayson murmured. "He can take you home."

"We need to talk about this," Stas said. "It's not safe in the condo, Liz. You don't understand."

"And whose fault is that?" Lizzie threw back at her. "I want you packed and out of *my* condo by the end of the week. It's not like you're there much anyway. Maybe your vampire, or perhaps John, will give you a free place to stay, but you and I are done."

"Lizzie, you're hurt, and I get that, but you need to give us a chance to explain." The authority in Tom's voice shoved her close to the edge of her sanity.

"You lost that chance when I buried you," she fired at him. "You're just another version that I never want to know. The Tom Fitzgerald I loved is dead, and frankly, I owe *you* nothing."

Stas gasped, "Lizzie."

She didn't even look at her. It hurt too much. "I want to go home," she said for the thousandth time. "I'm tired of being lied to and manipulated. It wasn't enough that I had to learn the truth from Kiel, so then you all tricked me *again* with that wake-up routine. And something tells me I didn't go to sleep by myself, either. I'm done. *Take me home.*"

"Okay. We can go," Jayson said.

Four words.

She understood them, yet didn't.

"I don't need a babysitter, Jayson," Lizzie told him. "You can stay here. I'll be fine on my own."

"It's not like—"

"Isn't it?" she countered before he could finish. "You said yourself that you were sent to New York City to protect me, right? And, what, when you didn't learn enough, you befriended me?" His expression confirmed her suspicions, which fractured her already broken heart even more. "You could have done all that without the added benefits," she added quietly.

How many times did he say they were just friends? She realized now what he'd been trying to do—push her away from any romantic notions. He never wanted to sleep with her, hence all those platonic kisses. It'd been an attempt to pacify her, but she had taken matters into her own hands during his party and kissed him, leaving him no choice but to respond.

No wonder he said they weren't having sex and refused to let her reciprocate.

He never wanted her. She didn't compare to his usual fare, something his friends had been happy to point out.

It'd all been a job to him. An obligation.

Why did that hurt most of all? Because everything else had weakened her to this point, or was it because she had started to care about him more than everyone else in her life?

I'm such a fool.

To ever think a man like him would want her…

At least she had confirmation about her feelings for Tom. His rejections had never hurt like this.

"I need to go," she whispered, her insides aching. "Now."

Because any longer in this room and she would break. She needed her room, her bed, and solitude before the tears came.

"Teleporting you back to New York so soon will make you a little queasy," a soft voice said. "But I will take you, if that's what you really want."

She met a pair of silver eyes filled with understanding and sadness. *Jacque.* The one who teleported her here, according to Jayson.

"You'll take me to my condo?"

"I will," he promised, holding out his hand. "If you'll allow me."

She didn't even think, she just pressed her palm to his. He could dump her in a fiery pit, and it would still be better than this place.

"Close your eyes," he whispered. "I'll tell you when to open them again."

The air shifted around her as she did as he suggested, and her stomach turned over at the unwanted inertia. It reminded her of an intense wind tunnel that stopped almost as quickly as it began.

"We're here," he murmured. "You can look now."

They stood in her living room again, and she nearly wept with relief. "Thank you."

He walked over to her sofa and bent to write something in the notebook lying open on the coffee table. "That's my direct line. Add the number to your phone, and call me when you're ready to come back. You're upset, and rightfully so, but they're still your family, Lizzie. And they love you."

Jacque disappeared before she could argue, leaving her more alone than ever before. Just as she wanted.

And yet, it only seemed to rip her apart even more.

I'm alone.

Well and truly alone.

Nothing would ever be the same now.

She didn't make it to her bed as originally planned, but instead she collapsed on the carpet and let all her emotions go.

It wasn't until much later—as Lizzie read Jacque's note—that she realized she couldn't call him even if she wanted to. That required a phone, one she didn't have because she'd left it at Cam's apartment with her purse.

CHAPTER FIFTEEN

A Free Spirit

Sleep deprivation logged at seven days
and subject showing no signs of
degradation. Benefactor requests
simulation continues to test
endurance.

—Entry Log 105.07.4-7

Jayson rubbed a hand over his face as Jacque disappeared with Lizzie.

"That went well," he muttered. Her pain had been a visceral thing, silencing anything he would have said.

You could have done all that without the added benefits. Her soft words had affected him in a way no others ever had. Because he *should* have protected her without touching her, but he had given in to the impulse instead.

Remorse mingled with frustration, because although he knew it was wrong, it had felt so right. How could he apologize for something he didn't fully regret?

"I expected her to be angry, but this…" Stas trailed off, her face paler than usual. "She can't stay there alone."

"She won't," Jayson replied. "I'll be there." It wasn't up for discussion. Lizzie didn't want a babysitter. Fine. He would be a guard instead.

Tom nodded, agreeing with Jayson's plan. He'd settled back onto the couch with Amelia at his side, but he didn't appear at all relaxed. His fingers traced his jaw, though Jayson doubted it still hurt from Lizzie's punch. The hit had been impressive, and startled most of the room, but also impactful on an emotional level, which showed in Tom's expression now.

"I can't leave it like this," Tom said. "When Jacque gets back, I'll ask him to teleport me to see if I can convince her to talk to me."

"I really think it should be me," Stas replied. "I know her best and—"

"You are not returning to New York City." Issac's tone brooked no argument. She opened her mouth to try, but he silenced her with an empathic, "No. This is not up for debate, Astasiya. Ezekiel knows you're a fledgling. Why he has not seen fit to act on that knowledge, I do not know, but this changes everything."

She was already shaking her head. "That's not your call."

"Indeed?" He arched a brow, daring her to disagree. "You seem to forget that your life is not the only one at risk in this situation. Should Ezekiel inform Osiris of your fledgling status, who will receive the harsher sentence?"

Her eyes widened, but the Ichorian wasn't finished.

"I have broken every Blood Law in an effort to support your decisions, Astasiya. And while it may be admirable, it ends now. I will not debate this with you. Call Jonathan and tell him you require a vacation, or quit, I do not care. As of this moment, you are not to leave Hydria until we determine Ezekiel's motives."

"And you?" she countered, clearly furious. "Will you be staying as well?"

"That remains to be seen," he replied coolly. "I have progeny to consider, as well as a company to run."

Stas folded her arms. "And I have nothing."

"You will have nothing if you are dead." A simple reply that didn't quite cool the fire brewing in Stas's eyes.

If Issac was trying to divert her attention away from the pain of hurting Lizzie, he was doing an excellent job of it. But Jayson suspected it ran deeper than that. Everything the man said was true, even if Stas didn't want to believe it.

"Why do you get to risk your life and I don't?" she demanded.

"Because I'm not nearly as valuable as you are," he replied without missing a beat. "Lucian has painstakingly allowed you to put yourself at risk with the CRF for a greater purpose under the promise that I keep you safe, and I can no longer guarantee that."

Her gaze narrowed. "And what happens when Ezekiel tells Osiris anyway?"

"That's for me to worry about."

"Fuck you." Tears brimmed in her eyes. "Fuck you for even thinking that! You believe you're the only one allowed to worry here? I sat through that Conclave, Issac. What Osiris did... You can't possibly think I would be able to sit by and allow that to happen to you, that I wouldn't fight for you."

"I know you would." He didn't flinch under the display of emotion. "Which is why you're staying here. I can't protect myself if I'm busy worrying about saving you." He palmed her cheek then her neck when she tried to move away from him.

"Don't, Aya. You're upset, and understandably so, but you cannot allow your sentiments to override the logical course, or we'll both regret it."

She looked ready to say more, when Jacque appeared, his expression somber. "I left her with my number in case she desires a lift back here," he said to the group before focusing on Jayson. "Ready?" The teleporter knew him well.

"Yep."

"I would stay out of sight for a few days," Balthazar suggested from his spot against the wall. He'd been observing the argument between Issac and Stas with a serious expression. All the Elders had agreed months ago that should her safety ever become a bigger issue than it already was, they would take measures to keep her in Hydria.

Unfair, but necessary, as Issac was right—Stas's gift for persuasion would be crucial during the next immortal war. And her life held more value than his, from a strategic point of view, anyway.

"I can't just sit here and do nothing," Stas said, shaking her head against Issac.

"It's for the best," Tom murmured. "As much as it sucks, they're all right. Your life is worth more than a few CRF secrets. We have what we need to keep Lizzie safe. There's no need for you to stay there anymore."

Stas freed herself from Issac's hold. He didn't try to touch her again but did watch her in that keen way he mastered through his brief centuries on Earth. "But we don't have Lizzie."

"Let me handle that," Jayson replied. "Give me a week."

Balthazar nodded. "From what I gathered of her emotions and her thoughts, Jay is our best hope right now."

Stas scoffed at that. "He barely knows her."

"I know enough," Jayson replied, irritated. This behavior had gone on long enough. He understood her distrust in the beginning, with everything being new and overwhelming, but now she just needed a swift kick in the ass. "You need to start trusting and respecting our experience, as it far outweighs yours."

Shock registered in her expression, replacing the frustration. "I... That's not..."

"It is," he insisted. "Your inability to have faith in our world has hindered your relationships with us from the beginning. I understand that you are not ready for immortality, but you need to accept your future. Perhaps you can use the next few weeks in Hydria to explore the world you'll be joining."

He didn't wait for her response. Rather, he focused on Jacque. "Let's go. Lizzie has already been alone too long."

~*~

Lizzie hesitated. If she knocked and no one answered, what would she do next? Call the cops from the phone she didn't have on her? Tell them that vampires exist and to please go check the Arcadia?

She almost laughed at the absurdity.

No one would believe her, and all the people she could confide in were liars.

"Just knock," she chided before the tears could start again. She already felt hungover from crying all night, not sleeping, and failing to eat or drink anything this morning. Or maybe the headache was a result of all the questions ricocheting through her head.

Who the heck knew, but she needed her purse and phone.

Her knuckles rapped against the door softly at first and harder as panic stirred. When Cam answered a minute later wearing her silky pajamas and a scowl, Lizzie threw her arms around her neck and hugged the life out of her.

"Do you have any idea what time it is?" Cam asked as she patted Lizzie on the back. "And why are you trying to suffocate me?"

"I was so worried," Lizzie admitted, her eyes dampening with relief. At least Kiel had told her the truth about Cam. She pulled away to look around the living area. "Is Kristin here too?"

"No, she took Zach home with her. Speaking of, Lars is still in my room, so… What do you need?" Typical Cam, eager to return to the man in her bed.

"Did he…?" Lizzie flinched as she spied the red mark on Cam's neck. "Never mind." He'd bitten her but hadn't killed her. *Yet.* "I need my purse."

"Oh yeah. It's still in the dining room. You can lock up on your way out."

She grabbed her friend's arm. The words she really wanted to say—*He's a vampire!*—refused to exit her mouth. So she settled on asking, "Are you sure about him? I mean, you just met."

Cam giggled and shook her head. "Oh, virgin Lizzie. You're so cute. I promise I'll be fine." She patted her on the head like one would a child. "Call ya later, chick."

Lizzie watched helplessly as her friend skipped off toward the bedroom. Even if she told her the truth, Cam would never believe her. She would probably laugh and tell Lars, and that wouldn't end well for any of them.

If he hadn't killed her yet, he probably wouldn't, right?

She could call Stas to ask, or that teleporter guy, or even Jayson, but would they tell her the truth?

Lizzie found her purse and pulled out her phone. What would she say? *Hi, just calling to find out if this Ichorian in the bedroom is going to kill my friend.* She snorted. That sounded ridiculous. And she didn't trust them anyway. Not after everything.

She had no one to turn to.

Her parents couldn't be trusted, especially after what Jayson and Kiel had said about the CRF. Her best friend had lied to her for months. The man she once thought she loved had faked his death and left her to live in misery without him. Then the man she started to well and truly fall for had turned out to be a babysitter sent to charm her into revealing information.

215

And her sorority sisters were shacking up with bloodsucking monsters.

She stared at her phone as if it could provide all the answers and noticed the nineteen missed calls. All from her mother. She'd sent a handful of text messages as well.

Lizzie had probably missed some sort of function. Or maybe they'd called to check up on her.

She snorted. *Yes, because they care.*

The last message came in twenty minutes ago. It wasn't like her mother to give up. Lizzie bet someone had been sent to her condo to check in on her, meaning she couldn't go home.

Not that she wanted to anyway.

Stas's stuff was still there. She could drop in at any moment to retrieve her belongings and move out, and Lizzie didn't want to face her or watch it happen.

If she called Jacque, he would teleport her to Hydria, which would be miserable but would at least provide some answers.

She shook her head. *Not ready for that either.*

"Damn it," she whispered, her eyes squinting as she strove for answers.

A piece of shiny plastic in her purse caught her eye. A credit card without a limit. One tied to her father's account, but with her name.

She checked the outer pocket for her passport as a plan formed. The devil popped up on one shoulder, while an angel sat on the other. She usually listened to the haloed creature, but today, the horned one spoke her language.

This isn't a good idea.

Are you kidding? This is a fantastic idea.

It's unsafe.

So is New York City, apparently. What could it hurt?

Everything!

Live a little.

I have to work tomorrow.

Seriously? That's your best excuse? Send an email and take the week off. You've earned this.

"Yes," she agreed. "I have." Living in a box and obeying the rules led to a lonely existence. Everyone else lied, cheated, and hurt her. Why couldn't she do something spontaneous and a tad dangerous?

There's a vampire in the other room, she thought with a laugh. She'd visited a club full of them last night, teleported to Greece to meet several more immortal beings, found out her best friend was apparently a part of that world for months without telling her, and also saw a man come back from the dead.

Yeah, a little trip on her father's dime was *nothing* compared to all of that.

A vacation was just what she needed. Somewhere to help her relax and think, away from all the distractions and troubles. When she returned, Stas would have moved out, and Lizzie could go on with life as normal.

Or not.

Either way, she deserved this excursion.

Decided, she sent an email to work stating she needed the week off. Her lesson plans were already done. A substitute would have no issue taking over.

That done, Lizzie left Cam's apartment and headed to the airport. Her navy shift dress was appropriate enough for a plane ride, and she could buy new clothes with her father's card when she arrived. He rarely monitored the account, and even if he did, he would just settle the bill as usual.

Sometimes it paid to have a rich father.

~*~

"We have a problem," Jayson said as soon as Mateo answered the phone. "Lizzie's at the airport and just bought an airline ticket, but I couldn't get close enough to find out where."

"I see," Mateo murmured. "Which desk?"

Jayson gave him the name of the airline.

"Any idea what card she used?"

"If I wasn't close enough to hear her, I obviously didn't see it," Jayson replied, his patience thinning thanks to the runaway redhead. She'd led him on a merry goose chase through Manhattan to a random apartment building before walking to Penn Station and boarding a train to Newark. He'd texted Luc to give him an update but hadn't anticipated her actually purchasing a plane ticket.

"Give me five minutes." Mateo ended the call as Jayson watched Lizzie go through airport security.

"Minx," he murmured. He sent a report to Luc with a shake of his head.

The woman needed a stern lesson on how to make smart decisions because this was not one of them.

He understood her fragile mental state, but to board a plane in response? Such an immature and bratty move. It weakened his regard for her intelligence as well.

He answered his phone as it started to vibrate. "Talk to me, M."

"Do you have your American passport handy?"

Jayson frowned. "No. It's in the condo."

"Okay. I suggest you ask Jacque to pop over and retrieve it for you because you're running out of time." A ding popped on Jayson's phone while Mateo was talking. "Congratulations. You've just been booked on the last available *Polaris Business* seat to Rome, and your flight leaves in sixty-seven minutes."

"Tell me the seat is next to hers," he growled.

"Of course. Safe travels, Jay." Mateo hung up again, and Jayson swore the man was laughing as he did.

"Fuck." The woman chose Italy for a last-minute flight? Did she not understand that the CRF was dangerous? That her existence was a mystery to them all?

He shook his head. Of course she didn't know, because she'd never given them the chance to explain. But to hop on a plane to Europe? Childish.

He punched in a message to Jacque, requesting his passport, and was still shaking his head when his floppy-haired friend arrived with the item in question.

"I'm very glad to not be the cause of that look," the teleporter said as he handed over the navy-blue booklet. "Try not to punish her too badly."

Jayson grinned. "Oh, when I get my hands on her, she'll never do anything this imprudent again." Fleeing the country, of all things. Damn foolish woman.

"Right, have fun with that." Jacque didn't sound so sure and even took a step back.

"I intend to," Jayson replied. And he meant it.

Because he was done playing nice.

Yes, he withheld information, but only to protect her.

No more.

If she wanted the truth, he'd wouldn't just give it to her; he'd show her.

~*~

Not for the first time, Lizzie wondered if she'd just made the stupidest decision of her life by boarding this plane. Then they came around with champagne, and she stopped worrying.

She watched the airfield workers out the window while she sipped her bubbly. The late-afternoon flight had worked much better than the option to Paris. Lizzie worried she would lose her nerve if she had to wait too long, so she'd selected Rome after reviewing all the departures on the board. Most European flights left later in the evening, but this one departed at half-past-five. She would watch a movie, try to eat something, and, hopefully, sleep.

The seat beside her crinkled as someone settled into it. Their business class chairs were close enough for chatting but also provided ample room for privacy. She'd still hoped the seat would remain vacant. Alas, her luck never

219

prevailed.

"Welcome aboard, sir," the flight attendant purred. "Can I get you anything for takeoff? A drink, perhaps?"

"Mmm, yes," a familiar voice replied. Lizzie's lips parted as she realized just *who* had taken the seat beside her, but rather than acknowledge her, he remained focused on the flight attendant.

"I would love a whiskey neat, at least for takeoff," he said with a wink.

Flirtatious much?

"Of course, sir," the brunette replied before sauntering off while Jayson watched her with a smirk.

Lizzie wanted to hit him. Not just for checking out the attendant so brazenly, but for sitting beside her without a word. For following her. For acting like he didn't even see her staring at him right now.

He rested his elbow on the oversized armrest and eyed the woman's legs while she fixed his drink at the front of the cabin. It was as if Lizzie didn't exist, yet he'd clearly followed her onto this plane.

"What are you doing here?" she hissed, unable to hold back her irritation.

"That is an excellent question, Elizabeth." He buckled his seat belt before finally meeting her gaze with a decidedly unamused expression. "Rome?"

She swallowed, her ire disappearing. The energy rolling off him did not match his usual playful vibe. He seemed more powerful somehow. Because she knew the truth? Or was it something else?

"You know, it's a good thing this is a long flight," he continued. "It'll give us plenty of time to talk."

"Oh no, you're not—"

"International flight regulations state that no passengers can disembark once the boarding doors are closed, and I was the last one in line. Which means"—he glanced over his shoulder before refocusing on her—"you're officially stuck with me for the next eight hours and thirty minutes."

He relaxed into his chair just as the brunette approached with his drink. "Thank you, sweetheart," he murmured.

"Anything else?" she asked in a sultry voice.

Jayson ran his eyes over her and smiled. "Perhaps later."

Lizzie wanted to punch him again. As if the last twenty-four hours hadn't been hell already, he had to hit on the flight attendant right in front of her? Could he be any more heartless?

She'd only been in his bed two nights ago. Granted, that'd all been her own doing. She'd practically begged him to kiss her in the kitchen, though he was the one who invited her to his room—to pacify her, apparently.

"I'll be back to check on you once we're in the air," Flirty Skirt murmured.

"I look forward to it," he replied while Lizzie rolled her eyes.

Flirty Skirt added a sway to her hips as she left, eliciting a grin from Jayson.

"Maybe you should spend the eight-hour trip talking with her," Lizzie suggested.

"I doubt we would spend much time holding a conversation," he replied before sipping his whiskey. "And I'm not here for her. I'm here for you."

Lizzie masked the pain of his words by rolling her eyes and scoffing, "Right. Babysitter Jayson."

"Oh, Elizabeth, you have no idea how wrong you are on that." He captured her gaze. "*Babysitter* implies that I see you as a child, which is distinctly different from finding your behavior childish and immature."

"Excuse me?"

"You heard me just fine. I could beat your ass red for this stunt."

Her mouth fell open. "Did you just threaten to *spank* me?" She pitched her voice low but couldn't help the squeak at the end. Because he did not just say that!

"I haven't decided yet, but you'll be the first to know when I do."

She gaped at him, speechless. No one had ever threatened to spank her, not even in her youth. Jayson couldn't be serious. Men did not punish grown women in that manner. Did they?

Jayson's lips were suddenly at her ear, sending a jolt of electricity down her spine. "You would enjoy it if I did, which I'm not sure you deserve."

She shivered. His words held a promise she didn't understand, one that elicited forbidden feelings she had no business entertaining on a plane, let alone with him.

Vampires are real, she reminded herself in an attempt to stay grounded.

Eh, yeah, but that's old news now, her hormones responded. *And they're called Ichorians.*

So she was losing her mind. Awesome.

Jayson's palm went to her knee, bringing her back to the present.

Energy simmered beneath her skin as his hand traveled upward and slid under the fabric of her shift dress to her inner thigh.

She shouldn't have liked that nearly as much as she did.

He lied to her.

Everyone had.

But his touch seemed to unravel her frustration and replace it with a much hotter emotion. One that tightened her stomach in anticipation.

Her brain fired important questions at her unresponsive mouth—she couldn't seem to move her tongue or form words. The man had captivated her with his touch.

Wizardry.

"For the record, I may be far older than you can imagine, but that does not mean I have ever thought of you as a child." He licked the shell of her ear, pebbling goose bumps down her neck. "You are a gorgeous woman, Elizabeth. And babysitting is not an activity I consider in your presence. Far from it." He nipped her ear before returning to his personal space.

He left a rattled, confused mess in his wake. Lizzie was supposed to be angry with him, not... feverish and... whatever.

And he'd only befriended her to learn more, not because he liked her.

Except he called her gorgeous again.

And the way he'd just touched her was *not* very friend-like.

"Buckle your seat belt," he said as the plane pulled away from the gate. "Once we're in the air, we'll play a game."

It took her three swallows before she managed to say, "A game?"

"Yes. One where I make the rules and you obey them."

Yeah, she definitely didn't agree with that plan. "Good luck with that." The words lacked their designated punch. Damn hormones.

His brown eyes smoldered as he met and held her gaze. "I've been easy on you, Elizabeth. That ended the moment you decided to forgo common sense and flee the country on a whim."

She opened her mouth to contest that point, but he silenced her with a glance.

Okay, so maybe it had been stupid of her to get on a plane to Rome, but it wasn't like she didn't have several good reasons to react that way. Escaping had sounded like a solid plan at the time. She just hadn't anticipated anyone following her.

"By the end of this flight," he continued, "you will understand why I've managed to survive as long as I have and how I earned the title of 'Elder' among my kind. Afterward, you will agree to play by my rules because you want to, not because you have to."

That was never going to happen. "You clearly don't know me at all." There. That held a little bit more confidence.

Except he silenced that budding self-assurance with a predatory smile—a king grinning at his chosen conquest.

"Oh, that is where you're wrong." His gaze dropped to her mouth before sliding back up. "Your body speaks to me on a level you don't yet understand, but you will, and soon."

CHAPTER SIXTEEN

The Treaty of 1747

Benefactor is satisfied with subject's
intelligence quotient and requests
increased focus on subject's
information recall functions.

—Entry Log 106.09.4-7

If Jayson called Lizzie by her full name one more time, she would scream.

He ordered her meal for her—*Elizabeth will have the filet*—then ignored her protests and made small talk while referring to her by her full name the entire time, and now he'd just requested a dessert drink for *Elizabeth* again.

Lizzie never thought she would actually miss her

225

nicknames, but she certainly did now.

"What if I didn't want a dessert wine?" she asked, irritated.

"In that case, I'll have two."

"Do you always order for the women you stalk?" She'd started referring to him as a stalker since he disliked the term *babysitter*.

"Only the misbehaving ones," he replied as he relaxed into his seat and flipped through the array of movies on his private screen.

This was hardly what she had in mind when he mentioned a game. It seemed to be more a display of power than anything else and perhaps a subtle way of implying that he knew her tastes. Because the dinner he selected was the one she wanted, and she did enjoy dessert wine with chocolates.

But that wasn't the point.

He couldn't just waltz onto this plane and watch a movie. Not after everything she'd been through these last two days. The whole purpose of her escape was to forget, and as he'd made that impossible, he might as well give her some answers.

"Were you really born in Babylon?" she demanded.

"Yep." He continued playing with the movies instead of regarding her.

"To the son of a war god?"

He snorted. "Artemis fancies himself one, but he's just an Ichorian who can control and manipulate metal."

The background noise from the plane drowned out their conversation to others, spurring her onward on this quest for information. "Explain what you mean by that."

"Pick up your spoon," he said instead.

"I hardly see—"

He cut her a look. "You will, if you listen."

She blew out a breath. "Fine." She lifted the spoon. "Happy?"

He didn't respond, but the spoon bent in half, causing

her to yelp and drop the item back onto her tray.

The passenger across from them gave them a curious expression, and Jayson said loudly, "Right. No horror movie."

"How did you do that?" she hissed. The metal returned to its real shape while she watched in fascination.

"Ichorians pass their supernatural talents on to their progeny, meaning Artemis gifted me with the ability to control metal. That spoon is a parlor trick, by the way. I can sense every nut and bolt on this plane, as well as all the watches, necklaces, belts, you name it. If I wanted, I could manipulate them all at once, or one at a time."

Her lips parted. "Really?"

He shrugged. "It's important to note that not all immortal gifts are created equal. I've met telekinetics who could only lift a stapler and others who could lift an entire house. Those of us with stronger skills live longer."

"So your father could do the same?"

"He can, yes." He finally met her gaze. "Artemis, the Ichorian who helped create me, is still alive."

"And your mom?"

"She died a very long time ago," he murmured. "Ezra, my mother, was mortal. Artemis killed her when I was ten human years old."

Lizzie's eyes widened. "Why?"

"Because she was aging." Jayson paused as if considering what else to say, then shrugged. "He could have turned her, of course, but he was bored with her. And rather than let her go, he killed her in front of me. He considered it a lesson in mortality and why immortals should never grow too close to humans. They die."

"That's…" She couldn't even finish. How horrible to do that to a young boy.

"I spent most of my youth trying to please him and prove my worth so I wouldn't suffer the same fate, but on my nineteenth birthday, he slit my throat." Lizzie flinched at the bluntness of his words, but he continued, unfazed.

"He wasn't aging due to his Ichorian genetics and had hoped to assume my identity as the new ruler because he wanted to hide his immortality from the mortals. But I woke up the next morning. He tried again for good measure, but I recovered, and he proclaimed me his true Ichorian son."

The flight attendant returned at that moment with their dessert trays. She traded them for the dinner ones while Jayson murmured things to her in Italian. Her cheeks were flushed by the end, causing Lizzie to roll her eyes. The damn man had been flirting with the brunette all through dinner and again now.

It churned Lizzie's stomach and soured her taste for the chocolate laid out before her. She opted for the wine that came with it, needing the alcohol to numb her senses. If he walked off with the woman, she would lose it.

Not that he owed her anything. They weren't dating. She was just a temporary assignment to him. Nothing more.

Except when he touched her.

"What was I saying?" he asked as the brunette wandered off with an overstated sashay in her step.

"That you're a jerk?" Lizzie suggested. *Okay, maybe less alcohol.*

He grinned. "Jealous, Elizabeth?"

She glowered at him. "First of all, no. Second of all, stop calling me Elizabeth."

His lips curled all the more, revealing those two precious dimples. "I thought you disliked my nickname for you, or you used to, anyway."

"I... That's not the point. You're calling me Elizabeth like I'm in trouble."

"Ah, but you are in trouble." He selected a piece of chocolate from his tray and brought it to her lips. "Open."

"No, this—" He silenced her protest by sliding the decadent dessert between her lips.

"Yes, enjoy that while I continue my story." His gaze

dropped to her mouth, where she reluctantly chewed. Spitting it out would be a waste of a perfectly good sweet and also very unladylike.

"Artemis believed me to be his own creation of an Ichorian, but he soon discovered that I didn't have a taste for mortal blood, nor did I require it. And I also boasted not one gift but two."

He selected another piece of chocolate and pressed it to her mouth. She really wanted to refuse, but saying no to such decadence seemed sinful. Besides, if he wanted to give her all of his dessert, she wouldn't complain. But she also wouldn't share her own.

"My secondary talent is from my mom's bloodline. I can more or less manipulate how others see me and leave them confused about my physical traits. I do it constantly without thinking, to the point where I have to actively want to un-shield my appearance, such as right now with you. You're the only one on this plane who *sees* me."

She blinked and swallowed. "What about Ms. Flirty Skirt?"

His brow furrowed. "Who?"

Lizzie gestured to the front of the cabin with her eyes. "The flight attendant you keep hitting on." She had given her name earlier, but Lizzie didn't remember it. Probably because the woman only focused on Jayson every time she stopped by.

Amusement crinkled his eyes. "I rather like you being jealous."

She rolled her eyes. "I'm not jealous."

"You are," he said, grinning. "And to answer your question, her recollection of my features is fuzzy, but she knows I'm attractive."

"That's not arrogant."

"It's not," he agreed. "Because it's true."

Another piece of chocolate appeared before she could respond to that. She grazed his finger with her teeth on purpose, earning her a heated look.

"Careful," he murmured. "Or I'll take that as an invitation."

To what? she wondered.

"Back to what I was saying," he continued as he studied her mouth. "I wasn't an Ichorian at all, something Artemis eventually deduced, and a meeting was called. It served as the first Conclave, actually, though they didn't refer to it as such at the time. The word used isn't one I can clearly translate given the dead languages, but it essentially implied they were gods."

He swirled his wine thoughtfully before continuing.

"Ichorians from all over gathered to discuss me, only to find that there were others in existence as well. That was the day I met Balthazar, Lucian, Alik, Eli, and about twenty additional immortals with similar traits." He smiled fondly, as if remembering it now, and shook his head.

"Some called us a gift from above, while others considered us a threat. Needless to say, the governing board, now known as the Conclave, voted to keep us alive to test our worth."

Lizzie sipped her water before setting it aside and focusing on him. "What does that mean? Test your worth?"

He studied her for a long moment before saying, "Nothing good. Let's just say they explored our limits in terms of death, powers, and otherwise. Not everyone made it."

Her eyebrows rose. "But you said they were your parents, right? Like, Artemis was your dad, so obviously Balthazar had an Ichorian parent as well?"

"Our fathers," Jayson murmured. "My kind are created when an Ichorian male procreates with a human female. And as to what you're implying, yes, they essentially tortured their children in the name of research. The one thing they never did was taste our blood because the Conclave had decreed it as disgraceful. Everything else, though, was considered fair game."

Jayson tilted his glass to finish his wine and set it down with a finality.

"That's awful," she whispered, her voice masked by the airplane's engines.

Their flirty attendant appeared to snatch up the dessert trays and frowned at finding them partially eaten. Jayson said something to her in Italian again, eliciting more blushing. Lizzie was still shaking her head when the lady flounced off.

She gasped when he stole a piece of food from her plate and popped it into his mouth.

"Hey!" She tried to smack his hand when he did it again, but he was too quick.

"I promised Rebekah we would be done soon."

"Rebekah?"

"Sorry, that's Ms. Flirty Skirt to you."

Lizzie grumbled a few choice words under her breath. Of course the woman had a sexy name to go with her long legs and curves.

This time when he tried to feed her more chocolate, she refused. Her figure certainly didn't need the fatty enhancements.

"To shorten a rather long story, the Ichorians eventually decided we could be useful as long as we were maintained. They treated us as second-class citizens— peasants—and exploited us for their own purposes. They also killed any progeny who could potentially overpower them and allowed only the useful children to be reborn into immortality."

"So Immortals can be killed?"

He nodded. "It's not easy, but it can be done by severing the head or burning the body to ash."

Lizzie flinched at the image that evoked. "Gross."

"There's also the matter of our blood being toxic to Ichorians, something that wasn't discovered until about a millennium ago. I'll come back to that after I explain where *Hydraian* came from." He stole the final bite from her plate and followed it with some water. "Do you want more wine?"

She shook her head. Two glasses were enough.

He signaled the attendant with one of his grins, and Lizzie wondered if little Ms. Flirty Skirt could actually see it. She must have because she brightened under the attention and almost bounced all the way over to them. Lizzie would have to ask him to explain the facial manipulation thing more in depth. After he finished this new round of flirting.

The trays disappeared, giving them space to move around again. Lizzie tucked her legs beneath her on the oversized seat and angled her body toward Jayson. He rested his ankle on his knee, giving her a nice view of his strong legs.

Dressed in khaki pants and a sweater, he resembled a fashion model. He even had the windswept-hair look and alluring eyes.

"After several centuries of testing our mettle and determining the best ways to manage the population, we were given a place to live on our own with limited resources. It was a way to hold sway over my kind, something most of us recognized, but we weren't going to turn down the opportunity at some semblance of freedom. And that's when we colonized Hydria."

She couldn't believe they were discussing this all so casually, yet it all felt so much more believable coming from Jayson than it ever did from Kiel. "So that's why you call yourself Hydraians?"

"Yes. Luc, whom you met briefly last night—he's the blond one—is a master of strategy and suggested we develop a term to promote unity among our kind." He smiled, his fondness for the memory and the man palpable. A moment of history that clearly meant something, perhaps one of the first to bring him happiness?

"Luc's commonly referred to as omniscient, but that's

not quite right. His gift allows him to remember everything, no matter how trivial the details, and he's been alive for longer than I have and was born to an Ichorian with a similar ability. Between the two of them, they essentially know everything."

Lizzie caught the affection in his voice, so different from when he spoke about his own father. "It sounds like Luc's upbringing varied from yours?"

He chuckled. "It did, in more ways than one. My father created me for the sole purpose of assuming my identity after a certain period of time so he could hide his own immortality from the mortals. Aidan, Luc's father, actually loves him. He's also considered one of the oldest beings on Earth, and unlike most of his brethren, he craves peace and equality among the immortals. I believe it stems from his love for strategy."

"He sounds okay," Lizzie agreed. "Does his opinion cause issues?"

Jayson scratched his chin. "Well, yes, but as I said, he's old, and as such, he's respected. I mentioned that Hydraian blood can kill Ichorians, which was only discovered about a thousand years ago. The realization lent credence to those who already wished to exterminate our kind due to our dual powers, and incited centuries of violence."

He paused, his expression sobering.

Lizzie placed her hand over his on the armrest and squeezed gently, startling him from wherever he'd gone in his head. He cleared his throat and refocused, his eyes brimming with haunting memories.

"I lost a lot of friends, several of them among the oldest of my kind from that original meeting, but those of us who survived proved resilient. The Ichorians had gotten lazy over the years, their control over my kind was implied and expected, and they didn't realize that some of their children were extremely powerful, because our kind had learned early on to hide those talents.

"Alik, for example, can torture with his mind,

something he never admitted. The Ichorians thought his telepathic skills—gifted through his father's bloodline—were his primary ability. For the longest time, he pretended that a minor language affinity was his other talent, but in truth, he can cripple an army of hundreds with a single thought."

"That's terrifying," Lizzie admitted softly.

Jayson nodded. "Yes, but also very useful. Pair his strengths with my affinity for metal, Luc's strategy, Balthazar's flair for manipulating emotion, a few Hydraians who can control fire, and several other combat-related abilities, and you have quite a formidable army. It helped that we developed weapons coated in our blood that kill on impact."

The attendant appeared again with bottles of water and a smile solely for Jayson, but this time he didn't return it. He merely dismissed the woman with a few words and refocused on Lizzie.

"In 1747, an armistice was established between Hydraians and Ichorians that created peace in specific regions. Hydria, for example, is a safe zone for my kind, while New York City is a haven for Ichorians."

She considered his words with a frown. "Isn't your being in Manhattan a violation?"

"No, it expressly states that we can venture over borders at our own risk. Meaning, if the wrong Ichorian found me in New York, he would be within his rights to kill me."

"Kiel is an Ichorian and a friend?" It came out as a question because Kiel spoke fondly of Jayson and they obviously hung out, but they were supposedly also rivals. Had Kiel meant that in reference to their warring factions or something else?

Jayson blew out a breath as he uncapped his water and took a swig. "Ezekiel isn't so much a friend as a respected adversary who is trained to kill fledglings, otherwise known as the progeny of Ichorians, who have not yet been reborn as a Hydraian."

He shifted while Lizzie waited for more. It was all so complicated, but he explained it in a way that helped her understand.

Stas knew about all of this?

How?

And where does the CRF fit in?

"There's a unique poison that essentially burns Ichorian blood when ingested, thereby killing fledglings. We call it the Nizari poison, after the band of assassins—of which Ezekiel is the primary leader—known to administer it."

Lizzie's lips parted. "So not a friend."

"Definitely not, though he seems to be playing by his own set of rules lately. I imagine it's a result of boredom that will end when he craves death again." He studied her. "Did he say anything else interesting?"

Can you read my thoughts? she asked, suspicious. Because she'd just been thinking about her former best friend seconds ago and his subject change seemed odd, but his expression remained politely curious.

Coincidence?

Possibly.

Lizzie considered her conversation with Kiel. Despite being shocked and emotional, she remembered almost every word.

"He said he arranged for me and Stas to live together our freshman year." Which was odd. "He also knew her full name, which I never mentioned to you or him, and 'Astasiya' isn't an easy guess."

"No, it's not, which means he knows more about her than we realized," Jayson replied, his expression thoughtful. "Is that all he said?"

"About Stas? Yeah," she replied. "He mostly talked about his youth and how Osiris took him in as a boy and raised him alongside his own son, Sethios. In Babylon."

He studied her for a long moment. "He said he grew up with Sethios? As in they were the same age as

235

children?"

"Yes, that's what he implied, anyway." Lizzie had a knack for remembering facts and discussions; it was something that suited her well in college, because she never had to study.

"What else did he say about Osiris?"

She shrugged. "Not much, just that I would meet him someday and he's friends with Artemis. Why?"

He finished his water, his eyes narrowed in thought. When he finally looked at her again, she saw a sort of resolution in his gaze, as if he'd been battling something internally.

"Osiris is a being everyone fears, including Ichorians, because he can persuade others to do his bidding through vocal command." He let that settle, his expression hardening. "I'm guessing Ezekiel meant to imply that Osiris turned Sethios, or perhaps even raised him as a child similar to the way Aidan raised Issac."

"Uh… Aidan?" All these names were giving her a headache. He'd mentioned him already as Luc's father, but not in relation to Issac.

Jayson smiled, as if hearing that thought, and slid his hand to her nape, where he massaged some of the tension from her neck.

"The immortal who turned Issac into an Ichorian," he clarified. "He's also Luc and Amelia's birth father, but that's not important."

Jayson shifted into her personal space and palmed her cheek. "I promised myself the day we met that I would never lie to you, and I've kept my word, but I've also omitted quite a bit. Before today, I mean. But this is really something Stas should tell you, not me."

Dread pooled in her stomach, but she couldn't stop now. "You can't say that and not elaborate."

His thumb traced her bottom lip. "I've explained that Ichorians and humans produce fledglings—"

"What about a Hydraian and a human?" she asked

before he could continue.

"Hydraians can't procreate," he replied. "But that's beside the point. What I want you to consider is *why* Stas would know about our world, and it's not because she works for the CRF."

Lizzie frowned. "Are you implying she's immortal?"

"Not yet, but close."

"A fledgling?" How could Stas keep something like that from Lizzie?

He nodded. "Yes, and her power is similar to Osiris's in that she can persuade through voice."

Lizzie's eyes widened. "What?!"

"Shh." His palm tightened warningly on her neck. "We don't want to cause a scene."

"You just told me my best friend can tell people what to do," she hissed. "I'm allowed a reaction to that."

"You are, but a quiet one," he replied.

She glared at him, but he merely smiled, amused.

"I understand. It's an interesting development."

Understatement of the year. Their entire conversation and the last twenty-four hours had been an *interesting development* in Lizzie's mind.

"Um, what's Stas's other ability?" Her voice had come down an octave, but her pulse still thrummed wildly at both Jayson's close proximity and their discussion. So much for this all being easy to believe.

"We don't know yet because she hasn't been reborn." Jayson's expression melted into one of compassion. "She has refused the next step for several reasons, one of which is you."

"Me?" Her eyebrows hit her hairline. "Why?"

"Because she can't work for the CRF as a Hydraian. She needed to remain human to become a Sentinel and gather intelligence. At first, she stayed on to save Issac's sister from captivity—which is another story we'll get into later—and subsequently, to help you. Tom found a file with your name on it while working there but had to retire before he could gather more information."

His palm slid to her neck, where his fingers massaged the tense area at the top of her spine. It felt divine but didn't belie the horror of his words.

"Do you have any idea what the file says?"

He shook his head. "No. We've spent two months trying and failing to gather more information, and we were planning to tell you everything, but Ezekiel beat us to it."

"I-I don't understand. What could they possibly have on me?"

"Whatever it is, you're valuable to them." Jayson settled back into his chair but kept his body angled toward her. "Do you remember that first night I stopped by? I believe a Sentinel stopped by right after, yes?"

Lizzie nodded. "Charlie."

"Does that happen a lot?"

She shrugged. "Sometimes. My mother likes to send them to check up on me."

"In this case, he stopped by to check on your surveillance equipment. I set off an interference with my watch to test their reaction time. It was impressive."

Lizzie blanched, and his palm covered her mouth before she could react vocally. She wrapped her fingers around his wrist to yank it down. "Don't do that."

"Don't scream."

"I wasn't going to."

He arched a brow. "Don't lie, either."

"You're one to talk."

"I've never lied to you, Elizabeth." The severity underlining his tone made her shiver. As did the intense way he studied her. "It was not my decision to keep all this from you, nor was it my place to tell you, even when I wanted to."

Lizzie swallowed.

It was Stas and Tom who kept all this from her. Jayson did, as well, but in a different way. They assigned him to guard and befriend her. That he wanted to tell her the truth said a lot, assuming he meant it. His eyes said he did, but her heart refused to believe anything yet.

"I need time," she admitted. "To think this all through."

"And although I appreciate that, running off to Rome on a whim is not the answer." He dared her with his expression to refute that, but she couldn't. He was right, not that she would admit it.

"Did you sleep at all last night?" he asked, his voice softer than before.

She shook her head slowly. "Not really."

"Then let's get some sleep now and start fresh in the morning. We can do a little sightseeing before deciding on our next destination."

"Really?" She perked up at that idea. "You're not going to send me to Hydria?" She half expected a welcoming party to be waiting at the airport for their arrival.

"Wherever we go next will be your choice." His lips curled as he added, "Just know that I'll be tagging along."

She toyed with a strand of her hair that had fallen over her shoulder. "You don't have to do that." It seemed unfair and dangerous from what he had said. "But I'm not ready to face them yet," she admitted, torn.

And to stay in Hydria? It would require leaving all she'd ever known.

Not that she had much to be thankful for in Manhattan. Her parents wouldn't miss her, and her friends would move on, just like they always did. She couldn't remember the last time she spoke to anyone from high school. Some of them kept in touch via text messages during freshman year, but everyone sort of moved on with their lives. That was when Lizzie met Stas, and their bond had felt so much more real than anything else in Lizzie's life.

Her chest ached with the loss of that friendship. It was irrevocably changed by the events of the last few months, and she wondered if they would ever be able to come back from this.

Jayson stood and stretched his arms over his head, revealing a sliver of skin between his red sweater and khakis.

Talk about a distraction.

Except she wasn't the only one who noticed.

Flirty Skirt gazed at him with a question in her eyes, but Jayson ignored her and turned to place his hands on Lizzie's armrests. His face was a scant inch from hers as he bent into her personal space.

"As irritated as I am with this last-minute adventure, I also understand your desire to run. Which is why I'm willing to overlook the foolishness of your actions, this time."

He tightly grasped her chin and forced her to meet his unwavering gaze. "But, Elizabeth, if you ever pull a stunt like this again, I will bend you over my knee and express my displeasure in a way that will leave you thinking about me for weeks. And I won't hesitate to do it in public, either. Do you understand me?"

Her mouth went dry. "You wouldn't—"

"I would," he promised.

She squirmed in her seat, uncomfortable by the feelings he'd awoken. A spanking should *not* intrigue her. It was wrong, yet the power in his stance as he leaned over her and the steadfast way he held her gaze unleashed something inside of her. A foreign desire that felt wanton and inappropriate, and oh-so right.

"What are you doing to me?" she whispered.

His mouth went to her ear. "I'm learning your limits, sweetheart. Now let's get some sleep."

CHAPTER SEVENTEEN

A Self-Guided Tour

Memory implants are complete.
Surrogates to be provided detailed
reports for future interactions.

—Entry Log 118.02.4-7

Lizzie woke to Jayson speaking Italian.

A peek through her thick lashes showed Flirty Skirt had returned. She had her hip popped against Jayson's armrest. His chair was upright while Lizzie lay curled in a ball on her flat-bed seat, and he seemed very alert.

The flight attendant blushed at whatever he said, and nodded. He fished his phone out of his pocket, murmured

LEXI C. FOSS

something sexy, and handed it over for her to type into. Which she did while smiling triumphantly.

Lizzie observed the exchange through narrowed eyes. Apparently, this was why he agreed to sightseeing and staying a little longer. He hadn't been able to sleep with the woman on the plane, so he was making other arrangements.

It shouldn't hurt.

But it did.

They weren't even dating, and he'd been clear about the purpose of their relationship, but why flirt with Lizzie? Unless she'd misread all his signals. Her experience in these matters was minimal at best.

He mentioned something about Balthazar as he returned the phone to his pocket, causing Lizzie to arch a brow. Tristan implied that Jayson enjoyed sharing women—was that what he meant?

Her stomach turned over.

They hadn't revisited their conversation from the other afternoon—the one where she learned about his penchant for bedding more than one woman at a time. And they'd yet to discuss his friend's comments from the party, either.

She clearly misread all his signals. One moment she swore he liked her, and the next, she was a mission again.

I need to get off this plane.

Lizzie sat up to check the flight monitor on her screen—one hour left. Good.

Jayson said something about her in Italian now, which caused the flight attendant to nod eagerly before scampering off.

"Rebekah is bringing you breakfast," he murmured.

Lizzie didn't acknowledge him as she shifted her bed upward into a chair. She tucked her legs beneath her and finger-brushed her hair, all while feeling his eyes on her.

Apparently, he expected a response.

Fine.

"I'm not hungry."

That's not petulant at all, Liz.

Screw you.

"That's too bad since you'll be eating anyway," he replied. "We'll be doing a lot of walking today, and I'll need you well fed for that."

She finally looked at him. Amusement radiated from every edge of his face. "And where will we be walking?"

"That depends on what sights you have in mind. I could provide a historical tour, if you're interested. Not the one provided by regaling tour guides, but one depicted from actual events." A boyish charm flirted with his features as he awaited her reply.

"You really want to show me around?"

"Of course I do. I wouldn't offer if I didn't."

Maybe his plans with Flirty Skirt were for after their day of sightseeing. Lizzie could attempt to exhaust him to the point of poor performance, though she didn't know if a man like Jayson ran out of energy.

Unwanted emotion poked her in the chest.

She had no right to be jealous. Sure, he kept touching her, but he also openly flirted with the flight attendant and exchanged numbers with the woman.

That was neither a faithful man nor one who would ever be interested in Lizzie.

"Why are you doing this?" she asked, confused. "Is it because you feel bad or something?"

He turned toward her. "Do I really need a reason for wanting to have fun with you?"

She stared at him. "You would have fun?"

He grinned. "Oh, undoubtedly. Probably more than I should, but as I've already broken all the rules with you anyway, what's a little exploration to add to the list?"

She frowned. "Rules? What rules?"

"Luc is a fan of edicts," he replied vaguely. "Now stop changing the subject and tell me where you want to go when we land."

His chocolate gaze pinned her in place, compelling her

to comply.

Sightseeing could be fun… And he was right about the advantages of having a guide who walked the streets a thousand years ago. Two or three thousand, even.

How will I ever wrap my head around all this? she wondered.

Oh. The purpose of his request hit her smack dab between the eyes.

He was offering her a distraction. Because he pitied her, or something else?

Does it matter? No. She welcomed the reprieve with open arms.

"Uh, well, I've seen all the traditional points of interest, but it's been a while." She went with her parents about ten years ago? Her memories of that trip were foggy at best, reminding her more of a dream than a true experience. "Is there anywhere you recommend?"

He considered. "You've already seen Rome, right?"

"About a decade ago, but yeah."

"Did you visit Pompeii?"

She frowned. "That's not in Rome."

"I'm aware of that." He reached over to tug on a strand of her hair hanging near her breast. "Have you been?" he asked as the back of his hand skimmed her breast. If it was intentional, he didn't show it, but her body reacted anyway.

She forced herself to shake her head since her suddenly dry mouth no longer understood English. Because no, she'd never been. Her mother preferred shopping and fashion to archaeological sites.

"Then we'll head south for a day trip, have some Neapolitan-style pizza, and spend the night in Rome, if that's your preference." He let go of her hair and brushed his knuckles over her cheek. "You blush so prettily, Red."

Flirty Skirt chose that moment to return with the breakfast tray. No doubt well-timed on the flight attendant's part.

Jayson's hand fell to Lizzie's shoulder as he addressed the woman in English. "Thank you, Rebekah."

She replied in Italian as Lizzie busied herself with the table. She accepted the tray with a forced smile and muttered a "Thank you." Her mother taught her to be polite in all circumstances, this one notwithstanding.

Jayson's thumb traced the column of Lizzie's neck as he asked for two cups of coffee. Again in English. When he requested two sugars and a cream for Lizzie, her eyes widened. That was her preferred way to drink coffee, but they'd never shared a cup together.

"How did you know how I take my coffee?" she asked as the brunette wandered off.

"Observation," he murmured, his thumb circling her pulse point. "I've learned a lot about you these last two months—not in a stalker way but in a security-detail sort of way."

"Bodyguards need to know how their charges take their coffee?"

He smirked. "Perhaps not, but you stop by that coffee shop on Broadway every day before work."

Lizzie's eyebrows popped up. "You followed me?"

"Yes." No shame, just a straight response. "I wanted to see where and when the CRF intervened in your life."

"And did they?"

"Only once a month."

She frowned. "When?"

"Brunch," he replied. "Let's discuss it more after you eat. We'll be landing soon, which means you need to hurry up."

She wasn't so sure she wanted to eat at all now. "Brunch?" she repeated. "That doesn't make any sense."

"How about you work on that omelet while I explain." He worded it as a suggestion, but his tone indicated it to be a demand, not a request.

A compromise. Okay. She could agree to that even if the idea of breakfast didn't appeal to her.

Lizzie sliced off a piece of egg and, with a raised eyebrow, put it into her mouth.

Jayson grinned, appeased, and dropped his hand to the armrest between them. "All right, I'll tell you what we know, but I'm warning you right now that it's not much."

~*~

"A brothel," Lizzie said, her brow furrowed. "With a rock bed."

Jayson chuckled. "It kept the men from lounging around afterward."

She studied the small, preserved room of Pompeii and nodded. "I wouldn't want to lie there, either."

Their little venture to this archaeological site served as the perfect distraction from their conversation on the plane. Of course, every few minutes, Lizzie would mutter something about how unreal this all was, especially since Jayson possessed intimate knowledge of the former Roman city.

She ran her fingers over the walls before exiting into the sunshine. Her red hair glimmered alluringly, but it was her new outfit that captivated his attention.

Fitted jeans, black boots, and a flowy top.

Sexy. As. Fuck.

Lizzie picked up the outfit at the airport while he arranged transportation. It'd taken all manner of restraint to travel here instead of finding a boutique hotel with a decent bed. Even now he wanted to pull her into one of the less populated sections, push her up against a stone wall, and devastate her mouth.

He clasped his hands behind his back instead.

"Does this place bring back memories?" she asked softly.

He shrugged. "It was primarily a trading port, so I never spent much time here. I preferred Rome." For a variety of reasons, but mainly for the women.

"No time in the brothel?" The teasing quality of her voice seemed forced, as did her smile.

"Do you really want the answer to that, Red?" He meant it as a taunt but also as a lesson. *Don't ask for details you don't really want to know.* He suspected that would be an issue between them given his age and her innocence. It was a challenge he wanted to overcome, but he didn't quite know where to begin. Or why he even felt the need to try.

"Probably not." Her gaze went to the ground. "Never mind." She picked up the pace, but he caught her hand and tugged her back to his side.

"Where are you running off to?" He linked their fingers and forced her to slow down.

"I wasn't, I mean, I just—"

"To answer your question," he said, interrupting her, "I don't pay for pleasure." He let that sink in before adding, "So, no, I did not waste any time in that brothel."

"Oh, I didn't mean…" She trailed off as color brightened her beautiful face.

"Yes, you did," he replied softly. And he couldn't really blame her. They had barely covered the surface of his experience, something that no doubt intimidated her, and rightly so. Still… "I can't apologize for my history, Liz." He squeezed her hand. "But I can try a new approach for our future."

She stumbled—something easy to do on the stone road, but he suspected his words were the true cause.

"Our future?" she repeated.

"Yes." He started to smile, when the hairs along his arm danced in warning.

Gunmetal.

Jayson's gift engaged on instinct alone, mentally grabbing the incoming bullet and dropping it to the ground long before it reached him.

A sniper. His location up in the hills gave him a perfect view of *Via dell' Abbondanza*, which meant Lizzie and Jayson needed to get off the main street. The former residences and shops surrounding them provided an ideal place to play hide-and-seek.

Jayson sensed two approaching handguns paired with blades.

Sentinels on the ground about a hundred yards out. He didn't bother searching for them. A battle among the tourists would result in unnecessary fatalities.

Only one option: run.

Jayson wrapped his arms around Lizzie and pulled her backward into a restricted area of Pompeii.

"What—"

"Sentinels," he explained as he yanked her between a pair of stone pillars and darted for another set. The way he forced her about would have caused a scene if anyone could see them. Fortunately, this area was roped off to the public and masked by ancient walls.

Thank fuck for preservation.

His back slammed into an old doorway as he subtly dismantled the Sentinels' guns with his mind. They were still close, but scattered, and wouldn't notice his meddling—something Jayson would use to his advantage as needed. He fucked with their knives for good measure as well and checked for anything else they could use as weapons from afar.

"Jayson," Lizzie breathed, her nails digging into his forearms.

"Sorry, Red," he murmured, easing his hold. He'd grabbed her harder than he meant to—a reaction to the approaching weapons. "We need to go."

"H-how do you know—"

"Guns," he replied quickly. "Now follow me." He grasped her hand and tugged her toward a side exit that was clearly not part of the original architecture.

His ability continued to scan for metal associated with gun power as he pulled a phone from his pocket. He'd texted Luc with an update when they arrived and also sent a message to Jacque to remain on standby.

Jayson had suspected the CRF would arrive and ruin their little field trip at some point, hence the necessary backup plan.

Jacque picked up on the first ring. "Yo."

"The CRF found us," he explained as Lizzie sputtered beside him. "We need a teleport. Now. Get B and have him explain to you where the *apodyterium* is located. He has fond memories of that place."

"On it."

The line went dead as Jayson leapt over a rope. He turned, grabbed Lizzie's hips, and hoisted her over it as well.

"I'm capable of doing that on my own," she snapped.

Jayson grinned despite the circumstance. "Probably, but this is more fun, Red." He winked and laced their fingers together. "Keep up."

She grumbled something incoherent, increasing his amusement as they moved at a brisk pace. At least her fiery personality hadn't died with the arrival of the CRF.

"We need to get rid of your phone," he said as they entered another home. They'd left her purse in the trunk of the car due to the Pompeii bag restrictions, but she brought her mobile, something he suspected the CRF was tracking. Or they had one inside her, like they did with Amelia.

Lizzie didn't argue. She handed him her mobile and watched as he smashed it into the corner of the room. "You're buying me a new one."

"Sure, sweetheart."

This time she took his hand in anticipation of being guided, eliciting a grin from him. She should have been terrified, but trust shone bright in her gaze. He supposed it helped that she didn't know about the sniper or have any idea how many Sentinels were on the ground.

"Remind me to kiss you later," he murmured. Completely inappropriate timing, but Jayson adored a strong-willed woman.

Her brow furrowed, but he didn't give her a chance to reply.

The *Stabian Baths* he desired appeared as he maneuvered them through another set of stone walls, and he increased their speed as they hit the open area.

Several tourists wandered about taking photos, providing what could have been decent cover if not for Lizzie's notable hair.

The CRF would identify her in an instant.

"In there," he said, gesturing to a solid doorway leading to the women's bathhouse.

"It looks like a dead end."

"Yep," he agreed as he guided her inside. "Keep moving."

She did, but slowed when they hit an open area filled with impressive mosaics. "Wow," she whispered as she tried to focus on walking and not admiring.

"I promise to bring you back here someday," he vowed. "But right now, I need your undivided attention. Move."

She nodded and continued the way he guided her until they hit a dead end. Jacque hadn't appeared yet, which wasn't a good sign.

"Uh, what now?" she asked, voice quiet.

"We wait or fight." He didn't have any weapons on him thanks to traveling by air, but he shouldn't need one. Jayson excelled in all manners of martial arts and a few other techniques not of this time period. Not to mention his affinity for metal.

"You're sure the CRF is here?" Lizzie whispered.

"Yes." He scanned the perimeter with his senses. The Sentinels appeared to be splitting up, which suggested either Lizzie's phone was the source of their tracking or something in these old walls was interfering with the signal.

"Okay." She sucked her lip into her mouth and chewed nervously. "I didn't see anyone I recognized."

"Not surprising. As much as I dislike them, the Sentinels are well trained."

She nodded. "Most of them are recruited from Special Forces, or the like. I always knew something was off with them. Nothing ever added up. Why all the traveling and secrecy?"

"They still do some good around the world," Jayson admitted. "But mostly to maintain their cover."

He sensed two guns enter the baths.

Four.

"They're coming," he warned. "Step over the rope and press your back to this wall."

She studied the mosaic on the floor and flashed him a skeptical look. "Isn't that illegal?"

Despite the situation, humor touched his chest. Just for a moment. Then he lifted her, set her where he wanted, and caged her against the wall with his body. "Don't move." Not that she could.

"But—"

He pressed a finger to her lips as a couple of tourists wandered in through the room's only entrance. They took in the sight with matching grins, snapped a few photos of the mosaic floor beside Lizzie's feet, and left.

I love this country. Displays of affection went unnoticed and undiscussed.

Jayson's amusement was short-lived as the gunmetal approached.

From the placement and nearness, he counted a pair of Sentinels carrying a duplicate set of firearms.

Easy.

CHAPTER EIGHTEEN

Trust and Conviction

Benefactor did not approve blood
tampering. Subject shall remain pure
and be tracked through other
reasonable means.

—Entry Log 101.02.4-7

"Try not to scream," he whispered as he stepped away to position himself on the other side of the entrance. Her rounded eyes touched his heart, but he needed to focus.

The Sentinels thought they were armed, giving Jayson the advantage.

Five.

Four.

Three.

Two.

As the first soldier stepped through the threshold, Jayson slammed his hand into the muscular man's throat, temporarily disabling him.

Unfortunately, that gave the Sentinel's partner enough warning to react. The blond tried to fire his useless weapon and threw it at Jayson when he realized it no longer worked. He followed it up with a punch that Jayson dodged and a kick to the ribs.

Evenly matched in size and strength, it became a dance of brute force.

Jayson went for the hit, but his opponent kept blocking and returning the favor.

Then the Sentinel made a fatal error by noticing Lizzie against the wall. Familiarity touched his features, and Jayson used the distraction to his advantage.

His fist collided with the blond's jaw, knocking him off balance and right into Jayson's knee. The Sentinel tumbled to the ground, where Jayson leapt on top of him and wrapped his hands around the man's throat. He sputtered and tried to grapple with him from the floor but failed.

"I'd say this isn't personal," Jayson said. "But that would be a lie." Because he recognized this jackass as the one lurking in Lizzie's building a few weeks ago. He'd been the one sent to check up on her after Jayson fucked with the surveillance equipment in her condo.

The blond's eyes dimmed as his oxygen supply depleted.

It would only be a few more—

"Jayson!" Lizzie squealed as the other Sentinel attempted to fire his weapon from the ground. The mechanism didn't trigger or move, causing him to pull out a knife instead as he climbed to his feet. He'd recovered faster than anticipated.

"Oh, that looks fun," Jayson said. He bent the blade with his mind while the blond beneath him lost consciousness.

"Code H, bathhouse," the Sentinel mouthed, but no sound came out as his windpipe had not yet recovered. So much for requesting reinforcements. And it seemed they didn't realize he was a Hydraian until now. Fascinating. What, did they think the sniper missed?

Jayson stood and took a defensive stance, when a familiar presence arrived, followed by a bullet firing into his opponent's skull.

Well, that was one way to handle the situation quickly, but a hell of a lot less fun.

"Next time, you need to be more specific," Balthazar chastised from behind him. "There were several baths I frequented in Pompeii, not just this one."

"There's only one *apodyterium*, B." Jayson turned as he brushed his hands against his jeans.

"In the historical records, sure," his friend replied. "But my memory is much vaster than a mere text."

"Can we go?" Jacque asked, holding out his hand. He and Balthazar both stood in the center of the roped-off area, while Lizzie remained plastered against the wall, eyes wide.

Right.

Not a good time to debate history with Balthazar.

He jumped over the rope and went to check on his startled companion. She flinched as he caressed her face. "Easy, Red. It's okay."

"You... you killed Charlie," she stammered.

That must have been the blond's name, and the way she said it sounded like she knew him well.

"He's just taking a nap, Liz. He'll wake up in a few minutes."

She met his gaze and blinked. "They tried to kill you," she whispered urgently.

"They usually do." He pulled her away from the wall and into his arms. "We'll have to finish our tour later."

"But this... I ..."

"Shh," he murmured as he hugged her. "We'll talk more once we get somewhere safe. Close your eyes, Red." He gestured for Jacque to join the group hug with Balthazar and grimaced as the sensation of whirling hit his abdomen.

Jayson's living room materialized around them, followed by a startled yelp from the naked woman on the couch.

Amelia.

One of the most alluring females in existence with her dark hair, striking blue eyes, and porcelain features. She resembled an angel, though she didn't look so angelic right now with the blond, male head between her legs.

Not what Jayson wanted to walk in on considering he loved the woman like a sister. Good thing her real brother wasn't with the welcoming party, or hell would ensue.

Tom's reflexes didn't disappoint as he yanked a blanket from a nearby cushion and tossed it over Amelia while also jumping to his feet in nothing but a pair of tented boxer shorts. His unashamed expression morphed into shock at seeing who stood before him.

These two lovebirds really needed to finish building their own home.

Lizzie trembled, her face tucked safely into Jayson's chest and away from the romantic scene.

"Not bad," Balthazar said, eyes grinning with mischief. "I'd deduct points for execution, as you get a better angle from, say, the counter, but overall a flat seven. Jay?"

"Don't you fucking knock?" Tom demanded.

"Not in my own fucking house, I don't," Jayson returned. "And I'm not rating that scene, B."

Bright pink splotches colored Amelia's cheeks as Lizzie froze. She'd obviously recognized Tom's voice.

"Sorry, we weren't expecting you," Amelia murmured as she found Tom's hand and gave him a healthy tug. He landed beside her but remained fixated on Jayson, or rather, the redhead in Jayson's arms.

"Yeah, the CRF found us in Pompeii. Which reminds me: I need to scan Lizzie for tracking devices." Not that it mattered here. The Sentinels would never attempt to enter Hydria, but there were other types of technology that could be running through her system.

"Mine was at the base of my neck," Amelia said softly, her complexion paling. "Tom removed it."

"I'll check there," Jayson replied as he drew soothing circles on Lizzie's back. She hadn't said a word or tried to move during their exchange. He pressed his lips to her ear. "You still with me, Red?" His words were whisper soft and for her alone.

Her fingers curled into his thin sweater so hard that he felt her nails through the fabric. "I-I can't."

The broken reply prickled his protective instincts.

"Let's go talk," he murmured, low enough for only her to hear. To the others he said, "We'll be in my room."

"Whoa, hold on a minute." Tom was on his feet again. "I don't think that's a good idea at all."

Jayson lifted Lizzie into his arms and cocked a brow at the young immortal. "That wasn't a request."

He didn't wait for or acknowledge a reply before starting down the hall to the master bedroom and kicking the door closed behind him.

Jayson stood in the center of the room, holding Lizzie, and admired the view out the balcony windows.

He missed his home, Hydria, the water, and the sunshine. But never had it felt quite like this. It was as if a missing piece of him had returned, except it had nothing to do with the scenery or his room and everything to do with the woman cradled against him.

The weight of the moment slammed into his chest, warming him inside and out. Everything about it seemed right, as if he was destined to be here, right now, with *her*.

Jayson never believed in fate or soul mates. He'd lived far too long for any of it to be real, but this connection forming between them surpassed logic.

He wanted to blame the serum or claim it was some sort of unique pheromone in her blood meant to seduce him. But no one else felt it except him.

It's all Lizzie.

Her intelligence floored him almost as much as her heart did. Sincerity flowed from her in waves, caressing everyone she met, and he adored that about her. She was charming, witty, and so beautiful it hurt.

And he was so done for, but fuck if he cared anymore.

All that mattered was her.

He slowly lowered her feet to the floor and held her close while she steadied herself. Her nails bit into his biceps—a physical indication that she didn't want him to let her go, which was fine by him.

"Talk to me, Red," he murmured as he palmed her nape. He gently prodded the area by her spine for a potential tracker beneath the skin. No bumps or obvious marks. He checked her hairline, but everything felt natural there as well.

He slid his hand to her face and eased her head back. Big brown eyes locked on his as her lips trembled.

"I-I can't," she stammered. The same words from before.

He studied her pale expression. The fear from Pompeii had been replaced by a deeper emotion, one that darkened all her features and creased the edges of her mouth.

Pain.

Ah, he understood now.

"You're not ready to be here." He tucked a loose strand of her hair behind her ear. "Okay, Liz. We can leave, but I need to check you for tracking devices first." Because he didn't want the CRF following them.

She blinked. "W-where?"

"Where will we go, or where do I need to check?" he asked.

"The former," she whispered.

He traced her lip with his thumb. "Somewhere remote,

just the two of us, while we sort all this out. But I need to know the CRF can't follow us there first."

Relief shone bright in her gaze as all her tension melted into warmth. She crumpled into him with a sigh. "Thank you."

His lips touched her forehead, then her temple, as he held her close and luxuriated in the rightness of it all.

Her arms wound around his neck as she hugged him with far more strength than he expected. He returned the embrace and rested his chin on her head. "How do you feel about Santorini or Turkey?"

"Aren't they close by?" she asked, voice small.

"They are, but both locations are beautiful." He paused, waiting to see if she would respond to that, but she stayed silent.

Hmm, we need something farther away.

Most European countries were out due to surveillance cameras, same with the United States and several countries in South America. The CRF had access to several systems worldwide, all with facial recognition software.

An island somewhere would be better.

The Caribbean was too close to New York City for his liking.

"How about the South Pacific?" he wondered out loud. "Tahiti, Fiji, or something similar?" All remote areas with little camera footage outside the airports. Since they would be using a teleporter instead of a plane, that wouldn't be an issue.

"Like Bora Bora?" she asked softly.

He grinned. "Sure, if you like that idea." They could go wherever she wanted. One of the perks of living forever was amassing unfathomable wealth. Most of his funds went into keeping Hydria healthy and thriving, but he maintained a private account as well.

She tilted her head back to see him, and the difference in her expression floored him. No more pain, only mild curiosity. He had accomplished that with a few words of understanding. Jayson rather liked the way that felt.

"That sounds warm," she said.

"There's a lot of water for cooling off."

"Bora Bora," she mused with a laugh. "Really? We can go there?"

"Well, we can't return to New York, and you're not ready to stay here, so why not go somewhere exotic. French Polynesia is private, beautiful, and far away from everyone. It sounds perfect to me." *And you'll pretty much be living in a swimsuit the entire time.* Nothing to complain about there.

She started to laugh, then paused, her eyes going wide. "I... Wow. I can't believe this is real life. I was in New York, Rome, Pompeii, now Greece, and now you're talking about the other side of the world." Her brow wrinkled as she laughed again with a touch of deprecation in her tone.

"The CRF sent people to kill me, and you're, like, three thousand years old, and Stas is a fledgling. Her boyfriend is a vampire, Tom is alive, and you totally kicked Charlie's ass. While I'm over here, just me, with a few added hormones. But why? I don't..."

He did not like where this rant was headed, nor did he like her paling cheeks or the look of despair shining from her beautiful brown eyes.

"This is all a mess, isn't it?" she continued, voice dropping to a whisper. "I'm a mess, I mean. And you're... Oh, you can't leave your home for me, Jayson. That's not fair to you, and I'm—"

He threaded his fingers through her hair and kissed her, hard. Her mouth opened, perhaps in protest, but he didn't care. That little rant set his blood on fire. Every word chipped at her confidence right before his eyes until she stared at him with an expression he never wanted to see on her face again.

Uncertainty.

Aimed at him.

And his feelings, his pride, and his place in her life.

Hell. No.

His tongue parted her lips and wasted no time in staking his claim. She moaned against him, spurring him on in his pursuit until every inch of her mouth belonged to him.

Mine.

No questions.

No arguments.

Fact.

"All bets are off now, Red." He licked a path down her neck. She knew the truth now, which meant no holding back. Luc's "no fucking" rule no longer applied, at least in Jayson's mind.

"I-I don't understand."

Oh, he doubted that. Her body understood every inch as it arched into him, begging for more.

But he could put it into words, if that's what she needed.

"Mmm, I intend to devour every inch of you, Lizzie." He brushed a kiss against her pulse and another over her jaw. "Inflict more pleasure than you can even imagine." His nose skimmed her cheek as he drew his mouth closer to hers. "And see how much of you I can make blush just by using my tongue."

Her gasp tasted sweet against his lips.

"Yes, I think you understand just fine," he whispered before taking her mouth the way he wanted—exploring, licking, and memorizing.

Lizzie melted against him, and he suspected the arm around her lower back was all that kept her upright. He would have grinned in amusement if the kiss hadn't devastated him just as intensely as it did her.

All Jayson wanted was more.

And so he took it.

The restraints of last week no longer applied.

He could take this woman how he wanted, for as long

as he needed, in any way he desired. Over, and over, and over again.

Except he craved this woman on a level he didn't know existed. It went beyond lust and physical desires and hit him so much deeper. Her touch burned his soul, implanting her memory there for decades, maybe centuries, to come.

It overwhelmed and consumed him, but fuck if he could stop.

And as her arms tightened around his neck, holding him even closer, he knew she yearned for this connection as much as he did.

Her little mewls of satisfaction only deepened as he palmed her ass to pull her flush against his aching cock. Over two months without a woman's touch, yet only she could satisfy him now. No one else would do.

She slid her palms down his arms to his hips and under his sweater to explore his heated skin. Eager little minx.

He adored how she came undone in his arms.

Beneath all the innocence was a passionate woman waiting to be unleashed.

He'd meant this to be a demonstration, not a claiming, but damn if he didn't want to dominate her right here and now. The alluring woman held more control over him and his actions than he cared to admit.

But this was neither the time nor the place. Especially with their unwelcome audience.

He'd felt the metal move as someone opened the door, and recognized the newcomer by the gun in his hand.

Only one person would be naïve enough to enter Jayson's bedroom armed. The man probably carried it out of habit, but the lack of a knock suggested a threat. As did the wave of angry energy rolling off him from the doorway.

Jayson slowly ended the kiss and brushed his lips over her cheek while maintaining his possessive hold.

"I wouldn't," he warned, his voice low with unveiled

fury.

Lizzie's hands stilled against his abdomen. "What?"

"He's talking to me," Tom replied, his tone equally livid. "I'm just here to check on her."

"And as you can see, she's fine."

"Is she?" Tom countered, sounding every bit like the older brother. Jayson would have laughed if it didn't piss him off.

Lizzie had tensed up again during the unwelcome conversation, infuriating him more. To the point where he wanted to put the young immortal's head through a wall for interrupting what was otherwise an enjoyable experience. He understood the protective reaction but also loathed the display of distrust.

"I suggest you remove yourself and your firearm from my room before something happens that upsets Lizzie more." A suggestion underlined with threat.

"Worried I might kill you?" he asked, cocky as ever. Jayson usually liked that trait in Tom, but not today.

"As entertaining as it would be to test the strength of your powers against mine, it would upset Lizzie greatly to watch *you* die," Jayson replied, confident. Tom was a strong Hydraian with impressive gifts, but age and experience would win this battle of wits.

Jayson finally met Tom's gaze over Lizzie's shoulder and let him see the severity of this transgression. "Amelia is like a sister to me, Tom. As such, I understand your concerns, and I'm willing to let this one instance slide. But try this again, and there will be consequences."

There was a reason Jayson had survived as long as he did, and it would be best for Tom to remember that. He let that conviction show in his eyes for a moment longer before returning his attention to the rigid woman in his arms.

"We'll be leaving soon," he whispered. "I promise."

She nodded slowly as faith dilated her pupils. That look undid him. He didn't know how he'd managed to convince her to trust him, but he would never take it for granted.

"I still need to scan you, and I think Luc will want to talk to you about a blood sample. Afterward, we'll go wherever you want, for as long as you need, okay?"

"Blood sample?" she repeated, sounding uncertain.

"He's out of options since the CRF serum doesn't tell us much."

"Oh…"

"But you can say no," he assured. "Everything that happens will be your choice. Always." And that applied to more than the research. He meant that in the bedroom as well.

She nodded again. "I've never been to Bora Bora."

He grinned. "You'll love it."

"Okay," she agreed, her lips curling into a small grin.

He nuzzled her nose. "Okay."

Their brief exchange, though meant to be private, must have appeased Tom as well, because he had left without a word.

Trust, it seemed, was the theme of the day.

CHAPTER NINETEEN

A Lesson in Confidence

Benefactor denied request to remove
pleasure receptors, stating subject
should feel satisfaction. Upgrade is
forthcoming.

—Entry Log 116.11.4-7

Lizzie expected a hotel room with beach views, not this gorgeous, secluded cabin on the ocean. There were others like it, but each one was strategically placed to give a semblance of privacy. And it came equipped with a private dipping pool, as well as an open deck to the salt water below.

And one giant bed.

"This is incredible," she said as she opened the balcony doors.

Jayson's scanner hadn't picked up any devices—indicating they were free to enjoy their stay without interruption—and the two large suitcases Jacque had teleported with them suggested they would be here for a while.

Lizzie had mentioned her job, not that it mattered anymore, and Jayson said someone would handle it for her. Whatever that meant. Something told her she wouldn't be working for a while, if ever again.

Being coddled should have bothered her, but after the last few days, she welcomed it and didn't ask any questions. She was just grateful to be away from Hydria and Tom. And Stas, too. The latter had showed up at the end of Lizzie's medical session with Luc and tried to express her regret, but it fell flat.

Lizzie wasn't ready.

She understood the reason Stas and Tom kept everything from her, at least on a logical level, but that didn't fix her broken heart. She needed time to think, and she couldn't do that with them barraging her with apologies.

This—the sea, the fresh air, and the new experience—was what she needed. And the fact that Jayson knew and understood that floored her.

She should be just as angry with him, but all the blame fell at Stas's and Tom's feet instead. Mostly because they were the ones who lied to her for months, even years.

Not Jayson. Everything he told her was a version of the truth with missing details. They were important omissions, but not nearly as devastating as the ones her best friends kept from her.

Tom was alive.

Stas controlled people and would someday be immortal.

Two very important facts that true friends would never

withhold.

Jayson's only fault was knowing the truth and not saying anything, but it was never his place to tell her. She understood that after their discussion on the plane, and perhaps even before that.

Her initial hurt had been the result of her intense feelings for him and the overall situation. But it took time to learn someone's faults and secrets, and their friendship was still very new. She thought that might be why she could be so angry with Stas and Tom, but not with Jayson.

Or maybe it went deeper.

Her connection with him defied comprehension. Staying in a room alone with him should terrify her, yet all she felt was satisfaction and perhaps a little bit of anticipation. Especially with the way he was looking at her now.

"Jacque bought you some clothes," he said as he wheeled over the suitcase.

She frowned. "He did? But how did he know my size?"

"I gave him the information he needed."

She glanced at the bag then back at him, uncertain. Her sizes varied by store, something her mother loved to ridicule her about. Because apparently, Lizzie had control over the fashion industry. "Uh, are you sure you got it right?"

His eyes roamed over her slowly and thoroughly, leaving her a little breathless. "I'm confident in my measurements." He set the suitcase on a luggage rack and unzipped it. "But feel free to try them on, Red. I'll be changing into swimming trunks."

She swallowed as he sauntered off with his own bag in the direction of the oversized bathroom.

Swimsuit. Yeah. She could handle that.

Her whole sense of time was backward after hopping from Rome to Hydria to Bora Bora, but she thought it was morning. A glance at the clock confirmed her theory.

Talk about the longest day ever. She could get used to

having a teleporter around.

Lizzie peeked at the contents laid out before her and grinned at the array of color. Sundresses, flip-flops, and several swimsuits.

Perfect.

Her jaw dropped as she found the lingerie. The French designer brand was one she knew well, but not one she ever purchased from.

"Oh, crap," she breathed. The gorgeously crafted handmade items were nothing like her usual flair, and very sexy.

Jacque picked these? Her cheeks warmed. *Oh dear.*

"I definitely think you should try those on," Jayson said as he entered the bedroom in a pair of black swim shorts. No shirt.

Her mouth watered at the sight of all that delicious muscle on display and, at the same time, dropped open at his comment.

"I... These..." She cleared her throat. "I'll just be putting on a swimsuit."

She grabbed one blindly and walked swiftly to the bathroom area. A huge round tub, a marble shower, and a double sink took up about a quarter of the space. The toilet was off to one side with an oversized walk-in closet across from it. Another long marble counter ran the length of the adjacent wall.

So much space for two people. No wonder Jayson only reserved one room.

Lizzie removed the outfit she purchased in Rome and folded it on the counter, and picked up the string bikini.

She held it up and nearly swallowed her tongue.

Not a full-piece bottom, but a thong with little strings at the sides.

That's what she deserved for rushing the selection process, but seriously, who wore thong swimsuits?

Lizzie pinched the bridge of her nose. She should have checked the swimsuit before undressing herself. Walking out there in a towel to dig through the suitcase would attract attention, as would putting all her clothes back on and starting over again.

Damn it.

Why would Jacque buy her such sexy outfits? Was it a European thing? Maybe all the women in Hydria wore thongs. Jayson probably wouldn't notice, right? Or he'd be comparing her to all the other women in his life.

No. She couldn't go there, or she'd lose all her confidence.

Right. Okay. She would wear it and cover up with a towel. Jayson would be none the wiser, especially if she jumped into the water after him.

The deep-red bikini top fit her perfectly, as did the bottom, though that didn't surprise her. Not a whole lot of fabric on a thong.

She found a towel, wrapped it around herself, and wandered barefoot into the bedroom, where Jayson stood waiting with the hotel phone in his hand. His other hand rubbed his chest idly, bringing Lizzie's focus to all that muscle again.

So hot.

Especially the way he drew his palm up to the back of his neck and squeezed, accenting his biceps.

Immortality seemed to gift men with insane sex appeal. Between Jayson, Issac, and Balthazar, the female gender didn't stand a chance. Neither did the males, for that matter.

As if hearing her thoughts, Jayson turned and winked at her while listening to whoever was on the phone.

"That sums it all up nicely, thank you." He hung up. "I arranged for an early dinner on the beach for after our swim. I figure we'll be hungry again by four or so."

"Uh, sure." She gestured toward the deck. "Okay. After you."

His gaze danced over her as he sauntered toward her instead of the open doors. She backed up into the wall and gulped as he entered her personal space without preamble.

"Why are you hiding?" he asked, voice deceptively soft. The heat from his chest radiated against hers, but he didn't touch her. Not physically, anyway.

"I-I'm not."

He traced the top of the towel, just over her breasts. "Liar."

Jayson tugged on the knot, and her hands flew up to catch the fabric before it fell. Butterflies took flight in her abdomen as he grinned at her instinctual reaction.

"I warned you, Red." A sharp yank sent the towel to the floor. "I'm done holding back."

Lizzie tried to cover herself, but he captured her wrists and pressed them against the wall on either side of her head. Warmth pooled between her legs at the show of dominance, causing her to squirm and Jayson to grin.

His gaze touched every inch of her bare skin, leaving her hot and bothered by the end of his exploration.

"This color looks amazing on you." Approval deepened his tone, sending a shiver down her spine despite the warm air. "I think we're ready to renegotiate limits."

She swallowed. "What did you have in mind?"

He slid her hands over her head, where he clasped one big palm around both her wrists. It left her feeling exposed and powerless, but she trusted her captor. And she was more than ready to further explore with him.

"This isn't about me, but about you, sweetheart." His free hand slid down her arm to her collarbone, and lower. Her nipples pebbled as he played his fingers over her cleavage. He tweaked one stiff peak without warning, eliciting a moan from Lizzie as she arched into him. It hurt, but the way he massaged it afterward felt so, so good.

"Mmm, I can work with that," he murmured as his touch shifted south. Her breathing escalated as he traced her belly button and ventured lower to the small patch of fabric covering her mound.

His eyes held hers as he slowly drew his thumb over

the top of her bikini bottoms to her hip bone before continuing the path of her swimsuit along the crease of her thigh. Electricity hummed in her veins as anticipation thickened the air between them.

"Not a limit," she breathed, telling him with words and her body that she was ready for whatever he wanted.

But rather than take what she offered, he skimmed his knuckles along her thigh, around to her bare ass. He cupped one cheek and applied pressure, forcing her hips to meet his.

"Do you feel that, Lizzie?" he asked, his voice low and seductive. "Do you feel how much I want you?"

God, yes. She nodded.

"Words, Lizzie." He pinched her ass in reprimand, then soothed it the same way he did her nipple. "Do you feel how hard I am?"

She swallowed and started to nod again, when she realized his demand. "Y-yes," she managed to say, though it sounded more like a groan.

"Good." His hand slid to the strings decorating her thighs. "Never belittle yourself by hiding, Red."

He held her gaze as he continued. "I promised never to lie to you, and I make no exception now when I say, you're gorgeous, Elizabeth. I've thought that since the first moment I laid eyes on you, and my attraction has only grown." He punctuated the point by pressing his groin into her again and drawing another moan from her throat in the process.

"I went easy on you the other night, sweetheart," he whispered darkly. "But your limits have expanded, and I intend to explore them thoroughly."

"Yes, please," she breathed as she arched into him again. They could swim later. Or during. She didn't care as long as it meant more of that pleasure he introduced her to over the last week. It was unlike anything she had experienced, and she yearned for more.

He tugged on the bow at her hip until it came undone.

Her heart rate kicked up a notch as he explored her freshly exposed curls with his thumb.

"I bet these are red too." His lips caressed her mouth with each word. "I can't wait to see how you blush down there while I'm tasting you."

Her knees trembled with the image his words evoked. What would it feel like with no barriers?

The other side of her bottoms came undone and fell to the floor between her legs. He licked her bottom lip before nibbling gently. "Hang on, Red," he whispered as he released her hands. "I'm going to devour you now."

That was the only warning he gave as he went to his knees before her and kissed her *there*.

"Oh God…" She tried to grab the wall and failed.

It was wicked, wet, and so very wild.

Her head fell back on a moan as his tongue explored her intimately. She thought the pleasure from the other night was intense, but it was nothing compared to this. His hands on her hips were all that kept her from falling.

His name fell from her mouth as a plea to never stop, but he controlled every move. She was a slave to his demands and the pace he set with his mouth.

"More," she begged, not knowing what she meant but knowing she needed something. Her thighs shook with the mounting pleasure, and she wondered how long she could remain standing.

He took the choice away from her by rising to his feet and kissing her soundly on the mouth. The taste of her own arousal knocked her legs right out from under her. Jayson lifted her into his arms without missing a beat and carried her to the bed.

The soft sheets soothed her heated skin, but only the man crawling over her could ease the ache between her thighs. She threaded her fingers through his thick hair and forced him to kiss her again. He grinned against her lips but placated her silent demand by sliding his tongue into her mouth and staking his claim on her soul.

Deep down, she knew no one would ever come close to making her feel as Jayson did. His skills set the bar too high, and she wouldn't have it any other way.

"Make love to me," she whispered. *Fuck me* were the words he probably wanted, but she couldn't seem to say them. They felt dirty and vulgar and so inappropriate for this moment.

He palmed her cheek and kissed her far too softly. "*Love* is not a word I use lightly, Lizzie." Another caress of his lips was followed by his tongue lightly dancing with hers as he untied the strings at her nape. He drew his nose across her cheek and pressed his mouth to her ear. "But it's a word I may just use for you."

Her skin burned as he trailed kisses along her throat to her breasts. His nimble fingers slid beneath her back to unfasten the top and tossed it aside. She bowed off the bed as he sucked her nipple deep into his mouth with a force she hadn't expected. Pain mingled with euphoria, confusing her nerve endings and heightening the pulse between her thighs. When his hand wandered down to explore her wetness, she moaned.

It was as if he had every button on her body memorized. He knew where and how hard to press to drive her insane with need.

Her hands were in his hair, tugging and pulling, as her body trembled uncontrollably beneath his.

And then he entered her. Not in the way she originally requested, but with two fingers twisting in a delicious pattern that brought tears to her eyes.

Heaviness weighed down her limbs as she fought for her elusive climax, but it evaded her.

Lizzie groaned in frustration as Jayson pulled away, and subsequently froze at the sight of him removing his swim shorts. He did so slowly, as if performing a striptease meant only for her, and tauntingly revealed the part of him she'd yet to see.

She licked her lips at the beautiful sight of him fully

nude and longed to explore him for herself.

He caught her hand and brought it to his mouth for a warning nibble. "Touch me now and we'll be doing this an entirely different way," he murmured as he settled between her thighs.

"I don't care how it's done," she breathed. "I just want you."

His erection prodded her slick folds and found her entrance with ease. Her hips flexed in encouragement, but his palms held her down.

"Minx," he murmured, his tone holding a touch of admonishment. "You're forgetting who's in charge again." His thick head slid inside her while he spoke, causing her to still beneath him. "This is going to hurt, Red."

Her lips parted to reply, but a shocked gasp exited instead as he penetrated her innocence in one swift move.

His warning did not prepare her for the severe reality of the experience. She thought it would be slow and didn't expect to be split in half by his impressive length.

Tears pricked her eyes, and not the good kind. She clung to his shoulders, begging him not to move again.

"Breathe." He nuzzled her neck. "Concentrate on me, sweetheart. Feel my mouth"—he licked a path along her throat—"and my touch."

His hands drifted up her sides to cup her breasts. She whimpered as his thumbs thrummed her stiff peaks.

"That's it, Red. Feel me." He nibbled her jaw while his fingers worked magic around her nipples. She pressed into him and jolted at the reminder of the fullness below, but it didn't throb in the way she expected; it was more of a tingle.

Lizzie lifted her hips to test the friction and found the movement far more pleasurable than she anticipated. Another shift had her moaning in approval.

His hot length branded her insides, claiming her as his in a way no other man ever had or would. He would forever hold her virginity, a gift she would never give anyone else, and she was oddly at peace with that.

His mouth took possession of hers as his body began to move. Slowly at first, almost teasingly so, before steadily increasing in power and in ferocity. He grabbed her hip to control the pace as his opposite hand cupped her cheek.

Her arms were around his shoulders, holding on for dear life as he wrecked her inside and out. Every thrust pushed her closer to the edge of something intense, and each swipe of his tongue against hers felt like a promise of souls.

Mine, some part of her proclaimed.

An irrational response, but one she couldn't deny in this moment.

All that mattered was the man mastering her body.

Her nails scored his back, marking him as he continued to devastate her future. Because no one would ever compare to Jayson and the feelings he evoked inside.

"You're so perfect," he whispered against her lips. "So fucking perfect." His hand shifted from her hip to the top of her sex where he found her swollen nub. It sent shocks to every inch of her being and created a dark yearning she couldn't ignore.

"Put your legs around me," he urged. She locked her ankles together against his ass and screamed as he slid deeper and harder into her.

"Oh, Jayson…" Her eyes rolled into the back of her head. That new spot, coupled with his expert touch, obliterated her grasp on reality.

Sensation and breathing were her only thoughts.

And pleasure.

Such intense discomfort, yet rapturous.

She couldn't think.

Couldn't breathe.

Couldn't move.

Just reveled in the motions and the feel of his body commanding hers.

"Shatter for me, Lizzie," he demanded. "Let it all go,

and come for me."

Her pulse hammered through her thoughts as her body yielded to his command. His thumb pressed down while he slammed into her harder than before, and her world went black, then light, as an explosion went off inside her.

Sounds she didn't even know she could make spilled from her mouth as she trembled from the most intense orgasm of her life. It rolled through her over and over and over again.

Sight failed her.

She was a puddle of bliss and nothing else.

Jayson groaned her name as he followed her over the edge after a few fierce thrusts. Warmth spilled inside her, joining her arousal and spiraling them both into a sea of ecstasy.

Lizzie panted from the onslaught of it all as her heart beat an unhealthy rhythm.

All her friends complained about their first times, but Lizzie could honestly say she had no regrets. Because that was phenomenal, and as soon as she could speak, she would ask for another round.

Jayson chuckled against her neck. "Don't worry, Red. We'll continue this exploration after we take a dip in the ocean."

She tried to respond but couldn't. It didn't surprise her at all that he sensed her wishes; he'd more than proven his ability to read her body language.

He went to his elbows on either side of her head. "How do you feel about swimming naked?"

CHAPTER TWENTY

Flirtatious Behavior

Subject is viable for conception.
Benefactor searching for suitable
candidate for initial testing.

—Entry Log 118.01.4-7

Lizzie resembled a mermaid on the beach with her damp red locks hanging alluringly over her blue sundress. She'd taken Jayson up on the skinny-dipping offer, something he thanked her thoroughly for. Twice. And she appeared well pleasured as a result.

"Why are you staring at me like that?" she asked.

He grinned. "Your naïveté floors me, Red." The

woman had no idea how sexy it was to watch her twirl her tongue around that straw. He kept envisioning his cock in its place.

Jayson's goal to ease Lizzie into their sexual relationship rested on thin ice. He wanted to introduce her slowly to his darker cravings, but if she kept licking her straw like that, he'd have her on her knees in the next five minutes with his dick down her throat. And wouldn't that be lovely for the waitress to see?

Lizzie's cheeks hollowed as she sipped her drink while watching him, and damn if it wasn't the most innocently erotic thing he'd ever seen.

"If you keep doing that, we're not going to make it through the main course." Because he'd be devouring her instead.

Her eyes widened as the straw popped out of her mouth. "What do you mean?"

He curled his finger in a beckoning manner. "Come here, Red."

Lizzie glanced around the mostly unpopulated area of the beach. Jayson had requested a private dinner near the water rather than in one of the restaurants. It meant their waitress left them alone for longer periods, and allowed for a more romantic experience, but anyone could walk by.

She licked her lips. "I don't—"

"Now."

"Uh." She cleared her throat. "Yeah, okay."

She stood, walked around the table meant for four diners, and stopped beside him with an arched eyebrow. "Happy?"

"Not yet." He relaxed into his chair and patted his leg. "Have a seat."

"You realize I'm not a dog, right?" she muttered as she did as he requested.

He wrapped an arm around her waist to pull her firmly into his lap, right where he wanted her. His mouth found her ear. "Do you feel that, Lizzie?" He knew she did by the way she froze after settling her ass on his hard cock. "That's because all I can think about is replacing your straw with my cock."

Her lips parted at his vulgar words as two splotches of pink painted her cheeks. "Oh…"

"Yes, *oh*," he murmured as he settled his palm on her exposed thigh and slid upward. "You drive me crazy, Red—in the absolute best way possible—which is why all this 'going easy on you' is very *hard*. Do you understand?"

He traced the seam of her new panties with his index finger and held her steady when she tried to squirm. No one could see what he was doing, something he ensured by angling her body the way he did, but Lizzie wouldn't know that.

"We've only begun to scratch the surface of what I intend to do to you, Elizabeth." He pressed his thumb to her clit and massaged the little nub through the handmade silk while she fought to breathe. "My appetites exceed traditional standards—a result of age and experience."

He sucked her earlobe into his mouth as he applied more pressure below. Her arousal seeped through the thin barrier while she tried to shift to close her legs. His palm prevented her thighs from touching, and his arm around her torso tightened in warning.

"You're going to come for me," he whispered. "But you're going to do it quickly before our dinner arrives."

"Jayson, I don't know…" She trailed off on a whimper as he increased the intensity and pace of his touch. The dampening fabric confirmed her enjoyment even as her mind rebelled against it.

A crack in her mental barrier was all he needed.

"Focus on the pleasure, sweetheart. Do you feel how hard I am right now? You're doing that to me, Red." He drew a hypnotic pattern with his tongue over her pulse before nibbling gently. Her breathing shallowed as her body tensed, all thought of their surroundings lost, just as he wanted. He hadn't meant to deliver this lesson over dinner, but he couldn't ignore the opportunity to play.

Jayson nuzzled her neck as she started to shake. "That's it, love. Give in to the sensations." He slid his palm up from her waist to her breast and pinched her erect nipple. "Let me feel you come, Lizzie. Now, sweetheart."

She shuddered and whispered his name as a benediction. He would never tire of that sound or the moan that followed as she crashed headfirst into oblivion and shook uncontrollably on his lap. His dick begged him to bend her over the table and fuck her until she screamed, but he reined in his yearnings and focused on the woman coming apart in his arms.

So much to teach her...

He would need years, maybe decades, to fulfill his craving for her.

I'm so fucked and don't even care.

His forehead rested against her shoulder as she came down from her high. He knew when reality returned, because she tensed and tried to scramble off his lap.

"Do that again, and I'll force another orgasm out of you, Red." He punctuated the point by roughly thumbing her sensitive bud. Her body jolted against his as another of those delicious whimpers left her mouth.

"What are you doing to me?" she asked breathlessly.

"Training," he replied against her neck. "And you're responding wonderfully to it." He removed his hand from between her legs and lifted his thumb to trace her lips. "Lick," he demanded.

She did with a tremble. "Oh God..."

"Mmm, I'll accept that nickname." He took hold of her chin and tilted her head back for a kiss. "You taste amazing, Lizzie. I think you'll be my dessert later."

Her cheeks darkened to that luscious shade he adored. "O-okay, but only if I get to taste you too."

The woman had no idea how fucking hot those words were, especially when spoken so innocently.

"I will absolutely be taking you up on that," he

promised. "After we eat dinner." He helped her stand and fix her dress just as the waitress strolled over with a tray of plates.

"Excellent timing, Jana," he said with a boyish grin. "That smells amazing."

The petite female beamed at him as she started decorating the table with food. "I hope you enjoy, Mister Jayson."

"I'm certain we will," he murmured with a wink. "Thank you."

"Can I get you anything else?" The touch of innuendo in her tone should have intrigued him, but it didn't. Not in the slightest. In fact, it sort of irritated him considering his obvious date, but some women would see that as a challenge. Still, he couldn't be rude.

"Not at the moment," he replied with another grin he knew women adored. "Thank you, though."

"You'll let me know when you're ready for dessert?" Another insinuation, one that reminded him of his plans later.

"I definitely will." He smiled a little too eagerly as a vision of Lizzie sprawled out naked in their bed graced his thoughts. It would be a very pleasurable night indeed. "Thank you, Jana," he said in a polite attempt to dismiss her.

"You are most welcome, Mister Jayson." She flashed him a promising look before flouncing away with her tray, leaving Jayson to shake his head in amusement. The female was pretty enough, but nothing compared to the beauty across from him.

He unfolded his napkin and eyed the array of dishes on the table. French cuisine was one of his favorites, but his companion didn't seem nearly as excited by the fare. Odd—she'd been thrilled about the menu when they ordered.

"What's up, Red?" he asked, confused by her furious expression. "Why are you glowering at me?"

Lizzie's eyebrows rose. "Seriously?"

Well, that was a response a man never wanted to hear.

He sipped his water and waited for her to say more.

"You're a jerk," she finally said, throwing her napkin onto the table. "No, I'm sorry; that's not the right term. You're a *player*. Of course, I already knew that. I'm the idiot for thinking this, us, or whatever..." She shook her head. "You know what? Never mind. I'm not hungry." She pushed away from the table, but he caught her wrist before she could walk away.

"Sit. Down." Two words. Softly spoken. Underlined in demand.

"Or what?" she countered. "You'll force an orgasm out of me at the table again and later seek the waitress out for dessert?" Her eyes shone with unshed tears as she looked imploringly at him. "I can't watch what happens next, Jayson. Just..." She sucked in her bottom lip as it trembled. "Please let me go." The broken quality in her voice undid him.

"Lizzie—"

"Don't, please. I just..." She sniffled, her eyes closing. "I'm fine."

He stood and pulled her into his arms because she was very clearly *not* fine. She stiffened, which both infuriated and shattered him. How had their dinner gone from pleasurable and promising to *this*?

And what the hell was she talking about with dessert? Why the fuck would he want that from the waitress when he had Lizzie?

"You're going to have to help me out here," he admitted. "I just finished telling you what I wanted to do to you after dinner, but you're implying I want the waitress instead. How did you come to that conclusion?"

She scoffed and tried to push him away. "You can't be serious."

"I'm very serious," he growled, irritated by her words and antics. He threaded his fingers through her hair and tugged her head back so he could read her expression as he added, "I've been nothing but honest with you from the beginning. Yet you're acting like I've deceived you in some way and are saying unflattering remarks regarding my personality, and I want to understand why."

She swallowed as the first signs of uncertainty filled her features. Now they were getting somewhere. "You were flirting with the waitress just like you did with the flight attendant," she said. "In front of me. Like I'm not here."

"Flirting?" he repeated, frowning. "I was being polite."

"By hitting on them!" she snapped, her fire returning. "I saw the woman on the plane give you her number, and you just promised the waitress to follow up on her offer for dessert, which I know has nothing to do with food. I might be inexperienced and naïve, but I can recognize sexual innuendo, Jayson."

"I see." He debated which point to tackle first and settled on the waitress. "Do you know what I was thinking about when Jana asked about dessert?"

Lizzie paled. "I don't want to know."

"No?" He arched a brow. "That's too bad because it was quite the picture in my head and starred you—very naked—in our bed."

Her eyes widened. "What?"

"And as for Rebekah," he continued, ignoring her confusion. "She gave me her number to pass along to Balthazar, because their preferences in the bedroom are well-suited." He considered whether or not to add this next part but decided holding back would only harm them at this point.

"She propositioned *us* on the plane, Red. It seems threesomes with handsome couples are her thing. I politely turned her down and suggested she reach out to B the next time she's in Greece."

Pink splotches decorated Lizzie's cheeks as her mouth popped open in surprise. "A threesome?" she whispered, scandalized.

"Yes, it's not uncommon. But as I told Rebekah on the plane, I have no intention of sharing you with anyone. Ever." The words came out with more conviction than he anticipated, but it felt good to admit it out loud. "I won't even share you with Balthazar." Those words were for himself more than for her and sent a shock to his heart.

Jayson never denied Balthazar when he wanted to bed a woman.

But Lizzie?

Oh, he would be fucking denying that.

Jayson's blood boiled at the thought of B touching *his* redhead.

Well, that's new.

He always shared.

Not her.

"You're hurting me," Lizzie said, voice strained.

Jayson relaxed his arm around her back, as well as the hand in her hair. "Sorry, Red." He hadn't meant to squeeze her—or even realized he'd done it. "My mind wandered to something unpleasant."

She swallowed and nodded, her brow creasing. "So, um, you didn't plan to see the flight attendant in Rome?"

"Of course not. I expected the CRF to find us, though I hoped they wouldn't. At no point did I intend to see her again, nor do I have any interest in our waitress."

"But you agreed to dessert?"

"Yes, with you," he murmured, grinning. "If you heard desire in my response, it was not directed toward her, Red. Only you."

She pursed her lips, and he could tell she wanted to say something but kept second-guessing herself. When she shook her head and forced a smile, he knew this conversation was far from finished.

"Say what you need to, Lizzie. Don't dance around it or hide. I expect honesty between us and will accept nothing less. That's the only way we'll ever work."

She blinked. "You talk about us like we have a future."

"Don't we?" He searched her beautiful eyes for answers but only saw more questions. "You need to help me out here, Red. I thought you wanted something long-term. Am I wrong?" He had better be right because short-term wasn't going to work for him. Not with her.

"What's long-term to a man of three thousand years?" she asked. "I mean, from what I gathered from your friends, you enjoy bedding multiple women at a time and eating breakfast as a giant group after a night of sexcapades. Oh, and Tristan insinuated that you usually share. So, as the man with all the experience, you tell me—what should I expect?"

"I don't know," he admitted as he combed his fingers through her damp hair. "All my relationships have been ones of an open nature. Eternity is a long time to promise yourself to one person—something all my former long-term lovers understood. They usually took other partners to keep things interesting but came to me when they wanted something familiar, and vice versa."

She scrunched her nose and pinched her lips to the side. "Okay, so an open relationship where I sleep with whomever I want and you do too?"

His stomach twisted at the thought of another man touching Lizzie. "Absolutely not."

Her eyes rounded. "But that's what you just described."

"No. I mean, yes, I did, but that wasn't in reference to us." He dropped his arm from her waist to palm the back of his neck.

Why was this so difficult? Jayson understood women, adored them, bedded them all the time, and yet this one had him tongue-tied and irrational. She'd just thrown up the alternative to bed her for as long as he wanted with the option of remaining open, and he'd turned it down without hesitation.

He needed his head examined.

Jayson did not do jealousy. He was a free spirit, and her description fit him perfectly—except when it came to her.

"I don't want you to take other partners, Lizzie. With or without me, the notion of another man touching you is enough to drive me mad, something I can honestly say has never been an issue for me." He let go of her completely to take a step back, both of his hands going to his hair as he paced in front of her.

"I don't want to share you, either," she said quietly. "It hurts when you flirt with other women. A lot."

Her gaze fell to the sand as her shoulders hunched, indicating that those words were not an easy admission. But they were words he needed to hear.

Jayson developed his charming candor with females over the centuries with the primary purpose of attracting them to his bed. It came so naturally to him now that he didn't even think about it, he just acted. And it clearly hurt Lizzie.

He cupped her cheeks to tilt her head upward again and swallowed hard at the pain radiating from her beautiful eyes. "You were right," he murmured. "I am a jerk."

She started to shake her head, but he stopped her response with a brush of his lips against hers.

"I thought my firsts were well and truly in the past, but this—us—is definitely brand new to me." His fingers slipped into her hair as he pressed his forehead to hers.

"You make me want to try something different, Red. Something I've never considered before. But it's going to take patience and time because my habits are very old, and I'll need you to tell me when I'm hurting you, just like you did tonight. Can you do that, Lizzie? Can you be honest and tell me when I'm doing something that wounds you?"

The begging quality to his voice was one he didn't hear often, but Lizzie brought out a side of him he rarely allowed anyone to see. He considered it his weakest link, but also his greatest strength.

His heart.

He wouldn't say he loved her—they didn't know each

other well enough for that—but he could see the potential *to* love her. She touched him in a way few ever had, and every part of him itched to stake his claim.

Mine.

A natural drive he rarely felt around a woman, but Lizzie caressed every possessive instinct he owned. The dominant in him understood patience, while the soul in him recognized his potential mate.

Lizzie licked her lips and parted them twice before replying, "I can call you a jerk when I need to."

He grinned. "Yeah?"

She nodded, her lips curling. "Maybe an asshole too."

He pulled back in mock surprise. "Did you just curse?"

"I curse. Sometimes. When it's warranted." Her brow came down. "My mother always said people used bad words when they couldn't think of anything more intelligent to say."

"Yeah, well, your mother's a fucking bitch, so I think I'll ignore that ineloquent deduction."

Lizzie laughed. "You say that like you know my mom."

"I may not have met the woman, but I watched her with you at brunch that day, and my summary is more than accurate. It took considerable effort not to throw her through the window."

Lizzie's eyes rounded. "You were at brunch?"

"Hormonal drinks, remember?" he prompted. "Speaking of which, we should probably eat our now-cold food. Unless you're still not hungry?" He cocked a brow, daring her to deny her need for sustenance. If she claimed not to be famished, his ego would be wounded.

Fortunately, she nodded in agreement. "Dinner." She gazed up at him through her lashes as she added, "Followed by dessert."

"As if that was ever a question," he murmured against her lips. "And tomorrow we'll have breakfast in bed."

Lizzie's lips curled into an impish smile. "I think I like the sound of that."

CHAPTER TWENTY-ONE

Let's Play a Game

Two weeks of sex and sun looked good on Lizzie. Her cheeks held a healthy glow, her eyes shone with the secrets Jayson had taught her, and her lips seemed perpetually curled into a smile. The lingerie helped with the latter.

She clipped her silk stockings into the garters and adjusted her cleavage in the lacy top. Jayson had given her a tutorial last week on how to wear all the fancy French

287

garments, and she'd enjoyed taunting him with that knowledge ever since.

Lizzie adored fashion. This newfound obsession with lace would not go away anytime soon. She loved how each set was strategically placed to appear revealing without actually showing anything truly intimate. And even more, she enjoyed Jayson's reactions.

Another once-over in the mirror produced an even bigger grin on her face.

Perfection.

A confidence boost was among the gifts Jayson had given her these last few weeks. After so many hours naked in his presence, it seemed silly to hide.

And the way he looked at her when she dressed up for him like this? Worth every ounce of hesitation.

She sauntered into the bedroom to wait for Jayson. He'd drawn her a bath in the oversized tub before venturing off to the market to procure some fresh fruit for the room, but she expected him to return any minute now.

Lizzie poured herself a glass of wine and admired the calmness of the waves. Jayson remarked last night that it reminded him a bit of home, something she took as a subtle sign that he wanted to return to Hydria soon.

Luc had visited twice, briefly each time, to ask a barrage of personal questions—similar to a physician—and to take more samples. She didn't really enjoy being his personal test subject, but she also wanted answers, so she allowed it.

Deep down, though, she knew if she *really* desired the truth, she needed to leave Bora Bora. The selfish side of her scoffed at the idea, while the part of her who adored Jayson dwelt on the unfairness of forcing him to stay here. Not that he seemed to mind, because he—

"Well, that's a sight to behold."

Goose bumps scattered down her spine at the familiar voice behind her. It came from a man she never expected to see again.

She swallowed her nerves as she turned to meet a pair

of amused brown eyes. All his fatherly appeal seemed to be replaced by a man she barely recognized. The way his gaze danced over her in an appreciative manner stirred up bile in the pit of her stomach.

"Doctor Fitzgerald," she managed.

"Come now, Lizzie, I think you can call me John while dressed like that." He gestured to the armed blond beside him. "You remember Stark, yes?"

She tried to nod but couldn't. Not with the way both men had her cornered by the water. She could jump, but where would she go? To the beach? Her dancer's legs didn't translate well in the water, not to mention her lacy undergarments would weigh her down. The two men would either catch her or beat her to the sand.

And they probably weren't alone, either.

"Shall we go?" Stark asked, his voice bored. He hadn't bothered to glance at her or her seductive attire, something she felt minutely grateful for, especially with the manner in which John kept glancing at her breasts and legs.

Twenty-four years and he always treated her like a daughter. But it was all a lie, and she could see that in his lecherous gaze.

"Not yet." John closed the gap between them. He fingered a strand of her hair as he asked, "Would you care to change before we go?" Innocently worded and belittled by the smolder in his gaze.

Lizzie always wondered why John appeared no older than thirty-five, but now she knew it was a result of his Ichorian bloodline. "I would," she admitted, unable to lie. From what she understood, he excelled at forcing the truth out of people, and it was no different with her.

"Please do," he gestured to the suitcase. "You'll understand why it has to be in front of us, though. I already lost you once and can't afford for it to happen again. You're an expensive investment, after all."

She shivered at the bluntness of his words. "What do you mean?"

"We'll discuss it along the way," he replied. "You have two minutes to change. I suggest you use the time wisely."

Lizzie considered telling him to go to hell but opted for sense instead. She couldn't try to run in this outfit without garnering a lot of attention. Jean shorts, a tank top, and tennis shoes would be far more appropriate.

A snakelike sensation crawled over her skin as he supervised her removal of the garter belt and stockings. Stark still didn't acknowledge her but focused on the perimeter.

Scanning for Jayson.

If she could find a way to delay their departure, maybe he would return in time to kick John's ass.

Lizzie finished her show of dressing by pulling a tank top over her head and folded her arms to hide herself from John's view. She'd managed to keep the important bits covered, but his grin said it didn't matter.

This John—despite the similar features—resembled a stranger and left her feeling cold, used, and inadequate.

She shivered as his smile grew.

"I think we should play a game and find out just how far this infatuation goes," he mused. "Would you like that, Lizzie? To learn Jay's true feelings?"

"Do we have time for that, sir?" Stark asked, an edge to his tone that wasn't reflected in his bored expression.

"Of course. Why else did we come prepared?"

"Because we assumed he would be here, sir."

"And I suspect he will be any moment now." John touched his ear. "Any sign of the Elder?" He nodded at whatever the person on the other side of his communication unit was saying. "Excellent." He glanced at Stark. "I told you Patel's gadgets would work."

The Sentinel shrugged one shoulder as he drew a gun. "We won't know for sure until he enters."

"Fair enough." Dark chocolate eyes met hers. "Be a dear and come stand by me, please." So politely worded and perfectly John.

And yet, everything between them had changed.

This man was a monster—an Ichorian—who founded an organization meant to hunt other immortals. And he'd done something to her, though no one knew what. Then there were the things Jayson had told her about Tom and a Hydraian named Amelia.

Lizzie would never trust Jonathan Fitzgerald again. And she certainly didn't want him to touch her.

"No," she replied, surprising herself and him. Years of elegance training kept her hospitable even in the most uncomfortable situations, but no more. What did she have to lose? He'd already implied she was an 'expensive investment.' That meant he wouldn't kill her, right?

"Sir," Stark murmured.

"I heard it," John replied as he stepped toward Lizzie. She started to back up out of his reach, not that she would get far on the deck, unless she jumped—

She fell to her knees as something sharp smacked her upside the head. Right above her ear. It throbbed and distorted the room.

An arm around her torso yanked her up against a hard body as something razor sharp pressed into her neck.

"Careful, sir, or the benefactor will not be pleased," Stark remarked, voice cold and void of feeling. He could have been talking about the weather for all he seemed to care.

"You let me worry about that." John's response came from behind her, confirming he'd been the one to smack and grab her.

Had he hit her with the blunt edge of the blade pressed to her throat?

"Try not to move, Lizzie. This isn't your average knife." He sounded amused by that, and she could think of only one reason why.

It's not made of metal.

She tried to focus on the firearm in Stark's hand, but it wavered in and out of her vision. The tears collecting in her eyes didn't help matters.

John shifted to place his back to a wall while holding Lizzie in front of him. The arm around her waist reminded her of a contracting band as he squeezed the air from her lungs. A whimper escaped Lizzie's throat, which resulted in a chuckle from her captor.

"That's for forgetting your manners," he murmured against her ear.

She had no idea he could be this cruel. Hearing about it from Jayson and seeing it were two very different experiences. No wonder Tom had faked his death. From her understanding, John didn't know. He also thought Amelia was dead. If only she could escape in a similar manner.

"I found those baby bananas you love, Red," Jayson announced as he entered the suite.

Lizzie opened her mouth to respond, but John's constricting arm warned her not to while Stark positioned himself defensively beside them.

Silence followed, suggesting Jayson suspected the disturbance.

"By now you've sensed our weapons are not of the traditional variety," John said by way of greeting. "But trust me when I say they are just as deadly."

Bags rustled against the ground before Jayson stepped around the corner empty-handed. He didn't look at Lizzie but focused on the man behind her. "Hello, Jonathan."

"Jayson," he greeted back. "I wouldn't come any closer unless you want to see what a diamond-encrusted ceramic knife can do against skin."

Jayson lifted his hands in surrender, his expression expertly blank. "You have my undivided attention."

"Do I?" John mused. "Excellent. I was just suggesting a game to Lizzie. Would you care to play?"

"Depends on the parameters." Jayson folded his arms. "What did you have in mind?"

"It's simple, actually. You see, that gun"—he gestured

to the one Stark had pointed at Jayson—"is filled with glass incendiary bullets. A new technology we devised specifically with you in mind. Your penchant for metal is a tricky one."

Lizzie trembled. Jayson told her the purpose for incendiary bullets. *They set the blood on fire, thereby permanently killing immortals.* Yet he merely yawned and waved his hand in a gesture to continue. "Go on."

"Well, the threat is clear, yes? But I'm willing to give you a choice. Consider it a way of respecting my Elders." The grin in his voice didn't seem to entertain Jayson at all. If anything, he looked about as bored as Stark.

Did he call Jacque for backup? Lizzie wondered. She tried to catch his gaze, but he remained fixated on the one behind her. John shifted his hold, raising his arm to cross her breasts instead of her waist, and she cringed at the intimate touch, but the knife at her throat kept her in place. At least her vision had cleared.

"Get to the point, Jonathan," Jayson demanded, his calm veneer cracking.

"I'll allow you to leave, unharmed, if you go now without Lizzie."

"Or?" Jayson prompted.

"Or Stark kills you."

"I'm not a fan of either option," Jayson drawled. "Surely you can be more creative than forcing me to choose myself over Lizzie."

"I admit, I assumed the choice to leave would be obvious."

"The last time an Elder trusted you, you shot him. I won't be making the same mistake."

John tsked. "Now, now, let's not live in the past. Not when we have a future to discuss." His fingers danced along Lizzie's arms, causing her stomach to churn. "All right, the third option is to let Stark collar you. It thwarts a fight and allows you to stay with Lizzie."

Her eyes widened. Jayson had mentioned the device

that controlled Amelia. "No, Jayson—" The blade bit into her skin, silencing her instantly.

"Your betters are talking, Lizzie. It's rude to interrupt." He squeezed her again, hard enough to draw out another whimper. "You broke my product, Jayson. I have to say, I'm displeased."

"I'd argue I improved it," Jayson replied, his voice underlined with emotion. "I accept option three."

John stilled behind her. "The collar?"

"Yes." No hesitation, and he still refused to look at her. If he did, he would have seen her imploring him not to do this. Not for her. Not ever. There would be another way. There had to be.

"Truly?" John sounded surprised. "For her?"

"Yes."

"First Issac. Now, the renowned Jedrick of Babylon?" John laughed humorlessly. "The world must be coming to an end."

Jayson cocked a brow. "Are we done playing this game?"

John chuckled. "Sure. Be a good Elder and kneel for Stark."

"Don't!" Lizzie shouted, unable to hold it in anymore. She tried to say more, but the air whooshed from her lungs as John crushed her with his arm. Her ribs and chest ached at the show of strength as her heart shattered in two at the sight of Jayson going to his knees with his hands loosely at his sides.

Still he wouldn't look at her, but she caught the tension in his jaw. He was holding back. For what, she didn't know.

You'd better have a plan, she thought as black dots danced over her vision.

"Really, Lizzie," John chastised. "You're acting like a child."

And you're acting like a dick.

Stark pulled a collar from his pocket and stepped

forward to wrap it around Jayson's neck. It sealed with a snick that seemed to ricochet through the room. He didn't move from his submissive pose even as the Sentinel backed away.

"Well, that worked out better than I expected." John sounded quite pleased as he finally loosened his hold enough for Lizzie to breathe. It struck her as odd that she hadn't passed out despite the darkness lurking in her gaze, but she didn't have time to think about it.

"I say we play one more round of truth," the monster behind her murmured. "Stark, send the text."

"Yes, sir."

Jayson finally looked up from the floor. "This isn't good enough for you?"

"Hardly," John scoffed. "There's a loose end that needs addressing."

"It's done," Stark informed. "I suspect we will know within minutes if your hunch is right."

As he said it, a buzzing sounded from Jayson's pocket.

"That would be your phone, I imagine," John surmised. "Let it ring."

Her lover shrugged. "As you wish."

"Oh, I'm enjoying this far more than I should."

"Enjoy it," Jayson replied. "It'll be short-lived."

"So confident for an immortal completely at my mercy. I did give you the option to leave."

Jayson's eyes smoldered as he narrowed them over her shoulder. "You did, and trust me when I say I won't be returning the favor."

"We'll see." John sounded more amused than frightened, something Lizzie suspected would be a mistake. Because Jayson's expression had transformed from polite boredom to lethally serious.

"We will," he agreed, voice colder than she'd ever heard it.

A frantic knock sounded at the door, sending relief to Lizzie's heart. That must be Jayson's backup, though why the Hydraian's would knock—

"Lizzie!" Stas's voice called through the door. "I know you're mad at me, but I need you to open up!"

Jayson flinched as John sighed. "And there's my answer."

"It would appear so, sir," Stark agreed. "Shall I let her in?"

"No, Lizzie will do that for us." The knife disappeared from her throat. "Be a dear and let Stas in, and don't even think to warn her, or Stark will put a bullet in Jayson's head. Actually..."

He removed his arm and turned her to face him, his expression excited.

"I'll allow you a choice, Lizzie. Warn Stas, Jayson dies. Don't warn Stas, Jayson lives, and, well, we'll see what happens."

"Oh, fuck no," Jayson growled.

Lizzie shook her head as tears collected behind her eyes. "That's an impossible choice." Jayson or Stas? She could never pick between them. As angry as she was at Stas, she didn't want to hurt her.

And Jayson... The idea of losing him twisted her up inside.

No.

She couldn't, *wouldn't*, let him die.

But Stas...

Another frantic knock had John grinning. "Tick tock, Lizzie. Make a decision. Now."

"I-I can't. You can't—"

"Shoot him," John instructed. "Now."

"No!" Lizzie jumped backward on instinct, placing herself between Stark and Jayson. "No. I'll... I'll decide. I'm deciding. I just..." She trailed off as a violent tremor shook her from head to toe.

Jayson's gesture of kneeling and accepting his fate left her without a choice.

She couldn't let him die. Not for her.

And John didn't know about Stas's immortality, at least according to their intelligence. That could be used to their advantage, as well as her ability to persuade.

Lizzie swallowed, her resolve solidifying.

This was the appropriate play and the only one that kept Jayson alive. Because the look on Stark's face said he wouldn't hesitate to pull the trigger, even if it meant shooting through her.

"I-I'll open the door," she decided as yet a third knock sounded, followed by Stas begging Lizzie to talk to her and Jayson's phone vibrating again.

"Excellent," John replied. "Escort Stas in here, please."

Lizzie nodded even as Jayson said her name in warning.

"You're not the only one who gets to make sacrifices," she whispered as she turned toward her fate. Her hands were shaking uncontrollably as she unlatched the door.

"Oh, thank God," Stas said as she threw her arms around Lizzie. "The CRF is coming. Jacque left for reinforcements, but I demanded he drop me off first to warn you and Jayson, who isn't picking up his phone."

Lizzie awkwardly hugged her back while her mouth refused to work.

Run, she wanted to say.

Stay, her heart begged.

Because Stark probably had his gun to Jayson's head, and the image sent a chill down her spine. She swore her soul cried at the thought. They had decided to be exclusive but never discussed their feelings.

This situation told her all she needed to know.

She loved him. More than she ever knew was possible.

Tom had been a crush.

Jayson? He was the real deal, and his life hung in the balance because of her indecision.

But her best friend... She loved Stas too.

An unfair choice.

She squeezed her friend as the emotions threatened to destroy her. "I'm sorry," she whispered. "I'm so sorry."

"Hey, that's my line," Stas murmured. "I'm the one who's sorry. I should have told you, especially about—"

"Don't," Lizzie said, cutting her off before she could say the name that would derail everything. *Tom.* "I... We..."

God, how could she walk her friend into the lion's den? How could she leave Jayson there to suffer?

He stayed for her.

He kneeled for her.

He took the collar for her.

It was about more than duty and protection for him. She knew with her soul that he felt the same abnormal connection, and saw it in the way he looked at her. Even if he wouldn't admit it out loud.

Love.

Or at least the beginning of it.

"You're shaking." Stas pulled back to grasp Lizzie by the shoulders. "I promise the CRF won't touch you."

Too late.

Stas's lips curled down as she studied Lizzie's expression and, worse, her neck. "How...?"

"I'm disappointed, Lizzie," John said as he joined them in the hall with a gun in his hand. "But not nearly as disappointed as I am with you, Stas."

Her best friend froze, her lips working on silent words as shock drained the color from her features.

"It's a shame," he continued. "You had so much potential, but I've suspected for some time that you were playing both sides. I assume your lover is as well, which is truly his loss. What me and my benefactor are creating is far greater than Issac can even imagine." He sighed dramatically. "Well, he can consider this a message. Goodbye, Stas."

The bullet cracked through the air before Lizzie could blink.

She yelped in response.

And screamed as the life drained from her best friend's

eyes.

It happened so slowly.

Her body seemed to float in the air, suspended in time as death registered.

And suddenly she was falling to the ground, her green eyes wide with emotions left unsaid.

Lizzie collapsed as her knees gave out. "No!" she screamed, her heart breaking into a thousand pieces. "NO!"

She shook her head as the tears fell.

This couldn't be happening.

He didn't kill Stas.

Her immortal genetics…

Except he said they were incendiary bullets—specially manufactured to kill immortals of all types. Fledglings included.

"No," she sobbed, her body folding over the ground as the weight of emotion crushed her spirit. "No, no, no…"

"Lizzie," John said, his voice holding a sharp demand. "I need your focus."

She shook her head, unable to yield. He'd just killed her best friend. Without a single ounce of remorse. As a fucking message.

NO.

Quivers racked her spine as she fought to breathe through the pain.

Then the unthinkable happened.

Another gunshot.

This one at the end of the hall, leading into the living area.

She glanced up into Jayson's vacant eyes and blinked in disbelief.

No.

He wouldn't… That… He promised…

"You made your choice," John murmured as he holstered his gun above Jayson's corpse. "He paid the consequences of your indecision. But don't worry, Lizzie.

You'll have a long, long time to live with the repercussions of this moment, as I suspect his life lives on inside you now."

She couldn't breathe, couldn't think.

Jayson...

Dead.

Because of her.

This had to be a bad dream.

Just yesterday he kissed her on the beach.

But his eyes...

So broken.

So... lifeless.

His lips were parted on words she didn't hear. Did he say her name? So shadowed in her own grief over losing her best friend, she didn't get a chance to say goodbye.

He would never know how she felt.

Jayson died thinking his sacrifice meant nothing, that she wasn't willing to make the same choice, that she didn't love him as he did her...

Oh, Jayson.

Something shattered inside her, rendering her immobile.

Her soul detaching from her body?

Her heart?

"I suggest we get moving," Stark said as he knelt beside her and pricked her arm with something.

She couldn't move.

Didn't care.

Escape meant nothing.

What was the point of living without the two most important people in her life?

Dead.

Because I couldn't decide.

Because I exist.

No longer.

Oblivion swallowed her, relieving her of this nightmare.

Blessed relief, lifting her to a dreamlike state where she

searched for Jayson, for surely he would meet her here.

Except all she saw was darkness.

A future without friends or love.

A future in a cage.

Home, her subconscious supplied. *Where we belong.*

She blinked inwardly at that thought.

That's not...

A vision of white lab coats, cameras, and endless tests flashed behind her eyes.

Memories or nightmares?

Home.

We're going home.

CHAPTER TWENTY-TWO

Welcome Back

Subject's vitals are steady. Will
commence resuscitation at 0800 hours.
Need to create new log for Subject
4-7.1.

—Entry Log 124.11.4-7

Lizzie awoke in a sea of white.

Walls, blankets, furniture, and curtains, all pristine. Even her pants and tank top were colorless.

A sense of déjà vu overwhelmed her as she sat up in the fluffy bed.

Sunlight streamed through the floor-to-ceiling windows.

Where am I?

A bandage on her arm suggested someone had recently taken blood from her. She removed it and examined the healing mark, indicating the invasive procedure was in fact recent.

She shifted to stand and winced at the weakness in her limbs. *How long have I been asleep?*

That strange feeling of having been here before swept over her again as she moved toward the glass. Evergreens and a clear blue sky stretched out for miles. She'd seen this before, but the memory evaded her.

A gentle knock preceded the opening of the room's only door.

Familiarity hit her in an instant, but she couldn't recall the bald man's name. His ancient green eyes spoke to her on a level she didn't understand, and as his lips curled, a feeling of foreboding twisted her insides.

I don't like him.

She didn't know why, but the feeling of hatred toward him superseded reason.

"Don't worry, little one. Your memories will be returned to you eventually." He clasped his hands behind his back as he sauntered toward her. "How do you feel?"

"Confused," she admitted. "Where am I?"

"In my home," he replied. "For now, anyway. Jonathan would prefer you in the lab, but I think this will prove a less stressful environment for you. You can return to him once you've given me what I need."

She swallowed. "Which is what?"

He smiled. "Your progeny."

My what? How?

Lizzie blinked as images surfaced behind her eyes.

New York City. Campus. Stas. Tom.

Jayson.

It seemed lost behind a cloud, the information she needed on the cusp of her mind...

"Yes, Jonathan felt inclined to introduce chemicals to

your system to keep you more compliant. As I do not want anything to jeopardize the life growing inside you, I've ceased the treatment. You are mine, after all."

"I—I don't understand."

"No, I imagine you wouldn't." He gave her a dismissive smile. "Reimagining your childhood was the only way to fulfill the final test, and I must say, it far surpassed my expectations. When they suggested giving you unloving parental figures, I questioned it, but the outcome worked just as they anticipated. You craved love and affection, thereby allowing others to easily manipulate your emotions. Fascinating, really. I can't wait to explore the depths of that programming myself."

She shook her head, not following. *Reimagining my childhood?*

"Now, your preference for dancing? That was my idea, as I've always enjoyed the ballet. And the beauty pageants were also my suggestion. Granting you second place after almost every competition instilled that drive to constantly do better while also ingraining a sense of elegance in you. I mean, the last woman I want is an insolent one."

He clasped his hands together. "Well, in any case, I'm pleased. I never expected an Elder to take the bait, but I'm thrilled that he did. It's the perfect final test before we begin."

Why the emotional profile?

And begin what?

A knock at the door caused him to turn with an arched brow at the female visitor. "Apologies, Sire, but Skye is having an episode."

"I see. Thank you, Jezebel. I will be right there."

"Of course, Sire."

Osiris, her brain finally supplied. That was this being's name.

How do I know that?

"We'll continue our discussion soon," he murmured. "For now, eat the food that is provided and behave, and

I'll allow you to remain unrestrained in your room. I may even bring you some books. Assuming you still enjoy them?"

She frowned. Fortunately, he wasn't looking for a response. He merely smiled as if amused. "It's lovely to have you here again, especially now that your purpose has arisen. Enjoy your afternoon."

With those strange words, he left, the door latching firmly behind him.

Lizzie blinked several times, confused.

More images trickled through her thoughts, these more erotic in nature.

Jayson kissing her. She touched her lips with the memory as her heart sped up. Her breasts tingled as she recalled his mouth teasing her nipples before venturing lower...

She moaned at the thoughts assaulting her, the very real memories of him worshiping her body and her returning the favor in kind.

Two glorious weeks spent learning each other intimately and falling in love. Her heart ached for him and fractured on a cry as the final image broke her mind.

His lifeless eyes.

"No!" she screamed as she collapsed onto the pristine floor. "NO!"

Jonathan killed him.

And Stas.

"Oh God..."

She dry-heaved, but her empty stomach denied the follow-through, leaving her light-headed.

Lizzie curled into a ball as the pain lashed at her nerve endings. Tears unlike any she'd ever shed poured from her eyes, dehydrating her soul.

"Jayson," she whimpered, craving him more than she ever had.

God, she thought Tom's death ripped her apart. It was nothing compared to this loss.

She felt incomplete—like half of her died with Jayson. He had touched her in a way no one else ever had.

And I'm carrying his child?

Was that what Osiris implied?

That Jayson had impregnated her? And Osiris intended to keep the baby?

Her blood ran hot and cold.

Jayson said he couldn't procreate, but Osiris implied she carried Jayson's life inside her. Jonathan had said the same.

How was that even possible?

What am I?

* * *

Lizzie needed a plan, some sort of diversion that allowed her to access the outside. Then she could lose herself in the trees. They stretched on for miles, but surely a road existed somewhere.

A chill skittered down her spine as someone knocked and opened the door without preamble. She expected it to be Osiris again and thought it was at first, until she saw the man's mouth.

Oh God... It was sewn shut with razor wire.

His green eyes, so much like Osiris's, met hers as he set a tray of food on the table in the corner. Beside it was a wooden chair.

"Th-thank you," she mumbled.

He bowed his bald head and straightened to study her. Curiosity lit his expression, and she thought he might want to say something but couldn't.

Those barbs resting against his lips looked painful. What could he have done to deserve that treatment?

"That'll be all, Sethios," Osiris said as he entered with a brunette in a lab coat.

The silent man bowed again before excusing himself quietly from the room while Lizzie frowned.

Wasn't that the friend Ezekiel mentioned growing up with in Babylon? The one Osiris raised as a son? Why on earth would he sew his lips together?

"Lizzie, sit in that chair." Osiris gestured to the wooden seat, and her legs moved of their own accord. She couldn't have stopped them if she wanted to.

This is bizarre.

She sat.

"Eat your sandwich," he added.

She picked up what she thought might be egg salad and took a bite. Again, against her own free will.

What the heck?

The hairs along her arms danced as the bread met her mouth again.

Compulsion.

Jayson mentioned Osiris's ability on the plane, yet that wasn't how she knew.

I've met this being before. The question was, when?

"This is Valerie." He gestured to the petite woman beside him. "I've borrowed her from Jonathan's research team and have requested her to oversee your progress."

The female's hazel eyes blinked once, the only confirmation that Osiris hadn't so much requested as demanded.

Lizzie commiserated with the woman. *This sandwich isn't even that good, yet here I am devouring it.*

"I'll leave you two to get acquainted," he said, leaving with the sound of another latch of the door.

Valerie set her bag on the floor and wandered the room with her arms crossed while Lizzie finished forcing the food down her throat. She didn't even like egg salad that much, but she couldn't *not* eat it.

Was that what Stas could do?

A pang rattled her chest. They never had a chance to discuss it, or anything, and the option to do so had been stolen from them by a bullet. To the head.

She sniffled into her glass of water.

If only Lizzie had agreed to return to Hydria, to talk to Stas... But no, she couldn't regret that decision, either. Not without regretting her time with Jayson, and she wouldn't give up those moments for anything in the world.

Valerie cleared her throat. "We should get started." She had a clipboard in her hand.

Lizzie swallowed and set down her drink. "Uh, with what?"

"I've already reviewed your records from intake, but I prefer to do my own exams." She gestured to the bed. "Over there, if you wouldn't mind." The hesitancy in her voice surprised Lizzie. She gathered from her reaction to Osiris that she might not want to be here, either, but the way her hazel eyes drifted from side to side confirmed it.

"Okay," she agreed, only because she suspected something unpleasant would happen to them both if she didn't.

The mattress creased beneath her weight as she settled against the headboard. Valerie's hands shook as she turned the page of the file to read the next page. Lizzie shifted subtly to see the top of the sheet.

Asset File: 4-7

Genotype: Nonhuman

Project Name: Rebirth

She frowned. "What is that?"

"A high-level summary of your progress," Valerie replied. "Have you ovulated this month?"

Lizzie blinked. "No, but—"

"Yes or no is sufficient." She wrote something down. "Do you know the date of your last cycle?"

"Yes." She didn't elaborate since she was told not to before.

Valerie met her gaze. "Date, please."

"No."

She arched a brown brow. "No?"

"No." If anyone was going to answer questions, it would be this woman. "Tell me what the file says."

"It's classified."

Lizzie couldn't help the laugh that bubbled out of her. "Look, I can tell you want to be here about as much as I do. How about we work together so we both survive?" Or better yet, perhaps they could help each other escape.

Unlikely, but worth a try. Maybe.

Valerie studied her for a long moment, then went back to reviewing her paperwork.

Lizzie blew a raspberry in frustration.

Okay, so that wouldn't work. She'd probably misjudged the doctor's reaction to Osiris. He did mention borrowing her from John's research team, which implied she worked for the CRF by choice.

So she was back to being on her own without a solid plan. The door locked from the outside, something she already confirmed, and her windows didn't open. They also appeared to be thicker than usual, not that she considered breaking them to be an option. Jumping from this height would result in injury and capture, thereby ruining that idea altogether.

Lizzie could—

"Asset 4-7 is the first successful attempt of birthing a child of Seraphim genetics from a mortal womb. All forty-six trials before this one failed or were exterminated due to unacceptable abnormalities at birth." Valerie looked up from the file. "Would you like me to continue?"

Lizzie processed the words but didn't comprehend them. "A Seraphim," she repeated. "As in the highest order of angels? The ones with the fiery wings?"

"Most people are not well versed in theology." Valerie flipped through a few pages and nodded. "Oh. I see Osiris designed your education curriculum. That explains it." She met Lizzie's gaze. "Yes. Seraphim are powerful immortal beings who are commonly worshiped in a variety of religions. And their wings are said to glow, though none of us can see them unless they take corporeal form."

Lizzie blinked. "Right." Why not? After everything else

she learned, why couldn't angels exist too? Maybe they were friends with Ichorians and Hydraians. She suppressed a hysterical laugh and instead asked, "And you're saying I'm part Seraphim?"

"According to your records, you *are* a Seraphim." She read a few more lines and shuffled the papers around. "It seems our International Affairs Chief, George Watkins, agreed to use his wife as a host in exchange for a higher-ranking position with the CRF. Considering all forty-six prior hosts died during the process, I'd wager to say he doesn't care much for the woman."

She seemed to be musing idly to herself more than talking to Lizzie, but the information seemed accurate. George and Lillian were certainly not a love match.

"Lillian's pregnancy progressed at an accelerated rate that nearly took her life, but she survived your birth and was paid handsomely as a result." Valerie's eyebrows shot up as she said that last part, no doubt at whatever figure Lizzie's "parents" received for their sacrifice. That explained the family's wealth and her father's, or rather, George's, obsession with the CRF.

This is surreal.

And yet, it felt right.

All those brunches and parties and parading around in high society like a puppet; it always left her feeling empty inside. And Lillian's constant hatred toward her didn't help. But now Lizzie understood why.

Because I almost killed her.

Not that it was Lizzie's fault or that she ever had a choice in the matter.

She wiped her clammy palms against her white pants.

"Does it say who my real parents are?" Lizzie wondered out loud.

Valerie pulled a paper from the stack and read it with widening eyes. "There are no names listed, but it says you were created from a variety of biological samples, all based on Seraphim genetics." Her hazel irises flared as she met

Lizzie's gaze. "And Osiris is the one who provided the live Seraphim subjects for testing."

"Why?" Lizzie asked. "Why did he create me?"

"To produce more Seraphim." Valerie looked at Lizzie's stomach. "You were genetically engineered to birth a new race of angelic beings, and if the child you are carrying turns out as Osiris anticipates, then the final phase will be for you to birth him a new son."

CHAPTER TWENTY-THREE

Move Your Ass

Jayson. The cool, unwelcome voice penetrated the darkness.

Fuck off.

I wish I could. Now wake the fuck up.

Oh, when Jayson opened his eyes, he would kick the telepathic bastard's ass. He enjoyed his peace and quiet, as it rarely occurred. Alik knew that better than anyone.

Seriously, I'm going to toss you in the fucking ocean if you don't start moving.

You'll be the one going for a swim, jackass.

I doubt that.

Jayson stretched his arms and rolled his neck as he stirred from the deep slumber. His body ached in a way it shouldn't after sleeping so soundly. And he had one hell of a headache.

He winced at the sunlight spilling over him and groaned.

"Alik," he growled, furious at the disturbance. But his voice didn't sound right. Too scratchy, like he'd just woken from death.

He sat up with a start and regretted it as the room spun around him.

"Shit." He fell back into the mattress. It felt like a cement truck had run over his skull.

"Good work, Lara," Luc praised. "We'll take it from here."

"Of course," she replied.

Why is a Hydraian healer here?

"Because you were shot in the head," Balthazar replied, irritated. "As was Stas, but she's not ready to wake up."

"We pulled you out early because we need to know what the hell happened, and you're the only one strong enough to handle it," Luc explained. "Start talking."

He would if he could, but his addled brain refused to commit to anything specific.

"Someone shot you with a glass bullet," Balthazar prompted. "Stas, too."

Jayson shook his head. "Where's Red?"

"Excellent question," Luc replied. "We're hoping you know the answer to that."

He tried sitting again, this time slowly, and eyed his familiar surroundings. They were in his room in Hydria, which meant Jacque had teleported him here. Without Lizzie.

Jayson massaged his temples as he fought to remember

what happened while striving not to panic. He went to pick up some fruit and other items from town and had been considering how to broach the topic of returning to Hydria as a couple. When he arrived...

"Stark and Jonathan," he said as fury clouded his vision. The image of a ceramic knife to Lizzie's throat, followed by the acceptance of the collar—he touched his neck to find it missing—then forcing her to choose between him and Stas. "They were incendiary bullets."

"No, they were hollow glass," Luc corrected.

Jayson shook his head. "Jonathan said they were glass incendiary bullets, but maybe the new technology malfunctioned?"

"I watched as Lara removed the pieces from your head," Luc replied. "They were definitely empty bullets, with no chemicals to stir up a fire upon entry."

"A ploy?" The note of disbelief in Jayson's voice conveyed his thoughts on that guess. Jonathan loved his games, but to miss an opportunity to kill an Elder? No. He wouldn't do that. "How soon did you arrive after Stas?"

"Within five minutes," Alik replied. "Your bodies were still warm when Jacque and I arrived."

Meaning Jonathan and Stark hadn't stuck around to confirm that their new technology worked—not that it would have been easy to tell. The incendiary bullets lit the blood on fire, killing an immortal instantly, but the corpse remained fine on the outside, minus the point of entry for the bullet. Impressive little things.

"Did you remove the device from my neck?" Jayson asked.

Alik frowned. "What device?"

"If you don't know, then they removed it before you arrived and took it with them." Because it was an expensive piece of hardware. He understood that, but the rest of it... Jayson scratched his jaw. "Something isn't adding up." Jonathan would have tested his tech before using it, but obviously, the bullet hadn't worked as intended. Why?

"You're thinking too hard," a cultured voice informed from the shadows. Ezekiel stepped out of his cloak, hands in the air in a gesture of surrender. "We all know my coming here is a huge risk to my person, so I suggest you hear me out before attempting to kill me."

Balthazar studied him. "How long have you been standing there?"

"Long enough." He smirked. "Upset that you can't access my mind, old friend? Shall we focus on that or the relevance of my appearance?"

"He's immune," Alik murmured. "That's new."

"Yes, I imagine you are quite displeased by that development," Ezekiel taunted. "Now, can we get to the point, or would you all prefer to continue wasting precious time?"

"Start talking," Jayson demanded.

"Brilliant." Ezekiel kicked back onto Jayson's chaise lounge, hands tucked behind his head, and crossed his boot-clad ankles.

"As to your discussion, they were indeed empty bullets, though Jonathan believed them to be of the incendiary variety. I would take credit for that parlor trick, but that would be deceitful and untrue. But that should not be the focal point for this discussion. As you all are apparently unable to determine Elizabeth Watkins's purpose—despite all the clues we have hand-delivered to you—I'm here to educate."

"We?" Luc repeated.

Ezekiel smiled. "Yes. But as I was saying, Elizabeth is the key. She was created by Jonathan as a token of appreciation for the CRF's benefactor." He glanced around. "Seriously? None of you know? Fuck, this is going to take longer than I expected."

"Keep talking," Jayson urged. "Preferably before I stick a knife in you."

Ezekiel tsked. "Tone down the threats and listen. You

all must know Jonathan didn't create the CRF on his own, and you have to wonder why Osiris would allow an organization who enjoys slaughtering immortals to thrive in the heart of Ichorian territory."

"Because he's the benefactor," Luc translated, his omniscient ability gluing all the puzzle pieces together before everyone else. "I've suspected their partnership before but never knew what Osiris could gain from it. From what you're implying, Elizabeth is his prize."

"Partially, yes. At least that's the item I've come here to discuss."

"Meaning there's more," Luc interpreted.

Ezekiel merely shrugged. "Isn't there always?"

Cryptic bastard. Jayson needed Ezekiel to start talking faster.

The assassin grinned, as if sensing the impatience in the room and enjoying it. "I assume you ran a few tests on her blood?"

"Enough to infer her purpose," Luc replied. "The serum Stark so politely donated to our cause was a mix of hormones meant to encourage pregnancy."

"Politely donated," Ezekiel repeated, amused. "He'll enjoy that classification. As for Elizabeth, she is a being beyond labels, but mostly a Seraphim without any of the abilities. Her aging has slowed, indicating she'll be immortal very soon, and yes, she was created for the sole purpose of breeding."

Jayson's blood heated, cooled, then heated again as his emotions warred. *Breeding.* "With whom?"

And he had better not say "Osiris," or Jayson would lose it. His grip on his temper was already waning; it would not take much to send him over the edge.

"Ah, the debate of who would be first wasn't settled until very recently." Ezekiel smiled. "When Osiris learned of your interest in his prized possession, he decided to let it play out. Your talents are extraordinary, and he's curious to see how her genetics bind with yours. It also served as a way to test her compatibility with Hydraians, which I gather was successful."

Jayson's heart stopped.

As did his breathing.

He couldn't mean...

"I believe congratulations are in order, Jedrick. You're going to be a father." Ezekiel brushed a piece of lint off his leather jacket.

"How do you know all of this?" Luc asked as if those words hadn't shattered Jayson's entire being.

I'm going to be a dad?

And Lizzie... Oh, hell... Lizzie...

"Where is she?" he demanded, not caring at all that Ezekiel had been in the middle of responding to Luc.

"As I was saying," Ezekiel murmured, "I know all this because I've been involved in her project from the very beginning. Not by choice, but that's a conversation for another time. What matters here, however, is that I've tasted her blood. Which, as you all know, means I can track her."

"You're the reason they found her in Bora Bora and Italy," Luc mused. "Clever."

Ezekiel shrugged. "As I said, it's not a project of my choice."

"Which is why you're helping us?" Balthazar guessed, speaking up for the first time.

"My reasons are my own," he replied. "But I'm happy to give you her location."

"Do that," Jayson urged. "Now."

Ezekiel gave him a disapproving stare. "You really will need to learn more patience, Jedrick. I hear children can be quite troublesome little beings."

Jayson wanted to introduce Ezekiel's face to the wall but refrained. Not only was the woman he cared about in jeopardy, but so was his supposed child. Assuming Ezekiel spoke the truth.

It could all be a deceptive con meant to trap them,

though his comments regarding the bullets added up. Jayson had seen the excitement in Jonathan's eyes when he pulled the trigger. He truly believed they were destined to kill.

And Lizzie's monthly hormone supplement did seem appropriate for a woman meant to conceive. If she was designed to breed with immortal beings, then her being pregnant now was a definite possibility. Especially after all the hours they spent in bed together.

He grimaced as pain touched his chest.

My Red.

She had to be so scared and alone.

And worse, she thought he was dead. That no one would be coming for her.

But he would. Even if it meant storming the CRF alone, he would cross the gates of hell for her.

Mine.

No one touched his heart.

Balthazar clapped a hand on his shoulder and nodded, as if to say, *I'm with you to the end.*

He returned the gesture and met Luc's patient gaze. "I want her back," Jayson said. "Osiris can kiss my ass."

"It may instigate a war," Luc cautioned. "Which I'm guessing is Osiris's goal."

"She's one of ours," Balthazar countered. "We don't leave ours behind."

"Is she?" Luc asked. "From what Ezekiel has implied, she's more Seraphim than Hydraian."

"She's carrying my child." Jayson let that statement settle before adding, "And even if she wasn't, she's still mine to protect."

"He'll go with or without us," Balthazar pointed out. "This bond they've formed supersedes logic."

"Alik?" Luc asked.

"Are you asking if I want to kill some Ichorians? Because I think we all know the answer to that already." He pushed off the wall. "Can I start with the one on the chaise?"

"And I believe that is my cue to depart," Ezekiel murmured. "I shall text you the address, Jedrick. But be advised that it's Osiris's home estate, and he's surrounded by some of the most powerful Ichorians in the world, including a clairvoyant."

He started to shift into his shadow form but reappeared to add, "Lucian, I am very sorry about what happened to Owen. He served a greater purpose in befriending Astasiya, and I am forever in his debt for his service. And I sincerely miss his company in my plight."

Ezekiel bowed his head in prayer and vanished from the room without another word.

Everyone gaped at the empty chaise lounge.

That was unexpected. Hell, the whole thing was unexpected.

But that's what Ezekiel excelled at—breaking the rules and looking out for himself first and foremost.

"A Nizari assassin protecting a fledgling? Now I've seen everything," Alik remarked.

"He could be lying." Luc's emerald gaze glowed in that eerie way that indicated the use of power. "However, I see no logical reason for him to add that information, or to give us any of the other details. Unless it's all a trap, in which case, he did an excellent job of convincing me it's not."

"Even if it is, I'm going," Jayson stated. "I'm not leaving her under Osiris's care."

"Tom and Stas will feel the same," Balthazar added. "And that means Issac will follow with Tristan and Mateo."

Jayson imagined other Ichorians would be willing to help as well, considering the alliance between Osiris and Jonathan defied the armistice. It meant the leader of their Conclave was actively allowing the CRF to hunt and kill immortals at will. Not many would approve of that agreement.

"Everything Ezekiel stated is logical and suits," Luc said, his green gaze dimming. "If it is the wish of the Elders to rescue Elizabeth, then you have my support. I fear it will incite a war, but I also believe that fate to be inevitable. And this is one battle I'm willing to fight."

Jayson's phone buzzed on cue. He pulled it from his pocket and read the address out loud to the others in the room. "Sounds secluded," he added as he set the phone aside.

"An excellent place to kill without drawing attention," Alik mused. "I'm game."

"We'll need a solid plan," Jayson admitted. He had a feeling they would have only one shot at securing Lizzie, and if they blew it, things would not end well.

"I'll call Aidan," Luc murmured as he started toward the door. "In the interim, please provide Issac your support. He's putting on a good show, but we all know he's not taking this well."

Issac might not be a Hydraian, but all of them considered him very much family. His pain would be felt through them all.

Balthazar nodded. "We're on it, Luc."

"Thank you," he murmured. "I would attend to him as well, but I sense my presence will only worsen his acceptance." With those solemn words, he left to strategize. Jayson was torn between following him, going to Issac, and leaving for the address on his phone.

But as always, it was Balthazar who grounded him. "Take a shower. Afterward, we'll talk. You can't help her on your own, but we can as a team. And given what Ezekiel said about her importance to Osiris, it's safe to assume she's unharmed. We'll get her back, Jay."

He nodded, believing his oldest friend. "You'd better be right."

"I always am," he replied, cocky as ever. "But seriously, grab a shower. This bloody look on you isn't appealing, and you smell like death."

Jayson tried to smile at the obvious attempt at a joke, but it fell flat. To feel complete, he needed his Red. Because without her, he had half a soul.

I'm coming for you, Lizzie, he vowed. *Just hang on.*

CHAPTER TWENTY-FOUR

Resurrection in the Light of Disaster

Subject was paired with a college
roommate. Name: Astasiya Davenport.
Age: 18. Origin: Havre, Montana. No
known conflicts at this time.

—Entry Log 118.08.4-7

Another nightmare.

Lost in the depths of the ocean.

Stas struggled against the binds, but her deteriorated limbs refused to move. She resembled a skeleton, lost in the waves of time, screaming for no one to hear.

Everything hurt, but her heart most of all.

So much loss...

It wasn't supposed to end like this.

"Aya…" Sandalwood and peppermint accompanied the nickname, but it didn't fit.

Help me…

Find me…

Free me…

Water suffocated her thoughts, granting her temporary peace in the world of silence.

Only to awaken again in hell.

Over and over and over.

A dark, unending dance of solitude and death.

When will they come for me?

"Astasiya." The voice grew stronger, pulling her somewhere new. Away from the familiarity of the ocean floor and into a world of sunshine.

Too bright, she thought, sheltering her eyes.

The vestiges of her nightmare disappeared into reality, revealing a room of mahogany and rich brown colors that didn't belong to her or the man holding her hand.

She swallowed, her throat dry from her deep sleep. A straw slipped between her lips, and she sipped on instinct, welcoming the freshly squeezed juice. It replaced the bitterness that always followed her visits to the deep sea.

Issac, she thought with a smile. He'd learned so much about her in their brief months together and knew exactly how to pull her from the nightmares in the sweetest ways. She waited for his kiss after the drink disappeared, but it didn't come.

Strange. He always kissed her after sleep.

She stretched her stiff shoulders and braved the light by opening her eyes. Issac sat in a chair beside her with his elbows braced on his knees, his expression carefully blank. A glance around showed they were alone and in one of Balthazar's guest rooms.

Stas struggled to remember how she ended up here.

She'd been staying with Eliza in Amelia's old home these last few weeks. The Hydraians had dubbed it the

"Fledgling House" since both of them were unturned immortals. Stas disliked the idea at first but admired Eliza's strength and conviction. She was a remarkable woman, especially considering everything that had happened to her prior to arriving in Hydria.

"How do you feel?" Issac asked, his voice soft.

"Groggy," she admitted as she rolled to her side and tucked her arm beneath her head on the pillow. It throbbed a little, likely from the nightmare. "Why aren't you in bed with me?" He wore one of his trademark suits, minus the tie, and his midnight hair was freshly tousled from his fingers. She loved this look on him but preferred him naked.

"Aya," he whispered, his voice cracking as he dropped his head into his hands. He visibly trembled, stirring alarm in her chest.

"What's happened?" She sat up despite her body's complaints. "Is Lizzie okay?"

The last she heard, her best friend was in Bora Bora enjoying alone time with Jayson. Definitely not the type of man Stas ever would have recommended, but at this point, all she wanted was for Lizzie to be happy. She deserved it after all the pain, and he seemed to be helping her work through the process.

Issac shuddered again, and Stas couldn't take it anymore. She reached for him, but he flinched away from her touch, almost as if she burned him.

"You're starting to scare me," she admitted, hurt that he would reject her in such a way. "What's going on?"

He shook his head. "I'm trying." His broken voice shot an arrow through her chest, eliciting an ache deep inside that fizzled and burned.

"What's wrong?" she whispered.

He ran his fingers through his hair and pulled on the strands. "Fuck, I'm trying, Aya. You..." His cheekbones hollowed with the words as he struggled to say whatever he needed to say.

This was a side of him she'd never seen, and it terrified her.

"Trying to do what?" she asked, tears in her eyes. "What's going on?" She grabbed his wrist and squeezed when he grimaced. "Tell me what happened, Issac. Now." The command slipped out of its own accord, but she couldn't pull it back, not even as his damp eyes met hers.

"You died, Aya." Three words, uttered so softly she almost didn't hear them. Or maybe that was the wind tunnel suddenly taking residence in her head that distorted the sound.

"What?" She couldn't have heard him right.

"You went to Bora Bora by yourself—without backup—and were shot in the head."

She blinked as the memory began to surface. So lost in her nightmare, she hadn't realized the truth of the moment.

"John," she breathed. "Where's…?" Her voice faltered.
Oh, fuck.
No.
No way.
This can't…

"I…" She released his wrist to feel her forehead and found nothing but smooth skin.

Her heart stuttered as her breath caught in her throat.

I died. Her mind fractured beneath the assault of those two lethal words.

I…
This…

She didn't want to believe it, would have begged for a different outcome, but the agony radiating from Issac's blue eyes confirmed the truth.

"I'm a Hydraian."

Her fingers went numb.

"I'm…" She couldn't say it again. That made it real. Too real. Just like the tears trailing down Issac's cheeks. And hers.

"No," she whispered, shaking her head over and over as if that would take it all back and fix everything.

She wasn't ready.

They weren't ready.

Her vision blurred as anguish ripped through her abdomen, tearing a scream from her throat. "NO!"

It wasn't fair!

She didn't want this future. She wanted *him*. The man she could no longer have. The man who meant everything to her.

Her heart...

And the despair emanating from him...

They needed more time.

"I can't touch you," she whispered. "But I need..."

Oh God, how would she survive without touching him? Without kissing him? Without his love?

All those tender moments and nights.

The unspoken words.

Those looks that said he wanted to devour her in the best ways.

His tenderness in the mornings.

All of it hung in the balance and shattered behind her eyes.

Forever cementing itself the past.

Too soon...

"Issac." Her soul withered as it sought the connection she knew it needed but couldn't have. She couldn't go to him. But, oh God, she wanted to.

"I'm so sorry." The words sounded foreign to her own ears. Was that shriveled, broken rasp her voice?

Issac merely shook his head, because what could he say? Nothing could be done now. She sealed her fate when she went to save her friend without thinking things through.

And she lost *everything* in the process.

Her decision had shattered their bond.

Stas broke under a sob meant to destroy her being, her

entire body convulsing uncontrollably.

This can't be happening.

Please…

I can't breathe.

Issac brushed his lips against her forehead in a devastatingly careful kiss, his fear of touching her evident, and yet saying so much. Sorrow, hurt, and *pain*.

Even now, he wished to comfort her, when they both knew he couldn't, and she longed to allow it.

It's all my fault.

I destroyed us.

"Oh God, Issac…" The words burned her throat and singed the air, forever separating them. Because he would never be hers again, not in the way she craved. Her heart would never recover. And her soul… It died when John pulled that trigger.

"Aya," Issac breathed, his internal suffering etched into that single word. He finally took her hand and squeezed, his head bowed as the tears fell silently from his eyes.

Stas couldn't help the whimper that escaped her. It felt as if her entire world had ended before it even began.

And now she had an eternity of suffering to live through. Alone.

She curled into a ball, her hand still clasped in his, and relived every memory of him behind her eyes. Every touch. Every kiss. Every word. She would dream of him every night, think of him every day, and miss him every moment. Even when he stood beside her, she'd miss him.

It would only ever be Issac for her.

Forever and always.

A silent vow.

"I love you," she whispered. She'd never said it out loud, and it wouldn't matter now, but he had to know… "It's only ever been you, Issac."

"I know, love," he replied, just as soft. "I know."

CHAPTER TWENTY-FIVE

Wall of Fire

Subject's infatuation memories with
Thomas Fitzgerald were implanted
today. Team psychologist says it will
counteract potential relationships
with unsuitable mates.
                    —Entry Log 118.05.4-7

"Stas is awake but won't be able to help us in her current state," Balthazar said as he entered the makeshift war room. "Issac isn't in the proper frame of mind to assist, either."

Aidan nodded. "It's for the best. Strategically, I recommend keeping Stas hidden for as long as you can. The sooner Osiris hears of her existence, the sooner he will come for her."

"There's no denying that her ability to compel would be useful in this situation, but I am inclined to agree." Luc flattened a drawing on the table. "Which is why we've devised a plan that doesn't include them."

The omniscient father-son duo had drafted over a dozen attack plans before settling on this one, all while the rest of the room observed. They spoke too quickly for anyone to completely follow their logic, but Jayson understood the main idea.

"How are we going to counteract the wards?" he asked as he folded his arms. Luc and Aidan had been discussing them just before Balthazar entered.

"We'll handle them," Luc replied, indicating himself and Aidan. "Between the two of us, we should be able to draw some ancient runes that will counteract the wards long enough for us to volley an attack."

"Yes, I suspect the point of them isn't necessarily to keep an army out but to give Osiris enough warning to relocate," Aidan murmured, his eyes that same emerald shade as Luc's. "Hopefully, that relocation plan does not involve Elizabeth, or we'll be playing a game of chase."

"That's where I come in," Ash said as she tied her light-blonde hair up into a ponytail. "Ring of fire."

"Exactly," Luc agreed. "But we'll have to stay back, just in case. Especially with Jeremy manipulating the earth."

Jayson nodded. "And if we see Lizzie—"

"I'll grab her," Jacque announced from his spot in the corner. He had three empty pizza boxes beside him and a protein shake in his hand. Teleporting burned calories at an insane rate, and they needed him fully charged.

"Good. Any questions?" Aidan glanced around the room. Several of Hydria's most powerful immortals had volunteered to help even though they didn't know Lizzie. Their support and unyielding friendship were why they would win a war against the Ichorians. Luc ruled with love and affection, as opposed to Osiris, who chose fear.

"Do you think my father will make an appearance?" Tom had his arms folded over the back of the chair he'd flipped around to straddle earlier. He hadn't said much but listened intently while Aidan and Luc debated.

Tom's previous sniper experience and general military knowledge would be very useful. Not to mention his perfect aim. And he seemed to have an uncanny ability to turn off emotions, because the man had to be furious about his father's actions, yet he didn't show it.

"Likely not," Aidan replied. "He's done his part by handing over Elizabeth to Osiris, and he believes he's just killed Stas and Jayson. The smart move for him would be to protect his headquarters, as he's now owed retribution from Issac for killing Stas and from the Elders for killing their brother."

"Why not take him alive?" Tom asked, causing everyone to look at him in confusion. "Sorry, I mean Jayson. I've been trying to figure out why my father would kill him. He's a powerful Hydraian, just like Amelia. Not that I condone it, but why not take Jayson back to headquarters for testing?"

"Because I'm too powerful for him to contain." Not an overstatement, but a fact. "He could have tried with that device, but I would eventually have found a way around it, and that would have ended very badly for him."

"Or it's his ego," Aidan suggested with a shrug. "When it comes to my progeny and the Elders, Jonathan does not think clearly. He wants power and craves theirs, while also seeking to appease."

"If it's ego, he would have claimed Eli's death," Balthazar pointed out. "Instead he framed someone else."

"To hide Amelia," Luc added. "But we don't know if he plans to make some grand statement later, or if he already boasted about his kills to Osiris. I'm inclined to agree that all of this has been about improving his ego since he's always been very touchy about his weak ability."

Tom snorted. "Small Dick Syndrome, not that I

inherited that problem from him."

Balthazar grinned. "We've all seen proof of that, Fitzgerald."

Jayson cleared his throat. "Are we ready? Because I can't stand around here doing nothing much longer. I need to see Lizzie, and soon." An understatement. This whole multi-hour planning session nearly killed him. All he could think about was holding his Red again and telling her how he felt. He never had the chance, and now he worried it would be too late.

Balthazar bumped his shoulder against Jayson. "We'll get her back, Jay. I promise you. No matter what it takes."

"How can you be so confident?" It hurt to ask, but he wanted to know.

"Because in three thousand years, I've never seen you regard a woman the way you do Lizzie. And I am determined to give that back to you." The solemn words were followed by one of his trademark grins. Balthazar never could be serious for long. "I also might want to see you play dad for a few years. Should be incredibly entertaining. I hope you have a girl."

Jayson smiled despite the circumstances as a picture of a beautiful little redhead crossed his thoughts. "She'll look just like Lizzie."

"She will," Balthazar agreed, clapping him on the shoulder. "Now don't lose that vision. Emotions can be a powerful motivator, Jay. Don't hide from yours."

~*~

Lizzie fisted the sheets of the bed while Valerie examined her as one would a lab rat. She drew blood, took on the role of gynecologist, and was now performing a spinal tap.

"Don't move," she cautioned as the needle slid into her back.

Ow, ow, ow...

LEXI C. FOSS

Her vision blurred with unshed tears, but she'd agreed to cooperate in exchange for more information. After the familial lesson and declaration that Lizzie was here to give Osiris a "new son"—which still freaked her out—Valerie had detailed Lizzie's genetic profile.

All her records indicated she was a full-blooded Seraphim without powers. She apparently didn't heal as fast as others, but the records provided proof of her immortality.

Because she'd been killed multiple times—in various ways.

And she had survived it all.

Yet she possessed no memory of any of it.

Lizzie couldn't decide if that was a blessing or a curse. Maybe Osiris could erase her memory of learning his purpose for her.

And what did that mean for the child in her belly now? Would he take the baby from her? She couldn't bear losing that final connection to Jayson.

Her eyes stung with suppressed emotion. An inferno of grief whirled inside her, waiting to be unleashed, but she swallowed it.

Osiris wouldn't win. He couldn't.

I'm not having his child.

She'd die first.

Or at least try.

"Done," Valerie said as she stepped back. "You can get dressed again."

Lizzie swallowed her response. *Thank you* had been on the tip of her tongue, which seemed inappropriate considering their situation. Her surrogate mother would say otherwise, but Lizzie no longer gave a damn. Not after everything she'd learned these last few weeks.

She pulled on the white drawstring pants and a matching tank top, gathered her hair, and let it fall against her back. Valerie placed all her medical supplies on a desk against the wall. Beside it was an empty bookshelf and another one of those wooden chairs.

The oversized room also came equipped with a marble bathroom with a large walk-in shower, two sinks, and a toilet. As far as prison cells went, this one wasn't bad. Although, she could do with some artwork, books, a television, or anything entertaining to keep her mind busy. Instead, she was surrounded by white walls, glass windows, and a few pieces of furniture.

The bed provided the only comfortable seat. Lizzie sat near the headboard and tucked her knees into her chest while watching Valerie bag and label all her samples.

Lizzie shivered, feeling violated and exposed.

I need to get out of here.

But she didn't know how or where she would go. She didn't even know where *here* was, for crying out loud.

Would anyone come for her? Maybe. Maybe not. She hadn't been very nice to the Hydraians, or to Issac, or Tom. Why would anyone want to help her after the way she acted?

Not to mention it being her fault Stas and Jayson were dead.

She dropped her chin to her knees.

Even if she escaped, would it be worth it? She would forever be a prisoner to her emotions.

I have a piece of him inside me.

She caressed her belly and closed her eyes. Would it be a boy or a girl? Would the baby have Jayson's milk chocolate gaze? His dark, luscious hair? His dimples?

Lizzie grinned at the adorable image of a small boy running around and causing mischief. She would call him Jedrick, in honor of his father.

Her fingers drew a heart—a tribute to the life growing in memory of their love. Because she had no doubt that she loved Jayson, just as she would their child. Time meant nothing in the face of her feelings. Her soul ached without her other half. That had to be love. And if it wasn't, then it translated to a word that didn't exist.

I'll take care of you, she promised as she palmed her flat stomach.

Because she would escape, if for nothing else than to save the life inside her.

"Are you ready to learn more?" Valerie asked softly.

"Yes," Lizzie replied without opening her eyes. "Please."

Papers shuffled as the doctor found a good place to start, but an explosion outside rattled the windows, silencing her before she could speak.

"What was that?" Lizzie asked as she sat up.

Another crash shook the foundation of the mansion and forced both of them to run to the windows. Smoke and fire danced in the yard.

Valerie closed the file and tucked it into her bag before walking across the room to peer outside. "They are trying to get through the wards."

"Wards?" Lizzie repeated as she joined her by the window.

"Seraphim create them, just like runes. I don't know much about the magic, but there are several surrounding the CRF, and it seems Osiris's compound has them as well."

"What do they do?"

"They mostly prevent entry." Another blast slammed into what resembled a force field around the estate grounds. "And strip immortals of their gifts. These appear to all be protective runes, and they're working."

Fire danced in the air, playing over a jagged line. "Are you sure about that?" Because it certainly looked as if they'd cracked the surface of that bubble.

"We should probably take cover," Valerie replied as a loud shriek sounded.

Lizzie cupped her ears at what resembled a raven's cry and screamed, "What the heck is that?!"

The doctor shook her head, her face paling.

A flash of light blinded them, and Valerie knocked

Lizzie to the ground just as the glass imploded inward.

"Shit!" Lizzie yelled as dozens of slivers sliced her exposed arms. The doctor took the brunt of it, having covered Lizzie with her body as they fell.

Ouch.

Valerie didn't move or speak, which was fine by Lizzie. That implosion had shattered her eardrums, leaving an incessant ringing behind.

Smoke billowed overhead, forcing her to cough. She tried to wiggle out from under Valerie, but the woman was dead weight.

"Move," Lizzie urged as she tried again.

It took some shoving, but she finally dislodged her with a heave and sat up to expel the bad air from her lungs. Only it continued to cloud her room.

"We have to get out of here," Lizzie said with a nudge to her companion. She still didn't move.

"Come on, Val…" Lizzie trailed off as she noticed the blood coloring the doctor's lab coat. She leaned around the woman and gasped at the jagged piece of glass sticking out of her back. "Oh God." She finally met the gaze of a very dead woman and scrambled back on a cry. "Shit!"

Valerie had saved her life by covering Lizzie during the fall. On purpose or by accident? She would never know. And as another vibration shook the floor beneath her hands, she realized there wasn't time to find out.

She ran to the door and tried to open it, but it didn't budge.

"Help!" Lizzie frantically pounded her fists against the door as she screamed. She still couldn't hear over all the damn ringing, so if anyone replied, she wouldn't know. But the door remained closed. The place above the knob seemed appropriate for a key. Would Valerie have one?

A glance at the dead woman left Lizzie gagging. Probably not, and she didn't have the stomach to check. But she could try her bag by the table.

Lizzie moved quickly, going through all the pockets

and zippers, and paused when she found the file with "Asset 4-7" printed at the top. She didn't have time to read it now, but she might later. Carrying the papers would be an issue, especially if she needed her hands.

Hmm...

Lizzie lifted her shirt and tucked part of the file into the band of her pants while resting the majority of it against her belly. Not the most eloquent look, but functional. She secured it by retying her drawstrings as tightly as possible and laid her tank top over the file before searching the bag again.

No key.

That didn't surprise her, as it seemed Valerie was just as much of a prisoner as Lizzie.

She returned to pounding on the door, her fists bruising from her efforts, as smoke continued to billow through the windows. It would be a lot worse if the fire were in the room with her, but, damn, it still sucked to breathe. And it couldn't be good for her unborn child.

The lock clicked as someone pushed the door open. She jumped back and met the green gaze of the silent male servant.

Sethios.

He gestured for her to follow him, and for lack of a better option, she did. His legs quickly ate up the hallway, and she kept pace behind him. The floor reverberated against her feet as powers far greater than her understanding annihilated the residence.

A set of back stairs appeared at the end of the corridor, and he pointed downward. She waited for him to lead, but he shook his head.

"Where do I go at the bottom?" she asked.

He mimed opening a door and scissored his fingers in a way that indicated running.

"Outside?" she asked.

One nod.

When she didn't immediately move, he pushed her

forward with an urgent expression. Then his lips ripped through the razors, causing her to cringe as blood poured from his mouth.

"Go now," he rasped. His eyes trained on the hallway they'd just run through, as if preparing for a battle.

"Sethios!" Osiris's voice ricocheted off the walls, sending a chill down her spine.

Her helper cracked his neck and grinned in anticipation. Or she thought it was a grin. She couldn't see through the gruesome mess of his mouth. "Run down the stairs, little one," he demanded hoarsely. "*Now.*"

Lizzie's legs started moving before her mind registered the action. She didn't pause to analyze the how or why; she just fled down the stairs as instructed and went through the door at the bottom. The papers shuffled against her belly but remained in place thanks to her waistband. Not that they would help her with this new predicament.

Fire blazed across the ground not twenty feet from her, forming an impenetrable wall. She darted right, only to find the same force field of heat and energy surrounding the entire back of the property.

Heat singed her skin as she went back the way she came, toward the front. Her pants stuck to her legs, her tank top to her back, and the file to her stomach.

She shook her head at the sight, her vision blurring with tears.

This was hopeless. Even if she found a way through the flames, she'd probably die of suffocation.

I can't give up.

She had no idea who had started the attack, but it offered her the only chance she may ever have to escape.

And maybe, hopefully, the assailants were on her side.

Because anyone who disliked Osiris was okay by her.

She took off at a dead run to the other side of the giant residence, hoping and praying to find a passageway. Her legs burned as she ran, but she pushed through the pain and ignored the scrapes to her bare feet.

The estate was long and vast, but she managed to arrive at the other side and ran right into a brick wall of male.

He appeared out of nowhere and halted her with an "Oomph" as her face met his chest. Hands grabbed her waist, and her vision swirled.

I'm going to be sick.

Wind whipped through her hair, and she stumbled as she fell to the sand.

A bright moon hung in a star-filled sky above as waves crashed against the shore behind her.

She spun in a circle and found herself alone.

No fire.

No mansion.

"Where am I?" she whispered into the darkness.

No one responded.

~*~

"Got her," Jacque announced as he returned to Jayson's side.

"How the fuck did she get outside?" Jayson demanded. He couldn't believe it when he saw that wave of auburn hair flying outside the manor.

Jacque gave him a look. "You want me to go back and ask her?"

"Someone obviously helped on the inside," Ash replied, her brow sweating from all the fire manipulation. "What now, boss?"

"Demolish it," he replied, furious.

"You heard the man," Ash said into the comms.

It'd taken far too long to get through all those damn wards, even with all of Aidan's and Luc's knowledge. They had to work quickly to find and draw runes over them, calling on millennia of ancient logic to solve the puzzles. A few booby-traps forced them to launch their attack prematurely, something that wasted a hell of a lot of energy, but once the protection spells fell, they were able to volley a sufficient attack.

And strangely, Osiris didn't return fire. So much for Ezekiel's comments regarding a clairvoyant and the substantial immortal gifts on site.

Grace stepped up beside him, her focus on the mansion. She stripped it with her mind, removing the roof first and sending it into the fire Ash created, followed by the walls.

Jeremy took a knee and palmed the ground, causing it to shake. His affinity for controlling stones of all kind came in handy during times like this, as did Jayson's ability to manipulate metal. He used it now to warp the support beams, not caring at all whom he crushed in the devastation.

Though, he suspected Osiris had long fled with his minions. Otherwise they would be outside fighting. "Why would he run?" he asked, his question directed at Luc over the comm. No one else would dare speculate.

"Our source mentioned a clairvoyant," he replied. "I imagine she provided him with the odds of winning, and they were not in his favor, so he chose to flee."

"Why not take Lizzie?"

"Perhaps he meant to, but someone intervened. We'll need her input to determine that."

Fair enough. Jayson destroyed the last of the metal structures while Ash, Jeremy, and Grace handled the rest. An entire army of Hydraians who volunteered to assist with this mission surrounded the estate, and he gazed upon them in pride.

The remains of the former palatial residence glowed as Ash weakened the flames until only a few embers remained. "That was a waste of a perfectly good home," she remarked as she wiped her brow.

"You did good," Jayson replied

"Of course I did." She grinned broadly and tossed her white-blonde hair over her shoulder. "Time to go?"

"Time to go," he agreed.

"On it," Jacque replied as he group-hugged four Hydraians, including Ash, and disappeared.

"He's going to eat all the food in Hydria after this," Jeremy said as he stood. He was one of the members of Jayson's guard, just like Grace, which explained why they were both flanking him on either side. The perceived threat might be gone, but one could never be so sure.

"You realize I can handle myself," he noted dryly.

"Says the jackass who was shot in Bora Bora after he refused to let his Guardians do their jobs," Grace sniped. "I'll be standing right here until Jacque safely escorts you back to Hydria, *sir*."

Jayson shook his head, bemused. There would be no talking her down, not that he intended to try.

Jacque appeared across the way, picked up the Hydraians walking toward the main camp, and disappeared. Jayson frowned as intuition inched along his spine. Two of those immortals were B's Guardians, but the Elders were nowhere in sight.

Not proper protocol.

"Luc, what's your status?" Jayson asked as his stomach twisted with foreboding. *Something isn't right.*

Silence echoed over the line.

Grace took a defensive stance, her ebony gaze flickering around the field as Jeremy knelt to touch the earth again. *Guardians sensing a danger to their Elder.*

Jayson cleared his throat and tried again. "Luc?"

"I'm sorry, but Lucian is quite indisposed at the moment," a cool voice informed. One that froze everyone in place.

"Osiris."

"Jedrick, or is it Jayson now? It's so difficult to keep everyone's names straight. Did you hear that Ezekiel is going by Kiel now? Such an unbecoming name." He sighed dramatically. "Anyway, I daresay you owe me a new home. Quite rude to drop by unannounced, but to destroy my property too?" He tsked. "And all over a woman. It reminds me of Troy."

"That's a myth."

"Is it?" Osiris mused. "Alas, we should chat more. In person. Assuming you want your *king* returned unharmed."

Grace and Jeremy shook their heads in prompt denial, while Jayson rubbed a hand over his face. Luc would tell him to stand down, but they both knew how Jay felt about following the rules. Exhibit A: Lizzie Watkins.

"Where?" Jayson asked.

"Finish sending your Guardians home, and we'll go from there."

"No," Grace stated immediately.

"Mind your Elders, young one," Osiris murmured. "They could save your life."

"Fuck you," Grace replied.

"Manners, child," Osiris chastised. "Make him scream, Alik."

Agony filtered over the speakers, causing Jayson to go to his knees at the familiar sound. It reminded him of when Luc almost died during the last immortal war.

"Now that is obedience," Osiris murmured. "Such a good little Elder you are." Jayson pictured him stroking Alik's head like a dog as he used his commands.

Jacque appeared, grinning proudly. "Eighteen down and…" His silver eyes widened. "What—"

More groans filtered through the earpiece, shredding Jayson's heart. Because that last one was Balthazar. Osiris must have snuck up on Alik when no one was looking and used him to take down the other two.

Fuck.

Jayson knew this had been too easy.

"More," Osiris urged as the screaming increased.

"Stop," Jayson begged. "I'll meet your demands."

"No, I quite enjoy watching them squirm. Centuries later, and I'm still impressed that you all managed to keep Alik's fantastic talent from me for all those years. It's fascinating."

LEXI C. FOSS

Jacque's eyebrows hit his hairline. "Where?" he mouthed, and Jayson just shook his head. Because he didn't know. These comms worked up to four miles away, and knowing Osiris, he had backup who helped him switch locations.

"Take Grace and Jeremy back to Hydria," he said.

Jacque shook his head, his loyalty kicking in.

"Aidan," Jayson mouthed. The master of strategy was still on the island and could advise them on how to proceed. For now, Jayson didn't have a choice but to comply with Osiris's demands. "And take care of Lizzie for me," he added, the unspoken *In case I don't make it out of this alive* hanging heavily in the air.

The teleporter nodded slowly. "Okay, Jay." He grabbed Grace and Jeremy before they could fight him and disappeared.

That left just Jayson and a very quiet Tom. He'd taken a position up in the hills somewhere, his sniper rifle at the ready even though he hadn't needed to use it. And he'd intelligently maintained radio silence the entire time.

Or maybe they'd discovered and killed him. It was hard to tell, but knowing Tom, he was healthy, alive, and scouting the ground for Osiris right now.

"I'm alone," Jayson announced.

"Excellent. Now disarm."

Jayson wondered if that meant Osiris could see him, or if he had men of his own stationed in similar positions to Tom. He made a show of removing his guns and knives, including the one in his boot for good measure.

"Done," he said flatly. "Now where are you?"

"I'm sending someone to retrieve you. I believe you're old friends."

Ezekiel appeared with a grin not a second later. "Jedrick, old friend, it's been a long time."

"You son of a bitch," Jayson growled. "I should have known."

Ezekiel sighed, "I don't think he's very excited to see

me, Osiris. I thought he would at least grin considering we haven't seen each other in over a hundred years."

Jayson blinked at the subtle comment. They'd seen each other hours ago, but it seemed his master didn't know that.

Or was it another ruse?

"I can hear that," Osiris replied. "Bring him to me anyway."

"As you command, Sire." His words were formal and respectful, but the gold flecks in his eyes flashed. He stared at Jayson, his gaze conveying some hidden message as he dropped a silver box between them. It was subtle and masked from onlookers by the position of their legs. He revealed a matching one in his palm before saying, "Shall we go, Jedrick?"

A tracking device? *What are you up to, Ezekiel?*

"Sure," Jayson replied. It wasn't like he had a choice. "Can't wait."

Chapter Twenty-Six

Fractured Bonds

Lizzie paced the beach, sniffling.

She was too afraid to call out for help. It may have been Jacque who brought her here, but she didn't know for sure. There were no house lights or people, only the moon and the black sand beach. It seemed to embody her life—a constant state of loneliness.

"Lizzie!"

The familiar voice froze her in place. "Stas?" No. That was impossible. She saw her die.

So now I'm going crazy. Awesome. Why not? It seemed appropriate, all things considered.

And she was freezing thanks to her sweat-dampened clothes and the cool evening air.

"Oh God, Lizzie." The words were accompanied by a pair of arms being thrown around Lizzie's neck.

She blinked.

And now she was feeling things.

Lizzie did hit that man's chest pretty hard...

"I'm so sorry, Liz. I'm so, so sorry. Everything is such a mess, and I don't even know where to begin. But you're my best friend, Liz. And I hate that you're mad at me, but I need you so much right now. So much it hurts. Tell me what I need to do. Please. I can't go through this without you too."

Stas is rambling.

Which could really only mean one thing: Lizzie had lost her mind. She'd created a babbling figment of her best friend to keep her company in the darkness.

Not the healthiest coping mechanism, but she couldn't help returning her friend's hug and indulging in a false sense of closure. Lizzie clearly needed this temporary reprieve from reality to heal, and so she would use it effectively.

"I should have forgiven you," she murmured. "I'm not thrilled that you kept me in the dark, but Jayson explained that it was to protect me."

Too little, too late, of course. But at least Lizzie understood now. It still hurt, but not nearly as much as losing her best friend.

"We should have told you," Stas said, sorrow in her voice. "I wanted to so many times, but I also didn't want to take your choices away from you and force you into this world. I realize now that by not telling you, I still stole your right to choose, and I'm so sorry."

"I forgive you." Lizzie squeezed her tighter. "I just wish you hadn't died on me."

"Me too," Stas whispered. "Me too."

They hugged for several minutes while Lizzie waited for her phantom to disappear, but the moment stretched on. Was there more to say?

"Is Jayson here too?" she asked, hopeful. It seemed appropriate for her delusional state. Maybe she would have the chance to say goodbye to him too.

"He's not back yet, but Jacque's been teleporting everyone in, so I suspect he'll be here any minute."

Lizzie frowned. "Teleporting from where?"

"Osiris's house, apparently." She pulled back with a huff. "They went without me. Something about keeping me as their secret weapon since no one knows I'm a Hydraian."

"Wait…" Lizzie used the moonlight to examine her friend. "You're immortal now?"

"Well, yeah. Jonathan shot me."

She swallowed her hope. "No, he killed you."

"And I woke up," Stas replied, her voice sad.

"But they were incendiary bullets."

Stas shook her head. "Hollow glass, actually. Which means I'm a Hydraian now." She paused. "Hold on, did you think I really died?"

"Well, yeah!" Lizzie blurted out, unable to hold back her conflicting emotions. She'd spent the last however many hours or days grieving. "You're not dead?"

"Does that mean I'm not forgiven?" Stas asked, voice unsure.

Lizzie shrieked and threw her arms around her best friend to hug the life out of her again. She didn't even care if this killed her, because she needed the comfort and had to assure herself that Stas was really alive.

Joy unlike anything she'd ever felt filtered through her chest, especially as another realization hit her. "Jayson's alive too?" She held her breath, waiting and hoping.

"Yes," Stas breathed. "And you're suffocating me."

"I don't care," Lizzie admitted as she squeezed her tighter. "You're here. You're really here."

And Jayson too.

Her heart thudded wildly in her chest at the thought of seeing him again as tears pricked her eyes.

He's alive.

She would see him again, and, hopefully, soon.

Except... "Did you say Jayson is at Osiris's house?"

"Yeah, he led the rescue mission," Stas breathed as she thudded Lizzie on the back. "You're gonna kill me again."

She let her go. "And he's okay?" she pressed, needing to hear it again.

"As far as I know, the mission went as expected, and you're here." Stas grasped her shoulders as if needing to steady herself. "It's been a hell of a day." A touch of wariness highlighted those words, causing Lizzie's happiness to falter.

She was missing something.

Everyone's alive. They should be celebrating, but Stas didn't seem joyous at all. Thankful, maybe, but not in high spirits.

Dying would be traumatic, Lizzie imagined. As well as waking up fine the next...

Oh. Oh, no.

"You're a Hydraian," she realized on an exhale.

"That's what I keep saying. And what the hell is stuffed under your shirt?" she rubbed her abdomen. "It felt like hugging a tree."

"It's a file," Lizzie explained, but she also saw right through her friend's attempt to change the subject. She was upset. Really, really upset. And then it hit her—why becoming immortal would hurt her so badly. "Issac."

She covered her mouth as Stas's face crumpled. Lizzie knew better than to hug her again. It would only encourage the waterworks.

Stas was silent for too long before she whispered, "I'm

not ready to talk about it yet."

"Oh, Stas," Lizzie murmured. "Oh God, it's my fault."

"No," Stas snapped. "Don't ever say that. Jonathan pulled the trigger, and I will kill him for it."

"Hold that thought," Issac said as he sauntered toward them. If he'd been watching in the shadows, he chose a heck of a time to make his presence known.

"We have a much larger problem to discuss." He glanced at Lizzie. "Welcome home, Elizabeth. I would allow this reunion to continue, but Astasiya is needed urgently. Amelia and Eliza have volunteered to keep Elizabeth company in the interim."

"What's going on?" Stas asked, her lips curving down as he came to stand beside her without reaching out to touch her. That missing gesture caused Lizzie's heart to break for her best friend.

They can't be together.

Because Stas died saving me.

"It seems Osiris has taken the Elders hostage," Issac murmured. "We tried to gather intelligence from the Guardians, but when we asked them what happened, they collectively slit their throats."

Lizzie gasped, her fingers going to her lips. "What? Is Jayson okay?"

"That remains to be seen," Issac replied, his tone far too formal for Lizzie's liking. "From what we have gathered, Osiris compelled the Guardians to leave the Elders unprotected. Then, in a grand show of power, he demanded they silence themselves when asked about the events of the kidnapping. It proves, unnecessarily, that distance does not dampen his power."

"Oh my God," Stas breathed while Lizzie tried not to faint at the gruesome image. "Will they survive?"

"Yes, with their memories intact." He paused to let that settle.

What a horrible thing to remember doing—and involuntarily, too.

She shivered. Osiris wanted her to have his child. What sort of monster would she have created for him?

Her stomach churned at the thought, followed by another more devastating one. It sliced through her chest, leaving her bleeding and pained.

"Jayson," Lizzie whispered, her voice cracking. To have him murdered, then resurrected, only to potentially die again by the hand of Osiris.

Oh God, her heart couldn't handle it.

"If Osiris intends to exterminate the Elders, he will do so in a grand fashion, which gives us time. My experience, however, suggests he's inviting us out to play, and Aidan agrees."

"You mean, you think he knows?" Stas asked, fear evident in her voice. "About your friendship with the Hydraians? About me?"

"I think he's always known," Issac murmured. "Ezekiel mentioned a seer. If that is true, it means Osiris has been playing us from the beginning. Although, Aidan believes a fortune-teller cannot predict all outcomes, and he has proposed a plan."

"Which is?" Stas prompted.

Issac studied her, his expression artfully blank. "He wants to send you to meet Osiris."

Stas paled. "What?"

"His plan hinges on Osiris being unaware of your talents, and he feels that the potential element of surprise is just what is needed to rectify the situation." Issac sounded so detached and very unlike the man Lizzie knew. Didn't he realize this behavior would only worsen the situation between them?

"What are your feelings on his plan?" Stas asked, her voice soft.

Issac remained silent for a long moment before replying, "My feelings on the plan are irrelevant. Aidan is a master of strategy, and I bow to his intelligence."

Pain filtered through Stas's expression at the far-too-logical response. Lizzie wanted to smack him for being so cold and heartless and would have opened her mouth to say so if her vocal cords still worked.

Stas nodded, taking on the same stoic air. "Well, so much for keeping me a secret. If I even am one, I mean."

"Indeed," Issac replied, his tone softening as he shifted.

The moon illuminated his features, causing Lizzie to stifle a gasp.

Sadness.

It emanated from his vivid eyes with such sincerity that it fractured logic. His formality may have hidden it in his voice, but that expression said it all.

The picture of a broken man.

"As always, you have my support, whatever you decide." He bowed his head in a way that spoke of reverence and torment—his throat convulsing with the words. "Always, Aya," he added in a whisper.

Agony destroyed Stas's features, breaking Lizzie's heart in two.

This was Issac's version of goodbye.

And her best friend had no choice but to accept it.

~*~

"Welcome, Jedrick," Osiris greeted, his hands open in a polite gesture belied by the scene before him. Luc, Balthazar, and Alik were all on their knees, heads bowed. A clear indication of where Jayson would soon be.

If he had access to his powers, he would choke the bastard with that gold chain around his neck. Alas, he seemed unable to use his gifts at the moment. No doubt a ward or a rune, or some other manner of voodoo created by Osiris himself.

Prick.

"Osiris," he growled as he stopped beside Luc. "Been a while."

"Has it?" Osiris blinked his ancient eyes. "I suppose it

is a matter of perspective, but it feels very recent to me." He shrugged. "Well, now that I have you all. Kneel."

Jayson dropped to the ground at the single-word command but held Osiris's gaze. A direct challenge, one he knew the Ichorian would not appreciate, but Jayson didn't give a fuck anymore.

"What now?" he demanded.

"Are you in a hurry, Jedrick?" Osiris asked, arching a brow. "Perhaps you're hoping to return to a certain redheaded female you erroneously assume is yours?"

"There are no assumptions, Osiris. She is mine in every way." And he would do whatever he needed to do to protect her.

"Oh?" Osiris turned to Ezekiel. "This continues to fascinate me. I understood the attraction—she's a gorgeous specimen—but that sounded more like love. Have you been guiding him on the process?"

Ezekiel's nostrils flared, but his lips curled into one of his trademark grins. *Hiding the pain?* "I'm not sure I would be able to provide him much guidance given the circumstances, nor have I seen Jedrick in over a century."

Jayson wasn't sure what fascinated him more: Ezekiel's outright lie or the implication behind the words.

"Yes, I suppose you have been preoccupied with other tasks." The taunt in Osiris's tone was not lost on Jayson. Ezekiel mentioned not having a choice in his work as of late; were the two related?

"In any case," Osiris continued, his focus shifting back to Jayson. "What would you be willing to give me in exchange for Elizabeth?"

"Considering she's already safe in Hydria, I'd give you nothing."

"Safe is such a relative term. It can so easily change, you see." He started pacing, hands clasped behind his back. "Ezekiel could bring her to me right now if I asked. I ensured their bond after her successful birth, as I did not fully trust Jonathan to uphold his end of our arrangement.

All it takes is a simple command. Would you care for a demonstration?"

Jayson bristled at the clear threat. "You son of a bitch, if you touch her—"

"I suggest you calm down before I decide to teach you some manners," Osiris chastised. "You could learn so much from Elizabeth. Perhaps I should allow you to keep her a little while longer, but I am still curious—what would you give me in return?" He strolled forward and ran his fingers through Luc's blond hair. "Perhaps your king? Would you sacrifice him for Elizabeth?"

Jayson's heart dropped to his stomach, impeding his ability to speak.

Luc for Lizzie?

He couldn't... wouldn't...

"Or perhaps your mind-reading best friend?" Osiris pet Balthazar with the words, almost as one would a cherished pet. "He's quite powerful. I could use him in so many ways or make an example of him at the next Conclave." He turned thoughtful. "Decisions. Hmm."

"Why?" Jayson managed. "Why do this?"

"Because you have decided to take something that belongs to me, Jedrick. Do you have any idea how long I've waited for her creation? How many times we tried to perfect it?" He paused, waiting. "No? Of course you don't, yet you dare claim her as your own? How incredibly ungrateful, after everything I've given you."

Jayson's lips moved, but no words escaped. How did one respond to a madman? The only thing Osiris ever gave any of them was death. Why would Jayson ever be grateful for that?

"Sire," Ezekiel murmured, gently interrupting the moment. "We are reaching the hour of the seer's prediction."

"Ah yes, the future." Osiris clasped his hands before him now and stepped back. "I so desire to know what it is our Skye cannot foresee."

Ezekiel's wince caught Jayson's attention.

Was it the name that hurt him, or the words?

"I would still love to know, though," Osiris added. "What would you give me in return for Elizabeth? If I vowed never to disturb her again, to wait for another of her kind's creation, what would you give me?"

"Your vow?" Jayson repeated, his voice hoarse with emotion. "Means shit to me."

"Perhaps, but that belies the point. I want to know what you would sacrifice for her. Give me a truthful answer. Now."

The compulsion wrapped around Jayson's heart and soul, forcing the response from his throat. He didn't want to say it, didn't want to think about what it meant.

Fuck...

It resembled a betrayal, a broken vow that was millennia old.

But deep within, he knew it to be true. As much as it hurt, he couldn't lie.

"Anything," he rasped, bowing his head in defeat. "I would give anything for her."

Because he loved her. More than anyone else in existence, including those he called his best friends and brothers.

A tear slipped from his eye as an ancient bond tying his blood to theirs splintered. For the first time in their existence, someone else had risen above their sacred connection.

"Fascinating," Osiris murmured. "Absolutely fascinating. I may just let you keep her after all, at least for now."

Jayson couldn't lift his head or say a word. What was there left to discuss? He'd failed his friends in the worst way, for a woman he cherished more than life itself.

It defied logic and all his principles, but Elizabeth Watkins was his to protect. And he would do everything in his power to fulfill that oath.

353

Even if it meant dying for her.
For she would forever be his heart.
I love you, Red.

CHAPTER TWENTY-SEVEN

And So It Begins

Subject's roommate has applied for an
internship with the CRF. Benefactor
informed of potential addition and has
given approval for hire.

—Entry Log 121.05.4-7

"This is a terrible idea," Tom stated.

"Maybe," Stas agreed. "But it's happening." She handed him a new earpiece meant for their team alone.

Several Hydraians, as well as Issac, Tristan, and Mateo, stood around them, dressed for action. Dark colors mingled with camouflage and a variety of weapons. Issac had worn dark jeans and combat boots, two items she didn't even know he owned. She'd donned long sleeves and pants, both forest green.

The plan was pretty simple. Send Stas in as a diversion, converge on Osiris and his minions while they were distracted, and free the Elders.

Aidan predicted their success to be around sixty percent. Better than all the other ideas, which were closer to forty.

Tom inserted his new comm unit. He'd muted the other one but kept it in his opposite ear to listen for any chatter between Jayson and Osiris.

"I have no idea where Ezekiel took him," Tom started, his words showering Stas in ice.

"Ezekiel?" she repeated, her voice hoarse. "He's here?"

"Yeah." He frowned. "Sorry, Stas."

She swallowed and shook her head. "No problem." Except anyone who could hear the frog in her throat would see right through that.

Issac raised a brow, silently asking, *Can you handle it?* He knew her reaction to Ezekiel the first time hadn't been favorable. The man murdered her parents—brutally. She sensed the others weren't as sure of his guilt, but Stas remembered that night vividly. Those ebony eyes were forever ingrained in her nightmares.

"Astasiya," Issac murmured.

Everyone was staring at her.

She shook her head again. "Yeah, I'm good."

Her demon didn't look so sure. This was usually the part where he would hug her, but he maintained a polite distance.

Already pushing me away, she thought sadly. Not that she could blame him. One drop of her blood would kill him instantly, and they both valued his life more than their relationship.

Stas would rather see Issac every day and not be able to touch him than to never see him at all.

Hurt and loneliness wrapped around her heart,

solidifying her resolve for the task ahead. She would focus on her inner frustration and devastation, and not on the fear Ezekiel evoked.

I can do this.

"I'm good," she repeated, stronger now.

Issac held her gaze for a moment longer before nodding. "Where did they go, Thomas?" he asked, his attention shifting to the plan.

"They disappeared into the underbrush." Tom gestured to the tree line. "I tried to track them but lost sight right about there." His finger lifted to a cluster in the distance.

"And that's where I come in," Brian, a Hydraian with decent tracking abilities, informed. Stas had seen the tall, lanky male wandering around Hydria but hadn't been formally introduced until tonight. His gift was the least defensive—being only able to track a scent, similar to a hound dog—however, their choices were limited.

"Hold on, mate. I sense something," Mateo said. "What happened there?" He nodded to the field beside what appeared to be a demolition site.

Tom followed his gesture. "That's where Ezekiel met Jayson."

Mateo grinned. "Brilliant. He left a tracker."

"You can sense that?" Tom asked, shock evident in his tone. Stas felt the same.

"I have a knack for technology," the blond replied with a wink. "Jacque?"

"Yep." He disappeared with the word and popped back not five seconds later with a silver rectangle in his hand. It'd happened so quickly that Stas didn't even see him appear and reappear.

Impressive.

Mateo plucked the device from his hand and started tinkering with it. Stas understood basic electronics, but she had nothing on this Ichorian. He flipped open a screen and grinned. "Now we have a location."

"They're still here," Issac said as he eyed the position.

"That confirms my suspicions. He's waiting for us."

Tristan stepped forward to study the map. "Do you feel it's a trap, Issac?"

"I believe he wishes to issue a statement of sorts, though I fear what that may entail." Issac ran his fingers through his hair and sighed, "As for a trap, there is only one way to find out."

"On it." Jacque disappeared.

Issac looked to the spot the teleporter had just vacated, and shook his head. "Not what I meant. We have no way of knowing what wards Osiris has constructed to capture us or—"

"Scouted," Jacque announced as he materialized beside Issac. "Elders are alive, and only Ezekiel and Osiris appear to be on site. I popped around in a few places with no interference, and I have a good place to drop Stas now."

Everyone stared at him.

"That was a dangerous maneuver," Issac noted dryly.

"Then you would be really displeased to know that I almost teleported to Luc's side just to see if I could nab him, but I chose to come back here and report instead. Shall I go try now?" The sarcasm in his voice would have earned a grin from Stas any other day, but not now. She agreed with Issac on that being a cavalier move, though she'd done several of her own these last few months.

"You've grown quite insolent in your short years." Tristan grinned with the words, clearly meaning them as praise. "I'm impressed."

Issac cleared his throat. "We need to focus."

"Yes, and we need to relocate," Tom said as he started to pack up. "Time for the distraction."

Stas nodded and reached for Jacque. "I'll meet you all there."

Issac grabbed her wrist before she could touch the teleporter, his sapphire gaze blazing as he said everything through those two smoldering orbs. Her heart skipped a beat at the familiar intensity.

He didn't want her to go. She assumed as much—even as she agreed—but it was predicted as the most successful option.

And she could do this.

With his support.

"Issac," she whispered, aware of their audience. "This is what Aidan suggested."

"I am aware," he replied, moving closer. "That doesn't mean I'm thrilled by it."

She dared to lay her hand over his heart, her touch tentative. "You'll be right behind me."

Emotion flared in his pupils as he cupped her cheek.

Fear, she realized.

"I've trained for this," she reminded him. "It's sooner than we expected, but I can do this." She needed his faith, and she let him see that with her eyes. "Please, Issac. You have to let me go."

The words stabbed her in the heart, and his expression said he'd felt it too.

God, it hurt.

She hated this.

Hated fate.

Hated her cursed immortal blood.

Hated everything.

But most of all, she hated the broken way he nodded in acceptance. It felt like the beginning of the end. They both knew it was inevitable, but to have the choice ripped out of their hands seemed so unfair.

It will always be you, her soul promised. *Always.*

"Be safe, Aya," he whispered.

Issac took a step back, his eyes glistening with unsuppressed emotion.

"Thank you." She would forever cherish his unfettered confidence in her to see this mission through. He hated it, but he also had faith in her success. And that meant more to her than anything in the world.

"I'll be waiting for you," she said as she held out her

hand for Jacque again. "Find me."

"Always," Issac replied.

Her environment changed as Jacque moved her deep into the forest about a hundred yards from the tracker signal. "Be back in a jiffy," he whispered.

Stas faltered as her emotions warred.

Focus, her brain demanded.

Cry, her heart begged.

There will be time to do that later.

She took a steadying breath and observed her surroundings from a crouched position. Their original plan had been to rely on Brian to point them in the right direction, but the tracking device worked much better.

The goal was to distract Osiris long enough to give the others a chance to take him and his minions down. It put a lot of the weight on her shoulders.

She shivered. *I can do this.*

It didn't help that she felt no different from before. Tom had mentioned the same when he awoke immortal. The others said it was "perfectly normal." Her gifts would trigger as she needed them.

Or so she hoped.

"We're in position," Issac murmured through the earpiece, his voice calming her in a way no one else could. "Give us a good show, love."

The endearment touched her soul, emboldening her.

He always knew what she needed.

She cleared her throat and grinned despite the dire circumstances. "That I can do."

All four Elders were kneeling at Osiris's feet in a clearing beyond the trees. Ezekiel stood beside him, hands clasped behind his back.

Where are all your minions? Jacque may not have found them, but Stas knew there had to be more.

Although, a man of Osiris's skill and power didn't really need an army.

Stas slipped between the trees, her boots silent over the

forest floor. Stark had taught her a lot these last few months, especially about stealth and combat. He called her a natural in training, something she attributed to her inhuman birthright.

And then there were the sessions with Issac. So many evenings spent honing her gift and practicing the art of compulsion. She learned that her commands weren't attached to a definitive time frame but remained in effect for as long as she held the thread of control. As soon as she dropped the link, the persuasion ended. That would be the trick to remember with Osiris.

"...do I choose?" His ancient voice slithered through the air, dampening her skin.

The same feeling of familiarity swept over her as it did the first time she met him. So did the sense of dread.

Pure evil lurked beneath his formal facade. She'd witnessed his proclivity for torture from the front row in his amphitheater.

Sick fuck.

"You'll have to compel me again for that response," Jayson growled as Stas stepped out into the clearing.

"Or I could use Alik." Osiris smiled. "Inflict pain on..." He trailed off as he noticed Stas's approach. She was surprised it took him this long. It indicated he might be alone after all. Minus the assassin standing beside him.

"Oh, don't mind me," she said, her voice boasting a confidence she didn't feel. "I'm just wandering."

Jayson's head whipped around, his mouth falling open, while the remaining Elders remained bowed and unmoving.

Victims of control.

"Well, well," Ezekiel said, grinning. "Welcome to the party, Astasiya."

Osiris cocked a brow. "Astasiya?" He studied her. "You're familiar to me." He sounded almost curious, if a little bored. "When have we met?"

"You don't remember?" she asked, feigning

disappointment. "I suppose you were busy preparing yourself for an evening of torture-filled fun." She stopped ten feet away and let her hands hang loosely at her sides.

Ancient green eyes looked her up and down, his expression indicating he found her lacking. "Your insolence is boring me. I'll deal with you when I'm finished. For now, stay—"

"Stop talking, Osiris." Three words, casually said but underlined in power. "It's rude to dismiss someone so quickly, especially when you know nothing about them."

His lips parted, but no words came out, causing his eyes to widen in apparent shock.

"See what I mean?" she asked as she wrapped all her mental faculties around that command and held it in place. If he couldn't speak, he couldn't persuade.

"Beautiful," Ezekiel murmured. "But, oh, don't mind me. I'm only here for the show." He displayed his hands in an *I surrender* pose and remained very still beside Osiris. "Please continue."

Stas considered muting him as well, but he appeared far more entertained than threatening. Osiris also appeared more amused than violent, his lips curling into an exuberant smile that nearly unsettled her resolve.

Apprehension prickled her nerves even as she forced herself to focus. She needed to free her friends. Then run far, far away.

Jacque had informed them all that Osiris had commanded the telepathic Elder to unleash his mental torture ability on the others. That seemed the appropriate starting place.

"Release your persuasive hold on Alik."

The tension in the air dimmed, but all three remained kneeling. Stas guessed all of them had been sent to their knees by vocal force.

She immediately dropped her command regarding Alik since it no longer held purpose, and tightened her mental grasp on the one forbidding Osiris to speak.

He appeared even more impressed now as he took her measure again. The bastard even applauded, which sent a tremor down her spine. She'd wanted to avoid his interest for as long as possible, but now she held his undivided attention.

He waved a hand as if encouraging her to do more.

And she had no choice but to comply if she wanted to save the Elders.

"Free Balthazar, Lucian, Alik, and Jayson from your persuasion."

Luc and Balthazar fell to the ground, their bodies trembling, while Alik sat back on his heels with a dead expression.

Jayson, however, stood. He'd obviously not experienced the same torture as his friends. "You shouldn't be here," he said in greeting. "Not that I'm complaining."

She ignored his remarks and unleashed her latest command, reaffirming her grip on Osiris's ability to speak.

The monster's grin widened in approval.

He spread his arms in a gesture that asked, *What are you going to do now?*

She'd expected more of a fight, but either the others had removed all the remedial threats or he really was here alone.

"Ezekiel, tell me where your backup is hiding." It took more effort than she expected to speak to her parents' murderer directly, but she managed with only a slight quiver in her voice.

The assassin smiled smugly. "You're looking at him, but I'm under strict instructions not to harm anyone." He glanced pointedly at his master.

Osiris shrugged, unconcerned. He still appeared to be far too amused for Stas's taste. She tested the speaking demand and found the binds strong and unbending.

"Are we ready to continue the show?" Ezekiel continued, his gold-flecked irises flickering to his left for approval.

Osiris nodded but kept his attention on Stas. He almost seemed delighted. Such a creepy emotion she never wanted to see on him again, especially in relation to *her*.

"Excellent. To the Ichorians on site, I have been instructed to inform you that your betrayal of your kind will not go unpunished, but for today, you are granted temporary amnesty." His gaze lifted over her shoulder. "And if you're thinking about shooting us, Thomas, I would advise against it. The seer predicted it would not end well. Besides, Astasiya seems to have Osiris well contained. Not bad for a pretty little angel."

The ancient one gave a subtle nod of acknowledgment, his eyes sparkling.

"How does that bastard know my name?" Tom growled through the earpiece.

"It would seem they expected this outcome," Issac replied. "Which would explain why Osiris merely tortured the Elders and didn't kill them. He wants us all alive, at least for now."

"And so, what, that means we should return the favor?" Tom asked incredulously.

"I am curious to understand the purpose of this meeting, so yes, I believe we should grant them the same reprieve. And as Ezekiel has insinuated, Osiris already knows we are here, which only intrigues me more. Besides, I'd say Astasiya has the situation under control." The pride in Issac's voice caressed her broken heart.

But that didn't mean she agreed that these two men should live.

They were murderers.

Evil, vile creatures who should be removed.

Kill them, a part of her encouraged. It would be so easy.

She could command the assassin to stab himself.

No.

She could force him to remove his own head.

A gruesome sight flashed behind her eyes, and her lips

flinched upward.

A few words were all she needed.

Remove your head.

Monstrous.

It would satisfy my need for revenge.

And you would never forgive yourself.

But they would be dead.

Do it…

Her lips parted as she considered the demand. *End them.*

The compulsion wrapped a cloak of darkness around her, causing all her hairs to stand on end. It would be so easy—

"Aya," Issac murmured through the earpiece. "Focus."

Stas blinked, startled out of her dark thoughts.

She immediately tested the silencing command and found it hanging by a loose thread. Her mind emboldened it immediately as she closed the door on her wicked yearnings. They were always there, lurking, and ready to take her over the edge.

Her power was intoxicating and addicting. And could be used to wield so much pain.

She met Osiris's gaze and saw pride brewing in his lurid stare. It sickened her to the core.

He knew.

Because he openly embraced the wicked urgings stirred by this power. She'd seen him in action, knew what he was capable of, and witnessed how much he enjoyed it.

I'm not you.

He merely grinned. As far as she knew, he couldn't read minds, but that all-knowing look left her unsettled.

"Osiris is secure," she said over the comms.

"Yes," Ezekiel murmured. "And as a sign of good faith, Osiris has granted permission for the teleporter to retrieve the Hydraians' precious king."

Stas narrowed her gaze. "I sense a trap."

"No trap, Astasiya. Merely a token of temporary

peace."

She studied the assassin and the content Ichorian beside him. None of this sat well with her, but they'd proven their knowledge of the situation at hand.

Because of the seer.

"I believe him," Issac said over the comms. "He has no reason to lie."

"I beg to differ, Wakefield. He has *every* reason to lie. Let me shoot him."

"Stand down, Thomas." The authority in Issac's tone rippled through her earpiece, soothing her in a way it shouldn't. "Jacque, grab Lucian."

Jacque didn't hesitate. He teleported to Luc and disappeared in a blink.

Ezekiel grinned. "There, that wasn't so hard, was it?"

"What was the point of all of this?" Jayson demanded, folding his arms. "A punishment for rescuing Lizzie?" He was still the only Elder standing. Whatever Osiris forced Alik to do to Balthazar had left him shaking uncontrollably on the ground, while the telepath sat motionless, staring off into the distance with dead eyes.

To be forced to torture your best friends... She trembled at the thought.

Ezekiel smirked. "Elizabeth is a key reason for our meeting tonight, yes. She's one of a kind, and Osiris would like her back."

"Over my dead body," Jayson growled.

"That can certainly be arranged," Ezekiel murmured as Osiris tapped him on the arm. They exchanged a long look that left the assassin grinning. "It appears my Sire has decided to grant her freedom. For now."

"For now?" Stas repeated. "What the hell does that mean?"

"I believe his objective has shifted, little angel." His gold-flecked gaze sparkled. "You are quite the enigma, darling one. And he's intrigued."

Ice dotted her spine as she interpreted his meaning.

"I'm his new objective."

"So it would seem, for you should not exist." He checked his watch and sighed. "We have crossed several foreseeable outcomes now. Therefore, I do believe it is time for Issac to appear. Please. Osiris would like a word."

The ancient Ichorian nodded, his attention finally leaving her to gaze expectantly to his left. Her demon sauntered into view a second later, his expression blank, as Tristan and Mateo flanked him on either side.

"A test of loyalty," Issac mused as he walked directly to her side. "You've known all along."

The ancient lifted a shoulder.

"Partly," Ezekiel murmured. "The seer warned Osiris of this outcome, as well as several others, but her vision of the ultimate threat remained unclear."

"Stas," Jayson replied as Jacque reappeared to grab Balthazar. He vanished in a flash, but no one commented. "Your seer couldn't identify her."

"Precisely," Ezekiel replied, pleased. "And now that it's done, we can go?" He regarded his superior, who shook his head.

Those ancient eyes gazed eagerly at Stas.

"You want to be able to speak," she realized.

A nod.

"Absolutely not." She refused to give him even an inch. "I say we kill you instead."

He gave her a disappointed look and turned to Issac. A silent conversation transpired between them as everyone else observed.

"Is there a way for you to remove his persuasion but allow him to speak?" Issac asked, his concentration on Osiris.

"You want to hear what he has to say?" She couldn't help the skeptical tone in her voice. He couldn't be serious.

"I do," Issac confirmed. "Especially as it likely pertains to you."

"I agree," Jayson added.

"I say we shoot him instead," Tom replied through the comms. He seemed to be the only voice of reason.

"I wouldn't," Ezekiel warned, shocking Stas. "The seer already foresaw the possibility, Thomas, and you will fail."

Stas's brow furrowed. "You can hear him?"

"Of course not, but I know what was predicted. And Skye is never wrong." His lips twitched with that last sentence as if he was actively suppressing a reaction. "That said, you could all try, but you have no idea what you're truly up against."

"Immune," Alik rasped.

Ezekiel's lips quirked at the corners. "Yes, as Alik discovered the hard way, Osiris and I are both immune to Hydraian and Ichorian talents. And the incendiary bullets in your rifle won't penetrate our shields. But again, feel free to try."

"That's great, except I'm controlling Osiris right now," Stas said, proving his theory wrong.

"Indeed you are, young one. Well done." Ezekiel clasped his hands in front of him. "Shall we agree to a temporary armistice and hold a discussion, or should Thomas attempt to pull the trigger?"

"Stand down, Tom," Jayson said, his voice holding no room for argument. "I want to hear what Osiris has to say."

"Likewise," Issac agreed. "Astasiya, please?"

She met his vivid gaze, startled. Please? Really? Stas could never deny him when he asked nicely, and he knew it. But he couldn't be serious.

"He's a monster."

"Perhaps, but he has allowed Balthazar and Lucian safe passage to Hydria. He also granted us temporary amnesty, and I believe him."

Stas openly gaped at him.

"Trust your Elders, child," Ezekiel suggested. "They've been playing this game far longer than you."

She glowered at the assassin but refrained from

replying. The man who murdered her parents saw fit to grant her advice. She had half a mind to demand he kill himself for sport.

The vision painted itself behind her eyes, eliciting a grin from a dark, dark place inside of her.

It would be so easy.

"Aya," Issac said, his hand brushing hers. "Please."

Twice.

She closed her eyes. The first time had been hard enough. The second, she couldn't ignore. "Okay," she whispered. "I'll do it."

They wanted Osiris's explanation, so she would give him back his voice. But they'd better at least consider killing him afterward.

Stas toyed with several phrases in her mind while the others waited. The command had to be concise with no flexibility to be interpreted as anything else, or this would go badly.

"Osiris, do not use compulsion on anyone within a one-mile radius of your current position."

He seemed much too pleased with her word choice and nodded, waiting.

She traced the mental strings to the order forbidding him from speaking and snapped the bonds.

"Thank you, child," he said. The fact that he felt the coercion lift implied far too much about his power. "You have much to learn, the first of which being that voice is never a requirement for persuasion. And as a second lesson, our shared gift is technically not called *compulsion*. My gifts have remained intact throughout our entire interaction, but I chose not to use them and will continue to do so now."

His amusement fled as he focused on Issac. Stas waited for Osiris to show his true colors and enact a horrid command, but he merely said, "The Conclave will be forever changed. I would request you all attend the next one, but I won't insult your intelligence."

Issac acknowledged the comment with a slight bow of his head, his version of respect. "I suspect we will see each other again soon, Sire."

Osiris returned the gesture. "You continue to impress me, Issac, even in your defiance. I may keep this entire interaction to myself, at least for now. Please give Aidan my regards. I will miss him."

"Of course," Issac replied in that cordial way of his, giving no outward reaction to the comment regarding Aidan.

"Best of luck to you. Until we meet again."

"Likewise, Sire."

Stas could not believe they were chatting like old friends. Just when she thought she understood this fucked-up world, the immortals in it went and held a pleasant conversation essentially underlined in threat.

Oh, by the way, I'm probably going to kill you soon.

Feel free to try at your leisure.

I will. No hard feelings, of course.

No, no, none at all.

Brilliant.

Seriously? This was why the world would end. They'd all sit back, enjoy a round of tea, and then beat the shit out of each other mentally.

Awesome.

Her inner sarcasm died as Osiris returned his ancient gaze to hers.

So old. So cruel.

"I daresay I am most pleased to make your acquaintance, Astasiya. Here I've spent the last few decades waiting to create a new protégé to replace my broken one, just to find that what I needed already existed. You." He turned to Ezekiel. "I'm quite impressed that Sethios managed to keep this revelation from me. His resilience truly is remarkable, yes?"

"Indeed, Sire," he agreed, his tone emotionless.

"Your gifts are quite rare, child," Osiris continued. "So

rare, in fact, that they reveal your ancestry, daughter of Caro and Sethios." His lips curled into an avid smile while she fought to breathe. "Or would you prefer I call you 'granddaughter'?"

Her eyes widened impossibly more as her throat went dry.

What?

Daughter of Caro and Sethios?

She opened her mouth to refute his claim, then closed it as a sense of rightness overwhelmed her.

Stas's parents' names were Caroline and Seth, though her father frequently referred to her mother as Caro. And *Sethios* wasn't all that far off from *Seth*.

But "granddaughter"?

Was that why he seemed so familiar?

Green eyes… The same shade as her own. Her father's, too.

No.

She shook her head in denial.

No. That was just… No.

That was impossible.

His son would be a Hydraian, and Hydraians couldn't procreate with humans.

Unless another Lizzie existed, which Ezekiel implied as a possibility. Was her mother a product of the CRF?

"Osiris and I are both immune to Hydraian and Ichorian talents."

"Except I'm controlling Osiris right now."

"Indeed you are, young one. Well done."

The conversation replayed through her thoughts on repeat. A ruse? A lie meant to provide false hope? A hint? A way to fuck with their minds?

Osiris turned to Ezekiel. *"Granddaughter* is the appropriate title, yes?"

"Yes, Sire." Dark eyes met hers, and she swore a hint of pain flashed in his features.

"Excellent." Osiris pinned Stas with a final stare. "I

look forward to our next conversation, my child. Might I suggest researching appropriate terms in the interim? Try, perhaps, *psychic persuasion.*" He winked and grabbed Ezekiel's arm. "I will see you soon, Astasiya."

"Until next time," Ezekiel added with a nod.

They vanished into the shadows, leaving Stas gaping at the hole they created, both physically and mentally. She hadn't even had a moment to process the idea of attacking him after that information bomb.

"Grandfather?" she whispered, her psyche shattering.

"I have you, love." Issac wrapped her in his arms. "I'm not going anywhere."

She moved into his chest on autopilot, needing his scent and comfort. "He's...? I don't..."

"Go to Elizabeth," Issac said over her head. "I can take it from here."

"We'll need to discuss this," Jayson said.

"Indeed," her demon agreed. "Later."

"Yes," Jayson said. "Later."

Issac's lips brushed Stas's temple. "We'll figure this out, Aya."

The double meaning in those words destroyed the thin wall she'd built around her emotions. "Issac," she whispered, shaking as the world around her tumbled down.

She clung to him as her legs gave out, and he caught her, just as he promised, and lifted her into his arms.

Her energy fled with the last of her control.

Grandfather...

What did that mean for her?

CHAPTER TWENTY-EIGHT

There's No One Like You

Memories firmly erased and humanoid
impressions implanted, as per the
direction of the benefactor. Subject
will be moved to the Watkins home
briefly for simulation purposes.
                    —Entry Log 118.03.4-7

Lizzie placed the file on the dining room table. "I have no idea where to start."

Amelia and Eliza sat across from her—two complete strangers who had taken it upon themselves to help Lizzie feel welcome in Jayson's home after Jacque had dropped her off.

The two women tried to distract her with a shower,

fresh clothes, and a very large cup of hot chocolate. Lizzie's mind never trailed far from Jayson or his current predicament, but she tried to play along as best she could. Especially since Amelia and Eliza seemed just as worried as her.

"I suggest you start from the beginning," Amelia said as her elegant fingers flipped open the folder.

She mentioned her familiarity with the CRF during the initial part of their conversation, something Jayson had touched on briefly while in Bora Bora. He also informed Lizzie that Amelia and Tom were romantically involved. The news left Lizzie feeling like an outsider. Tom—the man who treated her like a sister—had run off and fallen in love, and she had no idea. She felt as if she didn't know him at all.

"It looks like a series of logs." Amelia scanned the words while she spoke. "Little snippets of details throughout your years in the lab." She flipped to the end. "And out, I think."

"It's a code," Eliza said, her ebony gaze sparkling as she reviewed several entries. "The first digit is always one, but the next number seems to increase at specific intervals. How old are you?"

"Twenty-four," Lizzie replied. "Soon to be twenty-five."

Eliza nodded as she flipped to the back of the file. "Then yes, your age in the file is the next two digits. For example, this one is one zero four, so you were four years old when they created this entry. And I bet the second set is the month since it never goes over twelve. The last is your project name, four dash seven."

"Huh," Lizzie mused. "So it's a chronological catalog of my life."

"It's a qualitative log," she explained. "Typical for researchers in labs. I'm guessing there's a quantitative report somewhere as well, but the one you have is more important anyway. The other would just be numbers and statistics."

Lizzie thumbed through a few of the pages, looking for her eighteenth year. She wanted to confirm a theory that had been planted in her head by Osiris—the one about her memory. With all the insanity of the last day, she hadn't been given a chance to consider it, but now she needed to know.

Her eyes scanned the file from her eighteenth year, month eight.

Eliza and Amelia read with her, both of them paling at the information detailed on the page.

"So it's true," Lizzie murmured. "None of my memories are my own. They erased everything and gave me a false sense of identity." That explained the fuzziness of her thoughts and the recollections that didn't stick. Like Rome. "Interesting."

What did that mean for her personality development? Her polite convictions were literally programmed into her, as was her innate innocence. She never desired men because they instructed her not to.

She flipped to the end of the file to search for any notes on Jayson.

Nothing.

So they didn't pair her with him—not purposely, anyway.

There were a few notes about her infatuation with Tom, though. Amelia's cheeks flushed as she read the lines, and Lizzie cleared her throat. "I... It's not like that anymore."

"It's okay." Amelia smiled, her cheeks flushing. "I quite understand the allure."

Eliza rolled her eyes. "You two really need to take your home back and just move in. I can crash with B."

"We're building a home," Amelia said. "It's almost done. Then Jayson can have his place back."

"Seriously, you know the offer stands," Eliza pressed. "I understand why everyone gave me space at first, and I appreciated it, but really, I can handle sharing a house with B. He doesn't, well, you know."

Amelia's eyes sparkled. "I do. He's always treated me like a sister and nothing more."

Lizzie swallowed. "He intimidates me."

"Oh, I bet," Eliza replied. "But I hear you're handling Jayson just fine, which tells me B would not be a problem."

"I don't... It's not..." She shook her head, flustered. "Jayson is the one I want." At their startled gazes she added, "He's the *only* one I want."

"Well, that is the best welcome-home present I could have ever asked for, Red," a deep voice murmured from right behind her. "Although a hug would be wonderful as well."

Lizzie almost fell out of her chair in her attempt to reach him. He caught her hips and hoisted her into the air as her arms flew around his neck.

Real.

He's real.

She hadn't wanted to believe—had refused to let hope capture her heart—until she touched him.

And he felt very much alive, and hot, and hard.

Wearing designer jeans and a long-sleeved forest-green shirt, he was just as she remembered him. Even the windswept brown hair was right.

She pressed her nose to his throat, inhaling his cedar scent.

Very, very real.

His palms went to her ass as she wrapped her legs around his waist. The shorts Eliza let her borrow rode up her thighs, but Lizzie didn't care.

"You're here," she breathed. "You're alive."

He chuckled. "As are you." He slid one hand up to tangle his fingers in her hair and gently pried her face from his neck. "I missed you, Red," he whispered after catching her gaze. "So much it hurt."

"I missed you too." She caressed his face with her eyes, memorizing every strong, masculine line. "I thought you died."

"I'm right here, Liz," he murmured. "And I'm not going anywhere. I promise."

She leaned forward to kiss him, but the clearing of a throat stopped her. Lizzie lifted her gaze to the man standing in the foyer.

"Sorry, I don't mean to interrupt." Tom dragged his fingers through his blond hair, looking a little sheepish. "I just wanted to say that I'm glad you're okay, Liz." The hesitancy in his tone stung. He'd never been uneasy like this around her. Granted, the last few times they saw each other hadn't been all that pleasant for either of them.

Jayson tugged a strand of her hair to catch her attention. "Do you need a minute?" he asked softly.

She swallowed. He was offering her a chance to talk to Tom, but only if she wanted it.

Did she?

Things would never be the same between them—likewise for Lizzie and Stas—but that didn't mean she wanted to hate him forever. They might not be best friends after this, but they could still be friends. Even close, over time.

And if what the doctor implied about Lizzie's Seraphim genetics was true, then her time on Earth would be infinite. Just like everyone else on this island.

Amelia walked around the table to enfold Tom in a hug, her lips at his ear. He nodded at whatever she said, but his eyes were so sad. Lizzie had never seen him like this. Was he hurting because of her? Because she didn't want to talk to him? Because she refused to forgive him?

He died.

She attended his funeral.

And he lied to her in the worst possible way.

Yet the pain of losing him had nothing on the agony she experienced after losing Jayson. And she understood, on a logical level, why Tom kept her in the dark. He meant to protect her, as he always did. That didn't excuse his behavior, but his heart was in the right place.

"I'd like to talk to him," Lizzie decided. "But don't go far."

Jayson captured her mouth in a kiss that knocked her world off-kilter. "I think you'll find it nearly impossible to get rid of me now, Red." He kissed her again before helping her stand. "Let me know when you're done. We have a few items to discuss."

The promise in his words, whether intentional or not, doused her in ice water.

In all the excitement of seeing him, she forgot about something very important.

The baby.

Was that what he wanted to discuss? No, of course not. He couldn't possibly know.

Oh God. How would he react?

Three thousand years of sex without consequences... No way would he be pleased by this news.

It threw her history in both their faces. She was a woman created in a lab. What man would want someone like that? Lizzie's classification didn't exist. A Seraphim created in a mortal womb.

"Lizzie." Jayson's hands cradled her face. "Don't give up on me yet, sweetheart. Talk to Tom, and afterward, we'll catch up, okay?"

She swallowed and nodded. "O-okay." He obviously had no idea, or he wouldn't be so calm.

One problem at a time.

Talking to Tom would be a cakewalk compared to the father of her child. She forced a smile, and Jayson traced the edges of her lips.

"Trust in me," he whispered.

Adoration emanated from his soft brown eyes, causing her heart to flutter with hope. This was the man who kneeled, accepted a collar, and died—all for her. He might not be thrilled by the idea of a child, but he would at least be open to discussing it. As for her being different, he already knew and never looked at her differently.

A lifetime of insecurity and being told she would never be good enough exploded in a single moment as she realized, *To Jay, I'm good enough.*

Because he loved her.

And she loved him.

"Of course I trust you," she replied with conviction. She'd trusted him from the moment he waltzed into her apartment uninvited—an innate, gut reaction to her soul recognizing his.

"Hold that thought, Red," he murmured with a smile. "Tom first."

She returned the smile. "Okay."

He brushed his lips against her forehead and stepped back to address their audience. "I'm going to provide Amelia and Eliza with an update on what happened. We'll be outside."

Tom nodded. "I understand."

"Is everyone all right?" Amelia asked as Jayson opened the front door.

"Physically, yes." His reply whispered through the room, causing Lizzie to frown.

"What does he mean?" she asked, her question directed at Tom.

"Osiris forced Alik to use his mental abilities on Luc and Balthazar, and he's not taking it well. And Stas found out that Osiris might be her grandfather."

Lizzie's eyes widened. "What?"

"Yeah..." Tom rubbed a hand over his face and scratched his jaw. "I'm not quite sure how that works considering Ichorian genetics."

"Do you believe him?"

Tom shrugged. "Honestly, after the things he knew tonight? It's entirely possible. Or he's fucking with us at her expense."

"God," Lizzie breathed. "Is she in Hydria? Because I should go to her. She must feel so alone."

"Wakefield's with her."

"He is?" After the way he acted toward her on the beach, that surprised her. "You're sure?"

"Oh yeah." Tom shook his head. "I might have my own issues with him, but he does right by her. I'll give him that."

She nodded slowly. From what she'd witnessed, he cared deeply for Stas, even if he'd been a bit distant earlier. "She's in good hands."

"Not sure I'd go that far, but okay." The air changed subtly between them as the focus shifted from their mutual friend to the elephant in the room.

"Fuck, Lizzie, I hate that you're mad at me. I know I deserve it, and if you never want to speak to me again, I will do my best to honor it. But you need to know that I never meant to hurt you. Ever."

He palmed the back of his neck. "It all went down so fast. Did Jayson tell you what happened?"

She cleared the emotion lining her throat and forced herself to say, "He mentioned you saved Amelia from a bad situation. And he said you both faked your deaths."

Tom nodded. "That's high level, but yeah. John put me on an assignment to watch Amelia out in the middle of the woods, and the things they were doing to her..." His fists clenched. "Let's just say, I couldn't let it continue. But the only way to protect her was to convince John we were dead, and I couldn't bring you into that, Liz. Not without endangering you too."

"So you left me alone in New York City with a hoard of Ichorians and the CRF." She couldn't help the sarcasm or the annoyance in her tone. Because really? That was probably the worst place to keep her.

"I only saw a glimpse of your file, and I overheard my dad once talking about the serum you needed, and Luc wondered if it was something meant to keep you alive. We couldn't risk removing you from the potential life source without knowing for certain, which was why we sent Jay." He dropped his hands to his sides in defeat. "I realize it left you alone, but there wasn't a moment that went by when I didn't worry about you. I've always adored you, Liz."

"When did we really meet?" she asked, curious.

Tom frowned. "What do you mean? You were, like, ten or something. We met at one of those damn brunches. You don't remember?"

She shook her head and picked up her file. "According to this, I lived in a lab until my eighteenth year."

He stepped forward to take the paper from her, skimming it. "This is bullshit."

"I don't think it is."

"No, I definitely met you as a kid. I remember thinking you were like the sister I always wanted."

She smiled sadly. "I think they implanted that memory." Just as they did all of hers regarding the childhood crush that never blossomed into anything more. "It makes sense. They wanted you to assume the big-brother role to protect me, and they wanted to give me a love interest that would keep me occupied." So she wouldn't be tempted by anyone else until they were ready for her to breed.

And then she met Jayson.

Tom read the paper again and set it down, his eyes blinking. "That... that..."

"Is really messed up?" she supplied with a humorless laugh. "Yeah, it is, but it's probably true."

He stared down at her, his tan face paling. "I had no idea, Liz."

"I know," she replied. "I don't blame you, and I understand why you did what you did. That doesn't mean I'm happy about it, but it's enough to start forgiving you."

Moisture glistened in his eyes. "God, when did you grow up?"

She laughed. "Really, Tom?"

"I mean it. You used to be this fragile, demure little girl. But this new you, she's not demure at all. I approve."

She rolled her eyes. "Six years, at least in my mind, I tried to get you to notice that I'm a woman, and *now* you work it out. Figures."

He chuckled and mussed up her hair. "You're still like a sister to me, Liz."

"A womanly sister, though."

"Sure," he agreed, his brown eyes grinning as he pulled her into a hug. They stayed like that for a long moment, his chin on her head and their arms around each other's backs. It felt right. Not in the same way Jayson felt right, but in a friendship kind of way.

"I've always recognized your beauty, Liz," he added softly. "But I respected you far too much to act on it. Stas, too."

"And Amelia?" she asked.

"Amelia," he repeated, his tone deepening. "I never stood a chance at denying her."

Lizzie smiled, happy for him. "You love her."

"I do," he agreed as he pulled away. "More than I should."

"Good," Lizzie said, meaning it. "I hope she drives you crazy."

"Excuse me?" He managed to sound both amused and floored at the same time.

"What?" She batted her eyes innocently. "We both know you deserve it, Tom Fitzgerald. Oh, and by the way, if you *ever* die on me again, do not expect me to attend your funeral. I've done that once already, and I refuse to do it again. So stay alive. Got it?"

He swallowed. "Yes, ma'am."

"Great. Now, if you wouldn't mind, I need to talk to Jayson."

Tom chuckled and shook his head. "You know, I worried about the two of you, but I think you'll handle him just fine. In fact, I'm looking forward to it."

"And what does that mean?" she demanded.

He shrugged as he started toward the foyer. "Oh, nothing. Just musing out loud." He turned the handle. "Jay, she's all yours. And, uh, good luck, buddy. Bye, Liz!" He popped out of the house before she could get in another word.

"Rude," she grumbled.

Jayson locked the front door. "Sounds like you two worked things out."

"I wouldn't say that," Lizzie replied. "Pretty sure I might want to kill him again now."

His lips curled in amusement. "Tom seems to have that effect on a lot of people, though his talents are unquestionably useful, so we keep him around."

She giggled, and it felt good. After so many hours or days, she needed it.

And then she sobered as she realized the importance of their pending discussion.

"So much has happened," she started.

"Yes," he agreed. "And before you start us down that path, there's something I need to say."

She swallowed. "Okay."

He wiped his palms against his jeans as he approached, his expression serious. She tried to read the emotions in his chocolate eyes, but they were vacillating between too many for her to catch.

Jayson stopped in front of her and took her hands. "I've debated all night on how I wanted to do this and what I needed to say, but no matter what words I form in my mind, nothing measures up to the magnitude of this moment."

He paused to clear his throat and wet his lips with his tongue.

He's nervous.

"In my over-three-thousand years, I never thought it would be possible to feel this way. The notion of a family didn't exist for me, and I was always okay with that because I grew up knowing that inevitability. But now, life has given me the most precious gift I didn't even know I wanted, in the form of you."

She bit her lip to keep it from trembling. The intensity pouring off him was almost too much. It escalated her heartbeat to what had to be unhealthy levels and, at the same time, stilted her breathing. Because she didn't want to miss a single word, and even a simple exhale was too loud.

He held her gaze as he dropped to one knee. "I can't begin to explain how it feels, Elizabeth, to suddenly have everything you never knew you wanted, given to you on the whim of fate."

He dropped her hands to grasp her hips.

"Knowing you has changed me on an irrevocable level. I thought my yearning for you was a passing infatuation, just as the others who came before you were, but the desire grew with each day until I couldn't deny it anymore. And so I broke the rules, and tasted you, but, God, Liz, it wasn't enough." His grip tightened as he pressed his forehead to her stomach. "I don't think it will ever be enough."

Tears glistened in her eyes as he lifted her shirt to place a reverent kiss on her abdomen. He stared up at her with a look of worship as he kissed her belly button.

"A family, Lizzie," he whispered. "I never thought I could ever have a son or a daughter, or even a wife. And I never knew how much I wanted all of that until you. I will spend every day for the rest of my life thanking you, loving you, and cherishing you. And I will do whatever you need me to do to prove that I'm worthy of this amazing gift, Elizabeth. To prove that I'm worthy enough to love you, and to raise our child."

She sniffled as he clasped her hands again and straightened his back while still down on one knee. "I want to marry you, Elizabeth. I realize it's an antiquated tradition, and that humans rarely take their vows seriously, but I want to promise myself to you in front of all our friends and family. What we have is so rare, Lizzie. And I need to do this right, not just for us, but for our future."

He cleared his throat as affection poured from his eyes. "A baby," he whispered, his voice awed. "I'm going to be a father." His gaze shifted upward as if in prayer. "It's the miracle I never knew I wanted, Lizzie."

"Jayson…" She could barely see him through all the water clouding her vision. And if he kept speaking, she'd be a sobbing mess. Of all the things for him to say to her, she never expected this. But it was so perfect, so heartfelt, and so extremely right.

He kissed her knuckles and bowed his head over her hands as tears streamed down her face. "I have the benefit of time and experience behind me, and I can say with utter certainty that no one has ever made me feel the way I do for you. It might seem fast, especially to you, but I know in my heart that this is it for me. There will never be anyone else, and I will wait, for as long as you need me to, for you to feel the same."

Moisture gathered in his gaze as he looked up at her again. "Eternity is a long time, but I want to spend forever with you, if you'll have me." He kissed her wrist, his eyes holding hers even through the tears. "Elizabeth Watkins, will you marry me?"

CHAPTER TWENTY-NINE

Pizza Is Forever

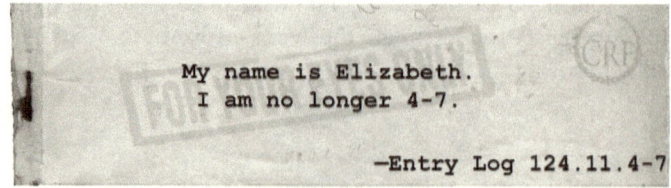

```
My name is Elizabeth.
I am no longer 4-7.

                              —Entry Log 124.11.4-7
```

Jayson's heart raced while he waited for Lizzie to say something. Anything. Even if the words *Fuck off* rolled out of her mouth, he wouldn't care, because the anticipation was killing him.

She licked her lips, opened her mouth, closed it, and opened it again, killing him more. Never had he needed an answer more than he wanted one now.

"Oh God, Jayson." She shook her head as more tears rolled down her pink cheeks. "No, that's not a no... hold on... I'm just... oh my God, I've gone and screwed it up already." She laughed and shook her head again. "Crap!"

Her face reddened even more, which he found both adorable and infuriating. The latter only because he wanted to kiss her, but he couldn't while she was still deciding how to respond.

She took a steadying breath, her hands gripping his harder than she probably realized. After several agonizing seconds, she finally met his gaze again and smiled.

"Yes," she said, her eyes matching the word. "Of course, yes. Always, yes. I... I don't even know where to start, but yes. I would love to marry you."

Adrenaline shot him to his feet as he wrapped her in his arms and kissed the life out of her. Her silky hair felt like heaven between his fingers as he coaxed her head to the angle he preferred. She melted against him, giving him what he needed as he returned the favor.

"I love you," she whispered. "I don't know how it happened, but it's true."

He smiled against her lips. "I love you too. And I also want you."

"Yeah?" She teased his mouth with her tongue. "Well, I *need* you."

"Minx." He lifted her into his arms to carry her to his room.

"Jay, this is a wedding-night tradition."

"In this house, it will be an every-night tradition. And maybe a morning one too."

She laughed as he dropped her on the bed. "Is that a promise?"

"Consider it part of the vows," he replied as he crawled over her. "Do you realize what you've agreed to, Red?" He pulled his shirt over his head while speaking.

"An eternity of staring at your abs?" Lizzie asked as she admired his torso. "No, an eternity of petting your abs."

She ran her palms over his abdomen.

He caught her wrists and pinned them on either side of her head. "No, Red."

"Yes, Jayson. Definitely, yes."

He chuckled. "Mmm, no, you've agreed to an eternity in my bed."

"Our bed," she corrected.

Jayson smiled. He liked the sound of that. "Our bed," he agreed as he trailed his fingers down her forearms. "Don't move your hands."

"Yes, sir." The taunt in her voice stirred all his darkest desires.

"I'm going to enjoy teaching you the art of pleasure," he murmured as he traced her curves down to the edge of her shirt. "But we'll start slow." He rolled off of her and onto his feet.

"Slow?" Lizzie went to her elbows. "I'm not sure I like 'slow' if it means you leaving me all hot and bothered alone in bed."

"You moved your hands," he noted as he pulled open the top drawer of his dresser. "My future wife is not very good at obeying commands."

She snorted. "Your future wife will never obey commands."

His lips curled. "Good. I don't want an obedient wife. I desire an impish one." He found what he wanted and returned to stand beside the mattress with his hands behind his back. "Take off your clothes."

Lizzie's tongue peeked out to lick her bottom lip as she ogled him openly. It took her about three seconds longer than he anticipated for her to comply. Her tank top went first, followed by the shorts and the lingerie underneath. Normally, he would require a slower reveal, but this worked for tonight.

He took his time studying her in the low lighting of his room. "You look amazing in *our* bed, Red. I think I'll keep you here for a while."

She relaxed into the pillows with a come-hither expression. The innocent woman he fell for existed beneath the surface, but a vixen prowled on the outside. His dick more than approved.

He let her see the item in his hand as he placed a knee on the bed.

"A blindfold?" she asked, her voice breathy.

"Starting slow," he repeated as brushed the silk over her cheek. Her flaring pupils told him she approved. "Close your eyes." She did, and he secured the fabric around her head. "Good?"

She nodded. "Yes."

He stood again to remove his jeans and did so as silently as possible. Her nipples pebbled under his gaze, and her thighs clenched—all signs he scanned for in an aroused woman. *Someone approves of the blindfold.*

"Do you feel my eyes on you, Red?" he asked, voice pitched low.

She nodded as her pink tongue darted out to dampen her plump lips. "I want you to touch me."

"Show me where," he said as he slipped out of his boxer shorts.

Lizzie touched her chest far too lightly for his taste. "Here," she whispered.

"Just like that?"

She shook her head. "No, harder."

"Show me," he murmured as he palmed his cock and gave it a lazy stroke.

She swallowed visibly but grabbed her breast and squeezed. Her moan teased the air in the sweetest way.

"Only there, Red?" His voice had taken on a husky quality caused by the show on his bed.

"N-no." She whimpered as her fingers traveled down over her flat stomach to the thatch of red curls between her thighs. "This is wicked."

"It is," he agreed. "Now tell me how wet you are."

"Oh God." Her back arched off the bed. "This

shouldn't be turning me on so much." Her hand slid lower, stirring a violent tremor from her. "So wet..."

She stilled as he knelt beside her on the mattress. "Let me see your hand, Red."

Her thighs squeezed together in protest. "I'm so close, Jayson."

"I know, sweetheart. Now give me your hand."

Lizzie trembled but relaxed her thighs for him. Her sweet arousal scented the air as she lifted her palm for his inspection, causing his abdomen to clench in yearning.

My future wife.

He drew his nose across her soft skin, inhaling deeply. "Mmm, I think that might be my new favorite smell, Red."

She squirmed beside him as he held her wrist. "You're killing me."

"The feeling is definitely mutual." He wrapped her fingers around his shaft and groaned at the sensation of her wet heat caressing his sensitive flesh.

She stroked him from head to base and back again, nearly undoing him. And that tongue of hers, licking her lips in anticipation, only worsened matters. He learned during their time in Bora Bora that she enjoyed sex of the oral variety, but he wanted to come deep inside her tonight, not in her mouth.

Jayson needed to claim her.

He gently removed her hand and grinned at her responding growl. "Someone's impatient." He kissed her wrist before stretching her arm over her head and introducing her fingers to the iron bars decorating his headboard. "Hold on to this, Lizzie." He caught her other hand and positioned it similarly. "Spread your legs."

She complied with a sweet moan, and he admired her damp, red curls. Her legs shook as she waited for his next move, but he purposely prolonged it, heightening the tension. He shifted subtly without touching her.

"I could admire you all night," he admitted softly. "So beautiful." He leaned over to blow against her sex, and she bowed off the bed in response. "Mmm, so needy too."

Sweat glistened over her skin. "Please, Jayson." Her raspy tone prompted his balls to tighten in anticipation.

Mine.

He knelt between her legs and drew a finger through her slick folds. "An eternity of loving you will never be long enough," he whispered reverently. "You're perfect in every way."

"Take me," she begged. "I need you inside me."

His palms slid beneath her ass to lift her pelvis from the bed as he thrust into her waiting heat. She cried out from the intense position, and he gave her a moment to adjust, even as his body implored him to take her the way he needed. *Hard and fast.*

"More," she demanded. "More, Jayson."

He smiled. "As you wish, future wife." He pulled almost all the way out and drove back in to the hilt on a groan that she echoed through the room. *So, so good.* He repeated the action faster and faster until her screams of pleasure rent the air.

God, he loved that sound.

And he would hear it for the rest of her very long life.

Fuck.

He wanted to own every inch of her, and he did with each hard stroke. Her legs quivered as her orgasm mounted, but he knew she needed more. He remained inside her as he lowered her to the mattress and found an angle that would send her over the edge.

His mouth met hers as he slipped a hand between them and found her clit with unerring precision. It took two circles to send her over the edge into oblivion, and, fuck, it felt amazing. Her walls clamped around him so tightly, so deliciously, he couldn't help but follow her into ecstasy.

"Lizzie," he groaned as his essence combined with hers in the most intimate way. But he couldn't stop. He craved more. And he wanted to see her eyes this time.

Jayson removed her blindfold and smiled at her sated

expression. Mmm, they were nowhere near finished. "Arms around me this time, sweetheart."

"Oh, yes, sir."

~*~

Lizzie was never leaving this bed. Ever. The silky sheets smelled of Jayson and sex. So much sex.

She smiled as she stretched languidly, feeling more than satisfied.

"All right, I need you to help me solve an age-old debate," Jayson said as he returned with a pizza box in his hands. He set the greasy deliciousness beside her on the bed.

She flipped open the top to grab a slice of pepperoni as she asked, "What's the debate?"

He took his own piece and relaxed into the pillows beside her. "B says pizza isn't a romantic food. I say he's wrong."

"He's totally wrong," Lizzie mumbled around the cheese in her mouth. "It's sexy."

"Right?" He took a bite, chewed, and swallowed. "I think pizza should be a requirement post-sex."

Lizzie nodded eagerly. "I approve of this rule."

He grinned. "Then it's settled. Pizza multiple times a day, post-sex. And they say marriage is hard."

She giggled. "Sex multiple times a day as well?"

"Obviously," he replied. "I'm making that a rule too."

She enjoyed another dose of cheesy goodness while considering. "You're going to take that back when I get fat." Lizzie frowned. "Oh God, I'm going to get fat."

He stole her pizza and flattened her beneath him. It happened so fast she didn't know where the food went. Hopefully, in the box.

Okay, maybe pizza in bed isn't very sexy after all.

He kissed her soundly on the mouth before nibbling her chin and neck. His lips created a path that led from her throat to her belly button, where he paused.

"Do you have any idea what the image of you carrying our child does to me, Red?" He looked up at her so she could see the heat in his gaze. "The problem won't be me not wanting you, Red; it'll be me wanting you too damn much."

She shivered. "I think I'll enjoy that."

"I'll make sure you do," he promised with another kiss to her stomach. "If the tests could already show that you were pregnant, I'd say this birth might be accelerated. Did the CRF files mention how far long they thought it might be?"

She shook her head. "We didn't get that far before you walked in."

"That's okay. We have several physicians in Hydria, including B." His expression darkened. "No, not including B. I don't like that idea at all."

Lizzie giggled. "I'm sure he would be professional."

"Oh, he definitely would be, but no. That's not happening. We'll talk to Lara. She's a Hydraian with healing abilities as well." He nodded, deciding. "Yes, I prefer that plan."

"Jealousy," Lizzie mused. "That's very interesting, Mister Masters."

"You're mine," he replied simply. "I'm not sharing."

"You've mentioned that." She smiled down at him, happier than she'd been in a very long time. "I'm okay with not sharing."

"Good." He relaxed his lower body against hers and rested his chin on her stomach. "You still owe me cookies."

She laughed. "I do. I'll bake them tomorrow."

"I think it's only fair that you bake them naked considering I've had to wait so long for them. While I supervise, of course."

"Will you also be naked?"

He shrugged. "If the chef requires it."

"She does."

"Then consider me naked." He grinned. "I better tell Tom and Amelia to find a new home." His grin slipped. "Actually, that may be more difficult now that several Ichorians are moving onto the island."

Lizzie ran her fingers through his hair while she asked, "What do you mean?"

"Well, rescuing you from Osiris didn't quite go as planned, and several of our Ichorian allies were outed in the process, including Issac."

She paused. "What?"

"Right, you weren't there. Let me fill you in."

He told her what happened after Jacque teleported her to Hydria, how Osiris managed to sequester all the Elders, and about his showdown with Stas.

"So now he knows which Ichorians are not on his side," she said when he finished. "And you think this will start a war?"

"Yes. Their defection tips the scales even more in our favor. Aidan's bloodline is very powerful, and all of them have officially chosen our side. It's possible more will request asylum as well, or go into hiding."

Lizzie considered everything he said while combing her fingers through his hair. He hadn't moved from her belly, his chin resting right over their future child.

What kind of world are we bringing you into, little one?

"I'll protect you both with my life, Red," he vowed, following her thoughts. She imagined the concern had flashed across her face.

"What about Jonathan?" she asked with a shiver. "He's still out there."

"Not for long." Something dark flashed through his eyes as he said it. "His time on Earth is short-lived. He's created too many enemies."

"But you said he's partnering with Osiris?"

He grinned. "My guess is that partnership is one-sided, in Osiris's favor. And I'm not worried. Jonathan will die. I promise you that."

She studied the conviction in his expression and decided, "I'm okay with that." It surprised her. Violence and death were two subjects she avoided. But the idea of Jonathan dying? Yeah, she could get behind that. "What if he's immune to your gifts like Osiris is?"

"Then we'll kill him the old-fashioned way. With a bullet." He kissed her belly. "I will do whatever I need to do to guarantee the safety of you and our child, Liz. I promise you."

"I believe you," she whispered. "Now come up here and kiss me."

He grinned. "Forgetting who is in charge again?"

"I might require another lesson on that."

He crawled upward to cage her between his hard body and the bed. "I'm happy to teach you, Red—every day, every night, for the rest of our very long lives."

She wrapped her fingers around his nape to pull him down for a kiss. "I love you," she breathed against his lips.

"I love you too," he murmured. "Forever and always."

* * *

Lizzie wandered up the hill in the direction of Luc's home. Jayson had given her directions earlier after saying Issac and Stas were staying with Luc for now.

His home wasn't near the other houses and seemed almost secluded up here, but the view was breathtaking. Dark blue waters rolling from almost every angle, white homes with blue tops, and cobblestone streets. So gorgeous.

Lizzie admired it all, including the adorable architecture of his home, before knocking softly. Jacque answered without his usual grin.

"Oh, hi." He palmed the back of his neck. "Uh, Luc's not feeling up for visitors right now."

"Is he still recovering from what Alik did to him?" Jay

had explained everything that happened, including what it meant for Alik to use his gifts on someone.

Jacque nodded. "Yeah. They all are. I can tell him you stopped by."

"Oh, I actually came to see Stas. Is she here?"

He shook his head. "No, she went down to the beach with Issac. Want a lift?" His eyes brightened with that last part.

He likes to be useful.

"Actually, yes, that would be lovely." She could totally walk by herself, but she didn't mind the teleport, and his responding smile at being needed confirmed her choice.

He held out his elbow, and she accepted. The scene dissolved into the beach a second later. "That's a really cool talent," she admitted.

"It's awesome," he agreed. "Exhausting, but awesome." He nodded toward the beach where Issac and Stas strolled hand in hand, deep in conversation.

"I, uh, I think they're officially ending things," Jacque whispered. "We should leave them alone."

"What do you mean?"

"I mean, I think they're finally having *the talk.*" He glanced at them with a grimace. "You know, breaking up."

"But…" Lizzie paused as Issac stopped to face Stas, his expression tightened with despair. "Couldn't he just, I don't know, not bite her?" It seemed simple enough to her. Most couples didn't bleed around each other, right?

Jacque gaped at her. "Whom is he going to feed from?"

"Donors?" Lizzie suggested.

"Feeding is a sexual process for Ichorians, and also, our blood is alluring. If he loses control for one second during intimacy, he'll die."

Lizzie frowned. "From what I've seen, Issac is very determined and in control."

Jacque considered, nodding. "True, but a relationship of that nature between an Ichorian and a Hydraian is unheard of."

"Just as I imagine having a bunch of Ichorians moving onto this island is unheard of as well," she pointed out.

"Touché," he replied. "Regardless, it's considered impossible, and the others wouldn't approve."

"It's not really up to them, though, is it?" Lizzie said, slightly irritated on her friend's behalf. "If they want to try, they should."

Jacque shrugged. "I guess we'll see."

Lizzie had hope. If anyone could figure this out, it would be Stas. Her best friend was the strongest woman she knew. "I should probably talk to her later," she said as Issac cupped Stas's cheeks and pressed his forehead to hers. "They look pretty caught up in their conversation." And it felt a little weird watching them.

"Back to Jay?"

"Yes, please. I owe him some cookies."

"Cookies?" Jacque repeated. "Sign me up."

Lizzie grinned. "I'll have to make a few batches, because Jayson doesn't share."

"As he shouldn't," Jacque agreed.

Stas tilted her face up for a kiss that Issac tenderly returned just as Jacque teleported himself and Lizzie from view.

Lizzie's lips curled into a smile.

Their story is nowhere near finished.

EPILOGUE

One Week Later...

Jayson stood outside Luc's door, hesitating. This had to be done. He had to walk in there and explain how he could pick a woman over his brothers, but the words escaped him.

An apology would be a lie. When Osiris demanded the truth, he gave it.

Anything. And he meant it. He would give anything to protect Lizzie, including the lives of his best friends.

Fuck, it hurt.

He never wanted to choose between them, but Osiris had forced him to express his feelings out loud. And now the three men inside this house knew.

Jayson rubbed a hand over his face as he searched for his confidence. He hadn't seen Alik, Balthazar, or Luc since the incident. No one had, aside from a handful of Guardians who assisted with their Elders' recovery. Jayson had given them all space, waiting for the inevitable summons.

It arrived this morning via Jacque.

Stop being a caitiff and knock on the fucking door, he told himself. *They know you're here.*

Hell, Balthazar could hear every thought. That he hadn't demanded him to enter yet, however, left Jayson feeling even more inadequate.

It wasn't like B to leave him hanging outside. Alone.

Unless this was to be his punishment.

Shit, if that's how they wanted to play, then so be it. He wouldn't apologize for giving his heart to Lizzie. She was worth whatever pain his friends intended to inflict on him.

Yeah, fuck knocking.

He turned the handle and let himself inside without announcing himself.

Balthazar stood just inside the house, leaning against the wall, wearing one of his trademark grins, and appearing completely at ease. A sense of tranquility settled across Jayson's shoulder at the sight of his best friend—healthy, alive, and smirking.

"Well, that was amusing." Balthazar cracked open the beer in his hand and held it out for Jayson to grab. "Welcome back, Jay. Sorry it took an edict to force you to come visit."

He gripped the bottle and cocked a brow. "Seriously? You ordered me up here to share a beer?"

"He wants to talk about your bachelor party," Luc said as he joined them in the foyer. The dark shadows beneath his eyes were the only indication of his suffering a week ago. "As we understand, congratulations are in order?"

"Yeah, the fuck is that about?" Alik demanded from the living area. "We have to hear these things from Jacque now?"

"I was letting you rest," Jayson said, only partly meaning it.

"Bullshit," Balthazar replied in an uncharacteristically irritated tone. "You were hiding. Choosing Lizzie over us is one thing. Not being able to confront us on it is an entirely different conversation."

"Trust," Luc added. "You didn't trust us to forgive you, not that we feel there is anything to forgive."

That wasn't entirely true. "I needed time to find the right words."

"And have you?" Luc asked, his gaze brimming with curiosity.

"Honestly?" Jay palmed the back of his neck with his free hand and blew out a breath. "No. I have no idea what to say. I can't apologize, even though I feel like I should. And I don't know how to explain any of it. Osiris forced me to choose—"

"He asked what you would *give* to save her," Luc interjected. "And you gave him the honorable answer, because if you would give less than anything to save her, then you wouldn't deserve her."

Alik walked into the foyer, hands in his pockets, brown eyes clouded with memories and pain. "Did you not accept me when I chose Jenika over all of you?"

Hearing the name sent a shock through Jayson's system. Alik hadn't uttered those six letters in several centuries, and the agony of it etched a pattern over his features that all of them felt to their souls.

"Alik," Jayson breathed. "You don't need to do this."

"Yes, I do." Darkness shrouded his features even as determination lit his gaze. "You all know I would sacrifice anything to bring her back, but that doesn't belittle our bond. We're brothers and always will be, but love, *true* love, surpasses all the rules. Including those implied by our history."

"He's right," Balthazar murmured. "What you have

with Lizzie should be cherished. We would never expect you to put us first, and you can guarantee that we will always be there to help you fight for it."

"Your happiness is our happiness, Jay." Luc clapped him on the back and pulled him into a hug. "I could sense how much that answer cost you, but I couldn't have been prouder."

"We all were." Balthazar joined the group embrace. "You'll always be our brother, Jay. No matter what."

"Loving her doesn't weaken you; it strengthens you. Hold on to that gift, Jay. Because you never know what life will throw at you next." The grave, but wise, words came from Alik.

He didn't join the group hug, not that any of them expected him to. Jenika's death had irrevocably changed him. None of them had understood, having never been in love themselves, but Jayson could appreciate that reaction now. Lizzie was his heart. Without her, he would cease to be.

Alik met his gaze over Luc's shoulder.

Now you know, he whispered telepathically. *Protect her, Jayson. Protect her with everything, and never stop cherishing your love.*

Jayson nodded once in reply, a solemn vow to do right by her. *Always*.

"You're going to be an excellent father," Luc whispered. "And an even better husband."

"After the bachelor party," Balthazar added with a pat on Jayson's shoulder as he pulled away from them.

Leave it to B to lighten the otherwise somber mood.

"After the party," Luc agreed as he released Jay.

Alik snorted and turned away as he said, "Yeah. Good luck convincing Lizzie to let him go."

Jayson welcomed the lighthearted change in topic but grimaced as he considered Alik's comment. "You're not planning anything too extravagant, are you?"

Balthazar grinned. "Would I call a meeting to discuss

anything less than phenomenal?" He waggled his brows. "Step into the living room, Jay. We need to review the blueprints and my proposed timeline."

The Story Continues with *Angel Bonds*

A love so forbidden, it transcends boundaries…
But even the strongest bonds require sacrifice.

Stas and Issac broke all the rules—and it's time to face the consequences. A necessary surrender leads to devastation, forcing Stas to choose between her heart and her future.

Will Issac remain by her side, or are they destined for different paths?

As word of an awakening power spreads, the immortal treaty shatters, and a looming battle of wills threatens to destroy everything in its wake.

The war has begun.

And death will reign.

Until an angel rises from the flames of destruction…

IMMORTAL CURSE SERIES
What's Next

Dear Reader,

Thank you for reading *Blood Heart*. I hope you enjoyed learning more about Lizzie and Jayson and watching them grow. Their relationship is one that has been with me for a long time, and as much as these characters made me cry, I loved writing this book. They will forever own a piece of my heart.

I originally planned to release *Angel Bonds* with *Blood Heart*, but this book took me on an emotional rollercoaster ride that left me reeling afterward. Diving right into Issac and Stas wouldn't have been fair to Jayson and Lizzie, so I'm taking my time with the transition and plan to release *Angel Bonds* in late August 2018.

But I have a surprise for you as well… *Blood Bonds*, featuring Stas's parents, will debut in early September. This novel is actually already finished, but it contains too many spoilers to reveal early. Therefore, it will be released two weeks after *Angel Bonds*.

For sneak peeks, early chapter reveals, and special excerpts, please join my reader group on Facebook or sign up for my newsletter. I love hearing from you all, and although I won't answer spoiler questions, I will provide some insight into the voices living in my head. ;-)

Thank you again for reading!

Cheers xx

Lexi

ACKNOWLEDGMENTS

It takes an army to finish a book. I'm so thankful to everyone for helping me along on this terrifying journey and for the support of my friends and family. Below are a few of the people on my team whom I truly could not do this without...

First and foremost, Matt: Thank you for your unconditional support, love, and care. You always know what to say, you're an amazing partner, and you are the love of my life. #DorksForever

Allison: Thank you for keeping me grounded in reality, for telling me when something needs to be rewritten, and for crying with me over a certain chapter nearly a dozen times. And thank you for your friendship and honesty. I <3 you!

Casey: Thank you for handling my baby with such care and grace! I appreciate all your feedback, and I love that you force me to perform at the next level. Your experience and guidance are invaluable. I hope you're ready for *Angel Bonds* ;-)

Louise & Melissa: You two are my foundation. Without your support and love, I'd flounder and hide indefinitely in my writing cave. I appreciate everything you do, and I cherish you both more than words can say.

Bethany: Thank you for editing my giant MS, and not balking at the word count. I'm so glad you still tolerate my commas, and I love that you try to teach me how to properly use them. It's never going to work, but I'll keep trying!

Jacy: Thank you for pushing me to provide my best work, for always finding my repetitive words, and for pointing out inconsistencies. Oh, and also for fixing my commas. Like I said to Bethany above, I'll keep trying, but we both know I'll never understand them.

Barb, Delphine, Jenny & Pam: You complete my editing team, and I appreciate you all so much! Thank you for catching all the things I miss in the final editing stages and for keeping me honest. You're amazing!

Barb, Delphine, Laura, Louise, Melissa & Tracey: Thank you all for beta-reading *Blood Heart* and helping me craft the strongest book imaginable. I appreciate all your feedback, comments, and edits and love having you on my team. Hopefully, you all are still speaking to me once you see the revisions I made, because I'll need your input on *Angel Bonds*.

Claudia: Thank you for the gorgeous art design.

Julie: Thank you for your amazing friendship and for helping me with the paperback typography. It's beautiful!

Famous Owls: Thank you for being such an important part of my team and for always making me smile. You all rock!

None of this could be possible without my ARC team, Itsy Bitsy, and IndieSage PR. Thank you, thank you, thank you!

And to the readers: Thank you for reading Lizzie and Jayson's story. The Immortal Curse series is my heart, and I can't explain what it means to me to share it with the world. Your support, kindness, and encouraging words keep me going. <3

ABOUT THE AUTHOR

Lexi C. Foss is a writer lost in the IT world. She lives in Atlanta, Georgia with her husband and their furry children. When not writing, she's busy crossing items off her travel bucket list. Many of the places she's visited can be seen in her writing, including the mythical world of Hydria which is based on Hydra in the Greek islands. She's quirky, consumes way too much coffee, and loves to swim. Cheers!

ALSO BY LEXI C. FOSS